Anchors

A Novel

Danielle De Sassano

Lions' Den Books

ANCHORS
A Lions' Den Book

Published by Lions' Den Books

All rights reserved
Copyright © 2024 by Danielle De Sassano
Cover art and photograph by Asya Blue Design

This is a work of fiction. Names, characters, places, and incidents either are the product of the author's imagination or are used fictitiously. Any resemblance to actual persons, living or dead, businesses, companies, events, or locales is entirely coincidental.

No part of this book may be reproduced or transmitted in any form or by any means, electronic or mechanical, including photocopying, recording, or by any information storage and retrieval system, without the written permission of the publisher, except where permitted by law.

978-1-7379330-0-7 ebook
978-1-7379330-1-4 paperback
978-1-7379330-2-1 hardcover

Library of Congress Control Number: 2023920218

Manufactured in the United States of America

First edition, March 2024

For the wanderers

CONTENTS

November 2006 1

December 2006 25

January 2007 45

February 2007 57

March 2007 81

April 2007 99

May 2007 133

June 2007 177

July 2007 217

August 2007 245

September 2007 273

October 2007 297

November 2007 337

Anchors

November 2006

1

ON THE NIGHT before Thanksgiving, Giovanni's on La Salle was packed beyond capacity. As rushed voices clamored around her, twenty-year-old Adrienne Deneau weaved through the marble-top tables to pick up a large spinach and anchovies from behind the counter. The fish smell drove Adrienne to suck in her breath. Anchovies were nauseating on a Zagat-rated pie or not.

On her way back to the crowded floor, Adrienne's best friend, Wendy Verona, desperately signaled her to the master register. A dozen takeout customers waiting before her, Wendy anxiously juggled cashing them out while answering the incessant ringing of the restaurant phone. Seething, she slapped her hand over the mouthpiece. "Adrienne! Where the *hell* is Jenni?"

Adrienne glanced at the second register. The POS was lit up and ready to go, but Jenni was nowhere in sight. She inhaled deeply, vying to remain cool in front of the customers. It had been the same nonsense since their manager, Roman, hired Jenni back in April. "I have no idea. Let me bring this pie out, and I'll come back to help you."

When she returned to the counter, Adrienne instructed the customers to split the line in two. "I can take some of you over here, folks!" Commanding authority was one of her strong suits, a useful skill for keeping order in Westford's most sought-after pizzeria. Instantly, the line broke, half heading over to her like cattle. Her first customer was Mr. Jensen, a regular and one of Connecticut's most powerful attorneys, picking up ten large pies. After Adrienne rang him up, Mr. Jensen slid two fifties across the counter. "I'll trade you. Give the other one to your pal." He nodded in Wendy's direction.

"Mr. Jensen!" Adrienne gasped. "That's too much money!"

"Don't argue with me, kid," he said, hoisting the pizzas. "You girls are slammed tonight."

When the line dissolved, Adrienne turned to Wendy. "I'm going to find Jenni."

Wendy shoved her cash drawer shut. "Tell her *she's* closing the registers tonight. I'm not staying late to pick up any more of her slack."

Adrienne walked to the kitchen. "Has anyone seen Jenni?" she called to the prep cooks.

Eight heads peered up from their various stations, all but one too busy to answer. "No Jenni here," Pedro, one of the dough pounders, said. "No Roman, neither."

Great. Behind the kitchen was the delivery area. Drivers bustled in and out of the back door carrying insulated bags. The ones waiting for orders sat on milk crates folding pizza boxes at warp speed. Adrienne turned to Connor, the delivery manager. He looked as strained as Wendy, with all four phone extensions blinking and screeching at him. "Connor, have you seen Jenni?"

Connor shook his head, grabbing the receiver and furiously scribbling a new ticket.

Past the delivery area, Adrienne yanked open the door to the walk-in. Still no Jenni. *Where is she?* Adrienne wondered.

Suddenly, the back door swung open, and a driver scurried in out of the cold, bringing the sound of Jenni's irritating voice with him. Adrienne caught the door and stepped outside. In the parking lot, her manager, Roman, sat smoking a cigarette on a milk crate. Behind him, Jenni, who was all of nineteen and easily the laziest person Adrienne had ever worked with, sat on her own milk crate with her legs wrapped around him. In her hands, Jenni held a hot-pink Motorola RAZR. "See how cool this is?" she was saying. "And it slides into my back pocket just like on the commercials!"

Adrienne let the door slam, startling them. "Are you kidding me right now?"

Jenni stared up at her. "What's *your* problem?"

"What's *my* problem, Jenni? It's the busiest night of the year inside, and nobody knows where the hell you are! I've got seven tables, Becca has the other seven, and Wendy's line was practically out the door! You're scheduled to be counter support tonight. Not doing whatever *this* is."

Roman mumbled something Adrienne couldn't make out, and Jenni stood from her milk crate, squeezing his shoulder. "I'll see you inside, baby," she cooed. She opened the back door, snidely motioning for Adrienne to go before her. "Are you coming?"

"Just get back in there," Adrienne snapped. "And you can forget about being early-out tonight. Wendy and I are leaving at nine. *Sharp.*"

Jenni gaped at her, slack-jawed, then whipped around and stormed into the restaurant.

Adrienne turned to Roman. At thirty-three, he was a big man—muscular Polish stock with light hair and ice-blue eyes. He smirked sheepishly as he crushed his cigarette. "I didn't make you front-of-the-house manager so you could cuss at the staff," he said. "It's not like you don't leave the floor to come out for a smoke."

"Not during dinner rush, I don't."

Roman shrugged wordlessly.

Adrienne tossed her arms up. "Oh, come on, Ro. I'm sorry you're not happy in your marriage, but we've had it with Jenni disappearing all the time. Even when she stays up front, she hardly lifts a finger as it is."

Roman glanced at the gold band on his finger and gave a conceding nod. Adrienne knew he knew she was right about everything—his unhappy marriage, Jenni's indolence, *and* his ongoing affair with her, which was public knowledge to everyone at Giovanni's. "I'll talk to her about running off," he said.

Later, Adrienne sat at the staff table to complete her server report. The dining room activity had ceased, but the delivery lines were still ringing off the hook. Wendy and Becca joined Adrienne as she pulled a fat wad of bills and receipts from her checkbook and sorted them. "What a night!" Becca exclaimed. "And I'm still here for an hour!"

"At least Adrienne didn't abandon you," Wendy said scornfully. "I honestly can't stand working with Jenni."

"You should work on the floor with us," Becca suggested. "Then you won't have to worry about Jenni leaving you at the registers all the time."

"Thanks, but no thanks. You know I don't wait tables."

"I'm just *say-ing* ..." Becca sang, turning to Adrienne. "How much did you make tonight, Dri?"

"Three-eleven," said Adrienne, grabbing her pile. "But don't forget that it's the busiest day of the year."

"I probably made about two," Becca guessed. "Wouldn't it be great to make this kind of money every day?"

Dream on! Adrienne thought. Her daily goal was to clear one hundred dollars in tips, but that wasn't always the case. Today's haul was a rare exception.

She and Wendy clocked out and wished their coworkers a happy Thanksgiving. Outside, Roman and Jenni were back on their milk crates, entangled in one another and giggling like fools. Adrienne sighed as she walked to her car.

Jenni was on her feet at once. "Seriously? *What* is your problem with me, Adrienne? Are you jealous of me or something?"

Adrienne exchanged looks with Wendy. "Jenni, I don't have a jealous bone in my body. But if I did, you're the last person I'd envy."

It was true. Jenni, with her lank blonde hair, pinched face, and enormous chest on a rail-thin body, had no physical qualities Adrienne could imagine desiring. Never mind her horrible work ethic or moral vacancy.

"Well, you must be jealous of something! Or you wouldn't get so mad whenever you see me with Roman! Do you want him? Are you jealous that he's *mine*?"

Roman remained on his milk crate, wearing the same sheepish smirk from earlier. Clearly, it struck his ego being the focus of an argument between two girls almost half his age.

Adrienne sighed again. "Jenni, he's *married*. From now on, I'll ignore you completely, okay? It'll be like you're not even here."

"She's not here even when she is," Wendy lamented.

Jenni's eyes bulged. "Y-you can't talk to me like that! You're a manager!"

Adrienne unlocked her car. "You're right, Jenni. I'm wholeheartedly abusing my authority. Just like *my* manager is abusing his." She shut her door in unison with Wendy and drove off, both girls shaking their heads as Jenni stamped her feet and shrieked at Roman.

Wendy

THIS IS WHY she loves Adrienne! She's never afraid to stand up and put anyone in their place! "That girl sure has some gall," her mother always says.

She remembers hating her parents when they'd moved to Connecticut ten years ago. At eleven, she didn't want to leave their small farm in Vermont. But her spirits improved when she saw Adrienne playing outside at the house next door. It didn't matter that Adrienne was seven months younger and a year behind her in school. They'd become best friends overnight, bonding effortlessly over their collections of Beanie Babies and shared love of Fear Street novels.

When they were younger, with their heart-shaped faces and deep-set eyes, people often commented how much they looked like sisters. Now, in their early twenties, Adrienne is the beautiful one. Those cheekbones. That hair. Long mahogany locks that cascade down her back. Not that *she* considers herself unattractive. At five-six, she's the perfect height, leaving Adrienne behind three inches ago. And after years of dyeing her hair every color of the rainbow, she's decided she looks best as a fiery blonde. She's the trendy one, and it gives her an edge.

One thing they'll always share is their ever-failing vision. Adrienne refuses to leave the house without contacts while she swears by her rectangle Vogues. Who cares if the frames alone cost two hundred bucks? Adrienne has always been more responsible with her money, but when *she* sees something she likes, all bets are off!

***

"YOU REALLY LET Jenni have it back there," Wendy sniggered as they arrived at the grocery store for last-minute Thanksgiving fixings.

Adrienne jerked the key from the ignition. "It's not only that she's a useless worker, Wendy, but I don't understand how she can so willingly get involved with a married man."

Wendy nodded. "I know all that infidelity stuff really bothers you."

Almost five years had passed since Adrienne's mother, Raina, had taken off with the Accountant. Since then, it had been up to Adrienne to care for her father and two younger brothers. "Roman has *kids*, Wendy. And it's like Jenni doesn't even care about potentially breaking up a marriage. Or a family."

"I agree," Wendy said. "And I feel bad that you have it rubbed in your face every day. Work shouldn't be like that."

Inside, they raided the bakery department. "I draw the line at baking," Adrienne said. She didn't mind cooking dinner for five, but dessert was always store-bought.

Wendy debated between a pumpkin pie in one hand and a pecan pie in the other. "What about your aunt and her boyfriend? They won't help you out with dessert?"

"My aunt is the appetizer queen. She specializes in stuffed mushrooms and overpriced cheese."

Wendy hesitated before putting the pecan pie back on display.

"What's wrong?" Adrienne asked. "You don't want to get both?"

"I left my tips in the register cup. I only have ten bucks."

Adrienne dug in her back pocket. "Here." She pulled out Mr. Jensen's tip and handed it to Wendy. "I almost forgot. Mr. Jensen told me to give this to you."

Wendy chuckled as she pocketed the fifty. "Thanks, Mr. Jensen! You gotta love rich people!"

2

ADRIENNE AND WENDY lived on Park Court, a working-class side street in southeast Westford. Westford Center, where Giovanni's was located, was often called the Manhattan of town—a central hub rich with boutique shops and extortionate menu prices. The main thoroughfare in their neighborhood was more likened to Brooklyn—boasting thrift stores and diners whose patrons came from all walks of life.

Adrienne had lived on Park Court since she was born, at 106, the little gray cape. Next door, Wendy lived at 110, the mustard-yellow two-story. So many lawn ornaments crowded Wendy's front yard it appeared the Veronas were merchants at an outdoor bazaar.

"Are you still coming over?" Wendy asked.

Adrienne nodded. "Just let me shower and peek in on Thany first."

In her living room, Adrienne's father, Jack, snored in his recliner while a *Bonanza* rerun blared from the television. The Deneaus had canceled cable when Raina left, learning to make do with the basic stations ever since. On the end table was one of many baby monitors Adrienne kept around to listen while Thany slept. Her six-year-old brother had idiopathic epilepsy, and the baby monitors came in handy if he had a seizure in his sleep. The good news was Thany had started a new medication in March, and so far, eight months had passed since his last seizure. Still, Adrienne prayed the episodes would remain less frequent than when he was younger.

She removed an afghan from the couch and covered her father. Then, considering the electric bill, set the sleep timer. In the kitchen, Dolly, the Deneaus' sheltie, poked her snout in and out of the grocery bags. "Dolly, stop!" Adrienne scolded, shooing her away.

She checked on Thany in his bedroom, then headed upstairs to the attic bedroom she shared with her other brother, Aaron. Much to their family's alarm, Aaron had enlisted in the Marine Corps on his eighteenth birthday back in August, shipping off to boot camp on Parris Island a month later. Since then, he'd only been allowed to communicate via letter-writing—no phone calls, no matter how much Thany begged. Aaron was due back right before Christmas, a homecoming Adrienne could wait for only because she'd long tired of sharing a room with him.

Before Thany was born, Aaron had lived in the smaller downstairs bedroom, while Adrienne lived on one side of the renovated attic. But when Thany came along, unplanned and then sick, Aaron moved into the other half of the attic so Thany could be closer to their parents. They'd moved all the old toys and boxes of holiday decorations down to the basement and partitioned the attic with tapestries. Adrienne and Aaron had made do with the arrangement for the past six years, but now more than ever, with her twenty-first birthday approaching, Adrienne continuously craved independence and a place to call her own.

She showered, then walked next door and let herself in through Wendy's hatchway. An only child, Wendy had the entire basement to herself. Ritually, every Wednesday after work, the girls gathered here to watch *South Park*, but with the show on hiatus, they'd likely watch one of Wendy's hundreds of movies as they always did in the off-season.

Wendy was updating her MySpace page when Adrienne walked in. "You smell nice," she commented, not turning around.

"Herbal Essences," said Adrienne. She gazed around Wendy's room, forever amazed by the abundance of *stuff* accumulated over the years. Wooden china cabinets, which Wendy had stained a rainbow of funky colors, stored thousands of books, CDs, and movies. Laminate shelves provided surface space for collectible dolls and meaningless tchotchkes—all testaments that Wendy had wasted every cent she'd ever earned on material nonsense.

Adrienne was thumbing through a shelf of paperbacks when Wendy called, "Oh my God, Adrienne, come here!"

She walked toward Wendy's swivel chair. "What?"

"Look at this!" Wendy pointed to the computer screen. "Rick got a job at Blockbuster!"

Adrienne focused on the MySpace profile Wendy was viewing—the profile of *her* ex-boyfriend, Rick, whom she'd dated from the fall of her senior year until finally breaking things off with him last May.

"You're still friends with Rick on MySpace?"

"Ech, no way! I saw him post in Connor's comments and clicked on his profile. It's not private."

Adrienne eyed the box captioned *Rick's Details*. Listed next to *Occupation*, read, *customer service at blockbuster*.

"It took him long enough to get another job," Wendy snickered.

Adrienne nodded. She'd met Rick, a friend of Connor's, during the lowest point in her life. He'd come to work as a dispatcher at Giovanni's, but despite being three years older than her, Rick didn't have a car or even a license, limiting him to answering delivery calls and folding pizza boxes. The perfect job for a stoner, she learned later. It was also Rick's first job, starting work older than anyone she knew.

In the two and a half years they'd dated, Rick made no advancements. He'd dropped out of high school before they'd met, lived rent-free in his mother's basement, and got high constantly, even at work. That was what had cost him his job, when Gio, the elderly owner, caught Rick and one of the drivers smoking a joint in the parking lot and fired them both on the spot.

When five months had passed, just after Adrienne finished with Tunxis Community College and Rick *still* hadn't looked for work, Jack intervened, forbidding Rick from entering their home. "I didn't raise you to date someone who brings you down, Adrienne! It's bad enough that he expects his mother to support him, but not my daughter!" Jack reminded her that by the time *he* was Rick's age, he'd had an associate's degree and was employed by a good construction firm. "I had this house, and I was engaged to your mother! If he has time to smoke dope, then he has time to get his act together. But he doesn't want to! That's no *man* in my book!"

Wendy, too, had helped Adrienne realize her only reason for dating Rick was her inherent desire to help people. And it was true Adrienne had tried to help Rick. Whether keeping him updated on the next cycle of GED classes or showing him want-ads in the paper, she was always finding ways to better his future. "I'm sorry, Adrienne," Wendy had finally said, "but Rick is the biggest slacker I've ever met. You're like Rene in *Mallrats* dating Brody. You can do so much better."

Adrienne found it ironic that such an opinion came from *Wendy*, who also lived in her parents' basement and didn't drive. But the parallels between them were far from the same. Despite not having a penny in savings, Wendy had at least finished high school and showed stability in the workforce. And even though she was still on an interlude from college, Wendy's plans to one day finish her education were ones that Adrienne knew wouldn't fall by the wayside. Rick was another story, presumably expecting to be babied for the rest of his life.

She turned away from the computer. "Good for Rick. I hope Blockbuster works out."

"Doubtful," said Wendy. "The way On-Demand cable is going, video stores will be a thing of the past."

Adrienne considered Wendy's theory as she took that morning's *Courant* from her nightstand. Ever since Wendy was a kid, Adrienne had known her to read the newspaper daily, cover-to-cover, just to know what was happening in the world. Adrienne used to read the *Courant*, too, but once Raina left, she'd canceled their subscription just like the cable, both now luxuries she couldn't afford.

She skimmed the Life section before switching to the classifieds. Since graduating Tunxis, Adrienne occasionally checked to see which jobs were hiring, but nothing she'd seen yet had struck her fancy. Nothing worth leaving Giovanni's anyway, where she'd spent almost five years working her way up. It was wiser to stick with what she knew until something better came along. But tonight, centered in the middle of the page, one ad caught her interest. Something about a cruise line in Rhode Island. She began reading just as Wendy abandoned her computer. "So, what should we watch tonight? No more *South Park* until March."

Adrienne set the newspaper down. "Oh ... I don't know. You pick something."

Wendy selected *Grandma's Boy*, but Adrienne couldn't focus, encompassed by an excited nervousness. She'd seen the word *stewardess* in the ad, and though she wasn't sure what a stewardess's job entailed, the idea of a cruise ship appealed to her. It had been a long time since she'd felt this curious about something, reaching for her jacket as soon as the credits started to roll.

"Don't you want to stay for a while?" Wendy asked.

"I can't. I have to be up early for the turkey." Adrienne pointed to the newspaper on the nightstand. "Can I have that?"

Wendy waved permissively. "Go ahead. I finished it this morning."

The living room was empty now, the afghan she'd covered her father with neatly returned to its spot on the couch. Adrienne looked in on Thany, then snagged a bag of Milano cookies and an extra baby monitor on her way to the attic. In bed, she propped herself against the pillows and flipped back to the classifieds, scanning the want ads until she found the one she was looking for. It was larger than the rest, intended to stand out.

EAST BAY, RHODE ISLAND
Northeastern Cruise Line Associates is now hiring stewardesses and deckhands for 2007. Long hours. Competitive industry pay. Rewarding time off. Applicants must be 18+, possess a high school diploma or general equivalency, and be citizens of the United States. Natives of southern New England strongly desired. Prospective candidates who meet the qualifications may apply to the address below. Join our adventurous crew of dedicated industry professionals and gift yourself the opportunity of a lifetime.

The opportunity of a lifetime. The words hovered as Adrienne nibbled on a cookie. How could something like *this* be anything but? Just hours ago, she'd been consumed with exasperation by the only job she'd ever known, every ounce of which was now diminishing as a volley of questions stormed her thoughts. Where exactly did the company travel to, and why had she never heard of it? What was a stewardess's job description?

How much money did they make? Would she have to wear a neck scarf and serve peanuts like the airline stewardesses in movies did? How big was the cruise ship? Did employees get their own rooms? A childlike exhilaration consumed her. Imagine getting paid to work on a cruise ship? Some of her favorite pastimes as a kid were beach trips. She'd splash in the water with Jack for hours while Aaron built sandcastles with Raina onshore. These days she tried not to think much about Raina, still harboring resentment toward her mother for leaving so abruptly; for leaving *her* to pick up the pieces.

Adrienne put the newspaper and cookies aside and walked to the half bath at the top of the stairs, removing her contacts and taking a long look in the mirror. Tonight, she didn't just see her physical self in the reflection staring back at her, but a young woman who, as much as she'd already lived through, hadn't ever *experienced* very much of anything.

3

ADRIENNE WAS UP before sunrise, a one-woman army prepared to lead the kitchen into battle. Every year, she cooked Thanksgiving dinner from scratch—meat stuffing for the turkey, mashed potatoes with sour cream and cheddar, fresh green bean casserole, and cranberry sauce. She moved around the kitchen whimsically, giddy with thoughts of becoming a stewardess. What harm could there be in applying? She certainly met all the qualifications listed in the newspaper.

By seven, the wafting aromas had roused her father. He entered the kitchen in his robe, his graying hair matted and askew from what Adrienne detected was another restless night's sleep. "Morning," Jack kissed her head. "The bird smells good." He walked to the coffeepot she'd readied and poured a full mug—black, the only way he ever drank the stuff. "Guess I better hit the shower before Claudette gets here," he said. "She always shows up so damn early."

Thany trudged in carrying a toy dinosaur. "Good morning, Adrienne. Happy Thanksgiving from me and Bronto."

Adrienne tousled his hair. "You, too, Bud! What do you want this morning? Cheerios or Kix?"

"Kix, please." Thany mounted himself on the phone book he used as a booster seat. "Is Aaron coming home today?"

"No, Thany. I already told you he won't be home until Christmas."

"Is he coming with Santa?"

Adrienne winked. "Even better. He's coming *before* Santa."

"Yay! I can't wait! We haven't seen Aaron in a million years!"

***

AUNT CLAUDETTE and her boyfriend, Dickey, arrived with an armada of hors d'oeuvres. After haphazard greetings, she left the cheese and crackers with the guys and followed Adrienne to the kitchen. Once the rest was in the oven, she uncorked a bottle of wine and poured two glasses. "How have you been, Dri? Still the hardest-working girl around town?"

Adrienne smiled, always fascinated to find her resemblance in her father's sister. With their tan skin, high cheekbones, and dark brown hair, she and Aaron bore a strong likeness to the Deneau side of the family. But Thany was the spitting image of Raina—sleek, jet-black hair mantled above a ruddy, cherubic face. "I'm good, Auntie. It's nice to have a couple of days off after yesterday." She sipped her wine, relaying the pre-Thanksgiving chaos and extramarital liaisons at Giovanni's.

"That's just incredible," Aunt Claudette said. "Doesn't the owner have any concerns about what's happening over there? You'd think being from the Old Country and all …"

"Gio is hardly around anymore, he's so old," Adrienne explained. "But he wouldn't be happy if he knew."

"Well, it sure doesn't sound like this Jenni does anything worth keeping her around the *workplace*. I don't know what's worse—a man who doesn't mind throwing his family away for some tart or a tart who doesn't mind wrecking a family."

Stung, Adrienne stared into her wine glass. Too late. Aunt Claudette had enough intuition to open a psychic hotline. "Oh, Dri, I'm sorry. I hope I didn't sound like I was talking about your mother. That whole thing with her was … *different* than this. I just meant the young girls like that Jenni from your work, honey. Those things never work out. And it's always the innocent ones who suffer the most."

"I know. But I don't feel like talking about Raina today."

Aunt Claudette took her hand. "I understand."

Once everyone polished off the appetizers, Adrienne and Aunt Claudette went to set the dining room table. Every year it was the same routine, small talk in the living room while they watched the parade, followed by Adrienne breaking out the good china they only used for holidays.

"What are your plans now that you're done with Tunxis?" Aunt Claudette asked. "Are you going to try for your bachelor's?"

Adrienne circled the table with placemats. "I'm not sure that's what I want right now. School will always be there, you know?"

"As opposed to what?"

"As opposed to … opportunities."

"Mmm. What sort of opportunities?"

Adrienne hesitated. As exciting as *thinking* about the cruise ship job was, *vocalizing* those thoughts panged her with guilt for even considering leaving her father and Thany.

Aunt Claudette sensed her uncertainty. "Dri?"

"I saw an ad in the *Courant* to work on a boat," Adrienne spat out. "As a stewardess."

"A boat? Like a cruise ship?"

Adrienne nodded. "There's a company in Rhode Island. They're hiring stewardesses for 2007."

"That sounds interesting! Are you going to look into it?"

Adrienne gave her aunt a *look*. "I can't leave my dad and Thany, Auntie. You know that."

"You certainly do a lot for them, Dri. But your father is a grown man, and believe it or not, he knows how to look after himself. That thing at the construction site happened almost … jeez, six years ago. And your mother's been gone almost five. That's more than enough time to have catered to my brother's every whim."

Adrienne remained quiet, disconcerted by Aunt Claudette's description of her role at home.

"And isn't Thany doing better? That new medicine seems to be a miracle, from what your father tells me. What's it called again?"

"Carbamazepine," Adrienne said. "But it doesn't prevent seizures. It just keeps them at bay. He could have another one at any time."

"I think working on a cruise ship sounds enlivening! It's good for a young girl to see new things, especially when you find something that speaks to you. I did a semester in Spain when I was your age, you know."

"Yeah, but—"

Aunt Claudette lifted a palm. "I'll work on your father. Lord knows it's about time he gave something back to you."

When the parade ended, everyone gathered in the dining room to feast.

"Auntie Claudette!" Thany piped up as Adrienne cut his turkey. "Did you know Aaron's coming home for Christmas?"

"I sure did!"

"Then he'll be all done with boot camp," Thany continued, "and we won't have to worry about him anymore."

Across the table, Jack grumbled. "The worrying's just begun. Next thing you know, my boy'll be in some desert fighting this ludicrous war while *Dubya* keeps running the country into the ground."

Thany scrunched his face. "Who's Dubya?"

"The president," Adrienne said. "President Bush."

"Now, Jack," Aunt Claudette said, "we don't know if Aaron will be sent over there. And even so, you have to remember it was *his* decision to enlist."

"Oh, come off it, Claudette! Of course he'll be deployed! He joined the Marines! They're always the first to go."

Dickey nodded compassionately. "Even if he does go, Jack, aren't you proud Aaron wants to serve his country? Now, I'm no father over here, but it sure would make me proud having a son who wanted to serve."

Jack banged his fist on the table. "Serving his country is something Aaron can do right here on American soil! Going overseas to shed blood for oil is something else. I raised my kids to be strong, not to bow to the *man* under the guise of humanitarianism!"

Aunt Claudette put down her fork. "Jack, it's Aaron's life. He's eighteen years old and can act as his own free agent. And the same goes if *Adrienne* wants to explore opportunities ..."

The last word lingered too long, and her father turned away from his sister. "What's this? Now *you* want to join the military, too?"

"No!" Adrienne cried. "You know I don't agree with the war any more than you do!"

"Then what *opportunities* is Claudette talking about?"

Adrienne sighed. "I saw an ad in the paper last night, is all. To be a stewardess for a cruise line that sails out of Rhode Island."

Jack had no time to process the information before Thany burst into tears. "No, Adrienne! I don't want you to go to Rhode Island! Then you'll be gone just like Aaron and Mommy, too!"

Adrienne motioned for Thany to come to her. It never ceased to amaze her when he mentioned Raina, believing he was too young to remember anything besides the sporadic visits she'd made over the years. He clung to Adrienne tightly, burying his face in her shoulder. "It's all right, Bud," she said. "I'm not going anywhere, okay? It was just something nice to think about."

She withdrew to bed early, struggling with Thany's emotional reaction, wondering if he would have responded the same if Raina had never left. Then there was the million-dollar question—*Would* Raina have left if not for Jack's work injury?

She hated thinking about any of it. Being called to her guidance counselor's office the spring she was a freshman. Mr. Khoo's news that her father was involved in a work accident, rushed by ambulance to the hospital. The status of his two coworkers, already pronounced dead. A senior crane operator, Jack had become trapped in the cab, a steel beam pinning his legs for hours. But though the doctors managed to save his legs, the initial prognosis he'd ever walk again looked grim.

The months following Jack's accident were awful. Adrienne finished her first year of high school with Cs and Ds, neglecting her homework as she did everything possible to help around the house. Then followed the longest summer of her life. Wendy was a constant presence, trying to cheer her up with board games and movie marathons, while Aaron holed himself up in the attic with his friend Bear and played video games. On Saturdays, Aunt Claudette made the fifty-mile drive from the shoreline with sandwich trays. Even the Veronas paid regular visits, stopping by with herbs and strange artifacts to assist Jack's healing. "I knew it was the echinacea!" Mrs. Verona prided herself when he began walking again.

Adrienne never told Wendy's mom that she disagreed. Intensive physical therapy and an act of God had put her father back on his feet. But by then he'd been approved for early retirement. "I've given the firm twenty-two years," he'd said one late August evening. "I won't give them another day if it means I might never see you all again." Two weeks later, when the planes hit the World Trade Center, Jack sat ashen-faced in his recliner. "You just never know …" he kept saying.

By October, the dynamic in their house had changed considerably. Jack became silently engrossed in Nick at Nite and crossword puzzles, while Raina became progressively absent. "Working late" at the insurance company meant not returning until Adrienne and Aaron were leaving for school, and whenever Raina *was* home, muffled sobs regularly sounded from the bathroom. Six months later, Raina announced she was moving. "Dad agrees the divorce is best for everyone," she'd told Adrienne and Aaron upon sharing her plans to relocate to Santa Fe with the Accountant. "And don't worry about me going after his pension. Vince will support me."

At sixteen, worrying about Jack's pension was the last thing on Adrienne's mind, but she soon learned that whatever the amount, it wasn't much. Her father didn't come right out and say it, but they were struggling without Raina's paycheck, especially supplementing Thany's medical expenses. Adrienne felt indebted to Roman and Gio for hiring her, proud she learned the restaurant trade quickly and could keep steady hours. Three years in, Roman promoted her to front-of-the-house manager, meaning she got eight dollars per hour instead of five, all while balancing community college. At home, she'd tended to Thany's epilepsy while keeping on Aaron about his chores and homework. Jack attempted to help where he could, but his new limitations complicated things, and the energy in their house became increasingly pessimistic.

Adrienne wouldn't deny how far she'd come since her family was ripped apart, but besides earning a general studies degree she wasn't using, she often found her personal growth lacking. For years, she'd longed to provide better for herself, to land a job with insurance and benefits, but now after the rash of emotions at dinner, she wasn't so sure. Would every prospective opportunity that removed her from Thany's daily life be met with such opposition? Nothing like this stewardess position had ever struck a chord with her before. Up until yesterday, the *only* thing that mattered was ensuring her family was well cared for.

4

ON BLACK FRIDAY, Adrienne and Wendy embarked on their annual shopping trip to New Haven. Every year since Adrienne had gotten her license, they'd avoided the crowds at Westford Mall and headed south to The Shops at Yale instead. The Shops had the only Urban Outfitters in Connecticut, making the forty-mile drive worth it.

"You've been quiet this morning," Wendy observed as Adrienne pulled into the parking lot. "Anything you want to talk about?"

Adrienne worried about upsetting anyone else with the thought of leaving home, but even with her lack of life experience, Wendy had been a helpful sounding board since they were kids, always knowing what to say. Inside the store, Adrienne relayed the events from yesterday as she and Wendy perused half-priced scarves.

"Since when did you take up an interest in boats?" Wendy asked, admiring a scarf printed with cat silhouettes.

"You know I've always liked the water," Adrienne said. "I guess I thought it would be a neat experience. See some new things, have stories to tell the grandkids one day."

Wendy shook her head. "No travel stories for me. I'm a homebody. But that's one thing I've always known, Adrienne, is that *you* have a ton more desires and ambition. Honestly, what's the worst that could happen if you apply for this job?"

Adrienne removed a knit scarf from the rack. "I could get hired …"

"Yeah, and then you'll have your adventure. Thany will get over it. It's not like you're going very far."

Adrienne considered this. The company was only one state away.

If the cruises were also local, that probably would alleviate some guilt.

"I say go for it," Wendy encouraged, "because *honestly* ... how much longer do you want to keep working with Jenni anyway?"

She had a point. There had been too many troubling incidents at Giovanni's since Jenni was hired, and how things were looking, Jenni had permanent tenure as long as her affair with Roman continued.

"So, you aren't upset?" Adrienne asked while they ate lunch later.

Wendy took a swig of Coke and raised an eyebrow. "Upset? I'd be sad to see you go, but I'm not selfish, Adrienne." She set the Coke bottle on the table. "Can I confess something to you?"

"Sure."

"Do you think I don't know how gridlocked *my* life is? Look at me. I'm twenty-one, and I'm a cashier at a pizza place. I left college over two years ago and haven't gone back. And I just blew my entire paycheck on stuff I don't need. *Again*."

Where was Wendy going with all of this?

"But you know what?" Wendy went on. "I've recently realized it's because I'm *content*. I can admit that. Nothing's driving me to push my limits, and that's because I've allowed myself to become like this."

"What are you saying?" Adrienne asked.

"Adrienne, you've sidestepped every obstacle thrown at you and kept going. You've done a lot for your family, and maybe it's time you did something for *you*. Who knows? Maybe you'll get hired, and you won't even like it. But at least you can say you tried, right?"

Adrienne smiled, always perplexed by the sage advice delivered by a self-proclaimed homebody. She knew she wasn't supposed to feel this old already, light-years beyond the high schooler she'd been a few years earlier, weighed down with responsibilities she hadn't asked for without ever getting to decompress. She often thought about others her age still enjoying their college years. She also thought of the famous quote on a poster in Mr. Khoo's office: *You miss one hundred percent of the shots you don't take.*

"I may as well share my news, too," Wendy said. "I was going to surprise you, but while we're on the subject of life changes ..."

"What?" Adrienne asked. "Are you going back to school next semester?"

"Nope. But I *am* going for my license on Tuesday. My parents said I can have the Tercel if I pass."

"Good for you, Wendy! What finally changed your mind?"

"That's what I'm telling you, Adrienne. I've done some soul-searching and decided it's time for a change. When you know, you *know*."

Adrienne folded her napkin into squares. "But what about Thany?"

"Why don't you give him something to look forward to?" Wendy suggested. "Something to distract him from your absence?"

"That's smart. I'm sure I can come up with something."

Wendy's eyes widened. "And you know what? If you get hired, I can even help with Thany every now and then!"

"Why would you do that for me, Wendy? Don't you know how much work it is looking after a little kid?"

"Puh-lease. Don't *you* know how many birthday candles I blew out wishing for a little brother? It'll be fun hanging out with Thany! Who knows? Maybe I'll even get your dad away from the TV long enough to play a game of Monopoly or something."

They shared a laugh, even though Adrienne knew that probably wouldn't happen. Her father had never been overly fond of Wendy or her offbeat parents, often referring to them as "backwoods hillbillies"—a pejorative Adrienne had never repeated.

"Come on, Adrienne. Honestly, where am *I* going? Maybe helping with Thany will teach me some responsibility. And *you* can finally have a break from all your daughter and sister duties."

She's not wrong, Adrienne thought. And for the past thirty-six hours, her gut had been urging her to apply for the job. How lucky she was to have a best friend who was so supportive, giving her the push she needed to pursue this very unexpected *opportunity*.

December 2006

5

ON THE FIRST Thursday of December, Adrienne left early to make the two-hour drive to Rhode Island. The MapQuest directions on her passenger's seat instructed her to take Route 6, a scenic drive that was easy on the eyes. Traveling across state lines, radio DJs kept remarking on the date's significance—the sixty-fifth anniversary of Pearl Harbor—and Adrienne found herself wiping away tears for all the lives lost in World War II. And also for Aaron, who she secretly feared would be sent overseas.

She'd gotten the call three days earlier. Northeastern Cruise Line Associates had received her application and was interested in scheduling an office interview as soon as possible. "Can ya do Thursday at ten?" a woman named Lorna had asked. "We undahstand that ya live outta state, so we've also got a two o'clock if that's bettah."

Ten was fine, Adrienne had told Lorna.

"Great! And ya can dress casual, hon. We're not a fancy place."

Sure thing, Adrienne had thought, thrown off by Lorna's accent and laid-back approach.

Entering Providence, it didn't take much for Adrienne to admire the small city's charm. Vibrant houses hedged the hilly outskirts, and a river snaked through the artsy downtown, highlighting waterfront parks and pathways. Providence was so much more inviting than Hartford that Adrienne wondered why she'd never been. It wasn't *that* far away. Then she thought of Thany's seizures, the aftermath of her father's work injury, and Raina's sudden departure. *Because you have responsibilities, that's why. There are people who need you.*

She followed the highway exits to East Bay, a waterfront community southeast of Providence. Soon, she was navigating down Bay Street, a narrow road in the town's historic district with iron streetlamps and a palette of mixed-use Victorians lining the sidewalks. Vintage storefronts with yesteryear signage heralded names of antique dealers, a shoe repair place, and even a record store. Adrienne felt like she'd time-traveled to a different era. Every shop was a mom-and-pop, as if the street and possibly even the town of East Bay itself forbade commercialism.

Further down, many places bore the name *Sanbourne* in some regard. The brick fish market and attached restaurant. The cluster of industrial buildings along the water's edge. There was even a cross street called Sanbourne Lane.

"That's strange," Adrienne said, comparing her MapQuest directions to the odometer. "I should be there by now." But all she saw to her left was a sandy parking lot full of cars and pickup trucks. On her right stood a double-wide trailer on a lift. Then she saw the sign on the telephone pole:

Northeastern Cruise Line Associates
PARK IN LOT

A stenciled arrow directed Adrienne back to the parking lot. She held the brake down and stared at the double-wide. *This is it? This trailer?* But what had she expected the office to look like? Before this very moment, she hadn't given it any thought.

Adrienne found a space and stepped out of her car, staring at the trailer across the street. "Here goes nothing," she said, crushing her cigarette in the sand. She couldn't identify which was more surreal—the robust smell of seawater, which until now she'd only associated with summer months, or the fact that she'd driven two hours for a job interview in a trailer.

A doorbell droned throughout the double-wide, welcoming Adrienne into an outdated front office. A few vinyl chairs and a water cooler made up the waiting area, with framed wall maps flanking the imitation wood paneling. Behind the reception counter were bookshelves with titles like *Islands of the Atlantic* and *Navigating the Intracoastal Waterway*. A countertop stereo played a popular John Mayer song.

Adrienne heard the accent in the distance. "I'm comin', I'm comin'!" the voice said hastily. A plump, heavy-chested woman, probably in her late thirties, appeared behind the counter. She smiled and stuck out her hand. "Adrienne, right? I'm Lorna. We spoke on the phone, remembah?" Lorna had a voluminous riot of red corkscrew curls and was dressed "casual"—in a tight thermal shirt, jeans, and knockoff UGG boots—a trend Adrienne had decided years ago she would never embrace. "Yes. It's nice to meet you."

"You too, hon!" Lorna shuffled through a manila folder behind the counter. "How was ya ride in? Did ya pahk across the street?"

"It was a nice ride. Very picturesque."

"That's good, hon!" Lorna found the papers she was looking for and swung her head over her shoulder. "Suzie! Tell Bev her ten o'clock is here!" Then she pointed to the vinyl chairs. "Make ya'self at home, hon. There's a bubblah if ya get thirsty."

Adrienne took a seat. This trailer ... this woman ... this *everything*, was the exact opposite of the environment she knew at Giovanni's. She was leafing through a travel brochure when an elegant woman in a blazer and pencil skirt emerged around the corner. She was tall, slender, and late middle-aged, with silver hair cropped short. Nothing about her appearance was casual, especially not the array of diamonds on her fingers. She smiled. "Adrienne Deneau?"

Adrienne rose and offered her hand.

"I'm Beverly Sanbourne, but you can call me Bev. Follow me." She strode back down the hallway, heading to the last office and situating herself behind an executive desk. Adrienne sat before her and looked around, taking in the potted ferns in either corner and the blown-up photographs on the walls. Many were black-and-white candids of a man in a pageboy cap, toiling away on boats. The largest was a portrait of a young man in a navy uniform, taken in the fifties or sixties, perhaps. Nothing in Bev's office mirrored the compactness of the trailer's entrance. It felt very Zen, as if the space was intentionally devoid of anything that might overwhelm her.

Bev picked up Adrienne's application. "So, I see here you're from Connecticut."

"Westford," Adrienne confirmed. "It's a suburb of Hartford."

Bev made a tsk-tsk sound. "I never liked Hartford much, if you want the truth."

Adrienne wondered if all job interviews started this way, considering she'd never had a proper one before.

"What I do like," Bev continued, "is your résumé." She unsheathed a pen and ticked off Adrienne's qualifications. "Five years of stability at the same restaurant, two of which you've served as a manager ... an associate's degree with an impressive GPA ... and ..."—she stopped and smiled hopefully—"born and bred in the Northeast, I presume?"

"Yes," Adrienne said, "born right in good old Hartford."

Bev set the paperwork down and spun one of her many rings. "So, Adrienne, what prompted you to apply for the stewardess position?"

"Well," Adrienne said, "I'm at the point where I'm ready for a change and thought this might be a good opportunity. I've only had one job, but I figured my customer service experience would probably qualify me to be a stewardess."

"It certainly does. And you're correct that working for my company presents a unique opportunity, especially for young people like yourself. I've never met anyone who's snubbed their nose at free travel, have you?"

Adrienne shook her head truthfully, not that she'd ever known anyone who'd been *offered* free travel.

Bev pointed to a photograph of the man sporting the pageboy cap. "My father started NECLA when I was quite young. We've come a long way since those days, but I adorn my walls with these pictures so the familial origins aren't forgotten. I think that's paramount."

Adrienne noted how Bev referred to the company as NECLA. The acronym was certainly much quicker to say than Northeastern Cruise Line Associates.

"I have two boats," Bev went on. "The *Amelia* and the *Beatrice*. They're small and intimate, as my father intended, but the *Amelia* has been out of commission for years. I used her for dinner excursions around the bay for a few summers, but she hasn't had overnight passengers since 2001."

Adrienne nodded, acknowledging that Bev had her full attention.

"We're a small company," Bev explained. "Very small. Our average passengers are around seventy, usually middle-to-upper-class retirees from across the country. Occasionally, we get some Canadians and Europeans, but not often."

The parted blinds gave sight to the bay behind the trailer. Abutting a wooden dock, Adrienne saw what passed for nothing more than a large yacht. "Is that one of the boats?" she asked.

"That's the *Beatrice*. The *Amelia* is drydocked, undergoing refurbishment, and the *Beatrice* is next in line. Sans the current cosmetics, they're completely identical."

"Oh …" The boat outside Bev's window starkly contrasted any cruise ship she'd ever seen on TV.

"Anyhow," Bev said, "this year, I'm looking for a crew with a gold-standard work ethic to man the *Amelia*'s revival. Does this sound like something you'd be interested in?"

"Yes, absolutely," Adrienne said, careful not to appear too eager.

"Wonderful. The steward department requires seven girls, and currently, I'm hiring four. You'll be working long days—fourteen to fifteen hours, with an afternoon break and a shortened day every rotation. You'll oversee the dining room, galley, and passenger cabins; set up, serve, and break down the three daily meals, and have housekeeping responsibilities between breakfast and lunch. What do you make of that?"

"Nothing I can't handle," Adrienne said. "I'm no stranger to long days."

Bev stared at her appraisingly. She was studying her, obviously so, for reasons Adrienne couldn't grasp. "How are your interpersonal skills? As a manager, I assume you have a good rapport with your coworkers?"

Adrienne tried putting Jenni as far out of her mind as possible. "Great, that I know of. I've never had any complaints."

"Given your obvious maturity, that doesn't surprise me. Working on a boat, especially a small one, takes grit, and it leaves no room for cattiness. You'll be living in close quarters, and unlike any job you'll ever have again, this is one you don't leave at quitting time. Your coworkers will serve as your roommates and peers, with no escape. Does that sound like a situation you're comfortable with?"

As long as I'm not surrounded by a boatload of Jennis, I'll be fine. But to Bev, Adrienne said, "Absolutely."

"Wonderful. For benefits, you'll be rewarded handsomely. I contribute one hundred percent health and dental premiums after your first sixty days, and, of course, you'll have free room and board. Three meals a day at no cost to you. And your meals are the same dishes served to the passengers—top-notch regional cuisine. I don't subscribe to the philosophy of producing a separate mess for the crew. It's my belief you must give the best to get the best, wouldn't you agree?"

"Definitely."

"There isn't much on board for leisure, but my past crews have never had trouble entertaining themselves, which you can take however you'd like. What *is* included is a small crew lounge and some exercise machines you're permitted to use when no passengers are aboard." Bev winked at Adrienne. "I've thrown a lot at you. Do you have any questions for me?"

"A couple," Adrienne said. "I'm curious why the ad said you were looking for natives of southern New England. I'm just wondering why that would matter?"

"To authenticate the passengers' experience. Most of my itineraries have ports of call in southern New England. The rest are along the Maine coastline and the Hudson River in the fall. It's important to me to employ a crew local to the region. Besides the point, my vessels are U.S. flagged and registered, which is quite uncommon in the industry, thus eliminating any international applicants."

Adrienne was glad she'd be staying local. If she got hired, it would be easier explaining to Thany that she wasn't going *too* far away. "The ad also mentioned competitive pay. What does that mean, exactly?"

"Another great question. I compensate my employees well above the industry standard. This season, I'm starting the steward department at ten dollars per hour on yard days and sixty-five dollars daily during trips."

A sinking feeling washed over Adrienne. *Sixty-five dollars? For fourteen to fifteen hours' worth of work?* This whole opportunity had sounded too good to be true! Those were slave wages, and she doubted they were legal. "I'm sorry," she said crisply, "but that's just over four dollars per hour. There's no way I can survive on that."

Bev raised her hand. "Please, if you'll let me continue. The sixty-five dollars is company *day-pay*. You'll accrue hundreds more in pooled tips each trip. And I provide a generous bonus if you commit through November first. If you're wise with your money, you could end the season in the ballpark of thirty thousand dollars."

"Really?" Adrienne exclaimed.

"Oh yes. I've known crew members who have left their checkbooks and bank cards on land and never spent a penny all season. That particular scenario is a rarity, of course."

Adrienne bit her bottom lip. "When does the season start?"

"I expect my crews to commit to full seasons. It doesn't always happen, but it's what I aim for. The steward department will begin in the shipyard on February twenty-sixth. You'll spend eight weeks stocking inventory and assembling the cabins, and you'll receive first aid, CPR, and HELM training, with certificates upon completion."

"February twenty-sixth?" Adrienne repeated. "And I'd work straight through until November first?"

"No. A few short breaks throughout the season will allow you to return home. And yard days are nine-to-five, Monday through Friday, until you set sail in April, during which time I only cover your course expenses. I may buy the occasional lunch, but otherwise, you're expected to support yourself until the season begins."

"Support myself?"

"Yes, dear. For food and travel costs. But your yard time is counted toward the first sixty days for the insurance. You'll receive your bonus when the season commences, after which you'll be eligible to collect unemployment."

Adrienne's mind was racing to piece together the bombardment of information. "So ... I would drive here and back for two months *without* reimbursement?"

"Yes. But I should share with you that I've received over fifty stew applications, and I've already capped my final selections. For what it's worth, I like you enough to offer you a position *now*, background check and drug test pending, of course."

"Why?" Adrienne asked. "Why me?" She'd hardly gotten a word in edgewise, and this woman was offering her a position *right now?*

Bev stared at her, hard and studious. "Why you? Because you have a nice résumé, you strike me as industrious, and you have a leadership quality to boot. And because instinct says you'll be an ideal asset to my father's legacy. You'll get the opportunity of a lifetime, Adrienne, and if you're smart about it, you'll profit nicely. If the commute is the only factor causing your indecision, I'd strongly reconsider."

There it was again, that phrase—*the opportunity of a lifetime.* Adrienne tried calculating how much the commute would set her back.

"What do you say?" Bev asked. "Shall I give you until Monday to decide?"

"Sure. That sounds great."

"*Wonderful.*" Bev shook her hand. "It truly was a pleasure meeting you, Adrienne. I don't think either of us will be disappointed." She opened a drawer and pulled out a few brochures. "Some of our itineraries. They'll give you a better idea of where the company travels."

Adrienne slid the brochures into her purse, thanking Bev and promising to be in touch soon.

On her way out of the trailer, Adrienne saw a girl sitting in the same chair she'd occupied a half-hour before. She was slight but athletically built, with wide gray eyes and a delicate bone structure. The girl's honey-blonde hair was as long as hers, and Adrienne wagered she must still be a teenager. She stopped to acknowledge the girl. For all she knew, this could be a new coworker if she accepted the position. "Hi. I'm Adrienne."

"Hailey," the girl said. She was trying to uphold a smile, but Adrienne could tell she was petrified. "Did you just come from a stewardess interview?"

Adrienne nodded, keeping Bev's offer of employment to herself.

"I'm *so* nervous," Hailey confided quietly. "I've never been on a job interview before."

"She's fine," Adrienne assured her. "Nothing to worry about."

Hailey put a hand to her chest. "Oh good. This sounds so exciting, doesn't it? I've never been *anywhere* before!"

Adrienne smiled at Hailey's youthfulness, wondering if *she* could've been capable of such innocent exuberance if she hadn't needed to grow up so fast. She was about to ask where Hailey was from when they heard Bev coming back down the hall.

"Good luck," Adrienne whispered. "I'm sure you'll do great."

"Thanks," Hailey said. "I *really* need it."

Hailey

Sheesh! What the heck did she get herself into? She stays strong as she follows Bev Sanbourne into her office, trying not to think about what her parents would say if they knew where she was right now ... where she'd *really* taken the Jetta.

"It's very nice to meet you, Hannah," Bev says. "I do hope the morning commute from Boston wasn't too overbearing."

Hannah? She tenses. "Um, my name is Hailey, and I'm not from Boston."

Bev stares doubtingly at the paperwork on her desk. "I was expecting a Hannah Donofrio for my ten-thirty."

"My last name is Decker."

Bev frowns. "Please excuse me for a moment."

From out in the hall, she hears Bev reprimanding the woman who'd set up her interview. *Laura? Lorna?* She's too nervous to remember even though she just met the woman ten minutes ago.

Bev is still sore when she returns with *her* application. "Well, I certainly apologize for the confusion, Hailey. Same initials, apparently." She flips the application around. "But I'm also confused about *this.* Am I correct in understanding that you have *no* work experience?"

She nods, feeling shame with each passing second.

"Quite frankly, I'm looking for candidates with at least *some* experience. Tell me, Hailey, why did you apply to be a stewardess?"

Okay, breathe, Hailey, she coaches herself. *You can do this.* "I want to support myself without relying on my parents anymore," she says, quick and assertive. "And I want to see new places." She hesitates before spilling her secret. "Before today, I've never left Connecticut."

Bev cocks her head. "You've never left *Connecticut?*"

"No ... not before this morning."

Bev squints at the address portion on her application. "You're from *Franklin,* Connecticut? Where is that?" She whips a road map from her desk drawer. "Show me."

She points to the tiny dot in New London County. "Right here. It's a small town with less than two thousand people. We don't have our own emergency services, and I had to commute to Griswold for high school."

Bev stares at the map in disbelief. "But you can't be thirty minutes from the border of Rhode Island! Or Massachusetts, for that matter!" Her eyes narrow. "How old are you, Hailey?"

"Nineteen. My birthday is on Halloween."

"You're telling me that in *nineteen* years, you've never left the third smallest state in the country?"

She trembles. "No. I-I've never even left New London County. My family is very strict."

She waits for Bev to say something to break the uncomfortable strain between them, but when Bev stays silent, tears surface, and she stands from her chair. "I'm sorry," she says. "This was a mistake. I shouldn't have applied to work here."

She's touching the doorknob as Bev says, "The position is yours if you want it."

"What?"

Bev passes her a tissue box. "Hailey, by the time I was your age, I'd seen the world three times over. As far as I'm concerned, any young woman brazen enough to venture this far from her comfort zone is *immediately* qualified."

She takes a tissue but doesn't sit down.

"Please, Hailey," Bev says. "Take this for what it is and consider it the most fortunate mistake of your life. Now, let's get to know one another better, shall we?"

Bev

SHE'S PLEASED with today's hires. She's always liked the ones with fire in their bellies. *Inconceivable* about that Hailey's situation, though. Of course the girl deserves the opportunity! But it's that Adrienne she's most proud of securing, positive she'll accept the position. She'd liked her the moment she laid eyes on her. Tenacious, mature beyond her years, and what a beauty! She can see Max Hardigan's face on yard day now, certain when Max sees Adrienne, that her reign will be threatened. And maybe that's exactly what the girl needs.

She's already advised Peter to mind his stepdaughter's antics, but be it from a distance, she's been around the girl long enough to know that's a warning bound to go over like a lead balloon. "You know I'll never fire her," she'd told Peter, "but Max and the Cavanaugh girl better not terrorize this year's crew as I heard they did last season on the *Beatrice*. If Max wants to look down on the world, that's her prerogative, one I'm sure will catch up with her when life matters most. But if she can't make nice, she doesn't make trouble either. You tell her to stick with her group and leave the others alone."

6

THREE DAYS BEFORE Christmas, Adrienne left work after lunch to prepare for Aaron's return from boot camp. She washed his bedding, put fresh towels on the chair in his room, and picked up his favorite snacks at the grocery store.

Thany zoomed around the living room with Dolly on his heels. "Today!" he kept yelling. "Today! Aaron's coming home today!"

Adrienne laughed nervously. "Take it easy, Bud. You don't want to overexert yourself."

But Thany's ecstasy was contagious, and even her father couldn't suppress an elastic smile. "There's nothing like having the whole family together for Christmas," he said. No one mentioned Raina, though Adrienne was already mentally preparing for her mother's Christmas Day phone call. Raina had also sent presents—three boxes Adrienne had tossed in the hallway closet.

At five o'clock, they piled in Jack's truck and headed to Bradley Field to meet Aaron. They waited at the bottom of the escalator, huddled together amid the hubbub of holiday travelers.

"There he is!" Thany called after twenty minutes. "There's Aaron!"

Adrienne looked upward. Dressed in military fatigues and much too tan for December, Aaron was descending with a duffel bag.

"They shaved his damn head," Jack said, shaking his own.

"What did you expect?" Adrienne whispered.

Thany jumped on Aaron when he reached the landing, and Jack hugged his sons while Thany remained in Aaron's arms. "Welcome home, my boy," he said softly. "Glad to have you back."

Adrienne hung back until their reunion ceased, stepping forward to hug her brother. "Hey, Dri. You hold down the fort while I was gone?" Aaron chuckled forcedly, and Adrienne tried reading his expression. He seemed happy to be home, but she sensed something else, a detached look in his eyes that suggested he was returning to them from something he couldn't explain, something there was no coming back from.

They ordered delivery from Giovanni's. Jack's expression hardened when Aaron devoured an entire pie. "I don't even want to know what they fed you down there, son. This is probably the first decent meal you've had since September, isn't it?"

Aaron scooped a heaping portion of antipasto onto his plate. "You can't call much of what they gave us *food*."

"So," Jack said tentatively, "did they say, er, did they say when you're heading back?"

"February second," Aaron said between mouthfuls.

Jack nodded. "And did they say where you'll be based?"

"I requested to be stationed at Camp Lejeune in North Carolina. No idea when I'll be deployed."

Jack took a swig of root beer. Too long a swig, one that allowed him to blink back tears. "As long as you're safe, son," he said. "All your old man wants is for you to come home in one piece."

Later, Adrienne found Aaron in their room, sorting clothes into his dresser. "Thanks for getting me set up," he said. "You didn't have to do all that."

Adrienne smoothed the corner of his bed and sat down. "Is there anything you want to talk about?"

"Like what?"

"Like anything that happened while you were away …"

"It's nothing you don't hear about, Dri. The brainwashing, the abuse, that shit's all real. Whatever you think in your head probably happened."

"I don't know what to think," Adrienne admitted.

"Then you're better off not knowing."

"So, why go back? Can't you get a discharge or something?"

"That's not how it works. Besides, why do you think I left? You think I want to keep living here with Jack and his depression? He's half the reason I enlisted. Or keep sharing a bedroom with my *sister*? No offense."

"Then get a job, Aaron," Adrienne pressed. "Move out and work somewhere. Or go to school. I don't understand why you'd want to subject yourself to that lifestyle if it's as bad as you say."

"I'm not the genius, Dri," Aaron said. "I can't focus on a million things at once like you. One good thing that happened in boot camp was learning discipline. I *like* being in a structured environment. A couple of guys I met down there said the same thing."

Adrienne paused. If those were Aaron's true feelings, what else could she do except support him? "Well, if you think the military is the best path, I'll stand behind your decision. I just don't want anything to happen to you, Aaron. You're my brother."

Aaron nodded, stern and composed.

Adrienne headed toward the tapestries. "February second, huh? Guess that means you'll miss my big send-off."

"*Your* send-off? Where are you going?"

Adrienne told him about NECLA and how she'd accepted the stewardess position shortly after her interview, her deciding factor that she'd be remaining in the Northeast. She could be home in just a matter of hours if an emergency occurred.

"Good for you," Aaron said. "You're doing yourself a favor getting out of here. Whatever you're looking for, you'll figure it out once you're gone. Trust me."

7

CHRISTMAS MORNING was one of the happiest Adrienne could recall. She'd set her alarm for three A.M., knowing Thany would be sound asleep, and transformed the living room to resemble a Sears catalog. Presents were stacked and layered under the tree, bulging stockings swung from the mantel, and the cookies Thany left out vanished, just crumbs remaining. Lastly, Raina's presents were pulled from the closet and placed on the couch.

By daybreak, Adrienne was back in the living room, curled in her father's recliner while everyone opened their gifts. She'd gone overboard this year, partly out of guilt for taking the job with NECLA, which Thany was still struggling to accept, but couldn't help basking in the reactions of her father and brothers every time their faces lit up.

Her father and Aaron were easy to shop for—crossword puzzles, coffee, and gift cards galore. But Thany made out better than everyone, unwrapping plenty of books, board games, and toys. The big draw was Thany's nontangible present. Thanks to Wendy's suggestion, Adrienne surprised him with the news that she'd enrolled him in the neighborhood Cub Scout den.

Jack had been apprehensive at first, but Adrienne encouraged him that Cub Scouts would be as good for *him* as for Thany. He'd finally come around, agreeing Cub Scouts was a happy medium. Thany couldn't play sports, but Scouting would allow him to interact with other boys outside of his first-grade class. An optimistic warmth took hold as Adrienne watched Thany pore over his new Scout handbook, and Jack gathered him in his lap so they could read together.

When Raina called, Adrienne acknowledged her gifts and handed the phone to Aaron, who shook his head and passed it to Thany. Their little brother rambled on to Raina for ten minutes, like two old friends catching up.

"My turn," Aaron said when Thany hung up. He bounded upstairs, returning with shopping bags in hand and a shiny two-wheeler over his shoulder. "No more training wheels for you, Bud."

Thany ran to the bike and tried climbing on, his ruddy little cheeks aglow. "Wow! A big kid bike! Thanks, Aaron!"

The morning continued with a rush of excitement the Deneaus seldom experienced. Aunt Claudette and Dickey were away for the holidays, but Wendy and Aaron's friend Bear joined them for brunch. After, the guys took Thany outside to try his new bike. Adrienne and Wendy stayed in the living room, sipping moonshine eggnog from Wendy's dad as they exchanged gifts.

Wendy had passed her driver's test and was now the proud owner of the seafoam Tercel her parents had driven down from Vermont. Adrienne gave her seat covers and a gas card, and Wendy presented Adrienne with a photo album she'd crafted, full of pictures of their ten-year friendship. "In case you get homesick," she offered.

Adrienne smiled. No matter what Jack said, Wendy was a true friend. They'd worked out a plan for Wendy to take Thany out on Sunday afternoons once she left for the boat. She'd put aside money, which she'd give to Wendy in April. It was a win-win for everyone, an unofficial Big Brothers Big Sisters program.

The day's activity left Thany more hyper than Adrienne was comfortable with. Even after Wendy and Bear departed, he was still in full gear. "You need to take it easy," Adrienne reminded him as she washed dishes. But on the same token, she tried remembering what Christmas felt like when *she* was six. The difference, of course, was that she wasn't epileptic.

She was scrubbing a Pyrex dish when she heard a commotion in the living room, running from the kitchen with sud-covered arms. Thany lay writhing on the carpet, Jack and Aaron at his sides. Adrienne grabbed a throw pillow. "Turn him over in case he spits up," she told Aaron. She lifted his twitching head and stuck the pillow under, rubbing his shoulder blades. "It's all right, Bud. It'll be over soon."

They watched the wall clock. A second past five minutes and they'd have to call an ambulance. Fortunately, no fluid discharged from Thany's mouth, and he quickly entered the postictal phase—doctorspeak for the disorientation an epileptic experienced post-seizure.

"Nathaniel, can you hear me, son?" Jack asked. "Are you okay?" Thany blinked, and Jack scooped him off the carpet. "You two get back to enjoying your Christmas," he said. "I'm taking him to bed."

But the magic was gone. They'd been through Thany's seizures so many times and no one ever had much to say when they ended. Without a word, Aaron walked upstairs while Adrienne resumed her spot at the sink. A few minutes later, she felt her father's hand on her shoulder. "What are those tears for?"

Adrienne turned off the faucet. "I think I made a mistake taking this new job, Dad," she confessed. "Look at our family. It's broken enough already. And look at Thany. He needs me."

"Look at *me*, Adrienne," Jack said. "Anything that will happen to Nathaniel will happen whether you're here or not. Your brother knows you love him, and that's all that matters."

"Are you trying to get rid of me?" she asked.

The pain in her father's eyes was deep-rooted. "I'm just sorry I haven't done more for you. After your mother left, Adrienne ... the way you up and cared for your brothers ... went out and started working ... you kept us whole. Did a better job than I ever could. And I know it's taken a toll on you. All that stress ... those cigarettes ... Maybe getting away will help you quit."

He'd always despised her habit. How he'd yelled the first time he'd caught her smoking was forever branded in Adrienne's memory. She wiped her hands on a dishtowel. "I just worry so much, Dad. Not just about Thany and Aaron, but about you, too."

"And that's why you need to go," Jack said. "Otherwise, you'll wind up like your old man. And that's the last thing I want for any of you kids. Worrying doesn't solve anything, Adrienne. Make some new friends and have some fun for once. You deserve it more than anyone out there."

January 2007

8

ADRIENNE WAITED until exactly one month before her start date to give Roman her notice. The little money she'd saved over the years would afford her to get by without working at Giovanni's straight through. That way, she could spend extra time with her family.

The arctic air sent chills through her jacket when she went outside and found Roman smoking a cigarette on his milk crate. Adrienne sat next to him and lit her own. "I'm putting in my two weeks. February ninth will be my last day."

Roman stared at her soberly, a look she knew meant her departing Giovanni's was the last thing he expected to hear. "And where're you gonna go?"

"I got a job on a cruise ship out of Rhode Island."

"Mind if I ask why?"

"It's not because of Jenni, if that's what you think. I just want a chance to try something different. Travel … have a job with benefits …"

"What about your family?"

Adrienne thought his question brave, considering how he'd always skirted around mentioning her family in the past. "Aaron's still home from boot camp, and Wendy's going to hang out with Thany while I'm away."

Roman looked across the parking lot, maintaining a reserved silence. Adrienne suspected his quiet stemmed from regret for not seizing any moments when he was her age, that his affair with Jenni was, in part, making up for opportunities lost in his youth. Not that he'd ever admit it, but she'd known him long enough.

"Well, you have my blessing if that's what you're looking for," he said eventually. "You've paid your dues here."

"Thanks, Ro. That means a lot."

He walked toward the door, surprising Adrienne when he turned and said, "There'll always be a place for you here if you come back."

"We'll see," Adrienne said. "I'm sure whatever's meant to be will work itself out."

Roman

HE REMEMBERS the night she walked into Giovanni's like it was yesterday. Just turned sixteen and hungry for work. She'd seen the Help Wanted notice in the window, and he'd given her an application and working papers for her parents to sign. She was back—signed, sealed, and delivered—at opening the next day. "I'll take any shifts you can give me," she'd told him. "I'm a quick learner, and I'm good with people."

He'd put her on the registers first. Never had a girl who memorized the POS so fast. Over the summer he'd moved her to the floor—lunch shifts, where there wasn't a high demand for beer and wine since she was too young to serve. She'd reminded him a lot of himself—walked into the place when he was eighteen and never left. She was personable and efficient, just like she'd promised, and he came to rely on her.

That October, he got a call from a guidance counselor named Sam Khoo. Turned out she'd been skipping all her afternoon classes to come to work. "There's nothing I can do about it," he'd told Khoo. "Her father signed the working papers. I hafta go by what he says, not the school." That's when he'd first learned about her home life. Dad had been injured at work and took an early retirement. Mom had met someone else and split to New Mexico. She had two younger brothers, one just a toddler and sick with epilepsy, and the school suspected she was working to supplement the family income. "I didn't know any of that," he'd said. "Whatever problems she's got at home, she leaves them at the door when she's here."

He was glad the school worked with her to graduate on time. He's never said it, but he admires her for taking on so much so young. Could've played that hand another way, but Adrienne was smarter than that, and it made him proud. He'd never even heard her complain until Jenni came around last year. But, ah, what're you gonna do? Sure, he still loves Shannon, but she'd let motherhood and her career take over. You tell him what kind of husband wants to work sixty-hour weeks to be neglected at home? Things are what they are for now. He's making up for his marriage troubles, and Adrienne's doing what she needs to so she doesn't wind up like him, miserable and full of regrets at thirty-three.

Connie

WHAT A WHIRLWIND of change these past six months have brought! Just last summer, she would've laughed if someone said Bev Sanbourne would request *her* to lead the first season of the *Amelia*'s revival. Not that fourteen years of managing events at the Wampanoag Club doesn't qualify her to be a cruise director. Or her summers off from college working as a stewardess in the eighties. She recalls the long hours fondly. And the seemingly longer ones making up for them at night.

She's always thought she would've stayed with NECLA if she hadn't gotten pregnant during the summer of '87. May of '88 had brought Macy, Brett, the deckhand who'd fathered her, never to be heard from again. Not that she'd tried hard to find him. She has enough love for Macy as a million parents, and Macy's never noticed the snub.

She can't believe Macy is eighteen already, just starting her second semester at the University of Colorado Boulder. How lucky she is to have such an intelligent beauty to call her daughter. She misses her so, but that's why she's agreed to help Bev for 2007. Being on the water again should help take her mind off the empty East Greenwich apartment. Hell, she's only just turned thirty-nine. Still spry enough to relive her youth ... well, *maybe*.

She's fortunate to have kept in touch with Bev's son Mattie on and off throughout the years. If not for him, she might never have been considered for the position ...

9

WHEN SHE REACHES NECLA, Connie's amazed at how little Bev has aged. Bev's once-blonde hair is silver now, and her face a bit more wizened, but she's just as polished and impeccably dressed as Connie remembers. They embrace warmly. Dozens of phone calls and emails over the past several months, but this is their first time seeing each other in nearly two decades. Not that Mattie hasn't kept them filled in about the other.

They discuss the *Amelia*'s itineraries over delicious haddock sandwiches that Bev's other son, Andrew, delivers from Sanbourne's Fish Market. Bev shuffles through some papers on her desk. "I have your stew applications here. You must just be itching to learn about the chosen seven."

"I'm curious," Connie admits.

Bev hands her two applications. "I've got two girls coming in from Connecticut this year. One from the Hartford area with five years' experience, and the other from a one-horse town called Franklin. No experience, and hired by complete fluke."

Connie skims the applications of Adrienne Deneau and Hailey Decker. "Her first job? Are you sure the Franklin girl can handle it?"

"Certain. Hailey and I have spoken at length, and I firmly believe she'll make an excellent addition." Bev slides two more applications across the desk. "I've also selected a very enthusiastic girl who hails from Falmouth. Katherine Fowler—a recent JWU graduate and quite passionate about hospitality."

Connie reads over Katherine's application and then the one behind it. "Wait a minute ... Bev, are you giving me a *male* stew for the season?"

Bev grins. "Noah Mitchell from Tiverton. Boating experience since he could crawl and a personality worthy of his own daytime talk show."

"Is he …?"

"Flamboyantly," Bev finishes. "Almost makes my Mattie seem straight as a gun barrel."

"I'm sure I'll love him. Who are the other three?"

"The other three are returnees. One of whom is an admirable young woman named Mackenzie Logan, a true world traveler."

"And the other two?"

Bev steeples her hands. "The other two don't need an introduction. I'm giving you Max Hardigan and Brynne Cavanaugh for the season."

Connie sighs, summoning her composure. *There it is. The missing piece Mattie so conveniently left out.* "I don't know, Bev … Max Hardigan and Brynne Cavanaugh? Has Mattie officially resigned yet?"

"Oh heavens, yes! After six consecutive seasons? My son threatened to quit if I didn't give him 2007 off. He's already frolicking around Fort Lauderdale, as I'm sure you're aware. No plans to return until the *Beatrice* is ready."

Connie swallows hard. *Mattie! That sneaky queen!* And she's already given notice at the Wampanoag Club!

"Look," Bev says, "I know those girls have quite the reputation out there in East Greenwich, but I feel strongly they're better off aboard my boats than further dishonoring their characters here on land."

"I've just heard a lot of stories, Bev …"

"I've heard stories as well, but whether they're half-truths or fully loaded ones isn't for me to decide. Besides, you know I owe it to Peter."

Connie nods stiffly. Sensing her tension, Bev asks, "Have either of those girls ever given you, *personally*, a hard time?"

"Well, no …"

"And what about your daughter?"

"Macy? No, of course not."

"So, there you have it. You've all lived in the same town for years without issue, so it's unlikely one should occur during the season. Wherever your apprehension stems from, shift it aside. Peter will see to it that they keep in line."

Connie

Maybe Bev is right, she thinks on the drive home. Ever since Macy was one, *home* has been a two-bedroom apartment above Morton's Florals on historic Main Street. Across the street is Salon Medusa, the boutique hair spa owned by Max Hardigan's mother, Michelle. For years, they've been quote-unquote "neighbors," and for years, there's been no trouble. Still, Macy, who'd been a year behind Max Hardigan and Brynne Cavanaugh in high school, was going to *die* once she heard the news.

The scandal involving Max and Brynne had become the talk of East Greenwich right as Macy was finishing seventh grade. Fifteen months later, when she'd become a freshman at the high school, she came home spilling the beans. "*Everyone* talks about them, Mom," she'd said one evening.

"Oh yeah?"

"Yeah. Everyone knows they're the girls who got expelled from Saint Agatha's last year. *And*, people say that Brynne Cavanaugh is a prostitute."

She'd had to bite her tongue at that one. "What about Max Hardigan? What do they say about her?"

"Mom, she is *so* mean. Everyone says she's the biggest bitch they've ever met. Even the junior and senior girls stay away from her."

"How does she treat you? Is she mean to you?"

"No, she's never bothered me."

"That's good." She would've wrung Max Hardigan's neck had she ever tried corrupting her Macy. Through other parents, she'd heard all kinds of small-town speculation surrounding Max's and Brynne's expulsion from Saint Agatha's. But if even a fraction of what they said was true, it was still enough to make sure Macy never befriended *either* of those girls.

She calls Macy during her evening soak in the tub. She's been trying to give her space at college, the whole *independence* thing. They talk about Macy's classes and a potential new boyfriend until Macy changes the subject. "Did you go to NECLA yet, Mom?"

"This morning. Bev gave me the rundown for the season. You'll never guess who she's putting on my boat …"

"Who?"

"Max Hardigan and Brynne Cavanaugh."

Macy gasps, and she pictures her sitting at attention, wide-eyed and waiting for more. "Oh crap! Are you serious?"

"Serious, baby."

"You better sleep with one eye open, Mom! Those girls will give you a run for your money!"

Yes. Which is exactly why she'd negotiated one hundred fifty dollars for day-pay after learning East Greenwich's Most Wanted will be on her roster.

Brynne

SHE CAN'T REMEMBER not knowing Max. They'd met in ballet when they were two and have been inseparable ever since. Even as a toddler, Max, who was two years younger than her biological sister, Desi, and six years younger than her stepbrother, Petey, never wanted anything to do with either of them. "*Brynnie* is my sister!" she'd tell Michelle and Peter when they were small. "Not stupid, ugly Desi!"

She didn't have siblings and was fascinated by being Max's "sister." And it was because of *her* that Max was even called "Max" at all. *Mackenzie* was a mouthful for a two-year-old to pronounce, so on the first day of ballet, when the little blonde girl toddled over and said, "Bwynnie, dance wif me," she'd responded as best she could—"Okay, *Max*." Ever since then, Max had thrown cringeworthy fits whenever anyone except Peter called her *Mackenzie*.

Michelle's first husband was killed in a car accident when Max was an infant, leaving Max forced to respect the man who swooped in and saved her family. Peter, who was twenty years Michelle's senior, met her at a wedding in Virginia and fell in love with her white-blonde hair and bewitching sapphire eyes. He'd proposed after a month, flying Michelle and her two daughters to Rhode Island and purchasing the big brick colonial on Ashland Farm Drive. It wasn't long after that when she and Max met in ballet.

Last year, she'd practically jumped to join Max as a stewardess when Max's boyfriend, Marco, accepted the officer-in-training position at NECLA. *Please* get her out of East Greenwich! *Please* let her learn some skills and earn her own money! She had no interest in Maureen's multi-million-dollar inheritance. Her mother had never worked a day in her life, and she was determined *not* to follow suit.

In her own quiet way, she'd been looking forward to befriending the other stewardesses when they'd arrived on the *Beatrice*. You think she doesn't know how small Rhode Island is? Working for a company on the other side of the bay gave her better odds of not running into people already weary of her reputation. But with her constant air of superiority, Max earned them both a literal boatload of enemies before even embarking on the first trip.

Now, she realizes how naive she was, hoping to compensate for her friendless high school years, hoping for alternate companionship while Gordon was working in Boston and Max was preoccupied with Marco. She doesn't stand a chance for new friends this season either. Not with Macy Lacasio's mother working as the cruise director, and God only knows how many other girls from last season coming back.

But she's decided to return anyway. With Marco still needing three hundred hours for his captain's license, it's the only way she can be with Max, who would follow *him* anywhere. And she follows Max. Without her, she has no one.

February 2007

10

ON HER LAST DAY at Giovanni's, Adrienne was squatted behind the counter looking for register tape when the front door opened, and heels clicked against the hardwood floor. Adrienne stood up, surprised to see Roman's wife approaching her. Shannon, her black hair secured by a jaw clip, was still in her lab coat, on break from the pharmacy at the corner. "I hear it's your last day, Adrienne," she said, pulling a wrapped box from her purse. "I'm on lunch, but I wanted to drop this off and hear about your new job for myself."

Adrienne was puzzled. "You didn't have to do that, Shannon. I mean, thank you, but why did you buy me a gift?"

Shannon glanced toward the kitchen and lowered her voice. "Is *she* here?"

"No," Adrienne said. "She doesn't work on Friday afternoons."

Shannon checked her watch. "Well, then, it's been a while, hasn't it? Let's catch up." She headed for the staff table with the gift box.

Adrienne was astounded by Shannon's placidity compared to the last time she'd seen her. Just thinking of that broiling July day made her shudder, a memory she knew would haunt her forever.

Seven months ago, a record-breaking heat wave meant nobody was leaving the comforts of their air conditioners, especially not for pizza. But Gio had insisted the restaurant stay open, and Adrienne had spent the morning cleaning the iron table crevices while Jenni pranced around in booty shorts, fawning over Roman and rubbing his neck with ice nuggets. Adrienne had shielded her eyes, shaking her head whenever Roman responded with a sensual groan.

At one-thirty, Roman left the kitchen to update the POS systems, grinning as Jenni hugged him from behind, pressing her chest into his back. Adrienne had turned her own back to them, reworking a section of clean tables to avoid the mock sex show. She'd been facing the front door when Shannon walked in on her lunch break, watching in horror as Shannon's insouciant expression morphed into a sick fusion of heartbreak and shock.

"I knew it!" she'd screamed, charging past Adrienne. "I *knew* you were fucking her!" She'd pummeled Roman with her fists. "We have children, you son of a bitch!" Then she'd turned on Jenni. "And you! So help me *God* if I ever catch you outside, you little whore!" She'd ripped her wedding bands off and hurled them at Roman, angry tears streaming down her face. "Don't come home tonight!" she'd bawled, running toward the door.

It had been Adrienne who'd answered the restaurant phone when Shannon called, weeping. "I have to get a *divorce* now! I should have listened to my gut months ago when he started acting distant!"

Shannon's anguish had reminded Adrienne of when her father had learned about the Accountant. But Jack wasn't reactionary, internalizing his pain and isolating himself from the family. "I'm sorry, Shannon," she'd said. "My mom screwed around on my dad, too."

"How *long?*" Shannon had pressed. "And how come no one told me?"

Adrienne cursed Roman. "We started noticing during the spring. I'm sorry, Shannon, but this is my job. Please think about the position I'm in."

Shannon had let out another wail. "I'm sorry, too! I'll never go against my woman's intuition again!"

Adrienne had only seen her once since then, for a split second on a gray afternoon when she'd dropped five-year-old Zoe off with Roman. Now, the Shannon who sat across from her looked unrecognizable from the spurned woman who'd blasted through Giovanni's last July. This Shannon looked complacent, assumedly accepting her husband's infidelities, looking the other way instead of getting that divorce. Her eyes told Adrienne not to discuss the matter, that *she* would broach it if at all.

"So, Ro told me you're leaving to work on a cruise ship."

"I start in the shipyard in seventeen days," Adrienne confirmed.

Shannon spun the saltshaker with her thumbs and forefingers. "I sure wish I did something like that when I was your age. Could've taken my life in a whole different direction."

"Yeah ... I'm really looking forward to the experience."

Shannon's mood lightened. "I'd *love* to go on a cruise! What fun from what you see on TV! All the entertainment! The casinos! The pampering! I'm sure you'll have a blast in your off-hours."

Adrienne laughed. "It's not that kind of cruise ship."

Shannon winced as Adrienne described the *Amelia*'s void of glamorous amenities. "Well ..." she said, "you'll just have to find organic ways to stay entertained." Then she asked about Adrienne's family.

"Wendy offered to keep an eye on them," Adrienne said. "I'm really lucky that she lives next door."

Shannon smiled. "I've always liked the two of you. Becca, too. It's not easy knowing your husband works around pretty girls all day. All this time and I never worried until ..."

Adrienne took a breath as Shannon's voice cracked. "I understand, Shannon, really. I'm firmly against infidelity."

"Oh, look at me ..." Shannon said, sliding the gift box across the table. "Here, sweetie. It's just my way of saying there aren't any hard feelings for not telling me what was going on. And to thank you. Five years of working with Ro, and you were nothing but a friend to him."

Adrienne unwrapped a jewelry box and lifted a silver bracelet from the cushion inside. A variety of anchor charms dangled from the chain.

"I got it at Sterling's," Shannon said. "No big deal. Just a reminder to stick to your roots. No matter what happens, don't ever forget where you come from. Or stray from your convictions."

Adrienne ran a finger over the fine detail work. "Wow. This is so thoughtful, Shannon. Thank you."

Shannon stood and hugged her. "No, thank *you*, Adrienne. You're a great kid. I hope you get everything you want out of your new job."

"I hope so," Adrienne said, walking her to the door.

Suddenly, Shannon said, "Who knows? Maybe you might meet a guy."

"Meet a guy on a boat?"

"Yeah! Wouldn't that be romantic!"

"Maybe ... but it'll be a small crew. I don't think I'll have many options."

"Only time will tell, sweetie." Shannon held the door with her elbow. "I guess I can tell you this now, but Ro and I never cared for that boyfriend you used to have. We always thought he was too ... *shiftless.*"

"Shiftless," Adrienne repeated, admiring Shannon's word choice. She couldn't have described Rick better herself, knowing her father, Wendy, and everyone else would agree in a heartbeat.

Nicky

BEV WANTS TO SEE HIM? Lorna bettah not've lost his check again. Last time it took a week for a new one—a wicked pissah! And she can forget about him goin' on direct deposit! He's been tellin' 'er *no* for six years!

Bev's waitin' for him in the trailah. "Mr. O'Hara! My favorite Napoleon without the complex! What a pleasure to see you!" She hugs him even though he's coated in dried paint. "Come to my office, dear. I have a problem that I'm hoping you can help with."

A problem, huh? He puts out fires in 'er damn shipyahd five days a week.

"How are things in the yard, Nicky?" she asks when they sit.

"The yahd's the yahd," he says. "No big news here."

"The *Amelia* is coming along nicely, then? You know I prefer to avoid the hangar in this weather."

"Oh yeah, she's a real beaut, Bev. The *Beatrice*'ll have nothin' on 'er when we're done."

"Wonderful. Nicky, I'd like to discuss you working on board the *Amelia* this season ... as opposed to staying in the yard."

Work on board? That's a good one! He thinks back to last summah when he filled in for the damn rookie who broke his leg on a Maine trip. Bev bussed him up to Freeport, and he'd spent ten days livin' on board. Now she wants him to do a full season? Nah, he's a yahd guy ... unless she plans on payin' more. He decides to hear 'er out.

"I need an engineer," she says. "And all your coworkers in the shipyard are married with families. You'd still have deckhand duties, of course, but your principal responsibilities would be minding the engine room and troubleshooting and repairing as needed. I'm willing to offer you eighty dollars in day-pay—plus tips—and don't forget you'll have the free insurance."

Eighty bucks *plus* tips? Not bad. That's more than he's makin' now. "Ya drive a hahd bahgain, Bev. Anyone I know gonna be on board this year?"

Bev looks like she's ready to reel him in. "Why, yes, actually. Your friend Jordy, as you know, and Marco Gagliardi will be assisting Peter as the second mate. I do believe you know a few returning stewardesses as well."

He leans back and props his hands behind his head. "Oh yeah? Which ones?"

"Well, Mackenzie Logan is returning for the season, and of course Peter's stepdaughter and her friend will be there. You're familiar with Max Hardigan and Brynne Cavanaugh, aren't you?"

He chuckles. "Not as familiah as I wanna be."

"Oh, Mr. O'Hara ... why does that answer not surprise me?"

He shakes his head as he leaves Bev's office. He likes his nine-to-five in the yahd, drivin' home to Fall Rivah and talkin' sports with Poppy. Don't mattah the season, as long as Boston's playin'. But money talks.

Aye, maybe he can use some change. And havin' Brynne Cavanaugh on board shuh don't hurt. He tries not to think about the stories he's heard in the yahd. There's just somethin' about that girl that drives him wild. Is he ready for a monogamous relationship? Hell no! But when he pictures himself settlin' down, the first girl that comes to mind's the tan one with short brown hair and knockahs that belong in a centahfold. Not that he's seen 'em ... *yet*.

He wondahs if Brynnie's still got that boyfriend. No biggie if she does, at least not for now. There's willin' girls in every port, and he's got *no problem* sniffin' 'em out.

11

SCHOOLS WERE CLOSED on Valentine's Day. Winter had come late to Connecticut, the first storm of the year powering heavily through the night. When Adrienne went to Thany's room to tell him, he said, "Aw, nuts! That means Cub Scouts is canceled, too!"

Thany's den meetings were held every Wednesday night in the local church rec hall. Adrienne adored seeing him dressed up in his uniform each week, listening to him chatter with such vibrancy when he and Jack returned home. She hadn't left for NECLA yet, but Thany had grown accepting of her upcoming departure now that he had Cub Scouts on the brain—just as Wendy had predicted.

After breakfast, Adrienne let him play in the snow. When the mail arrived, Thany ran it inside. Shuffling through bills and spam, Adrienne spotted a pink envelope addressed to her in Rick's misshapen scrawl. *Oh no …* The card inside pictured a teddy bear with a word bubble—*A Fresh Start for a Lonely Heart?* The inscription disturbed her more.

> *Happy valentines day Adrienne.*
> *I still think about you alot and I miss you.*
> *What do you think about a 2nd chance???*
> *Always yours. Rick*

A second chance? Was he kidding? The past nine months she'd been free of Rick had been a breath of fresh air, offering her a new take on her self-worth. Theirs was the only relationship Adrienne had ever been in, but she knew now that what she'd had with Rick was a joke, a far cry from true happiness or real love—whatever that was. This spelling-and-punctuation-errored attempt at reconciliation seemed so infantile she almost felt bad for him. *Almost.* But Rick had worn her down, given her such a hard time when she'd ended things. "What do you want from me?" he'd whined. "I'm a late bloomer! You knew that when we started going out!"

"And for all this time, we haven't *gone* anywhere!" she'd fired back. "I've done everything I can for you since I was seventeen and haven't gotten *anything* in return!"

"But I love you, Adrienne!" he'd whimpered, begging her to stay.

This was supposed to be love? His childish pleas sickened her, and she'd never felt surer of any decision she'd ever made.

Now, Adrienne couldn't remember what she'd seen in Rick, couldn't believe he was delusional enough to think she'd ever get back with him. She'd left the relationship feeling cheap and used, persecuting herself for all those wasted years she could've spent with someone who treated her better. She ripped the card in eighths and disposed of it. *Go find someone else to put up with your shit, Rick. You'll see how long they stick around.*

Rick was the farthest thing from her mind these days, a fading memory that grew bleaker with each passing moment. He could daydream about having her back all he wanted, but it was *over*, and a new relationship wasn't on Adrienne's list of priorities. She hoped to someday find a boyfriend who valued her, but for now she had a new adventure on the horizon. One that was as far away from Rick as possible.

Brynne

SHE'S TRYING ON her new dress when the telephone rings. It's black. Sleeveless. A collared Marc Jacobs. It feels tight against her chest, but she hopes Gordon will love it. She finds the receiver on her canopy bed, next to Pearl, her cat, and sees Max's name on the Caller ID.

"Brynnie?" Max is using her breathy voice. "Oh my God, Brynnie! Have you seen the news?"

She hits the speakerphone button and tells Max she hasn't. "Why?"

"*Brynnie* ... Britney Spears shaved her head!"

She listens to Max prattle on, never understanding why she delights in the corruption of innocence. She'd behaved the same when Christina Aguilera transformed into Xtina when they were fifteen. "I love this!" Max had gushed. "She'll sell *so* many albums!"

She smooths her dress as Max rambles, speculating all angles of the pending Spears-Federline divorce and Britney's ongoing meltdown. "Brynnie? Are you still there?" Max asks after several minutes.

"I'm here."

"Brynnie, I feel *horrible*! I just remembered today is your birthday! You aren't hurt, are you?"

She *is* hurt, but she doesn't let on. It's happened before, and Max always has an excuse. This year, she's determined not to let it bother her. She's entering a new decade, starting with Gordon taking her away for the night. They'll have dinner on Federal Hill, then check in for their reservation at the Biltmore. Gordon's promised her the Grande Suite. *You only turn twenty once, love.*

She'd hoped to spend the long weekend with him, but he has patients through Monday. It's no easier dating an anesthesiologist than dating a man thirty years older. But she's grown used to the grotesque glares whenever he comes down from Boston to take her out, learning to ignore the onlookers after two decades of watching *Maureen*.

Her mother has been a regular on the yacht club scene since before she was born, letting her fortune accrue interest while being wined and dined by fat cats and sugar daddies until tiring of them. Even now, in her early forties, Maureen attracts men effortlessly, partly due to her stunning Irish roots but mainly because she isn't shy about what she wants: Black-tie soirees and lavish excursions on yachts paid in full. Handsome lovers who will fuck her properly and stay the night. Often, Maureen keeps more than one lover, and they aren't always men. By thirteen, she'd lost count of how many of Maureen's partners she'd crossed paths with in the mornings. Many commented on *her*. *You've got a real looker there, Mo.* One asshole even asked if he could get a two-for-one deal.

She'd never asked Maureen who her father was. It was hard enough stomaching the whispers that her mother was the harlot heiress of Kent and Newport Counties, but not as painful as it would be to hear Maureen admit the true reason she'd never met her father was that Maureen had no idea who he was. "He's probably Portuguese," Max suggested once. "That would explain why you're so tan."

Instead of wasting her life wondering, she looked for a father in every middle-aged man she'd been with since they started picking her up during high school. She looked for a father until eighteen months ago when she met Gordon, down from Boston for the weekend to join friends on a yacht charter. He'd reminded her of Richard Gere in *Pretty Woman*. Up until then, she'd been a loose variation of Vivian Ward. Except, unlike Vivian, she'd never given men her body for money.

Katherine

SHE STILL CAN'T BELIEVE her luck! Working on a *cruise ship* for the next eight months? What an *amazing* opportunity! She'd had to keep from shrieking when she'd received the phone call from Beverly Sanbourne, offering her the stewardess position after she'd interviewed. She'd emailed Professor Dahl immediately, sharing the great news and thanking her again for the referral.

And her father was *sure* double majoring in Travel-Tourism and Hospitality Management at Johnson & Wales was a waste of money! Even though she graduated *early*, which she never fails to remind him. She was practically gloating when she hung up with Beverly. "You see, Daddy? I *told* you something would come my way!"

Her father wasn't convinced. "Don't count your chickens just yet, Katherine! I'm not counting mine until you can prove this won't be a repeat of what happened at the Biltmore!"

Ugh, the *Biltmore*. Her *first adult job*. Terminated shortly after she'd accepted the overnight front desk agent position. "This isn't a good fit," upper management had told her, remaining tight-lipped when she'd pressed for further explanation. "You were hired as an at-will employee, Miss Fowler. We wish you better luck with future endeavors."

Well, look at her now! Future stewardess for Northeastern Cruise Line Associates! Who needs the Biltmore and their evasive ways? She's going to *wow* Beverly Sanbourne with her hospitality expertise! So long, overrated hotel with mediocre benefits and subpar management! Next stop, on board the *Amelia*!

12

ADRIENNE ARRIVED EARLY for her first day of work. Lorna had called the week before, instructing her to bring two forms of identification and to park in the lot closer to the shipyard. The shipyard gate was already open, permitting Adrienne access to a sandy lot on the bay.

The shipyard wasn't nearly as big as she'd envisioned. Nor was the newly renovated *Amelia*, now that she was finally seeing it in person. The white boat was docked parallel to a rock jetty, two hundred feet at most and a quarter of that in width. The *Beatrice* was no longer behind the trailer, presumably already undergoing renovations.

Heavy machinery and loud voices boomed from a tented hangar across the way. Men in work coats and hard hats were entering the site, toolboxes and thermal mugs in hand. They reminded Adrienne of when Jack used to leave for work, similarly dressed. She'd never given any thought to his job sites before, now stopping to recognize this outdoor work environment was very much a reality. Not everyone had the luxury of being surrounded by eight-hundred-degree pizza ovens during New England's notoriously cold Februarys.

A Volkswagen Beetle crept toward Adrienne as she lit a cigarette. It was an obnoxious baby pink, with plastic eyelashes fringing its bulbous headlights. The car parked, and a girl around Adrienne's age sprang out and headed straight toward her. She was doughy-faced, with cornflower eyes and light brown hair held back by a padded headband. She wore a business suit and flats, causing Adrienne to reconsider her jeans and Adidas. She thrust her hand out. "Hi! I'm Katherine Fowler!"

Was this the cruise director? She seemed a little juvenile. "Hi, I'm

Adrienne. I'm starting work on the *Amelia* today."

"Me too!" said Katherine. "So, where did you go to school?"

Adrienne looked at her quizzically. "You mean high school?"

"No, college."

"Oh, I went to Tunxis."

Katherine stared disapprovingly at Adrienne's cigarette. "Where is that? I've never heard of it."

"Connecticut. It's a community college."

Katherine appeared genuinely puzzled. "How did you get hired without a four-year degree?"

Now it was Adrienne's turn to be confused. "Uh ... the ad didn't say anything about needing a bachelor's ..."

"Oh. I was referred by one of my professors. I graduated early from Johnson & Wales. So ... where in Connecticut are you from?"

"Westford," Adrienne said, finding Katherine more interrogative than curious.

"I'm from Cape Cod. Falmouth, specifically."

"That's nice. We're supposed to go to the Cape, aren't we?"

"Mm-hm!" Katherine pulled a folder from her purse and removed a NECLA brochure. "I took copies of all the pamphlets when I interviewed. We're doing Coastal Cape Cod & the Islands seven times this season, but we aren't stopping in Falmouth. Only Hyannis and Provincetown. Have you ever been?"

"No, I haven't."

"Here, I'll show you." She pointed to a small map of the Cape. "Hyannis is a village in Barnstable, which is mid-Cape and home to the Kennedys. Provincetown is up here at the tip. It's where all the gays live."

Adrienne raised her eyebrows. "Wow, you're so ... prepared."

Katherine smiled and tucked the brochure into her folder. "I need to be. I double-majored in Travel-Tourism and Hospitality Management."

Adrienne wondered if she should've prepared more. Had she missed some instruction from Bev? She was relieved Hailey was pulling up in a green Jetta. She remembered Hailey from the office. Timid but normal. Hailey waved nervously, and Adrienne was glad she'd also opted for jeans and sneakers.

The next car was a black Mercedes-Benz. The driver wore a peacoat and carried an enormous Chanel purse, approaching them with a refreshing effervescence. Her hair was fantastic—spiraling, waist-length blonde curls. She introduced herself as Logan.

"Logan?" Katherine repeated. "As in the man's name?"

Logan flashed a brilliant smile, balancing on one leg to re-stuff her jeans into knee-high boots. "As in my *last* name," she laughed, shaking her head as she regained her stance. "I don't think I'll ever get used to skinny jeans. I hope this fad doesn't last too long!"

"Why do you go by—" Katherine started, but she was cut off as a silver Honda Civic sped dramatically into the lot, Nelly Furtado quaking from its speakers.

"*Someone* wants to make an entrance," Adrienne joked as the car jolted to a stop.

The girls watched as a guy with diamond earrings and a dark pompadour emerged. "Heyyy!" he called. "I'm Noah!" He circled them, cologned in musk and citrus notes, pecking their cheeks with an exaggerated "Mwah!"

Connie, their cruise director, arrived at nine. She was taller than everyone except Noah, with shoulder-length auburn hair. Connie, too, wore jeans, and Adrienne wondered if Katherine felt self-conscious for being the only one who overdressed. "Five out of seven isn't bad for the first day!" Connie said, rubbing her gloved hands against her thighs. "Thank you for all being on time, especially those from out of state." She looked at her watch. "We're still waiting on two more. I'll give them a few minutes before we head on board."

As they waited, two guys in work coats appeared from inside the *Amelia* and walked toward the bow. One was *short*—five-five tops—with friendly brown eyes. He wore a Red Sox cap and carried a coil of rope over his shoulder. The other was taller and of heavy bulk. A Celtics beanie was pulled past his ears, and his face was pitted with stubborn acne, probably left over from adolescence.

"Ahoy, ladies!" the short one called down jocularly.

The group stared up at him.

"Nicky O'Hara!" he continued. "Twenty-three, single, proud

Irishman! I like beer, Boston sports, and long walks on the beach with a pretty lady!" He laughed. "And this here's Jordy! He don't talk much."
Jordy glowed with embarrassment. "Shut up, Nicky!"
Nicky ignored him, nodding with smug approval. "Yep! Bev shuh did a fine job with the stews this year!" He squinted in Logan's direction. "Is that Logan? Bev told me ya were comin' back, but I didn't believe 'er!"
Logan laughed airily. "They couldn't keep me away from you, sailor!" She waved at Jordy. "Hey, Jordy! Good to see you again!"
Katherine whipped around. "You've worked here before?"
"Mm-hm. I was a stewardess last season, too."
Their group was following Connie to the boat when a black Infiniti convertible flashed into the lot, kicking up sand as it swerved into the spot next to Katherine's Volkswagen. The top was down despite the bitter temperature, and the stereo played full blast. Logan looked at Adrienne. "*That's* someone who wants to make an entrance."
Nicky playfully tossed his rope coil over the rail. "Batten down the hatches, Jordy! Trouble's finally here!"
"And *there* are six and seven," Connie said through her teeth.
Everyone watched with intrigue at the Infiniti's production of closing the convertible top. Finally, both doors opened, and a girl materialized from either side.
"You're ten minutes late," said Connie.
The blonde, exiting the driver's side, held up a Dunkin' Donuts cup and glared abhorrently at Connie. "There was a *line* at the drive-thru."
Her tone was wildly inappropriate. Not that Adrienne hadn't spoken so candidly to Roman, but certainly not on her first day of work.
Connie stood rooted in place. "J-just because Peter is your stepfather doesn't mean you can show up whenever you want, Max."
Was it Adrienne's imagination, or was there a quaver in Connie's voice? And who was Peter?
No one could stop staring as the girls advanced closer, wholly entranced by their beauty. The brunette waved simply, introducing herself as Brynne. She had dark eyes set against an olive complexion and a slightly upturned nose. Her ears were elegantly pin-cushioned with diamonds and pearls, showcased by a stylish bob.

There was no denying Brynne was attractive, but Max, who didn't bother introducing herself, was riveting, unequivocally the most beautiful person Adrienne had ever seen. Her platinum hair and sideswept bangs were smooth as sealskin, professionally teased, and held up with bobby pins. Her large eyes were like sapphires, accentuating chiseled cheekbones and a dimpled chin. She possessed a beauty that deserved an encore, the work of a master sculptor rather than conceived and grown in a womb.

"It's a little early to have ya top down, aye, Max?" Nicky joked from his spot at the bow.

Max threw him a middle finger and smiled wickedly.

"I'm just *sayin'* …" Nicky went on. "Ya've got precious cahgo in there." His face reddened as he looked over to Brynne. "Aye there, Brynnie," he called down, a huskier quality in his voice.

Brynne took a sip of coffee. "Hey," she said, barely audible.

"*Well*," Connie spoke up, looking at her watch. "As long as we're getting to know each other, let's do it on board where there's heat."

Katherine

SHE RECOGNIZES ONE of those two girls from *somewhere*. *What's her name? Brianne? Brianna?* The tardy one with all of those ear piercings. She studies the girl as Connie leads them up a steel ramp called the *gangway* into a lounge, where Brianne/Brianna and the one named Max seclude themselves away from the group.

Then it hits her. *From the Biltmore, of course!*

The girl used to come in *late*, always with a handsome, middle-aged man who preferred the suites on the top floors. At first, she'd thought they were father and daughter, but not after Mr. Silver Fox requested a single bed. She recalls that Brianne/Brianna would be dressed to the nines—slinky gowns with plunging necklines ... sparkly jewelry that caught the light of the lobby chandelier—and a full face of makeup always packed on dark and heavy.

Now, she looks at the girl sitting next to her rude friend. They're both dressed *so* unprofessionally in their velour tracksuits and UGG boots. Brianne/Brianna has also put on eyeglasses to read the W-4 and I-9 forms Connie passes around. Can she be sure it's the same girl from the Biltmore? The girl doesn't seem to recognize *her*. But then she takes a second look at those ears, those *piercings*, and she's positive it is. One hundred percent positive.

13

AFTER COLLECTING their forms, Connie suggested they familiarize themselves with the pax lounge, *pax* being short for *passengers*. "It's one of the most popular areas on board," she said. "You'll be in here often, especially on embarkation days."

Nicky and Jordy had returned to the hangar, their only purpose aboard being to start the boat's engine. Max and Brynne, also NECLA returnees, didn't show any interest in the renovations, but Adrienne joined the other three new hires and Logan in exploring. They'd entered the pax lounge through a sliding door next to a built-in bar. Panoramic windows crescented the lounge's perimeter, with banquette-style seating underneath. Loveseats and matching club chairs surrounded various tables, and a massive flat-screen television hung from the boat's forward. "Seventy inches," Connie said. "But it's only used for movies or for slideshows when we have lecturers. There's no cable on board." Overall, Adrienne didn't find the lounge extraordinary, nor did she get the impression that NECLA catered to passengers whose primary expectations were with the boat's interior. The company's selling point was its intimacy.

Connie led the group into a hallway. They were on the sun deck, she explained, which had the highest-priced cabins and most optimal views. The boat could hold up to seventy-four guests plus crew, and the sun deck boasted twenty-three cabins, with the rest on the deck below. Past an off-set library, Connie opened a door in the hallway. "This is one of the housekeeping closets. We have three, and you'll be using them every day."

Adrienne peered inside the deep room. It was empty except for a horseshoe of metal shelves.

"I know it doesn't look like much," said Connie, "but soon, you'll be stocking these closets with everything you'll need for housekeeping."

Max let out a deliberate yawn. If Connie saw, she didn't let on, taking a key from her pocket. "You'll all get a master key for housekeeping," she said, unlocking a cabin door. "Who wants to look inside? They're cramped, so I suggest you go two at a time."

Adrienne hung back with Noah to make room for Hailey and Katherine to enter. Logan, Max, and Brynne all stood off to the side. "It *is* small!" Katherine confirmed when she stepped back into the hallway. Hailey followed behind her, nodding in agreement.

"Our turn, girl!" Noah grabbed Adrienne's elbow and led her into the cabin. Adrienne blinked when they crossed the threshold. *These* were the most expensive cabins? Twin bed frames were bolted to walls on either side of a window, complete with a shared nightstand and reading lamps. Storage was a wardrobe with three drawers.

Noah opened a door revealing the puniest bathroom possibly ever—a three-by-three box with a vanity basin and a wall-mounted toilet more resembling a child's potty than a standard throne. "Girl! It's tighter than a nun's snatch in here!" He stepped on a chunky pedal that released a whooshing sound. "Ha! Even the head on my dad's boat is bigger than this!"

Adrienne looked around. "Where is the shower?"

Noah eyed a corded attachment and stared down. The rubber floor had a drain in the center. "I think we're standing in it."

Were they stuck in a bad sitcom? This "bathroom" they were standing in was toilet, sink, and shower, all in one. There was no way people paid thousands of dollars to vacation like this, was there?

"The cabins will look cheerier once we bring them to life," Connie said, reading their faces. "One of our many tasks these next two months."

They spent the morning touring the *Amelia*. On the main deck, they toured the dining room, galley, and remaining cabins. Five foreship cabins arced around the bow, and the other ten split between two hallways that wishboned to the stern. Outside was an area called the *lazarette*, commonly known as the *laz*. "The laz is only accessible to crew," Connie said.

"And if any of you smoke, it's the only place you're allowed to light up."

She led the group down the portside hallway to a narrow staircase barricaded by a chain. "Down here, we have crew lounge, galley stores, and guys' quarters—a.k.a. *your* new home," she said, nodding at Noah.

Crew lounge had a couch, loveseat, and a television on a shelf. It also had two doors. The first door led into galley stores—a room full of deep freezers and shelving to hold the food provisions. The second door connected to guys' quarters, where they let Noah enter first. Adrienne, Hailey, and Katherine followed while Logan, Max, and Brynne waited behind. Adrienne wondered if anyone else noticed how Logan kept separating herself from the other two.

Guys' quarters were dark and airless. When Noah switched on the lights, Adrienne relaxed upon seeing the crew's living conditions far exceeded those in the passenger cabins. Inside were four bunk beds opposite a row of lockers, two standard showers, a two-sink vanity, and two toilet stalls. "Ugh, thank *God* these showers are normal-size!" Noah said dramatically. He gave guys' quarters a quick once-over. "I mean, it's not the Ritz ... but I can make it work down here."

They ate lunch on loveseats in the pax lounge, all except Max and Brynne, who stayed on the portside banquette.

"Girls ..." Connie said, "I'd like for everyone to sit together."

Max's eyes seared through Connie like knives. "We're fine over *here*."

What's with all the animosity? Adrienne wondered. And why did Connie keep allowing Max to speak to her like that?

Connie suggested they tour girls' quarters and call it a day.

"Aren't these nine-to-*five* workdays?" Katherine objected. "I thought we were getting paid for forty hours a week."

"It's been a long first day," Connie said. "We'll resume the regular schedule tomorrow."

Max cleared her throat. "Brynne and I have already *seen* girls' quarters. My stepdad's the fleet captain, in case you didn't *know*."

Her stepdad is the captain? And that made it okay for Max to defy their boss?

"Yes, Max, I'm aware," Connie said. "You two can leave now if you'd like."

Everyone else transitioned back to the main deck. In the foreship hallway, Connie opened a *Crew Only* door and headed down a steep staircase. She stopped on the landing and pointed to the doors on her left and right. "Port and starboard," she said. "Each side has two double berths, four lockers, and a head. These are the most compact crew quarters on board, but just remember you'll only use them to shower and sleep. Otherwise, you'll be upstairs."

A succession of gasps emitted when they entered the starboard door. The bunks in the front bunk room were angled, meaning whoever slept up top had to climb *over* the bottom bunk to get into bed. The same went for the rear bunk room, behind which was the exact bathroom setup as the passenger cabins.

"Why do the *men* have better accommodations?" Katherine asked, reading Adrienne's mind.

"Uh-uh, girl!" Noah rounded on her. "Don't give her any ideas! I'm not switching into this mess for anyone!"

Connie smiled. "Bev's dad didn't think it was appropriate to board female stews so close to areas accessed by other crew members. Once the season starts, the chef will be in and out of galley stores all day."

Logan nodded. "Plus, everyone hanging out in crew lounge at night."

"That's right," Connie said. "But no one has any reason to use this stairwell except you girls."

"You said the room on the port side is identical?" Adrienne asked, holding out hope that it might be larger.

"Mirror images," Connie said sympathetically. Then she offered some words of comfort. "I was a NECLA stew in the eighties. I worked on both boats, and I can guarantee you'll feel more emotionally comfortable down here. These quarters are much more private."

"It's not that bad," Logan seconded. "It totally takes some getting used to ... but living down here just becomes second nature after a while."

When Adrienne, Katherine, and Hailey still looked bummed, Connie brought the group upstairs to her cabin for perspective. Back in the dining room, she opened a Dutch door, revealing a closet-size office. "This is the cruise director's office," she informed them, pushing open another door inside. "And these are *my* windowless confines."

There was only room in the cruise director's office for one person besides Connie, who let them each check out her living space. Adrienne was the last to look, appalled by the size of Connie's room. The claustrophobic space was bittier than a prison cell, containing a bed frame, two drawers, and another undesirable three-by-three bathroom.

"So, now you see," Connie said, "the best advice I can offer is not to let this way of living get to you. There's too much money and too many memories at stake to back out because of your quarters."

Adrienne understood what Connie was saying. Her future living situation was way worse than sharing the attic with Aaron, but not bad enough to walk away from this extraordinary *opportunity*.

"However," Connie added, "boat life isn't for everyone, and I understand feeling uncomfortable about living this way." Her eyes diverted specifically toward Katherine. "So, if anyone isn't sure they can handle these living conditions, the time to turn back is now. Otherwise, welcome to the *Amelia*."

March 2007

14

NONE OF THEM turned back. In fact, Adrienne returned to the shipyard with twice the enthusiasm she'd felt on Monday. The two-hour drive twice a day was going to kill her gas budget and sleep cycle, but she was determined to power through until officially moving on board in April, keeping in mind that the commute was only temporary, that the opportunity ahead would be well worth the lack of sleep and family time. She was glad no one else had bailed after the first day either. She'd sensed a connection to Noah, Hailey, Logan, and even Katherine, and was curious to see their friendships evolve.

Their first order of business was separating linen in the dining room, courtesy of a local company who'd left them knee-deep in product. For the next three days, the stews needed to sort it all—various bedding, bath towels, tablecloths, and napkins that came in a motley of whites and blues.

If Adrienne had been unsure about Max's and Brynne's aversion toward everyone when they'd met on Monday, her suspicions were confirmed in the days that followed. Each day, Max and Brynne took their shares of the linen and isolated themselves across the dining room, showing no desire to socialize. They didn't greet the other stews or Connie in the mornings or say goodbye when they all left at five o'clock, and they showed zero interest in joining the group during their half-hour lunch breaks. "Get used to it," Logan said nonchalantly. "They did the same thing last season on the *Beatrice*. We got over it."

"But why?" Adrienne pondered. "Why be so antisocial when we have to live together all season?"

Logan tossed a chunk of curly blonde hair over her shoulder. "Who knows? Because they're spoiled East Greenwich girls? Anyway, it's their loss, not ours. Max especially can be a real bitch, so watch out for her. She totally thinks she's above everyone because her stepfather is the captain, and her boyfriend is an officer-in-training. He might be an officer this year, but I'm not sure."

"All together on one boat?" Hailey asked.

Logan nodded. "They were last year, too."

"A family affair!" Noah quipped.

Katherine shook her head in disapproval. She'd quit wearing business suits after the second day, arriving to work in street clothes like the rest of them. But just like her ever-changing headbands, Katherine's opinionated personality had yet to wane, and Adrienne was noticing this was just Katherine's way, that she and the others would have to learn to accept it. "I think that should be against company policy," Katherine said. "Working with family automatically leads to favoritism and leaves *us* at a disadvantage."

"Try telling that to Bev," said Logan. "This company *thrives* on family."

Adrienne considered Katherine's viewpoint while she folded a stack of washcloths. "Maybe not," she said, offering a different perspective. "Bev cherrypicked us from how many others because she saw qualities she liked? Maybe that means we have the advantage, and they only have connections."

"Ohhh, tell it like it is, girl!" Noah acclaimed loudly. "*Cherrypicked!* Let *me* start saying that!"

By Friday, the week had flown by. They spent the day moving their linen mountains to the three housekeeping closets, labeling the shelves until the dining room no longer resembled a floating laundromat.

"I appreciate all your hard work this week," Connie said when she dismissed them. "I'll see you back here on Monday."

As Adrienne set off down the gangway, she was confused to see Max standing cross-armed next to her car. Max's Infiniti idled a few spots away, her stereo pulsing raucously.

"Hey …" Adrienne said, approaching Max. "What's up?" They'd

started work four days ago, but this was their first proper interaction. It was also the first time she'd seen Max without Brynne by her side.

Max narrowed her sapphire eyes. "I just thought you should know we heard what you said yesterday."

Adrienne thought back. "What did I say?"

"Your comment about being *cherrypicked*? Did you think Brynne and I couldn't hear you? How you think that Bev hired all of you for some *special* reason, and we're only here because we're connected?"

Shit. Adrienne wasn't about to backpedal on what she'd said, but that didn't make the situation any less uncomfortable. "You are connected, aren't you?" she asked. "That's my understanding."

"Your understanding? From who? You don't know anything about Brynne *or* me, and we bust our asses as hard as any other stew. Who cares that my stepdad has connections to the Sanbournes? Bev's brother was his best friend, not that it's any of *your* business."

Where was all this hostility coming from? This anger Max had been directing toward everyone all week?

"Look ..." Adrienne said, "I think we got started on the wrong foot. I'll admit I was surprised you've been so unfriendly toward us. You act like we did something to you."

"I'm not here to make friends," Max snapped. "I'm here to *work*. I can run circles around the rest of you, and Bev knows that. So the next time you think she *cherrypicked* you because of special qualities, think again. There is *nothing* special about you."

She got in her Infiniti and slammed the door. As she pulled off, Adrienne could see Brynne sitting stone-faced in Max's passenger's seat, staring straight ahead as though she wanted no part in what happened.

Brynne

OF COURSE Max would set them up to be friendless again. The only thing worse than the stews rejecting her is that Connie does, too. She hates Connie's cold stares of revulsion, reserved equally for her and Max. *Get over it already, will you?* Though she and Max are twenty now, the story of their expulsion has been kept alive by the East Greenwich rumor mill for years. And unlike most rumors, the people who still talked about it didn't need to embellish any details. The truth was bad enough as it was.

It had all started when Desi joined the student exchange program. Desi, who had always been timid and would never be half as beautiful as Max, had wanted to take turns hosting with her Australian pen pal. It was simple. The pen pal would come to Rhode Island for the spring semester, and Desi would join her back to Australia once school ended.

The pen pal arrived on December 31, 2000. Lola was thin, blonde, and beautiful, with swooping high-arched eyebrows over the most incredible golden eyes. *She'd* knelt with Max behind the banister when Lola came through the front door, eagerly peering through the beams at the Hardigans' new houseguest. "She doesn't *look* Australian," Max had scoffed, shooting Lola the same catty glance she'd perfected for their Saint Agatha's classmates.

"What are Australian girls supposed to look like?"

Max just shrugged.

For three months, she'd listened dutifully as Max complained about "The Aussie" living in her house. "Can you believe Desi and I have to share our bathroom with her? Her shit smells like kangaroos! And all she talks about is Kylie Minogue and Vegemite! I swear, Brynnie, this is the *lamest* thing Desi has ever done!"

"I like her," she'd told Max once, ignoring her prejudice. She'd liked Lola's accent. Her carefree disposition. And especially her stories about Australia, particularly when she substituted words with her native slang. She also liked how Lola was helping Desi blossom. But Max being Max could find a reason to hate almost anyone she laid eyes on. The world was full of people who weren't worth her time.

She'd even forbidden Lola from attending her fourteenth birthday dinner, screaming that she only wanted *family* there.

"You're bringing Brynne," Desi had pointed out.

"Brynnie *is* my family, Desi! What rock have *you* been living under?"

For April vacation, Lola asked if her younger sister could spend the "holiday" in America. "What the fuck?!" Max had shrieked in protest. "This isn't a fucking homeless shelter!" As usual, Michelle and Peter had rolled their eyes, the trademark reaction of parents too caught up in their own lives to care much about the lives of their daughters. "Don't give your sister's guest a hard time about this, Max," was all Michelle had said. "You know how hard it is for Desi to make friends." Then it had been Max's turn to roll her eyes. "It's no one's fault but her *own* that she's so boring!"

She knew Max was up to something deviant the moment Lola's sister arrived, watching Max welcome Emma—who had just turned fourteen like them—with a hug, then pull her up the staircase where she had wine coolers waiting in her bedroom. Emma, so excited to be in America, had clung to Max's every move. And word.

"Teenagers in America have sex *all* the time," Max said provocatively, educating Emma on her version of American culture. "You should try it while you're here."

Emma looked from Max to *her*. "Even you?"

"Of course…" Max answered for them both. Not that she was lying. Or telling the truth. She and Max were dating two of the Gagliardi brothers, but only Max and Marco had started sleeping together. "My boyfriend's name is Marco," Max told Emma. "He says I give the best head he's ever had."

Max gained Emma's trust quickly, taking her shopping on Main Street and at Providence Place Mall. One afternoon, she suggested Marco drive them to Newport, seductively asking him to bring a friend for Emma. Marco arrived a half-hour later with his brother Adamo—her boyfriend—and a friend named Tristan. The six of them had gotten drunk on the Cliff Walk. Too drunk, as she remembered it.

"Tristan really likes you!" Max goaded Emma for the rest of the week. "I'm going to have a party when my parents stay on their boat this weekend. Do you want me to invite him?"

Of *course* Emma had agreed.

That Friday, after Michelle and Peter left for their weekly yacht club soiree, Marco arrived at Max's house with Adamo and Tristan. Desi and Lola had gone to Block Island for an overnight, so they'd all spent the evening drinking in the Hardigans' entertainment room, eventually breaking off into pairs across the house. "Go on!" Max whispered to Emma, leaving her behind with Tristan on the sectional. "I really can't believe you're still a virgin!"

In the morning, after the guys had left, Emma emerged from the entertainment room, distant and disoriented. Her red-rimmed eyes and disheveled clothes told a story her words couldn't. *She* tried offering Emma water while Max called Marco in hysterics. "What did your friend *do* to her, Marco?"

When Desi and Lola returned from Block Island, Emma pulled Lola into the bathroom and locked the door. They were both *gone*—bags packed and everything—in a heartbeat.

"What *happened*, Max?" Desi cried as their cab peeled off. "*What is going on?*"

Max had pushed Desi aside and ran to her bedroom. She cried uncontrollably, holding a pillow against her chest. "Brynnie, how was I supposed to know she was too *stupid* to handle her alcohol? How was I supposed to know Tristan would *do* that? I just thought they would hook up! I didn't know he was going to *rape* her!"

"Neither did I, Max ..." was all she could think to say.

15

ON ADRIENNE'S SECOND Friday in the shipyard, Logan beckoned her out onto the sun deck. "Adrienne ... have you been driving back and forth from Connecticut every day?"

Adrienne told Logan that she had.

Logan shook her head, each of her blonde curls dissatisfied and scolding. "No, no, no. Why don't you stay with me? My condo is only five miles away, and I totally have plenty of room."

Her condo? Adrienne wondered how Logan could afford a Mercedes and a condo so young. Surely NECLA didn't pay *that* well.

She discussed Logan's offer with her father first. "Do you mind, Dad?" she asked at home that night. "I'd still come home on weekends until the boat leaves."

"No," Jack assured her. "Gives me less to worry about knowing you won't be on the road as much."

Adrienne was grateful for his support, trying to ignore the guilt she carried now that she'd see even *less* of her family. But with Thany's first Pinewood Derby coming up, the timing was ideal, giving him a new focus instead of her gradually increasing absence.

She conferenced with Thany at bedtime on Saturday, explaining to him that staying at her new friend's house meant she could get some extra rest.

"Daddy already told me," Thany said. "He said you need your beauty sleep."

"Will you be okay with me gone during the school week?"

"Just as long as you don't leave forever. Forever is a *really* long time."

"Why do you think I'd leave forever?" Adrienne asked.

Thany squeezed his teddy bear. "Mommy did."

"Mommy didn't leave forever," Adrienne lied. "Mommy's just ... figuring things out."

Logan had invited Hailey to her condo, too. That Monday, after work, they followed Logan to Riverside, a quaint suburb not far from NECLA. She lived in a complex called The Bayview, five clusters of units bordering a cove. Across the street was a sprawling waterfront park.

"Wow," said Hailey as she and Adrienne exited their cars. "This is beautiful! Logan is so lucky!"

Adrienne agreed the area was gorgeous, a dream neighborhood straight from a picture book.

Inside, Logan's end unit had all the trappings. Stainless steel appliances and sea glass countertops in the kitchen. An oversized sectional and an enormous flat screen in the living room. Art was everywhere. Abstract paintings hung from the periwinkle walls. Statues and sculptures stood on every shelf and credenza. "I went to RISD," Logan explained. "My mom is an artist, too. I take after her."

How can she afford all of this? wondered Adrienne. Hailey's expression read the same. Factor in Logan's Mercedes and voguish wardrobe, and it was anyone's guess what her secret was. Maybe her family was well-off. Logan brought them up to a guestroom with a king-size bed. "It's a waterbed," she said. "Super comfy. You'll have to decide who sleeps in here and who gets the pull-out."

"You can sleep up here," Adrienne told Hailey. "It makes more sense for me to be closer to the door since I smoke." Not that she would have minded a king-size waterbed four nights a week, but the sectional she'd seen in the living room would do just fine.

Hailey's eyes danced with glee. "Are you sure?"

"Positive."

They ate dinner on tufted wingback stools, sampling assorted Italian delicacies around a bistro table. Adrienne thought she'd seen triple digits when Logan signed the delivery slip, but when she and Hailey offered cash, Logan brushed it away. "Please! I love playing hostess! Maybe you can buy me a drink sometime during the season."

Logan stared at her minibar until selecting a bottle of Vinho Verde. Adrienne accepted a glass, and surprisingly, so did Hailey. "I'm not *that* conventional!" Hailey giggled.

They'd learned a lot about each other these past two weeks, but Hailey had only confided in Logan and Adrienne how she came from a strict upbringing and was just finding her footing. And, coincidently, not only were the three of them originally from Connecticut but they'd all been born on holidays.

"I'm not sure how much my birthday counts," Adrienne said after sharing she was born on Easter Sunday. "Easter only fell on my birthday once since then."

Logan was born on Cinco de Mayo. "I'd totally take yours over mine!" she said. "There'd be such less pressure to go drinking!"

Hailey laughed. "I'd rather have either of your birthdays! My parents hate that I was born on Halloween!"

At twenty-three, Logan was an experienced globetrotter with an impressive list of humanitarian work under her belt. "I've been to five continents," she said as they ate. "I did Habitat for Humanity every summer during college, and then I spent the summer after graduation teaching English in Benghazi." She'd just completed her teaching contract when Hurricane Katrina struck New Orleans, flying to Louisiana to volunteer with animal charities until Christmas. "I learned about NECLA when I got home. I *totally* would've stayed longer after Katrina, but I get anxious if I'm in the same place for too long. That's why the boat is perfect—we're somewhere new every day."

"That's very noble," said Adrienne. "You're so accomplished."

"Yeah, really," said Hailey, "I would *love* to have your life."

Logan also revealed why she went by her last name, recounting her first season working alongside Max with annoyance. "It's so stupid how it started. Our first names are both *Mackenzie*, but she kept complaining to Hardigan—that's her stepfather—that 'Max' and 'Mackenzie' were getting mixed up. She got so angry everyone kept calling *her* 'Mackenzie,' that I finally gave in and told them to call me 'Logan' instead."

Adrienne choked on her wine. "You changed your name because of Max? How could you let her have that kind of power over you?"

"You don't know Max yet. It's not worth the fight with her. At least my last name is workable and not something totally horrid like *Quackenbush*."

Adrienne hadn't told anyone about her confrontation with Max in the parking lot, suspecting there might only be more drama if she did. "I guess ..." she said. "I just think changing your name to accommodate someone else is a little extreme."

"My family calls me *Kenz*," Logan said. "But that's not something I want to be called at work. It's too sentimental."

"What about your middle name?" asked Hailey.

"Fianna. After a grandmother I never met."

"Mackenzie Fianna Logan," Adrienne said, trying it out. "Irish much?"

"Scotch-Irish," Logan corrected. "Don't ask how I wound up with brown eyes."

"I like *Logan*," said Hailey. "It suits you."

"Yeah," Adrienne said. "I'd feel weird calling you *Mackenzie* now."

Logan tilted her head. "I like it, too. It's grown on me."

At bedtime, Adrienne helped Logan assemble the pull-out in the living room. "So ..." she tried staying indifferent, "do you rent this place?"

Logan fluffed a pillow. "No, I own it," she said simply.

"It must be expensive living right by the water."

Logan smiled modestly. "I make do."

Adrienne knew better than to continue. She didn't sense Logan was hiding anything, but rather her financial situation wasn't something she felt comfortable sharing.

I wonder what her parents do? Adrienne thought as she molded into the Tempur-Pedic mattress topper. The cushy material sent immediate relief through her body. That was just how the world worked. Some people didn't ever have to worry about money.

Logan

SHE'S ALWAYS THOUGHT there should be a handbook for people who win the lottery. If there were, she'd totally go back in time and make her parents buy it. She still struggles with a quick answer whenever people mention the material assets in her life. What *should* she say? The truth? *Our family was living a regular blue-collar life in rural Connecticut until my dad won the Powerball? We went from being working-class to multimillionaires literally overnight?*

She thinks she plays the money thing down well for a take-home of sixteen million. Not that the oversized cardboard check had been addressed to *her*. She was just twelve at the time, and Alannah was only ten. But there was trust money waiting for them. That was the arrangement their parents made with their new accountants and financial advisors. She and Alannah would get the "basics"—cars, tuition, homes, and moderate allowances—but they'd never see their trusts until their thirtieth birthdays. Three million apiece. That was the deal.

And if they wanted their money, they'd have to follow the rules. Good grades and college weren't optional, and right after graduation they had to find jobs or start volunteer work. They were responsible for handling their own bills and weren't allowed more than one non-family vacation a year. The consequences? Any obscene treatment of the money they had access to meant their trusts would be eliminated. "We'll donate your shares to charity if you abuse what we give you now," their mother had warned shakily the first time she and Alannah received allowances. "You can't imagine the people who *need* this money."

Before they'd won the lottery, their mother was a struggling freelance artist who worked out of the backyard shed. Their father was an hourly sales associate at The Wiz in Danbury, earning minimal commission. They had one car—a used station wagon—and had never taken a family vacation. She and Alannah had grown up wearing thrift store clothes, sleeping in bunk beds in a cramped room with one window and no closet—memories that flooded back every night in her bunk on the *Beatrice* last year.

"My dad was in sales ..." is the only answer she's ever given those who've pressed her about money. The truth would incite nothing but jealousy and hangers-on. And who needs that? She might have riches that others don't, but it's harder to make friends, harder to trust men or have relationships. Besides, she thinks she lives a humble life considering the wealth her family fell into. Two hundred thousand for a small condo is *nothing*.

Don't think she doesn't know how she'll one day be living. Sure, she likes nice things, but she's grateful her parents have stuck to their guns about raising her and Alannah this way. It's taught them integrity, humility, and character—totally traits money could *never* buy.

Hailey

Holy moly! She can't stop smiling and knows it isn't the wine. She only had one glass!

Logan is a guardian angel to save her from her parents four nights a week! They'd been so *sore* ever since finding out she lied to take the Jetta to Rhode Island. Especially her mother. "You went behind our backs, Hailey! We trusted you to always be honest with us!"

"But I'm *nineteen!*" she'd protested. "I want to do more than volunteer at church three times a week! I want to get out and see the world!"

"You're *barely* nineteen! Too young to be gallivanting around on some boat! You haven't the faintest clue what the real world is about!"

But Bev's job offer had given her the confidence to stand up for herself. "So, let me find out! Let me make mistakes and learn from them! Let me be *young!*" The tears had welled heavily in her eyes, but neither of her parents wanted to end the argument.

"I blame that school!" her father shouted. "We should have never allowed you to attend a public high school! Too much freedom too early! The way you rode us about cheerleading! And then that *show!*"

That school. That show. She'd had to *beg* their permission to attend Griswold High. Once they'd agreed, she'd pressed them again, this time to cheerlead for the Wolverines. Enough with the repetitive dance lessons in the basement of Franklin Congregational! She loved dancing, and she'd wanted to do it her way! She'd given them her word that the cheer uniforms were knee-length and modest, *pleading* until they'd approved.

Her first semester of high school had gone perfectly. Then came the Friday in February when her parents showed up unannounced to a half-time performance at a basketball game. That night, the squad had danced to two songs off the new No Doubt CD—"Hey Baby" and "Hella Good." Her mother pulled her out of the gymnasium the second the performance ended. "Indecent, Hailey! Indecent and vulgar!" First thing Monday morning, she'd been forced to turn in her uniform.

That was the last time she'd defied her parents until now. Sort of.

But this was getting ridiculous. She's *still* hiding Gwen Stefani CDs from her parents, for heaven's sake! She could never thank her brother, Jeremy, enough for stepping in, for threatening to drive her to NECLA in his police cruiser. Jeremy was five years older and a first-year officer for State Troop K. He still lived at home, saving money for land to build a house.

"Stop riding her so hard!" he'd laid into them. "This isn't the forties and fifties anymore! There are plenty of opportunities for girls Hailey's age now. And don't give me that crap that a woman's place is in the home! If anything happens, you can blame me! But at least give her a chance!"

She'd thrown her arms around Jeremy after the fight, sobbing tears of joy and gratitude.

"You know I'll always have your back, Hai," he'd promised her, "but I don't want you hating Mom and Dad. You can't blame them for being so old-fashioned. They just had us too late in life to have a clue."

She wonders what her parents would say about Logan's life. *Five* continents, and *she's* just leaving her county? She feels blessed to call Logan her friend. Adrienne, too. She pinches herself to make sure she isn't dreaming, sinking into the waterbed and falling into a blissful trance.

※ ※ ※

ADRIENNE DIDN'T STAY at Logan's for her twenty-first birthday. Instead, back home, Wendy took her to their favorite Mexican restaurant to celebrate. It was tradition for them to buy each other three books for their birthdays—one they knew the other wanted, one they'd read but knew the other hadn't, and something completely random. Wendy presented Adrienne with Kerouac's *On the Road*, the newest Stephanie Plum mystery, and an obscure nineteenth-century book called *Three Men in a Boat*. "It's supposed to be humorous," Wendy explained.

As Adrienne enjoyed her first legal Bud Light, Wendy slid another gift bag across the table. "They're so you don't get seasick!" she laughed when Adrienne pulled out Dramamine and a box of Sea-Bands.

"Seasick?" Adrienne uttered. She hadn't even thought of that. And why would she? She'd been working on the *Amelia* for four weeks, but technically, it hadn't gone anywhere.

Wendy sipped her sangria. "Can you imagine if you hadn't seen my newspaper that night? You'd still be stuck putting up with Jenni every day."

Adrienne raised her beer. "You're right. I owe this whole career change to you, don't I?"

"How much longer until you leave?" Wendy asked. "I feel like you've been working there for a while already."

"April twenty-fifth. The first trip starts the next day."

"Are you worried about the adjustment?"

"What do you mean?"

"I mean sharing a room with all those girls ... only getting a few random days off ... those sorts of things."

There was truth behind Wendy's words, soon-to-be realities inching closer. Living on board *would* be an adjustment, especially sharing girls' quarters with five others. But "free time" hadn't been part of Adrienne's life in years, and her schedule on the boat wouldn't differ much from the busy hours she already kept.

"No, none of that bothers me," she answered Wendy. "We've just been preparing so hard that the adjustment has kind of already sunk in."

April 2007

16

THE STEWS *had* been preparing hard, starting with the first two weeks dedicated solely to housekeeping. After stocking the linen closets came the lessons on cabin cleaning, including how to fold hospital corners and hide pillowcase excess like hotel professionals did. In the cabin heads, Logan taught the newbies the "trade secret" of removing mirror smudges—always with lint-free toilet paper, never paper towels or terrycloth. At the end of the second week, Connie had assigned mock cabin setups to determine who needed improvement and where. "You'll only have about fifteen minutes to clean each cabin," she'd advised. "That's not much time when they're full of the passengers' stuff."

Adrienne felt relieved when Connie acknowledged she'd mastered housekeeping. "You catch on quickly," she said after inspecting Adrienne's test cabin. "Your hospital corners are perfect." Connie praised everyone else's housekeeping efforts, too. Everyone except Katherine, who thought finishing first was good even though Connie had warned against rushing, and was sent back to remake her bed.

They'd transitioned to dining room duties during the third week. But when the new wares and cutlery were delivered, Adrienne was stunned at how limited her knowledge of food service was on a grand scale. She'd served silver bullets with the salads at Giovanni's, but ramekins, soup tureens, and monkey dishes went far beyond what resided in her china cabinet at home. She'd kept her feelings of inferiority to herself, letting Connie and Logan fill in the many blanks. But on the day Connie devoted their shift to dining room etiquette and standard rules of service,

Adrienne truly saw how much was left to learn.

"Connie, girl, I thought this was *casual* cruising," Noah kidded.

"That doesn't mean we don't give first-class service," Connie said.

She tested their setup knowledge for breakfast, lunch, and dinner, each meal more elaborate than the last. Adrienne was embarrassed about misplacing the wine glasses at her dinner settings, but Connie assured her that if that was her only mistake, she should consider herself ahead of the game. Adrienne could see she was doing better than Katherine, who miserably confused her silverware placements for all three meals, including facing her knives outward.

"Girl, I can't believe how *serious* they're taking this training," Noah said on the laz one afternoon.

As the only stews who smoked, Adrienne was growing used to their outdoor bonding sessions. "Mmm. Bev's definitely investing a lot into us."

Noah blew an exaggerated plume of smoke rings in the air. "I mean, I *like* this job, but I better still remember everything a month from now … that's all I hafta say!"

Adrienne worried she might not remember it all either. So much information was being thrown at them with only so little time to memorize it. Especially on the morning they arrived to find stacks of linen laid out for a crash course in napkin folding. "Don't worry," said Logan. "You retain everything, just like CPR. It all comes back to you when you need it."

They were lucky to have Logan's wisdom at their disposal whenever they second-guessed themselves or were unsure. It sure made up for Max and Brynne going out of their ways to avoid everyone. Adrienne wasn't the only one to notice, and all the stews agreed that Connie was spineless when it came to Max and Brynne.

"She's the *cruise director*," Katherine said with a trace of umbrage. "*She* has the authority, not them."

"You keep forgetting that Max's stepfather is our captain," said Logan. "He tops the chain of command. Not Connie."

"We haven't even met him," Hailey pointed out. "What's he like?"

"Hardigan? He's friends with Bev from way back. He totally takes his job too seriously."

"But is he an ass?" asked Noah.

"I suppose you could call him an ass."

"*I* still think Connie should stand up to them," Katherine said, getting back to Max and Brynne. "That should be part of her job. What happens when we start cruising and have to live together?"

Adrienne didn't admit aloud that she agreed with Katherine or believed there was more to Connie's resistance than she let on. She'd seen enough of the unwelcome looks and felt enough friction to know there must be more to the story, but she couldn't begin to imagine *what* the story possibly was.

Brynne

THE VISIT FROM the detectives came three days after Lola and Emma left. The girls had made it back to Australia, and their parents wanted Tristan and the Hardigans held responsible for Emma's alleged rape. Michelle refused to let anyone speak a word. "You'll only speak to my daughters with our attorneys present. And you won't speak to Brynne without her mother's consent!" Her strong Virginian accent nearly knocked the detectives off the front stoop. When they were gone, Michelle hauled back and slapped Max across the face. "Are you out to destroy our name? I have a business to protect, Max! And haven't you *any* idea how valuable Peter is to the community?"

She'd tried picturing Michelle in her twenties—a young widow rescued by a well-to-do sea captain, relocated from Norfolk to one of the Ocean State's wealthiest towns. At the time, Peter wasn't just a NECLA captain but an off-season private hire who sat on the boards of two yacht clubs. He'd put Michelle through hairdressing school and set her up in business after she became licensed, buying her the prime real estate on Main Street. The community fell in love with her immediately. Salon Medusa took off practically overnight, and soon Michelle did hair for the whole town, getting commissioned for weddings and proms well in advance. But Michelle always did *her* hair for free. Every time Maureen sent her along with money, Michelle refused to accept it.

All Max got out of her mother's fury was a bruised cheek and an indirect lesson on the importance of standing by your man, not giving a damn about her family's reputation. "Promise me you'll never say Marco and Adamo were here, Brynnie!" she pleaded. "You have to promise!"

She knew Max was worried because the Gagliardis were *affiliated*, so she promised, even though Adamo had taken her virginity that night, then broken up with her a few days later.

In the end, the only person Michelle and Peter brought to meet with their attorneys was their accountant. Justice would come in the form of a check. "My mom says it's taken care of," Max reported back. "No one is getting arrested. No one is pressing charges."

She didn't ask Max how much hush money the Hardigans had settled on, but no amount could buy off the town of East Greenwich. Thirteen thousand was too small a population for the story not to circulate, and she and Max were expelled from Saint Agatha's in no time. They spent their last weeks of eighth grade getting tutored in Max's living room, but because Saint Agatha's was private, their expulsion didn't apply to the public school district. Come that September, they were free to attend the town high school.

Tristan's family had up and moved out of state, but she and Max had scarlet letters attached to their names before high school even began, mothers keeping their daughters as far away from them as possible, including Connie Lacasio.

With a mob-affiliated boyfriend and a mother working damage control, Max couldn't have cared less. But *she* did. How was she ever supposed to move forward with her life, to be known as more than "Maureen Cavanaugh's daughter," or "the girl who was expelled from Saint Agatha's," if no one ever allowed her to forget?

17

THE REMAINDER OF the stews' time in the yard was dedicated to safety training. They learned how to discern the three main distress signals—Fire, Abandon Ship, and Man Overboard—and were all assigned muster stations—designated areas where the passengers gathered during the mandatory embarkation drills. Adrienne's muster station was in the main deck aft. She stood by the laz door wearing a life jacket—or PFD, as she was instructed to call it—and mock-counted her pretend passengers until the dry run was over. Connie also showed them where to locate the buoys, axes, and fire hoses, and with the spring weather tolerable enough to work outside, they even assembled an inflatable life raft up on the top deck.

Nicky and Jordy were still renovating the *Beatrice* until the season started, but regularly, they'd stop over from the hangar to visit. By now the stews knew Nicky and Jordy were childhood friends from Fall River and would both be working aboard the *Amelia* with them that season.

For as short as he was, Nicky was big-humored, with a penchant for using nautical idioms as part of his everyday conversation. "Bettah not be any land lubbahs on board this year!" he kidded in his heavy accent. "This type'a work here's sink or swim!"

Jordy was more reserved, assumedly self-conscious, and Adrienne made sure to be kind toward him.

On the Monday their certification classes began, a new deckhand named Kyle boarded with Nicky and Jordy for their week of lessons. Kyle was tall and gangly, with shaggy black hair and a dopey grin that never left his face. He was young, still only eighteen, and based on their murmuring, Nicky and Jordy weren't crazy about him. Adrienne recalled Shannon's romantic fantasy of meeting a guy at work, but the current selection didn't interest her, and the thought quickly fizzled off.

They spent the week in the pax lounge, first earning their CPR and first aid certifications from a Red Cross specialist, then being left at the mercy of a contractor hired to teach their HELM courses, spending two days listening to him drone on about onboard emergencies and crises involving large crowds. The material itself was interesting, but the contractor lacked enthusiasm, supplementing his lessons with ancient videos featuring unrealistic situations and lousy acting. Adrienne had never been so happy to leave NECLA that Thursday, more excited to be heading home for the long weekend than she was about receiving her certificates. Katherine was the only one who enjoyed the lessons, taking a notebook's worth of information and chirping about what great additions the credentials would make to her résumé.

The Thursday after Easter, Connie announced Captain Hardigan would be coming to give a pre-season talk the next day.

"Shouldn't we have met him by now?" asked Katherine. "I think six weeks is too long to go without being introduced to the captain."

"The other officers don't work in the off-season," said Connie, "but they'll all be here tomorrow."

On Friday, the crew regrouped in the pax lounge. The first officer to arrive was Marco Gagliardi—their second mate and Max's boyfriend. Max made a dramatic performance of kissing him possessively, letting everyone know Marco belonged to *her*. Marco was of average height and bronzed all over, with defined muscles stretching his V-neck and thick brows looming over his dark eyes and hooked nose.

Noah snickered. "Typical *guido*."

Marco nodded, acknowledging the stews, but Adrienne sensed if he weren't an officer, he wouldn't have paid them any mind.

Next aboard was Chef Ray—a short, stocky man with a white comb-over. Chef Ray made a point to shake everyone's hand, introducing himself with a smile before settling into a club chair. Then came Keith, the *Amelia*'s first mate. He was around Connie's age, with a reddish-brown goatee and a man bun, sitting next to Chef Ray without muttering a word. Connie had already told the stews they wouldn't see much of Keith throughout the season, that he was on a permanent 4P-4A shift. "The overnight," she'd explained.

Finally, Captain Hardigan arrived, entering the lounge with a hard-boiled presence, surveying but not speaking. He was mid-sixties, sturdy, and towering, his slicked-back hair leaving a runoff of white curls at the nape of his neck. He positioned himself at the lectern and said, "Good morning. My name is Peter Hardigan, and I am the fleet captain for Northeastern Cruise Line Associates."

He gave a few snippets of personal information—how he'd been raised locally before crossing the bay to East Greenwich—followed by a background of his time at the U.S. Naval Training Center. Then he said some words of tribute to Cecil Sanbourne's legacy in the shipbuilding industry. After a brief silence, he examined the crew and asked, "Does anyone know this week's historical significance?"

Katherine's hand shot up. "Easter!"

Hardigan wasn't amused, though it was plainly obvious Katherine wasn't trying to be funny. "Be that as it may, I was speaking of *maritime* history." When no one responded, he said, "This week marks the ninety-fifth anniversary of the RMS *Titanic*'s demise. How many have seen the film?"

Every hand in the room raised except Kyle's.

"Is that right, young man? You've never seen *Titanic*?"

Kyle smirked dumbly at Hardigan. "Why should I? The boat sinks, doesn't it?"

Hardigan ignored his smart-aleck response. "For those who *are* familiar, who recalls the scene where Bernard Hill locks himself in the bridge while the vessel sang her swan song?"

Most heads nodded, Adrienne's included.

"*Good*. Because you should know that I consider that detail a falsity. If one thing is to be learned from that tragedy, it is that the captain does *not* go down with the ship. Nor does the crew. Have I made myself clear?"

"But *I* thought—" Katherine began, but Connie touched her shoulder to silence her.

Hardigan cleared his throat. "I say this because my duty is to ensure that crew members never jeopardize their safety. Catastrophes at sea should not be treated any differently than those aboard an aircraft. In emergency circumstances, you must secure *your* PFD before assisting others."

They listened painfully to his many additional onboard rules. The engine room and wheelhouse were off-limits. Male crew members were prohibited from entering girls' quarters for any reason. Non-officers were to respect a midnight curfew, and no one could leave the boat without signing out first. Off-the-clock alcohol consumption wasn't allowed less than six hours prior to one's next shift, and finally, any crew member caught possessing drugs or alcohol on board would be terminated. "Furthermore," Hardigan added, "if probable cause presents, I reserve the right to order urine testing and search the crew quarters at any time."

Regarding the chain of command, Hardigan emphasized the hierarchy must never be deviated from. "I am not a babysitter any more than I am a circus handler. Any grievances in the steward department are to be reported directly to Ms. Lacasio. Any problems among the deck crew are to be reported to Keith or Marco. Issues that reach me will come only from those officers or Raymond. Are there any questions?"

Katherine's arm pierced the air. "Will there be a doctor on board?"

Adrienne found Katherine's question smart, wondering why the thought hadn't occurred to *her* over the past seven weeks of training.

"No, there will not," Hardigan answered. "Medical personnel are not employed aboard our vessels."

"But what if something happens? Aren't the passengers supposed to be elderly? What if one of them gets hurt? And what if something happens to one of *us*?"

"Young lady, all officers on board are certified with a full complement of emergency response training. There is no need for a doctor."

Katherine remained incredulous. "But this is a *boat*. What if something happens while we're sailing? Are we going to pull over?"

"*Pull over* is not the correct term for docking a vessel," Hardigan corrected her. "*Berthing* is. But while we're on the topic, let me remind you that vessels are the oldest form of transportation in history. Does anyone care to guess when the first vessels were used?"

Nicky was lounged in front of them, his legs outstretched on a nearby chair. "Since prehistoric times, Capt.," he said. "Folks used to make 'em from hollowed tree trunks. Called 'em *dugouts*."

"Impressive, Mr. O'Hara," Hardigan commended derisively. "You see, young lady? Since the prehistoric era."

"Okay …" Katherine said, "so what does that mean?"

Hardigan clutched the lectern and peered down at her. "What it means is that with *millenniums* of practice, there isn't reason to question maritime operations. What it means is that *should* we require further assistance, we'd drop anchor and summon the Coast Guard."

Katherine cocked her head. "You mean like a rescue boat coming to take someone to land?"

Hardigan looked at her incorrigibly. "*Yes*. No different than if you had to *pull over* and wait for an ambulance while driving."

Katherine didn't ask any more questions. Silently, Adrienne took pity on her, hoping that, like the stews had learned to do, Hardigan would cut Katherine some slack in the future. Once he got to know her better, of course.

18

THE FINAL WEEK before the season started was organized chaos at best. On Monday and Tuesday, the galley orders arrived en masse. The stews separated vegetables, dairy, and beverages among the three galley fridges, then brought the rest downstairs, lining the shelves in galley stores with economy-size foodstuffs, and filling the deep freezers with cuts of meat and three-gallon tubs of ice cream. The process was never-ending, leaving Adrienne sore all over. Just when she thought they were done on Tuesday, Chef Ray tasked her and Noah with stocking the fruit deliveries. They hauled corrugated trays of berries, pineapples, and melons to the outdoor fridge on the laz, filling it quickly so they could head out for the day.

The seafood delivery from Sanbourne's Fish Market came on Wednesday, along with lobster rolls Bev had catered for lunch. While they ate, Connie passed out envelopes. Inside were their name tags, ID badges, and TWIC cards—all the identification they'd need for the season. Adrienne studied her name tag. It was gold-colored and embossed with the NECLA logo. Her name was printed on clear labeling tape:

Adrienne Deneau
Stewardess

Cardboard boxes contained their uniforms. The stews were responsible for purchasing their pants and shoes, but NECLA took care of the rest. There were multiple components, and Connie began by distributing their logoed polos. Then came the T-shirts and ball caps to wear on galley days, followed by their formalwear—worn during dinner service and embarkations. The white formalwear shirts had buttoned shoulder straps for their epaulettes. Adrienne removed one from its plastic sheath. It was solid black and embroidered with a gold moon. Finally, Connie passed out their housekeeping attire—white gypsy pants and zippered smocks.

Noah dangled his smock at a distance. "Girl, are you *serious?*"

"For ninety minutes a day, Noah," Connie said. "Just ninety minutes."

The housekeeping uniforms were awfully unbecoming. Adrienne had long-gauged the other stews' clothing styles and knew this shapeless polyester outfit wouldn't do much for any of them.

Noah dropped his smock on the banquette in disgust. "I mean, I guess I'm just gonna hafta make it *work.*"

Thursday was Adrienne's and Hailey's last night at Logan's condo before spending their final weekend at home. They were moving on board next Tuesday, but as excited as Adrienne was to start her adventure, she also felt bittersweet, having enjoyed staying at Logan's the past six weeks. She'd grown fond of the spring evenings on Logan's deck, drinking wine and listening to the water birds honking and quacking in the cove. On Wednesdays, when Hailey and Logan took over the living room to watch *American Idol*, Adrienne had routinely headed to the park across the street to read her birthday novels. When it grew too dark to read, she'd walk the beach alongside the waves until reaching the edge of the peninsula.

Logan asked Katherine and Noah to join them that night, for a dinner that included a risky amount of wine consumption, considering they still had work in the morning. The conversation focused on which trips everyone was most eager for. By now everyone knew the brochures by heart and could recite the season's six itineraries blindly.

"I'm excited for Maine," Adrienne shared. The twelve-day Maine Marvels itinerary touted an extensive trek from Portland to Eastport. Counting the return trip, they would be in Maine for almost all of July.

"Oh, I *love* Portland," gushed Logan. "It's such an artsy city! And so progressive!"

Noah guzzled a mouthful of wine. "Uh-uh, girl. Wait until we do

Coastal Cape Cod & the Islands, okay? The gay clubs in P-town? Boy scouting all those hotties on Martha's Vineyard and Nantucket? You girls are gonna see another side of Noah!"

Katherine was the only one who abstained from drinking, opting for water instead. "I'm looking forward to the Bay State Colony and New England Newcomer cruises. I'll really be able to put my background to use with those, being from Massachusetts and all." She turned to Hailey. "What about you?"

"All of them," Hailey said breathlessly, "but Foliage on the Hudson if I *had* to pick. I've wanted to see New York City forever."

"Foliage on the Hudson is one of the best trips for scenery," said Logan. "The passengers go nuts taking pictures of the leaves."

"Is that your favorite, too?" Hailey asked.

Logan shook her head. "In my opinion, the best trip is totally Haunted Homecoming. It's just a super fun way to end the season. The whole boat gets decorated for Halloween, and we visit all the historical haunts in New York and Massachusetts. Plus, we spend three days in Salem, which is amazing. Last year, we dressed up on Halloween and painted the town red!"

Hailey smiled. "We'll be in Salem for my birthday."

"That's right!" Logan exclaimed. "Your birthday is on Halloween!"

"You were born on *Halloween*?" Katherine asked this like it was something Hailey should feel guilty for.

Hailey nodded, and Adrienne wondered if Katherine felt left out, not having been included in their after-work bonding at Logan's. It was a momentary thought, one she considered silly after reminding herself that as of Tuesday, they'd all be living together, including Max and Brynne.

She stared around Logan's table at her crewmates—her onboard family for the next twenty-seven weeks. She was glad they'd all managed to get along so far, hoping it would remain this way once they finally moved on board.

Noah

HE LEAVES LOGAN'S just after ten, feeling *hella* sassy from all that wine. He's merging onto the Mount Hope Bridge when his phone vibrates with a text. TJ Ferrier. Ha! Of *course* he wants to "hang out" while he's home from college. Whoever said there isn't a universe of straights with closet fantasies was *wrong*, let him tell you!

TJ Ferrier—the star quarterback who lived on Sea Coast Drive and only dated bulimic girls—first texted him two years ago. *Tutoring help? Yeah, right.* They'd studied trig in TJ's father's home office until TJ got panicky and asked, "Can you blow me, Noah?" Girl, of course he said yes! What gay in their right mind would turn down a baby-faced jock with a chiseled body and a firm ass?

He'd made TJ strip behind his father's desk and devoured him on the Angora carpet. It turned him on how TJ quivered … how he kept yelling, "Oh shit!" when he came—which didn't take long. He'd siphoned him clean for good measure, then wound up coming himself. When they finished, TJ pulled up his pants and got macho with him. "I'll fuckin' kick your ass if you tell anyone, Noah."

Okay, boo. He kept his lips sealed. Except for all the other times TJ texted him before leaving on a football scholarship.

He reads the text. Lover Boy's back home to celebrate his grandma's ninetieth birthday? Sure, they can meet tonight … right in his father's office like old times. He wonders if Papa Ferrier ever noticed the stains on the carpet. He and his nonagenarian mother should be oh so proud!

19

ADRIENNE OPTED to take the train on move-in day. The others were leaving their cars in the shipyard, but keeping her car at home would save money on insurance. "Makes more sense that way," her father agreed. "No point in dumping the car in Rhode Island for six months when we have room in the driveway."

When it was time to say goodbye, Adrienne knelt before Thany. "I'll be home soon," she said. "For Memorial Day. And I promise I'll take you to the parade."

Thany smiled trustingly. "Will you call me before then?"

"Of course, Bud! Every day! I want to hear all about school and Cub Scouts and your trips with Wendy!"

Starting that Sunday, Wendy would take him a few hours each week to do activities around the neighborhood. Adrienne had given her five hundred dollars, hoping it was enough to last the next six months.

Thany wrapped his arms around her. "I love you, Adrienne."

She felt like melting right there on the sidewalk.

Adrienne took a cab from Providence, arriving at the shipyard with everyone else. Nicky and Jordy were pulling luggage from the bed of Nicky's pickup, and Kyle was traipsing aimlessly, dragging a lone duffel bag up the gangway. Max and Marco emptied several suitcases and plastic storage drawers from Marco's Cadillac. *Where are they going to fit all of that?* Adrienne wondered.

She was gathered with the girls, waiting for Noah to unload his luggage, when a luxury BMW with Massachusetts plates arrived.

Brynne was in the passenger's seat, driven by a distinguished-looking man Adrienne assumed was a relative, until Brynne clasped his face in her hands, kissing him passionately.

"Oh my goodness!" Hailey exclaimed. "Is that her *father?*"

Noah slid his sunglasses down. "Uh-uh, girl. Looks like she has a *Daddy.*"

"A what?"

Katherine looked uncomfortable. Adrienne suspected she wanted to say something, but Katherine turned away from Brynne and her driver, not uttering a word.

Once all their luggage was on board, Logan suggested they move down to girls' quarters in groups. They'd chosen their bunkmates the week before. Adrienne and Katherine, and Hailey and Logan. Max and Brynne, they already knew, would stick together.

"Ha!" Noah cawed, rolling his suitcases across the dining room. "Good luck with that, girls! I'll be down in my lair if you need me!"

They were separating their luggage when Max appeared on the gangway. "Just so you *know*, there's seniority in the crew quarters. Brynne and I get the first pick of our bunk rooms."

"What do you mean *rooms*, as in plural?" asked Logan. "Aren't you sharing a bunk room like last season?"

"Not with only six girls, we aren't! There were *seven* girls on the *Beatrice*, which means this year Brynne and I each get our own rooms."

"Wait a minute ..." Adrienne said. "I assumed we were sharing three bunk rooms and using the fourth for storage."

Max smirked, her sapphire eyes challenging a rebuttal. "You assumed *wrong*. But if you want to clarify with Bev, go ahead."

Adrienne refused to take her bait. "No. Seniority rules, right? Take whichever bunks you want. We'll find a way to work it out."

Max brushed past Adrienne. "We'll take the port side."

They watched in bewilderment as Max disappeared from the dining room. "They're taking up a whole side?" asked Hailey.

"That doesn't seem right," said Katherine. "Now, we all have to share the *same* quarters?"

"It's not right," said Logan, "but it's true we'd have to share if there were seven girls. And, hey, we're better off being separated from them. We'll have to see them enough during work."

Everyone else slowly nodded in unison. There wasn't much else they could say.

They spent the rest of the afternoon getting situated. Adrienne and Katherine took the front bunk room, the upside not having to hear—or smell—anyone in the bathroom. But they were closer to the door, which caused a resounding echo up the stairwell when it slammed.

Adrienne let Katherine have the bottom bunk when she asked. Better her climb over Katherine than the other way around. And Aaron had issued a warning during a recent phone call. "Don't take a bottom bunk if you can help it, Dri. Some guys I know took a boat when they deployed to Iraq. They said when the guys up top got seasick, the guys on the bottom got *obliterated*."

Katherine had purchased brand-new blankets and sheets, all irritating shades of pink, just like her car. Adrienne didn't see the point. Why buy bedding when you could use what was on board? She helped herself from a housekeeping closet and got to work. As they made their beds, thuds and bangs sounded loudly from the portside quarters next door.

"What is that *noise?*" said Katherine. "Are they moving furniture?"

"The furniture's all bolted to the walls, remember?"

"Well, it sounds like they're moving *something*."

"Do you want to go over and help them?" Adrienne joked.

Katherine frowned. "No thank you!"

Adrienne jammed a carton of cigarettes on the shelf of her locker. Her father wanted her to use this opportunity to quit smoking, and Adrienne promised she'd try, knowing the regimented work schedule wouldn't allow her to take cigarette breaks at her leisure. She hung up her uniforms, then piled her shoes on the locker floor. A four-drawer dresser in the rear bunk room left them each just one drawer apiece. She folded her clothes efficiently, then headed upstairs with Katherine.

For dinner, Chef Ray prepared a sheet-pan lasagna, two loaves of fresh-baked bread, and two bowls of salad—one for each of the crew tables.

Jordy and Kyle were seated at the table closest to the galley, so Adrienne, Noah, Hailey, Logan, and Katherine joined them, filling in the empty seats. Nicky, Max, and Brynne sat with the *Amelia*'s officers.

Hailey glanced over her shoulder. "Are the tables assigned?"

Adrienne had noticed the division among the crew and was wondering the same thing.

"They're not *assigned*, per se," Logan said, "but there's totally segregation based on department. Remember that *Friends* episode where Joey went to work with Ross at the museum? It's kind of like that. We're the 'blue blazers,' like Joey, and the officers are the 'white coats,' like Ross."

"Then why are Brynne and Max over there?" asked Katherine.

Adrienne laughed. "They haven't eaten with us for two months. Did you think they were going to start now?"

Katherine turned to Jordy. "Why aren't you eating with them? I thought you and Nicky were friends?"

"Because I'm the company bitch," Jordy said flatly.

Kyle belched loudly. "No doubt, Jordy. I hear you, man. It's hard out here in these streets." He brandished his dopey smile even though no one was laughing at his strange humor or lack of table manners.

What an odd kid, Adrienne thought. Sure, meeting different people was one of the things she'd signed up for, but spending a season with Kyle was bound to bring forth some unusual moments.

Jordy

KYLE DOESN'T KNOW shit about being the company bitch. The kid's only been here a few weeks. *He's* been here for four years. He'll be the first to tell you that working on the boats is better than dealing with the guys in the yard. He fuckin' hates those guys. Yeah, he puts up with them during the winter, but not all year round. No way. He'd work the boats the whole year if he could, just not to hear their mouths.

So what if he doesn't have a license? Hitches rides in from Fall River with Nicky? Why bother if he can't afford a car? It was a mistake telling the guys he lives at home with Ma. Now he keeps quiet about his personal life. They don't know that Ma relies on him, that *she's* where all his money goes. She's got health problems. Sleep apnea. Obesity. Gout. She's on disability and food stamps. Can't even afford medical insurance on her own.

Nicky really looked out for him, bringing him to NECLA after things didn't work out at Atlantic Embassies. He's always looked up to Nicky, even after he got taller and started looking down. The guy's been helping him since they were kids, ever since Ma lost her job and they'd moved to Fall River. They found a two-bedroom duplex in Corky Row—where the Irish families lived—and he met Nicky outside playing street hockey with some other kids. Even back in those days, Nicky wore a Red Sox cap.

Turned out Nicky lived the next block over in a big three-family on Plymouth Ave., owned by his Poppy, who'd been raising him since his parents died. Back then, Nicky lived on the first floor with Poppy and Poppy's two Flemish Giants. *He'd* been terrified of those things, running around the house like cats and dogs. Now Nicky lives alone on the second floor, and they've got a tenant upstairs. It's a wicked good deal, from what Nicky tells him.

One day he'll have his own pad, too. He's just gotta keep working, keep dealing with the bullshit until he gets promoted. Maybe one day he'll even be a captain like Hardigan and Knowles. One day the guys in the yard are gonna see that he's not *anyone's* bitch.

***

AFTER DINNER, Connie handed out slips of paper. "Your job rotations," she said.

There were seven shifts in the steward department, which Logan had previously explained to them. Galley Stew and Galley Assist began at six o'clock and were responsible for helping Chef Ray with food prep and dishwashing. Crew Stew, Bar Stew, and Cocktail Stew started at six-thirty and performed meal service in the dining room. Crew Stew monitored that day's crew meals, and Bar Stew and Cocktail Stew oversaw the daily Cocktail Hour.

The worst shift, Logan had warned them, was Turndown & Activity Hour Stew, or, as Nicky called it, "T&A Stew." T&A Stew assisted Connie with turndown service and worked Activity Hour until ten P.M., but with the midnight curfew, there wasn't much time to let loose after work. The only benefit to the T&A shift was the Light Duty—"LD"—shift that followed the next day. LD Stew began work at eight and ended promptly at six, leaving whomever an evening off. They were free from food service and housekeeping responsibilities, sticking only to light cleaning duties.

The girls and Noah stared at the colored charts, deciphering the rotation. It was certainly no accident that Max and Brynne fell next to each other in sequence, but when Noah groaned, Adrienne knew it was because he fell on the other side of Max. Starting the next day, Max would be Noah's Galley Assist whenever he was Galley Stew. And on the days Noah would bartend during Cocktail Hour, Max would be right there with him in the pax lounge handling the hors d'oeuvres. Adrienne couldn't complain about her spot in the rotation. She was between Noah and Hailey and had no problem sharing responsibilities with either of them.

After parting ways with Connie, Adrienne joined Noah on the laz. They'd each claimed a regular spot, Adrienne perching next to the outdoor fridge and Noah occupying the plastic chair near the *Amelia's* forty-passenger launch boat. Between them was a bucket of cigarette butts.

"Who are you sharing a bunk with?" Adrienne asked after telling

Noah what happened with Max that afternoon.

"No one, girl. I'm all by my lonesome."

"How's that?"

"There's only four guys down there. Everyone has their own bunks."

"Four?" Adrienne repeated.

"The officers all have cabins," Noah said. "It's just me, Nicky, Jordy, and Kyle living downstairs."

Adrienne exhaled. "Lucky you. You have no idea how uncomfortable it'll be down in our quarters. Four girls packed in like sardines is a lot."

"Uncomfortable? Dri, how do you think I feel about living with three straight guys? How do you think *they* feel about living with me?"

"I thought you got along with Nicky and Jordy? They seem open-minded."

"Yeah, I guess you're right. Kyle's a frickin' weirdo, though."

"Yeah …" Adrienne agreed, thinking back to dinner. "I've noticed."

Brynne

SHE STIRS RESTLESSLY in her bunk, plagued with worry and regret. It was harder leaving Gordon this season, especially with his indifference toward her monthslong absence. "Go back to your cruise ship, love," he'd told her. "Go be with your friends."

What friends?

Gordon claims there isn't a rift in their relationship, but she can feel it. He's been increasingly distant since the pregnancy last fall, especially after learning it wasn't her first. She'd explained about missing her period after being expelled from Saint Agatha's, how she and Max took a bus to Providence to buy pregnancy tests, which they wouldn't dare buy in Kent County. Max had rubbed her shoulder on the bus ride. "It's probably nothing, Brynnie. You're just being paranoid." But when parallel lines showed up on every test in the drugstore bathroom, Max was visibly shaken.

She was hysterical. "How could this happen? I'm only fourteen! We used a condom!"

Max collected herself. "We'll get this taken care of, Brynnie," she'd said solidly. "There's no *way* you're going to be a teen mom."

Maureen had been tight-lipped when she drove them back to Providence the following Thursday. At the clinic, she'd signed the necessary legalese before leaving them alone in the waiting room. "I'm going shopping," she'd said, eyeballing her Rolex as if dropping them off on a playdate. "Call when you're ready."

They were escorted into an exam room, where a nurse took her blood and gave her a smock. When the nurse asked if she had any questions, only one truly mattered—"Does this mean I can never have children?" No, the nurse had promised. So long as there weren't complications, she'd be fit for childbearing for the next thirty years at least.

She'd chosen not to look at the monitor during her ultrasound, but Max did, craning her neck toward the screen and cooing, "Ohhh! It looks like a little gummy bear! Like one of the miniature ones!" Then she spun back around. "I'm here for you, Brynnie. I'm always here for you."

A poster of a palm tree was taped to the ceiling above the operation chair. The doctor and his staff had ordered Max into the hall while they began the sedation process. "Fifteen minutes, and this will all be over," the doctor had said. "Then you can go back to being a kid again."

The procedure was fleeting, just as he'd promised. She'd never told Adamo, and Max *swore* she would never tell Marco. But it was the memory she kept bottled inside that haunted her. For over five years, she'd tried terribly to put it out of her mind, up until last September, when she and Gordon had slipped up somehow, and she'd become pregnant again.

20

EMBARKATION DAY went off without a hitch—mostly. The entire crew reported to the dining room in their formalwear, and Adrienne had to admit they all looked mighty impressive sitting together during breakfast. Only their epaulettes differed, the various symbols and number of bars denoting their departments and ranks.

As they cleared their plates, Adrienne saw Connie take Katherine aside and ask her to switch her epaulettes. "Your moons are backward," Connie said. "They need to be facing in the other direction."

Katherine side-eyed her shoulders. "Oops! Sorry, Connie!"

"No problem, kiddo. Practice makes perfect."

After breakfast, Connie led the stews to the pax lounge for embarkation. The bulletin board in the lounge was now covered with essential trip information. There was the itinerary—complete with arrival and departure times, lists of optional shore excursions, and a crew roster.

They alphabetized name badges as they waited. Coastal Cape Cod & the Islands was their first trip, and seventy passengers were joining them on the six-day cruise. Connie explained how to show the passengers around their cabins. "You've been here two months," she said. "You should know every cabin like the backs of your hands."

The passengers arrived between nine and eleven. They showed up in taxis and shuttles, as couples or with friends. The youngest traveler seemed around sixty, but the rest were seventy-plus. Adrienne saw some canes and walkers, and there was one woman in a wheelchair who Nicky jauntily wheeled up the gangway. "All right there, pretty lady," he said, "just call on me whenevah ya want a ride!"

Giving cabin tours came naturally to Adrienne. It was fun seeing the excitement on the passengers' faces. One couple especially liked her demonstration on how to flush the toilet by foot. And no one complained about the all-in-one showers.

Once all the passengers boarded, the deck staff untied the mooring ropes, and the *Amelia* broke away from the dock. Within moments they were cruising the Narragansett Bay to Newport.

Connie initiated a welcome announcement from the lectern, then contacted Hardigan via walkie-talkie to start the muster drills. A shrill series of beeps followed, and Hardigan's voice came through the intercom, directing the guests to secure their PFDs and head to their assigned muster stations.

After her group was settled, Adrienne waited with them for the drill to end. As they stood in the hall, Katherine walked over and introduced herself. "Hi, everyone! I'm Katherine Fowler!" She began chatting, but Adrienne nudged her and said, "Hey ... I think you're supposed to stay at *your* station until the drills are over."

"No worries, Dri!" Katherine said. "All good!"

But when Connie appeared for a mandatory headcount, she beelined straight for Katherine. "Who's watching your muster station right now?"

"Oh, I already checked on my passengers!" Katherine said. "Then I came over here to introduce myself to these guests."

Connie drummed her pen against her clipboard. "Muster drills aren't for *checking* on the passengers, Katherine. They're for staying with your group and making sure everyone is accounted for."

Katherine's face fell. "Oh ... I thought that was only if something happened."

"That's why we *practice*, Katherine. In case something happens."

For the rest of the day, Katherine grudgingly complained to Adrienne every chance she got. "I don't think it was very professional of Connie to reprimand me in front of the passengers. Problems should *never* be addressed in earshot of guests. That's one of the first things you learn in Hospitality Management."

By bedtime, Adrienne had heard enough. "Katherine, it's the first day. Don't you think Connie is under stress, too? Besides, I don't even think the passengers heard her."

Katherine crossed her arms. "Maybe she is, but that still doesn't give her the right. There's a time and a place for everything."

"I agree. But let's drop it, okay? Tomorrow will be a fresh start, and I'm sure everything will be fine."

Before Katherine could say more, Adrienne grabbed her towel and shower caddy and headed to the bathroom to escape her.

21

ADRIENNE HAD TO BE in the galley at six on Tuesday morning. She was scheduled as Galley Stew, with Noah as her Galley Assist. Working in the galley meant you could wear any pants you wanted except jeans. Adrienne settled on a pair of sweats, but Noah had chosen his much-loathed housekeeping pants. He yawned loudly. "Girl, I don't own any cheap pants. These suckers are just gonna hafta cut it."

Chef Ray gave them their briefings. Adrienne was to presoak, sanitize, and send the wares through the dish machine. Noah was responsible for drying and putting them away. During mealtimes, they'd help pass food through the service window. Dinners were plated, but breakfast and lunch were served family style, with heaping platters of hot and cold options for each table. "It's a three-man job," Chef Ray said, no-nonsense, "and I expect you both to keep up."

Adrienne got right to work. She filled the sinks, washed the dirty wares, and still had time to help Noah prepare twelve bowls of berries and twelve platters of sliced fruit. Sure, she could do without rising at the crack of dawn, but the harsh lighting and drool-worthy aromas gave her a much-needed jolt of energy, forcing her to wake up.

The other stews came up at six-thirty, except for Hailey, who had the much-coveted LD shift. At ten past seven, Max, that day's Crew Stew, made her rounds throughout the boat, alerting the crew for breakfast. Anyone able to leave their posts hustled to the crew tables. Those who couldn't get away or were sleeping would have to wait for lunch and dinner.

The order that went into the schedule was impressive. Though she was used to the irregularity of *à* la carte service, Adrienne found working on a structured timeline came easier, even if it left no room for error. If anything, the deckhands had a more enviable schedule, working twelve hours on, fourteen hours off. Their pay grade was lower, but they still got an equal share of the pooled tips.

After breakfast, the stews changed into their housekeeping uniforms. Adrienne made the rookie mistake of zipping her polyester smock over her bra without a shirt in between. She was only on her second cabin when she began sweating profusely, the beads of perspiration seeping through her bra, making it damp.

Two of her cabins were on the sun deck, where she ran into Noah. He pulled out an earbud and said, "I think Katherine got in trouble."

"What for?"

Noah shrugged. "Girl, I was listening to my music. All I know is I saw Connie talking to her in one of her cabins."

Back in girls' quarters, Katherine gave Adrienne another earful. "Did you know we have to *remake* the beds if a passenger already made them?"

Adrienne pulled her galley T-shirt over her head. "None of my passengers made their beds."

"Well, one of mine *did*, so I left it. Then Connie made me remake it how we learned in training."

"That's standard practice," Logan said, walking out of the rear bunk room dressed for lunch service. "Even if they make their beds, we have to remake them to match the pictures in the brochures."

"I wouldn't sweat it, Katherine," said Adrienne. "It's the first trip. We're all going to have kinks to work out."

But on Sunday, while they were underway to Nantucket, Connie was vexed when Katherine showed up four minutes late to her LD shift. This time, Adrienne could understand why. Working the LD shift meant you had to be upstairs at *exactly* eight o'clock to circle the boat with the handbell. The same went for lunch at noon and again at six for dinner. Only after you rang the dinner bell could you leave for the night.

So far, no one had been late for their shifts, LD or otherwise, but when Katherine wasn't upstairs at 8:01, Connie took the handbell herself. When she returned and saw Katherine standing in the dining room, adjusting her headband and looking confused, she directed Katherine to her office and shut the door behind them. Katherine came back to the floor without a word to anyone, her usual perkiness eliminated entirely.

When they reached Nantucket, the *Amelia* didn't dock alongside a pier as it had at the other ports they'd visited. Instead, Hardigan anchored in the middle of the Sound.

"It's to avoid paying the totally exorbitant docking fees," Logan explained. "Nantucket is *the* most expensive port to dock in."

"How do the passengers see the island?" Hailey asked.

"The launch boat takes them," said Logan. "You'll see. Soon they'll line up on the laz and go over in groups. They usually spend the day there, so Hardigan gives them pickup times to come back."

"How about us?" Adrienne asked. "Do we get to see Nantucket?"

Logan nodded. "One of the officers will take us over this afternoon."

After serving lunch to the few passengers who'd stayed behind, Adrienne, Logan, and Hailey ran downstairs to change into their street clothes.

"That is *so* unfair," Katherine whined, abandoning her vacuum and following them. "I'd like to see Nantucket, too, you know."

"You get out at six tonight, Katherine," Adrienne reminded her. "You'll have all night to see it."

"Yeah, don't feel bad!" said Hailey. "We'll all be LD here at some point."

Katherine shuffled her feet. "I *suppose*."

Noah was already waiting on the launch. So were Max and Brynne. Max was cozied up next to Marco, who was piloting their excursion. "This it?" he asked. "Anyone else coming?" He backed away from the *Amelia* and steered toward the island.

The trip was short. In minutes, they were being helped from the launch by dock staff at Straight Wharf. Marco would return to get them at three, leaving them two hours to explore what they could of Nantucket.

Adrienne was unprepared for such opulence when they reached the cobblestoned downtown. From the crown-molded boutiques to the chicly dressed locals, the island was unquestionably exclusive, reserved for those with Black Cards and shoulder-draped sweaters. Sure, Westford had its share of affluent residents, but it also had plenty of working-class folks, and the two groups were used to cohabitating. Nantucket was tailored for the wealthy, the *privileged*.

Noah had dressed perfectly for the environs. He wore mint-colored shorts and massive white sunglasses that matched his crisp polo shirt. He hadn't been kidding about "boy scouting" either. Whenever they passed someone he found attractive, Noah made a big deal of lowering his shades and humming erotically.

"I think you're overdoing it," Adrienne said while they waited for Logan and Hailey outside of some luxe clothier that Adrienne had no interest in.

"Girl, I'm just getting started. Wait until we get to Provincetown, and I *really* give you a show."

Adrienne made a face. "This isn't all you want out of life, is it?"

Noah held his cigarette like a model, a pose he *never* struck on board. "What?"

Adrienne nodded toward a polished man who looked like he'd stepped out of a golf catalog. "To settle down in a town like this? Married to some snooty elitist?"

She hadn't meant her words to be interpreted as funny, but Noah chortled and said, "Of course not! But they're such *fun* to play with!"

Everyone except Adrienne carried shopping bags on their way back to meet Marco. Max, Brynne, and Logan carried several. As they neared the wharf, Adrienne saw a sign advertising kayak rentals. Maybe next time they came to Nantucket, she'd go kayaking instead. Otherwise, the port had bored her, and she didn't see much point in getting off the *Amelia* at all.

Katherine

SHE ZIPS OVER to ask Captain Hardigan about the launch schedule when he passes by as she's cleaning. It's only the fourth day, and she *already* needs a break from Constantly Nagging Connie. "Hey, Captain! What time is the launch boat taking the crew out tonight?"

"The launch isn't taking the crew *anywhere* tonight," he says.

She's confused. The schedule on the bulletin board says they're not leaving for Hyannis until tomorrow morning. So where exactly will they be *tonight* that the launch isn't taking the crew to Nantucket?

Captain Hardigan snaps when she probes him. "The launch isn't equipped to travel in the dark! When we dock in Nantucket, *everyone* spends the night on board."

"Sure," she says. "Safety first. I understand."

She's a little miffed, but she remembers Hailey saying they'll all be in this position at some point. Well, now she'll have plenty of time to redecorate her and Adrienne's room with all the goodies she picked up on Martha's Vineyard yesterday. It's so bare down there right now! So depressing!

✳ ✳ ✳

NOAH SUGGESTED they watch a movie in crew lounge after their shift. "I brought hella DVDs with me!" he said during dinner. "We'll make popcorn and sundaes and have a girls' night!"

"I'm beat," said Logan. "I'm totally calling it an early night."

"Yeah," Hailey agreed. "Me too. We both started work at six."

"Suit yourselves!" said Noah. "What about you, Dri?"

Adrienne nodded. "Sure. I'll ask Katherine if she wants to join us."

But when Adrienne entered the front bunk room with Logan and Hailey, she had to look twice at the makeover before them. "Voilà!" Katherine squealed. "Don't you love it?"

Adrienne wasn't sure *love* was the word. Eggplant-colored blankets curtained their entire bunk, and a new minifridge and full-length mirror were lined against the wall. "And look!" Katherine said, turning off the lights. "This is the best part! We had them in my dorm room at Johnson & Wales!"

A galaxy of glow-in-the-dark stars shimmered across the ceiling. Adrienne hadn't seen them since she was a kid, when Aaron received a package for Christmas one year. "Where did you—"

"On Martha's Vineyard yesterday!" Katherine interrupted. "I needed some retail therapy!"

"Good job, Katherine," Logan said.

"Yeah!" said Hailey. "It looks really cute."

"What do you think, Dri?" Katherine asked. "I picked a dark color to help block the light while we're sleeping. Plus, I know you don't like pink, so ..."

"It looks great," Adrienne said, wanting to keep Katherine esteemed. "Thanks for thinking of me."

Truthfully, she felt annoyed, wishing Katherine would have checked with her first. Not that Katherine had made over any of *her* things, but they were just starting to live together, and Adrienne hoped these little surprises wouldn't become common occurrences.

After changing out of her uniform, she smiled at Katherine as she headed to meet Noah. Maybe she'd ask her to join them another night.

May 2007

22

THE SECOND TRIP was Coastal Cape Cod & the Islands in reverse, cruising from Provincetown back to East Bay. Adrienne had liked the first trip well enough and was glad she'd seen each port, not getting stuck on board as Katherine had in Nantucket. Her favorite stop was Martha's Vineyard, where they'd taken a shuttle to Oak Bluffs to explore the pastel confection of gingerbread cottages. She genuinely appreciated everything she'd seen that week, even Nantucket. How could you know if you cared for a place without experiencing it first?

The crew had all of Wednesday to restore the *Amelia*. These were called "turnaround days," intended for deep cleaning the cabins and public areas. Connie assigned each stew a section of cabins, then told them to tackle the public areas in pairs. Adrienne hit the pax lounge with Noah, who brought his iPod dock and chose a playlist featuring Rihanna, Beyoncé, and his *favorite*—Nelly Furtado.

That night, Connie assembled the crew to explain the tip-counting process. She brought out a Pendaflex folder with cabin numbers labeled on the divider tabs. Each pocket contained an envelope, and Connie recorded their contents on a bookkeeping sheet. The tips ran the gamut from average to generous, and no one complained as she compiled the total. When Connie finished calculating, Adrienne realized that, including her day-pay, she'd earned almost one thousand dollars for the six-day trip. She celebrated inwardly, watching the expressions of her coworkers range from accomplished pride to sheer glee. They would split the pooled tips evenly, except for Keith and Hardigan, who had different pay grades.

Later, Adrienne and Noah were on the laz when Kyle appeared, his dopey grin plastered across his face. "You got a smoke, man?" he asked Noah.

Adrienne stared at his doltish expression, his lazy posture. Something about Kyle didn't gel with the rest of the crew. She couldn't put her finger on it, but he didn't fit. He didn't belong with them.

Noah shook his head, exasperated. "My pack's downstairs."

In the short time they'd known him, Kyle had become infamous for bumming cigarettes and lights not just from Adrienne and Noah but also Nicky, the only other smoker on board. "The kid's Bev's seasonal basket case," Nicky said one afternoon. "She hires one every year." They'd all grown tired of Kyle's scavenging but so far had yet to deny him. Noah shot Adrienne the evil eye as she handed Kyle a cigarette.

"Man, I can't *wait* for this paycheck!" Kyle said, taking the cigarette without thanking her. "I'm gonna do so much damage with all that bread!"

"Good for you, boo," Noah said sarcastically. "You should start with buying cigarettes and a lighter. Or matches, since they're free."

Kyle laughed strangely, like he believed Noah was joking around with him. "No doubt, Noah, man," he said. "No doubt!"

Adrienne wanted to like all of her coworkers. Before Jenni, she'd never taken issue with *anyone* at work. But certain crew members made it difficult. Max, of course, would have nothing to do with any of the stews except Brynne, who they deemed guilty by association. Then there was Kyle, who Adrienne suspected was far more troubled than a "seasonal basket case." Nicky and Jordy frequently complained of his sluggishness and general idiocy, but not wanting to be labeled "rats," they hid their disapproval from the senior officers. Besides, as Jordy had pointed out, if they said anything about Kyle, he could turn and snitch on them for smoking weed. And though Katherine was the prolonged novice in the steward department, even her issues paled against Kyle's peculiar ways.

Adrienne had decided to give Katherine's shortcomings the benefit of the doubt. Sure, no one else had experienced as many difficulties as her, but you had to let people progress at their own pace, so long as it didn't bring down the team. She kept this mentality until the first night of the new trip, when Jordy stormed into crew lounge, barking, "Who the hell was

Crew Stew today?"

Adrienne had just finished her first T&A shift and dropped in to join Noah as he watched a movie. "Not me. I was T&A."

"LD," said Noah, not looking away from the screen.

Jordy wore a nasty scowl. "That's *not* what I asked."

"What's with the attitude?" said Adrienne.

"I want to know who Crew Stew was! My shift's over, and I can't find any food in the galley fridges!"

"I think it was Katherine," Noah said.

Adrienne stood up. "Hang on. I'll go down to girls' quarters and ask her." She walked upstairs and across the dining room. Down in their bunk room, Katherine snored peacefully behind the blanket curtains. "Katherine ..." Adrienne whispered. "Wake up ..."

Katherine drew a blanket curtain back. "Hmm? What's going on?"

"Where's the crew food? Jordy wants to know."

"What crew food?"

"The leftover food you saved. You were Crew Stew today, weren't you?"

"Yes, but what are you talking about?"

Adrienne sighed. "You should probably come upstairs."

A minute later, they stood in the galley with Jordy and Noah. "Okay," said Adrienne, "the food left from lunch and dinner ... where did you store it so Jordy can make a plate?"

Katherine blinked. "I didn't save any food. Was I supposed to?"

"That's wicked fucked!" Jordy groaned. "You know we work twelve-hour shifts, right? I haven't eaten since breakfast!"

"I'm sorry! Today was my first Crew Stew shift. I didn't know I was supposed to save the extra food. No one told me to at breakfast."

"Girl, that's because you don't save breakfast," said Noah. "Just lunch and dinner."

"So, it's *gone*?" Jordy pressed. "All of it?"

"Yes," Katherine said. Then she pointed at the pastry case. "But look! There are still blondies and pudding cookies left!"

"I don't *care* about blondies and pudding cookies! I want food!" Jordy tramped out of the galley. "Nicky and Marco are gonna be wicked pissed, too!" he called back to her.

Katherine looked from Adrienne to Noah. "I really didn't know I was supposed to save the food. I thought Crew Stew just monitored the coffee station and let the crew know when to eat."

"Don't worry about it, girl," Noah said. "Jordy gets pissy when he doesn't eat, can't you tell?"

"Well, he didn't have to be so *rude*."

"It's just food," Adrienne comforted her. "He'll get over it."

As they started back to girls' quarters, Nicky walked through the dining room and said, "I hear you're in deep watah, Homegirl!"

"Who are you talking to?" Katherine asked.

"I'm talkin' to *you*, Homegirl!"

"Why are you calling me *Homegirl?*"

"'Cause if ya can't get on board with how things work around here, then you're goin' *home, girl!*"

It was clear Nicky meant the remark lightheartedly, but Katherine folded her arms across her chest. "What are you *saying?*"

Adrienne touched her shoulder. "Come on, Katherine. Let's go."

"No! I want to know what he means about me going home!"

"Relax, will ya?" said Nicky. "I was only bustin' ya chops about all the little hiccups ya keep havin.'"

"Well, *I* don't think that's very funny. You ought to mind your own business!"

Nicky bent forward with a courtly bow. "My apologies, swabbie!"

"Those deckhands are so unprofessional!" Katherine huffed as Adrienne followed her downstairs. "Like *they've* never made mistakes before!"

"I'm sure they have, Katherine ..." Adrienne said. *Just probably not every day.*

23

KEEPING HER PROMISE to Thany, Adrienne called home every afternoon. It amused her what a chatterbox Thany was on the phone, gabbing away about Cub Scouts and his first Sunday adventure with Wendy. "She took me to the flower store, and we bought little clay pots and zinnias! We got reds and pinks and yellows, and Wendy even bought me a watering can!"

Jack was more of a question-asker. When he wasn't nudging Adrienne about quitting smoking, he preferred hearing how things were going aboard the boat rather than talking about himself. Mostly she shared about the different ports she'd seen and how tasty Chef Ray's meals were—meals like veal osso buco and seafood bouillabaisse that would cost her a small fortune anywhere else in the world.

"I'm glad you're enjoying yourself," Jack said one night. "Anything eventful to report yet?"

"Not really," Adrienne said, unsure what he might be getting at.

"All confined on that boat, guess I figured you'd have some war stories."

Adrienne thought she sensed a subtle humor but quickly reminded herself who she was talking to. "No war stories yet, Dad, but you'll be the first to know if that changes."

Besides the idiosyncrasies of her crewmates, life on the boat had been relatively unremarkable. Things stayed that way until the second afternoon of the return trip, while in Hyannis, an anxious passenger surprised Adrienne during her LD shift. "Excuse me? Miss? I need help looking for something in my cabin. Right now, please!"

The nametag hanging from the woman's lanyard identified her as Nita Cagle from Stuart, Florida. Adrienne had shown Nita and her husband, Bruno, to their cabin yesterday. Bruno was frail and used a walker. In their cabin, he sat on a bed, his fragile hands on his knees, wincing in pain. "Are you okay, Bruno?" Adrienne asked.

"Oh, miss!" said Nita. "My Bruno had knee surgery recently. The doctor gave him some medication for the pain, but he's misplaced it. Would you check if it's rolled under one of the beds?"

"Of course!" Adrienne searched the entire cabin but found nothing. "I'm sorry," she told Bruno and Nita once she'd checked everywhere possible. "Let me find out who cleaned your cabin today. Maybe they can help."

The Cagles' cabin was in the housekeeping section belonging to Galley Assist. Adrienne cringed when she ran her finger across the rotation and saw Max's name. *Great.* Of all the days for Connie to be on a passenger excursion, today had to be it. Adrienne had no choice but to approach Max herself.

She knocked on the portside door. When it cracked open, Brynne looked like she'd just been woken from a nap. Behind her, the room was pitch-black.

"Is Max here?" Adrienne asked.

Brynne yawned softly. "No."

"Do you know where she is?"

"Try Marco's cabin, maybe?"

It was strange hearing Brynne speak, especially to her directly. "Thanks," said Adrienne. "Sorry to wake you up."

Marco's cabin was in the midship aft, across from the crew laundry closet. He answered the door wearing a pair of briefs. "Yeah?"

"Is, uh, is Max there?" Adrienne stammered, looking away.

Marco turned. "Babe ... *Babe!* That girl Adrienne wants you."

Max was at the door in a flash, yanking it shut behind her. She wore black boy shorts and a strappy top, but whatever she'd been doing in there, her sheeny blonde hair was flawless, bobby pins and all. "What do *you* want?" she hissed.

"Did you clean cabin 30P this morning?" Adrienne asked.

"*Why?*"

"The couple can't find the husband's pain medicine. I thought you might know where it was."

Max's face registered with disgust. "You think I took it?"

This had been a mistake. "No. I don't think you *took* anything. I thought maybe you'd seen it and could help them."

"I don't know what you're talking about, so *don't* bother us again."

Adrienne reported the lost medication when Connie returned from the Kennedy Museum. "It used to happen when I was a stew, too," Connie said, unconcerned. "Usually, they forget to pack their meds and don't realize until they're here and it's too late. I'll look into it."

Before dinner, Adrienne split a cigarette with Noah, sharing the mystery of the missing pills and her off-putting exchange with Max.

"The bitch was probably in the middle of a quickie," Noah surmised, raking a hand through his pompadour. "Must be nice having a built-in booty call on board."

"Wow, hostile much?" Adrienne joked.

"Girl, I just can't stand the bitch. You try working with her in the galley all day, okay? Then come talk to me about being hostile."

To date, Noah and Max had worked three galley shifts together, each more rivalrous than the last. Adrienne knew of several instances of Max bossing Noah around, finding fault with his every move even if Chef Ray didn't. One day, she'd even called Hardigan into the galley, knowing he'd berate Noah for wearing his earbuds during service. And just that morning, Adrienne had seen Max yanking the steaming racks from the dishwasher in a fury, slamming them down on the prep table so the hot water droplets splashed Noah. Whatever had brought this on, Adrienne hadn't asked, but Noah had whipped around and yelled, "Keep it up, girl! I am *not* the one!"

Chef Ray had shaken his head. "You see what I deal with when they're partners? A couple of queens fighting over an invisible crown in here. I couldn't make this up if I wanted to!"

Connie

WHAT A NIGHTMARE—spending all of Cocktail Hour helping the Cagles look for the Percocet. When she asked, for the third time, if they were *sure* they'd brought the prescription along, Nita Cagle snapped at her. "Of course we did, you ninny! I helped Bruno with a dose just before bed last evening!"

She urged them to have an emergency refill sent to the pharmacy on Barnstable Road, promising to pick it up herself on their behalf. But still, if they didn't leave the Percocet behind, where the hell is it?

Against her better judgment, she pulls Max from the galley during dinner to ask if she'd seen the medication while housekeeping.

"Are you serious?" Max snaps. "I already told *Adrienne* I don't know about any missing pills."

"Max, I just thought—"

"I don't give a fuck what you thought! Don't you know how much money my family has? I can afford to *buy* whatever I want!"

She feels as though she's been struck. The audacity of this ... this *child*. No wonder Mattie wanted the season off! Shaking, she goes to Peter in the wheelhouse. "I don't work sixteen hours a day to be snarled at by your stepdaughter," she tells him.

Peter doesn't look up from his newspaper. "Yes, I can agree Mackenzie is a very strong-willed young woman."

"She's insubordinate, Peter."

His face reads that he can't be bothered. "Ms. Lacasio, I have no more time for drama now than I did when you were a stewardess. For what you're getting paid, I'd expect you to possess the skills to resolve trivial crew issues. Otherwise, perhaps we should explore finding a *replacement* cruise director."

She leaves the wheelhouse before saying something she'll regret. *Peter will see to it that they keep in line.* Right. The entire Hardigan family is depraved if you want her opinion. How Bev hasn't seen through the nonsense for all these years is absolutely staggering.

24

They celebrated Logan's twenty-fourth birthday with a party in galley stores. They were anchored in Nantucket again, which meant no night out on the town. Instead, Nicky smuggled a rack of beer into their secret confines, where they sang "Happy Birthday" to Logan atop the deep freezers. "A family that drinks togethah, sinks togethah!" Nicky toasted.

Present company also included Hailey, Noah, Jordy, Kyle, and, oddly, Brynne, who sat beside Nicky, saying nothing. Soon, their group was engaged in a game of Truth or Dare. Adrienne hadn't played since middle school and agreed to participate on the terms that no one got too invasive or out of control. They were still getting to know each other, after all. The game was basically harmless. Nicky asking Noah if he'd sleep with a woman for ten thousand dollars. Noah daring Nicky to do something that scared him. "Your choice, girl!" Noah said.

A red blush crept up Nicky's face. He knocked back his beer, said, "You're on, matey," and kissed Brynne's cheek. She was as startled as everyone, but Nicky laughed and said, "Aye, at least I kept it PG!"

Adrienne limited herself to two beers. It may have been Logan's birthday, but drinking on board was a cardinal sin, and she didn't want to risk losing her job over something so avoidable. Kyle drank like he had nothing to lose, consuming the lion's share of the beer until Nicky grabbed it away. "That's enough, Kyle. I'm cuttin' ya off."

Kyle's eyes were swimmy. He tried getting down from the deep freezer, banging his head against the overhead light and causing it to swing astray. "C'mon, man … lemme just have one more!"

"I said *no*, all right? You're three sheets to the wind already."

They wrapped at midnight, Kyle staggering after Adrienne, Noah, and Nicky on their way to the laz. "One'a you guys got a smoke for me?"

Nicky yanked one from his pack. "Someone needs to find ya a job there, Kyle."

Kyle took a few drags and extinguished the cherry on the outdoor fridge, leaving a jagged black streak scarring the door.

"Ya gonna clean that up?" Nicky asked.

Kyle stumbled. "Don't worry about it, man. It'll … it'll clean itself."

Nicky grabbed a rag from his pocket and wiped away the ash. "I helped paint this whole boat, Kyle. Have some damn respect."

Kyle floundered across the laz to urinate through the rails, the streak of ash already light-years behind him.

"This fuckin' kid's a stooge," griped Nicky. "I'm gonna say somethin' to Mahco in the mornin'. Enough's enough here already."

Two days later, on a rainy morning at the Block Island Boat Basin, Adrienne was surprised to see Connie and Hardigan waiting in the dining room when the stews arrived to set up for breakfast.

"What's going on?" Noah mouthed, trekking in from guys' quarters.

Adrienne shrugged. It was too early for whatever this was. She suspected the officers had learned about Logan's party, but the energy Hardigan was externalizing didn't seem to indicate as much. Besides, *if* the officers knew about the party, wouldn't they have said something yesterday?

Hardigan did a quick head count. "Who's missing?"

"Katherine," said Connie. "She's LD today."

"Well, go get her! I want your entire department in here!"

Adrienne and Noah exchanged puzzled glances with Logan and Hailey. Max and Brynne walked toward the coffee station.

"Don't stray far, Mackenzie," Hardigan warned.

Max batted her eyelashes. "I won't …"

When Connie returned with a confused and sleep-rumpled Katherine, Hardigan instructed everyone to sit at the center banquette. Max and Brynne opposed, leaning against a beam with their coffees.

"Last night," he began, "Nita and Bruno Cagle asked Ms. Lacasio to rouse me after I'd retired for the evening."

Adrienne felt a knot forming in her stomach.

"It seems Bruno Cagle discovered his Percocet was missing again. The Percocet *refill* Ms. Lacasio just retrieved in Hyannis."

He scrutinized the stews. Was he waiting for a confession? Was one of *them* being blamed for the pills going missing? A small part of Adrienne sympathized with the sense of accusation Max must have felt on Friday. A *very* small part.

Everyone stared at Hardigan wordlessly, watching him tower over them until speaking again. "At this time, we have reason to believe the medication is being stolen. Unless someone comes forth with admission, a complete strip of your living quarters will begin effective immediately."

The stews all stole wild-eyed looks at each other. From their beam, even Max and Brynne were speechless.

"What about the deckhands?" Katherine blurted out. "Will they be questioned?"

"Young lady, I have had it with these inquiries of yours! It is none of your concern how I conduct business on this vessel!"

Katherine shrunk against the banquette as Hardigan ordered Connie to get started in girls' quarters. He stormed off, grumbling about Keith's whereabouts, while Connie headed in the opposite direction.

Once they were gone, the stews sounded off. None of them had ever experienced a violation of this nature. All Adrienne could picture was the careless ransacking of Andy Dufresne's cell in *The Shawshank Redemption*, the utter lack of regard for his possessions. It didn't help that Hardigan wasn't unlike Warden Norton, though Adrienne hoped Connie would go about searching their quarters more tactfully.

And if the pills *were* being stolen, who was the guilty party? Adrienne wanted to believe she knew her friends well enough to discount them as thieves, and though she didn't know Max and Brynne at all, her instinct said they probably weren't responsible either. Max surely fell under the umbrella of many unflattering titles, but "thief," Adrienne was almost certain, wasn't one of them.

Jordy

THEY'RE NOT GONNA find anything in *his* bunk. The weed's all Nicky's, but they won't find that either. Nicky hid it too well. *He* didn't bring anything unless you count a couple of *Hustlers*. Let 'em search. Hardigan and Keith don't get to him. Not like all those jack-offs in the yard.

He puts the search out of his mind, goes out on the sun deck to find the cabin with the backed-up head. *Fuck.* Which side did Capt. tell him? 71P or 71S? That's all he needs is to waste time in the wrong cabin. As he rounds the bow, he sees Kyle walking out of a cabin. Walking too fast if you ask him. Kyle jumps when he sees him, stuffs his hands in his pockets.

He picks up his pace. "What's up, Kyle? What were you doing in that cabin?"

"Oh ... uh ... that's the cabin Capt. said had the toilet problem."

He looks at the cabin numbered 74S and then back at Kyle. The kid's out of it. His pupils are like pinpricks. "They're called *heads*," he corrects him. "And you weren't in the right one. And why're your eyes all fucked up like that? What'd you just shove in your pockets?"

"Nothing ... okay, man?"

He takes a step forward, gets in his face. "No. Show me."

"Aw, c'mon, Jordy!"

"Now! Or I'll get the guys up here, and we'll take it."

"C'mon, Jordy! I thought you were cool, man!"

"*Last chance, Kyle!*" He says it like he means it, and Kyle reaches into his pocket and pulls out a prescription bottle. He grabs it away from him. "*You're* the one stealing pills from the pax?"

The kid's shaking like a leaf. "I gave it back, okay, Jordy? Just don't say anything, man, please?"

He grabs for his walkie-talkie. "No way, dude. I'm getting the officers. And if I were you, you'd better start packing."

✸ ✸ ✸

KYLE'S FIRING was unlike anything Adrienne had ever seen. Noah rushed upstairs to tell the girls how Hardigan and Keith tore Kyle's bunk and locker apart until finding the prescriptions, then made him pack his stuff and turn over his uniforms and IDs. Kyle was cooperating, according to Noah, but when he entered the dining room, flanked by the male officers, he began to protest. "Where are you guys *taking* me?"

"We are escorting you off of this dock!" thundered Hardigan. "You are not to return within one thousand feet of the vessel!"

"But we're on an island, man! You can't leave me here!"

"Sure can," said Keith. "You should've thought about that before stealing three bottles of pills."

When Kyle argued, Hardigan roared at him. "Another word, and I'll send for the New Shoreham Police! You better count your lucky stars that Ms. Sanbourne doesn't want to cause a scene on this island!"

They watched as Kyle was ushered away in the rain, but deep down, Adrienne felt disturbed. Certainly, NECLA had grounds for firing him, but leaving Kyle stranded on an island didn't sit right with her. Could the company really just dump an employee off somewhere? On the other hand, what Kyle had done was illegal. Maybe this was just NECLA's version of punitive action. Adrienne wondered if this was how all firing procedures were carried out, hoping she'd never have to witness another to get her answer.

The pill fiasco was over as quickly as it began, the saving grace for the female stews being that Connie had gone easy on them, leaving nothing *Shawshank* in her wake. Max and Brynne had lucked out especially, as Connie hadn't even reached their side before Kyle was apprehended.

The crew was forbidden from mentioning the incident around the passengers. Fortunately, all the guests had been off board, and Kyle's removal had gone unnoticed. But after work, everyone murmured in private. The theft was their first drama, and it livened things up. A war story on a small scale, although probably not one Adrienne would tell her father. Some things, she was learning, you didn't share past the boat.

Shane

HE WINCES when the dish soap stings the cuts on his arm. Doesn't hurt too bad, but it's annoyin' anyways. Last night was what? The fourth, fifth fight with Jess since Travis moved in? This time it was about food. "That piece'a shit's been eatin' us dry since he got here!" Jess kept screamin'. "Treats us like a fuckin' soup kitchen!" He got away fast when she started throwin' hands, but he didn't hit her back. Never has, no matter how bad she's hurt him.

He'd waited 'til Avery was in bed before tellin' Jess off. "Don't ever touch me or pick a fight in front of her again! One more time, and we're done, Jess! I fuckin' mean it!" As usual, she didn't believe him, even after he dared her to try. Finally, he'd found a spare blanket and spent the night on the couch. This mornin', he didn't even wanna look at her.

He takes a smoke break at two-thirty, right as the truck from Sanbourne's Fish Market pulls up. Every Tuesday, Sanbourne's delivers to his job at Dellagatta's. After a year here, he knows the place like clockwork. That's what givin' up the nightlife industry'll get ya when you've got no fallback plan—washin' dishes and minimum wage.

This week, it's his neighbor, Eric, drivin' the truck. They take a few minutes to shoot the shit.

"Nasty fight over there last night," Eric says. "Nati and I heard you guys across the street."

He shows Eric his arm. "She's still heated that my cousin moved in with us."

"Look at you, mano, you're miserable. How many times do I gotta tell you to get out? Jess is *loco*, no offense."

Eric's not wrong about that. "I threatened to leave if she does it again. All this fightin' in front of our daughter? Avery's not even three, and she knows things aren't right between us."

He admits he's been thinkin' more about gettin' out, but he can't do that to Avery. And where's he gonna go? He's already on the wrong side of his twenties—no special skills, doesn't know any trades or have any licenses. Even his cousin's got a better job than him, and *he* just finished a three-year bid at MCI Norfolk.

Eric loads his order onto a hand truck. "I know you'll probably say no, but my boss's mother needs a guy on one of her boats like *tomorrow*. They just fired some pill-popper for stealing scripts from the guests."

He looks at Eric but doesn't say nothin'.

"I'm just putting it out there, mano. A gig like that sounds like just what the doctor ordered for you. It'll get you outta the house ... plus, the pay ain't half bad from what I hear."

"Oh yeah? How much?"

"More than you're making now, I know that."

He outs his cigarette. "You're sayin' I should just quit here and uproot my life to work on some boat? You sure you're not the one poppin' pills?"

Eric laughs. "What I'm saying is you should drive to East Bay and talk to a lady named Bev Sanbourne. After what I heard last night, Nati and I are gonna be visiting you in the hospital soon." He slams the truck door and secures it. "I'm serious, Shane. I've seen some of the dudes they've got on those boats. Cool guys. And you get paid to travel and shit? I'd be all over a gig like that if I were you, mano."

He thinks about it. Twenty minutes later, he tells Gary, his manager, that somethin' came up, he's gotta cut out early. When he finds the place, he pulls up to some trailer and parks across the street.

"I'm here to see Bev Sanbourne," he tells the redhead inside.

She eyes him up and down ... nothin' he's not used to. "Do ya have an appointment?"

"Nah, sorry, I don't."

"What's this regahdin'?"

"A job openin'. A deck staff position, I think."

"Oh? And how'd ya hear about us?"

Now he knows she's just tryin' to make small talk. He plays along. "Eric Gonzalez referred me. He drives truck for the fish market."

She picks up the phone. Next thing he knows, some older broad's walkin' up to him. She gives him a once-over, too.

"I'm Shane Piroux," he says, turnin' on the charm. "You Bev?"

"I am indeed." She tells him to come to her office.

"I don't have a résumé," he says when they sit. "I was just referred about an hour ago."

She smiles, and he can tell she likes him. "What are you currently doing for work, Mr. Piroux?"

"Right now, I'm washin' dishes at Dellagatta's in Pawtucket. Before that, I worked security for six years."

"Do you have any prior boating experience?"

"No, ma'am, but I'm a hands-on guy, and I like to keep busy."

They talk about the job and then the money. As soon as Bev tells him the pay, he knows he's not lettin' this opportunity go. She says, "I usually don't hire crew members on the spot, but in this case, I'm desperate. You'll need to complete the forms and a drug test by tomorrow morning. Do you have any obligations preventing you from working through October?"

He thinks of Avery, thinks of Jess, and thinks of the job offer. "Nah, I don't," he says. "No obligations."

"Wonderful. My boat will be back from Newport later this evening. Plan on being here for noon tomorrow."

He's gotta laugh on his way outta the little trailer. Life would be great if all things were that easy. And that bit about workin' security was golden. Sure it's true if bouncin' six nights a week at the club counts. He won't deny it if Bev finds out.

Right now, all he's gotta worry about is Jess when he gets home. He can just see her flippin' shit now.

25

THE CREW HAD a few hours to explore Newport while the *Amelia* refueled. Hailey, Logan, and Katherine were going to tour the Breakers, but Noah invited Adrienne back to his house to wait while he did laundry. "Girl, I don't trust that washer-dryer in that crew closet," he said. "My clothes are too expensive to chance it."

They were picked up in a bare-rimmed Celica by Noah's best friend, Bethany, whom he introduced to Adrienne as his "fag hag." Bethany was full-figured and emo glam, with spiky raven-colored hair. Noah had talked about her enough that meeting Bethany in person felt familiar to Adrienne. They were both Tiverton natives and had been friends forever, but lately, Noah had grown frustrated with Bethany's lackadaisical approach toward life. "I love her to death," he'd said, "but all she does is sit on a stool at a toll booth. She's not motivated at all."

His complaints made Adrienne think of Wendy. Did judging your best friend make you a bad person?

Noah had also shared a lot about his home life with Adrienne. Except for Logan, who seemed to come from normalcy, dysfunctional families and the need to escape were proving common grounds for boat employment. Between Hailey's overprotective parents and the way Katherine spoke of her brassbound father, Adrienne understood why none of the stews acted particularly homesick.

In Noah's case, his parents had announced their divorce the day after he'd graduated high school, right after his father discovered his mother was having an affair. It startled Adrienne how Noah's background mirrored hers, especially how they both began smoking after their families split, using cigarettes to cope. Adrienne had started bumming them from Roman at work. Noah had picked up the habit from Bethany. When Adrienne had asked if he still talked to his mother, Noah said, "Fuck her. My dad was a tugboat captain for twenty-six years. He worked his ass off to support us. She was a fucking restaurant hostess. I mean, really? *Who is a hostess when they're forty-five?* My dad found out she was screwing one of the cooks and filed for divorce the next day."

That's when Adrienne had told Noah about Raina and the Accountant, then about Roman and Jenni.

"Shocker," he'd said about the latter. "The restaurant industry is *so* incestuous."

Noah lived in a clapboard house with faded shingles. Adrienne followed him and Bethany upstairs to a bathroom that doubled as the laundry room, chuckling at the sign above the toilet—*The Best Seat in the House.* Noah loaded his laundry into the machine, then led them to the kitchen and poured three glasses of lemonade. A large package waited for him on the stove.

"Yes, girl!" Noah cried, yanking a knife from a drawer. "More movies!" He sliced open the box and began pulling out DVDs by the handful. "I ordered these before we left. Let's watch one while we wait for my laundry."

Noah's movie collection was becoming a valuable asset on the boat. He owned hundreds of DVDs, all stored in thick binders he pulled out on nights they had nothing to do. Bethany scoured through his new additions until selecting *The Laramie Project*, which Adrienne had never heard of.

"You don't know who Matthew Shepard was?" asked Bethany.

Adrienne shook her head.

"I'm her first gay friend," Noah said proudly.

Bethany appeared unimpressed. "Have you ever seen *Boys Don't Cry?*"

"Once," Adrienne said. "A long time ago."

"Similar story."

Adrienne got chills throughout *The Laramie Project.* The savage way Matthew Shepard was beaten turned her stomach. Tied to a fence post and left to die in rural Wyoming? For no reason other than being gay? How could people be so cruel? So hate-filled? She worried about the movie's impact on Noah, but he didn't say anything, not even when he got up to switch his laundry to the dryer.

When the movie ended and Noah went back upstairs, Bethany leaned over and said, "He got bullied a lot in middle school. Kids called him 'Nomo the Homo' for a long time."

Adrienne felt sick. She couldn't imagine anyone trying to strip Noah of his sassiness or gregarious personality.

After a nonverbal ride back to Fort Adams, Adrienne turned to Noah as they walked to the boat. "Does it bother you to watch movies like that?"

"No, girl. When I see movies like that, I feel lucky."

"Lucky? Why?"

"Because, Dri," he sighed, "... if I was born ten years earlier ... or in one of those conservative states ... I might not even be alive today."

Shane

HE'S NEVER LEFT a job that way—just quit with no notice. He felt bad dippin' on Gary, but a dishwasher's easy to replace. Gary'll be all right. He knows it'll be harder leavin' home, mainly Avery. He's never loved anyone as much as he loves her. Broke his heart when the doctors said she had developmental delays. He didn't even know what that meant. They assured him and Jess she'd be okay. Said she's high-functionin', shouldn't be held back much in life.

Leavin' Jess is another story. She'd flipped when he told her last night. Threw things. Accused him of only thinkin' about what *he* wants. He did what he could to defend himself, yelled back at her. "You don't understand, Jess! You don't work! How long are we gonna keep survivin' on seven-forty an hour and food stamps? We need this money! This cycle of poverty's gotta stop somewhere!"

He had a sit-down with Travis afterward, told him it's okay that he keeps stayin' in the basement. "My home is your home, cousin," he'd said. He knows it's hard for Travis to find a place with his record, so they'd talked numbers. Travis'll put aside one seventy-five a month—a quarter of the rent—and he'll send the rent to his landlord by money orders. Travis can reimburse him whenever he comes home.

His mom and sister live way the hell down in South County, so he calls to let them know what's goin' on. His mom says she loves him, to be careful. Caela, his sister, tells him she's proud. Imagine that, his little sister, only twenty-one, tellin' him *she's* proud. Caela says she'll do whatever she can for Avery, promises she'll come up to see her every week.

He takes Avery in his arms while Travis heads to the car. Jess is in the bathroom, so he has a moment alone, just them. He pushes her hair to the side and kisses her forehead. "You deserve more than what we've got right now," he whispers. "I'm gonna do somethin' to make things better for us."

Then he puts her in the playpen and leaves. Doesn't even say goodbye to Jess.

26

CONNIE ASSIGNED Adrienne the outdoor cabins for turnaround day. With the temperature topping seventy, Adrienne was happy to oblige. She'd come to enjoy housekeeping—the one part of the job that allowed for solitude—and taken Logan's advice to bring music and headphones, immersing herself in a private headspace while she cleaned her cabins.

It was the *Amelia*'s first time back in East Bay since the initial trip. Vendors streamed about the parking lot delivering linen and food orders, Jordy pumped out the black water tank, and Marco and Nicky squeegeed the windows at warp speed, overcompensating for being a man down.

Adrienne had just retrieved the sun deck vacuum from Hailey when she saw a tan Buick pull up to the boat. A guy stepped out, dressed plainly in jeans and a T-shirt, and she watched him grab a suitcase from the backseat and give the male driver a fist bump through the window.

As the Buick pulled off, Marco and Nicky headed toward who Adrienne guessed was a replacement deckhand, watching them exchange macho-guy greetings from her vantage point. They were walking back to the gangway when the new guy glanced up and caught sight of her. Adrienne was held captive by his gaze, neither of them breaking eye contact for several moments.

Even from a distance, Adrienne found him attractive. He was at least six feet, with a round face and brown hair shaved close to his head. She sensed an edge to him, giving her a fluttery feeling that grabbed hold and clung to her. It wasn't just that the guy was good-looking. There was something about his walk, his minimalistic attire, and that mutual gaze that dared the other to look away.

She considered this new guy might only be temporary, maybe a yard worker she hadn't seen before. Kyle was only fired two days ago, and she wasn't certain Bev had time to replace him so fast. But an impulsive curiosity hoped he wasn't temporary. Something about that look they'd shared made her want to get to know him better.

When she finished her cabins, Adrienne sat on the laz. As she concentrated on the stillness of the water, unfamiliar footsteps jogged down the restricted staircase. The replacement deckhand, looking lost, appeared before her. He stopped short, smiling slowly when he saw her. "Hey. You happen to know where Marco is?"

Adrienne pointed to the door leading to the hallway. "He was just in the dining room. It's straight through there."

"Thanks." He walked over with a natural swagger and stuck out his hand. "I'm Shane."

"Adrienne."

His hand was huge, igniting a wave of warmth inside of her. He pointed to her cigarette when he let go. "You happen to have an extra one of those? I gave my last one to my cousin."

Adrienne opened her pack. "Only if you don't mind menthols."

"Nah, I don't mind. I smoke menthols, too."

She studied Shane's face. He was even more attractive up close, with poignant chestnut eyes that told her he'd seen as much darkness as she had, if not more. He looked strong. Not as cut and ripped as Marco, but lean and sinewy, built to withstand a lot physically. Then she noticed his left bicep. An armband tattoo stuck out from under his T-shirt sleeve. A tattoo and a long, knotty scar.

Nicky and Marco came through the door as she handed Shane a cigarette. "Ya ready to go there, Shaney-Boy?" Nicky called. "Mahco and I ah gonna show ya the engine room."

Shane tucked the cigarette behind his ear. "Thanks. Nice meetin' ya, Adrienne."

Adrienne smiled. "Nice meeting you, too."

Shane

IT'S NOT SO BAD. Eric was right—Nicky and Marco seem like cool dudes. He vibes with them fine. They take him up to the wheelhouse to meet Hardigan. Strict guy, but nothin' he can't handle. Hardigan tells him not to be late for his shifts, to treat his position with importance. No problem there. He only hesitates when Nicky brings him down to where the guys live and says, "The kid in the bunk next to ya—Noah—he's gay. But he don't bothah nobody."

"I don't know about sleepin' next to a gay kid ..." he tells Nicky.

"I promise ya, Shaney-Boy, the kid's hahmless."

We'll see. He's heard enough stories from Travis about bein' bunked up with a bunch of dudes.

Nicky tells him Marco's got his own cabin with his girl, asks if he has a girl back home. He tells Nicky about Jess, and Nicky laughs, shakes his head. "That's a damn shame, matey. There's a lotta good-lookin' girls on the boat this season."

He believes it, especially the one he just met.

He's not gonna pretend he's always been faithful to Jess. Girls have a way of pushin' up on him, and he hasn't always said no. But this is different. You don't shit where ya eat, and he's not losin' this job for more than triple his pay at Dellagatta's. Still, he asks Nicky about Adrienne anyways, just general curiosity.

"Adrienne? She's all right in my book. She can hang."

That's cool. He likes when a girl has a good personality. There was somethin' else about her, too. Somethin' in her eyes, that look they shared. He'd like to know more about her. Doesn't matter if nothin' else happens. He's just interested.

***

ALL THE GIRLS had something to say about Shane. So did Noah, who, against Hardigan's orders, was habitually popping into their starboard quarters at his leisure. Adrienne felt like she was in middle school again, attending a sleepover with Wendy and gossiping about which boys everyone thought were cute.

"I think he's sexy," Logan said. "Sexy, but not my type."

"I think so, too," Hailey admitted, "but he's not my type either."

Katherine disregarded the consensus. "*I* don't find him attractive. He seems ... rough."

"Girl, please!" cried Noah. "Homeboy looks just like that Wentworth hottie from *Prison Break*. And guess who sleeps in the bunk next to him?"

Lucky, Adrienne thought. Shane *did* resemble the actor from *Prison Break*—Wentworth whoever. Just taller ... and with chestnut eyes instead of blue.

"I've seen him looking at you, Adrienne," Logan said cunningly. "A couple of times, actually ..."

Adrienne's cheeks heated. She'd noticed, too.

"Ohhh, get it, girl!" Noah whooped. "Just tell me before you visit guys' quarters so I can tie a bow on the doorknob!"

"Oh my God, Noah! I don't even know him!"

Noah winked. "Better get on that!"

Noah

HA! Do these guys think he can't tell they're uncomfortable sharing a room with him? Girl, it blows his mind how homophobic some straights can be. Please. Are all straight guys attracted to every *girl* they see? Didn't think so. He'd set the record straight with Nicky, Jordy, and even that weirdo Kyle when he'd first moved in—"Don't flatter yourselves, boys. None of you do anything for me." Now, he tells Shane the same thing— "Just because I like dick doesn't mean I want *yours*."

Whatever. At least there's finally some eye candy on this boat, but Shane's too *bad* for his taste. He likes preppy guys. Toned jocks. Guys who know how to dress. And he might have hella hookups under his belt, but he's had a long-term boyfriend before. Devin. If he hadn't moved to Florida, they'd probably still be together. They'd hooked up again when he visited last November, and they still sext all the time, especially now that he's got his bunk barricaded in blankets. Katherine gave him the idea. He waits until the other guys are working their deck shifts, then gets off with Devin over the phone. Last week when Devin sent him a dick pic, he texted back right away—*I want you in my mouth.*

Devin keeps telling him to come to Florida again. Oh, he'll come, boo. Once this season's over and he has his play money. Then they can get each other off in person. Maybe this time, he'll stay the whole winter. Maybe this time, he'll never leave.

27

INSTEAD OF ORBITING the Cape and islands, the eight-day, seven-night Bay State Colony cruise was set to travel up the Massachusetts coastline, starting in Fall River and ending in Rockport. On the second night, in New Bedford, Adrienne decided to meet the crew after her T&A shift. She was tired, but not tired enough to miss joining her coworkers at the National Club, which Logan had kept raving was "totally divey"—the most authentic fisherman's bar they'd see all season.

Shane had spotted Adrienne ferrying a tray of sundaes to the lounge. "You comin' out tonight?" he'd asked, a glint in his eyes.

"Maybe …" she'd said coyly, already knowing the answer was *yes*.

"I don't like you walking over to that bar alone," Connie said later.

"Isn't it right across the street?" Adrienne asked.

Granted, "across the street" was a hike, but she'd seen passengers coming and going from the *Amelia* all day, many headed to the New Bedford Whaling Museum and others walking around the State Pier Maritime Terminal, taking pictures of all the fishing boats. If the city was safe enough for senior citizens to roam, why the concern for her?

"New Bedford can be a different place at night," Connie explained.

"What do you mean?"

"Seedy characters … people of the night … The economy is poor here, and there's a lot of drugs and crime. The Cheryl Araujo case was still recent when I was a stew. It happened only a few miles away."

Adrienne knew what case she meant, having seen *The Accused* at Wendy's house a few years ago. "I think I'll be okay, Connie," she said.

"Thanks, though."

"I'm just being a mom."

Adrienne picked up on Connie's leeriness as she walked across the State Pier parking lot. Like Fall River, where they'd docked yesterday, New Bedford wasn't known for the tourist traps and quaint architecture of Martha's Vineyard and Nantucket. While those ports were quintessential visions of New England, New Bedford was a blue-collar city riddled with evidence of dependency. Enough discarded baggies and nip bottles lined the curbs for Adrienne to get the message, but even so, the walk didn't bother her.

The National Club was in a dated building at the end of Union Street. A billow of cigarette smoke walloped Adrienne when she walked through the windowless door. The bar *was* a dive, just as Logan had promised. Rugged locals occupied the pool table, and an ancient jukebox blasted Michael Jackson. But the National's most eye-catching feature was the chalkboard behind the bar. It read:

If you don't have
(1) Money
(2) Cigarettes
(3) Alcoholic Beverages
Get The Fuck Out
No Bums, Leeches, Moochers, OR Low Lifes Allowed
~Management

The crew was at the bar's center, sandwiched between barflies and unkempt fishermen. They looked so out of place but were enjoying every minute of it, especially Logan and Hailey, who were merrily conversing with some old-timers who seemed dazzled by them.

"Dri, over here, girl!" Noah called. But as Adrienne passed Shane, he patted an empty barstool. "There's a seat here that could use some warmin' up." He lifted his Bud Light when she sat. "Can I buy ya one?"

Adrienne unzipped her purse. "That's what I drink, actually, but I'll get it myself, thanks."

"So, Adrienne," Shane said when her beer arrived, "where do ya hang your hat when you're not workin' on the boat?"

Adrienne laughed cautiously.

"What?"

"Nothing. I've just never heard anyone use that expression before."

Shane sipped his beer. "Guess there's a first time for everythin.'"

"Yeah, I guess there is. And I'm from Connecticut. Westford, if you're really curious. It's a suburb of Hartford."

"I've been to Hartford once," Shane said. "With my cousin, Travis."

Adrienne didn't correct him that Westford and Hartford weren't one and the same. "What about you? Where are you from?"

"Rhode Island. Grew up in Providence, but I live in Pawtucket now … if you're *really* curious."

Adrienne was back in seventh grade all over again, experiencing her first-ever crush on a boy. "Pawtucket …" she repeated. "I've never been."

Shane chuckled. "You're not missin' much." He slid his empty bottle aside and asked the bartender for another. "How long've ya been workin' on the boat?"

"This is my first season. Before this, I was a waitress at a pizzeria. I haven't done much traveling."

"Me neither," said Shane. "I went to Baltimore once before my daughter was born, but that's the farthest I've ever gotten."

Adrienne looked stilly into his eyes. "You have a daughter?"

"Avery. She'll be three in September. Her birthday's close to mine."

Adrienne saw Noah wink mischievously. "How old are you?" she asked, ignoring Noah.

"Twenty-five. Turnin' twenty-six this year. What're you? Twenty-three? Twenty-four?"

Adrienne shook her head. "I just turned twenty-one in March."

"Really? You seem a lot more mature than that."

"Responsibility will do that to you."

Shane nodded. "Yup, ya can say that again." He glanced at her sidelong. "You have a boyfriend?"

"I have an ex. And wasted years I'll never get back."

"Any kids?"

If he were anyone else, Adrienne would have found Shane's questions too forward. But in his case, she didn't mind. "Not of my own, but I've cared for my little brother practically since he was born. He has epilepsy. My best friend is helping with him while I'm away."

"That's cool of your friend to help out," Shane said. "My cousin's helpin' my wife with—"

"*You're married?*" Adrienne sputtered, coughing on her beer. She looked past Shane to see Max, Brynne, and Nicky staring at her, realizing she'd been too loud, emitted too much shock in her tone. But married? Really? She never would've guessed. And where was his ring? She certainly would've noticed if he wore a band, but Shane's ring fingers were naked, bare without indentations or tan lines.

Shane nodded again. "Yup. Married for just over two years now."

"Then what are you doing here?" She didn't know if she meant working on the boat or chatting *her* up at the bar. Maybe she meant both.

Shane looked away, concentrating on the chalkboard across from them. "The short story's that I needed to get away, and the money's too good to pass up. The long story can wait 'til another time if ya don't mind."

"No, I don't mind. I'm sorry. I didn't mean to sound so surprised."

"Don't worry about it," Shane said. "Everybody's got a story."

Adrienne lifted her bottle toward his, a peace offering. "Cheers," she said. "I'll definitely drink to that."

Logan

SHE LOVES THE NATIONAL! It's not a place you go for fancy drinks, but she totally adores the gritty ambiance and local culture. Nothing beats the stories from the sailors who patron the National while they're docked in New Bedford, and she makes sure to listen when they talk. So many are older and quite lonely, still working at sea, never having had families.

When one man, Crow, a mild-mannered fisherman with a crooked smile and a Sailor Jerry tattoo, asks her to untie her ponytail and let her hair hang loose, she does. He nods appreciatively, and she understands. She totally gets it.

Hailey

WHO SAYS you need palm trees for paradise? It doesn't matter *where* she is—luxurious Newport ... sketchy New Bedford! She's living a fairy-tale existence and wouldn't trade it for anything!

She *loves* having freedom! *Loves* how cute and old and sweet the passengers are! She looks at them and hopes to live happily in love into old age. Imagine being in *her* golden years, cruising the world with *her* husband! She captures everything she can with her new digital camera. She bought the same top-of-the-line model as Logan, even though it cost a fortune.

Can life be any more perfect than this? Thank you, Hannah Donofrio, wherever you are! And thank *you*, Lorna!

***

ADRIENNE DIDN'T KNOW it was Katherine's birthday until the morning of—when Katherine told her. They'd just arrived in Boston when Katherine sprang from bed as Adrienne dressed for her Galley Assist shift. "Hey, Dri! How do you feel about trading shifts with me today?"

"For the whole day? What are you scheduled for?"

"I'm Turndown & Activity Hour Stew tonight, but my parents are driving up to take me to dinner for my birthday."

"Oh, happy birthday! But I don't know about trading shifts, Katherine … I don't think we can."

Katherine crossed her arms. "I *am* turning twenty-one, you know, and I think asking my parents to wait at the Marriott until ten o'clock is rude. They already booked dinner at the Chart House."

Adrienne understood Katherine wanting to celebrate with her family, but why had she waited until now to say something? To appease her, Adrienne walked over to the schedule. "I don't know, Katherine. I'm already T&A Stew twice this trip. And it's not like we're trading LD days, too, so I wouldn't even get to sleep in tomorrow."

She suggested Katherine ask Hailey or Logan, but they turned her down, having made reservations for the Old Town Trolley. Knowing better than to ask Max or Brynne, Katherine broke for Noah up in the dining room. But Connie exited her office and said, "The rotation is *permanent*. No trading shifts."

Adrienne wanted to think Connie wouldn't have been so uptight if she'd known it was Katherine's birthday, but instead of taking Connie aside and discussing the circumstances, Katherine sulked, convinced Connie had it out for her. Adrienne felt bad, but she was also realizing Katherine brought a lot of issues on herself—always voicing her opinion and complaining about things. Worst was how Katherine constantly reminded them of her education—of her dual degrees and how she'd graduated early. *With honors.* So far, no one had called out her self-promotions, but Adrienne wasn't the only one getting annoyed, figuring it was just a matter of time before someone spoke up.

Katherine

HOW RUDE of Connie to stop her from trading shifts with Noah! And of the girls not to trade with her in the first place! She fills her parents in over an *extremely* late dinner. "This company is *so* unprofessional! When this season is over, I'm looking for another job!"

Her father snaps his fingers for the waitress and orders a third Manhattan. "Katherine, your mother and I did not drive two hours to hear you gripe! You should be so grateful that we're here at all, funding your birthday without so much as a *thank you*."

He's accusing her of being ungrateful? How can she thank him if the night isn't over? Her mother tries consoling her, but her father blows his top. "Another word about that blasted cruise director—Bonnie, or *whatever* her godforsaken name is!—and I'm going back to the hotel! If Michael and Diana had given me this much grief, I'd have shipped all three of you off to boarding school when I had the chance!"

She saves her tears until she returns for curfew. Imagine her father comparing her to her *half-siblings*! She barely knows them! Assuming everyone is asleep, she storms onto the lazarette to cry. This experience is *not* what she had in mind! Especially not her schedule! She's already checked, and she'll be anchored in crummy Nantucket for *four* upcoming LD shifts! No one else will be stuck there more than twice!

She's wondering if maybe Connie did this on purpose when she's startled by Max and her boyfriend. *What are they doing up so late?* She can't stand Max, but she decides to ask her about the rotation anyway—if it always works like this. Max cuts her off. "Don't get *me* involved in your problems with Connie! How stupid are you?"

She's too stunned to respond, meekly following Max and Marco back inside. She almost bumps into them when they stop short, and Marco unlocks his cabin. They both walk in and the lock clicks behind them. *Is Max living in there?* Now that she thinks about it, she does see Max entering work from that hallway in the mornings instead of coming up from girls' quarters. And she *wonders* ...

28

On Sunday, May 27, Connie relieved the stews after their cabins were clean. They were free to enjoy Memorial Day, but she expected everyone back by one on Tuesday to finish the public areas.

Adrienne hitched a ride with Logan to Union Station, where she got stuck waiting for the next southbound train. She lay on the lawn of the Rhode Island State House, staring up at the statue of the Independent Man while she daydreamed. So far, she hadn't told anyone about her growing feelings for Shane, feelings she felt certain he shared.

Since his arrival, Shane sat beside her at every crew meal instead of the other empty seat between Hailey and Jordy. He sought her out often, usually on the laz when they had time to spare, asking questions about her life and showing a genuine interest in getting to know her. He was chivalrous, holding doors and clearing her plates.

No guy had ever triggered feelings of this magnitude in Adrienne. The chemistry between them was strong, unfurling as she kept learning how much they had in common. Not just superficialities like preferring tea to coffee or having the same appreciation for nineties hip-hop, but they shared similar outlooks on life, held like-minded values.

Though there was an authenticity Adrienne admired about Shane, she was struggling with being drawn to a married man. But it wasn't like she'd known right away, and he hadn't exactly advertised it. For three weeks, she hadn't stopped thinking about his wife—wondering what she looked like, what she did for a living, and if she knew how lucky she was to have Shane as a partner.

***

ADRIENNE DIDN'T GET HOME until six. She took a cab from the train station, instantly bombarded by an overexcited Thany who couldn't stop talking about his afternoon with Wendy at the children's museum. "That sounds fun, Bud!" Adrienne said, yawning. She'd hoped to spend the evening catching up with her family and Wendy, but working thirty-two days straight was taxing, and she fell asleep on the couch soon after dinner.

Every Memorial Day meant getting to Westford Center early to find good parade-watching spots on the sidewalk, though parking was never a problem as Roman always allowed Adrienne to use the lot behind Giovanni's. When she went to Thany's room that morning, she was confused to see him dressed in his Cub Scout uniform, pulling the gold-tone slide up his neckerchief. "What are you doing, Than? Why are you wearing your uniform to the parade?"

Thany showed off his dimpled smile. "I'm *in* the parade, Adrienne! My den is marching, and I get to help hold the banner! I wanted to tell you last night, but Daddy said to let you sleep."

Adrienne didn't know whether to laugh or cry. She was thrilled Cub Scouts was having such a positive impact on Thany, allowing him his own little world of experiences, but until now, it hadn't occurred to her that important parts of Thany's life were transpiring in her absence. She wondered what else she'd missed out on. Or *would* miss once returning to work.

She stood with her father and Dolly at the corner of La Salle, in front of the pharmacy where Shannon worked. When Thany's den marched past, she pulled out her camera and took plenty of shots of him holding the banner, front and center among his new little buddies.

Her father looked on pensively. "Do you remember the night Nathaniel was born?" he asked.

Adrienne hadn't thought about that stuffy August night in ages, the night Jack called from Hartford Hospital, letting her and Aaron know they had a new little brother. When Raina went into labor that Sunday, they'd expected the new baby to be born within a few hours—on August twentieth. But there were complications. Not only was the baby breech, but the umbilical cord was twined around his neck. A "blue baby," her father had explained over the phone. When Thany had finally entered the world after midnight, it was Aaron's twelfth birthday, which he now had to share forever.

Adrienne turned to her father. "Yes, Dad, I remember."

Jack wiped a single tear. "My boy. The doctors didn't think he would make it."

After collecting Thany from the end of the parade route, Adrienne treated everyone to pizza at Giovanni's. The patio was open for the season, and Adrienne chuckled when she saw the *Reserved* sign on the table Wendy had held for them. When Becca came out with their drinks, she even put a water bowl on the ground for Dolly.

"That's how *everyone* should leave a job," Jack commended as he skimmed the menu. "Have your worth shown back to you even when you're not an employee anymore."

Until that moment, Adrienne had never considered leaving a job any other way. But thinking about how her father had left his, and what she'd seen with Rick and, most recently, Kyle, she realized how good she had it. She'd given Giovanni's her all for many years, and her efforts hadn't gone unnoticed.

Marco

MAX WANTS HIM to take her to the East Greenwich parade, but he's promised his Uncle Frankie he'll drive up to Federal Hill to talk business. Max pulls a face. "But, babe! Don't you know the parade was the first time I ever saw you? I told Brynnie I *knew* I'd spend the rest of my life with you."

"Our anniversary's in September," he reminds her. "That's the date that's important to me."

He's not looking forward to doing business with his uncle. Sweats bullets the whole way to Providence even though Frankie already told him he doesn't have to *sell* anything, just mule. There's eight kids in his family, and they all need to pay their dues. He's always known Frankie would call on him one day, just like he did his six older brothers. But none of *them* ever had to mule on the water. Frankie thinks it's genius. "Foolproof, Markie, foolproof! Took my brother seven sons for one to date the daughter of a sea captain? All your brothers, where's their brains at?"

He meets his uncle in the back room of Alessio's—the family's café on Federal Hill. There's other guys back there, too—guys who work for the family but not at their restaurants or bakeries. One of them stands watch at the back door. Arms folded. Doesn't say a word.

Frankie does all the talking. He listens to the game plan and knows he isn't allowed to say no. Last year was his first year at NECLA, and Frankie wanted him to feel it out. But this year, when he comes home in October, Frankie'll give him the money to bring to New York City. The contact there will hand over the weight for him to bring back to Rhode Island. That's it, over and done with. Frankie'll give him ten percent.

"Whaddaya think there, Markie?" Frankie asks. "A diamond ring for your little *Tesoro*? A down payment for a house? This is the American Dream, nephew! This is why we're here!"

He doesn't tell Frankie he only plans on this being a one-time thing, that he won't mule once he gets his captain's license. But for now, he'll play the same role as his brothers. They all did what they had to do. They all live honest lives now.

※ ※ ※

THE THIRTY-SIX hours away from NECLA were short-lived. As much as Adrienne had enjoyed briefly seeing her family and Wendy, she was eager to return to the *Amelia* to see her other friends and Shane. The next day, they'd embark on their first New England Newcomer cruise—a mixture of the previous two itineraries with new stops in Portsmouth, New Hampshire, and Portland, Maine.

Connie told Adrienne there was a package waiting for her in the office. Adrienne brought Noah along to collect it, smiling when she saw Aunt Claudette's return address.

> Dri,
> Just some treats to share with your friends.
> I sent one to Aaron, too!
> Miss & Love,
> Claudette & Dickey

"Jealous!" Noah whined, standing over Adrienne's shoulder. "I wish someone would send *me* a care package!" He helped her riffle through the box's contents—tubes of Pringles, bags of Sour Patch Kids and Skittles, cheese puffs, chocolate-covered pretzels, and three kinds of fruit snacks. "Yes, girl!" Noah cried. "All for when we watch movies!"

Adrienne called Aunt Claudette, who wanted to know *everything* about the boat. But Adrienne remained selective, focusing on the different ports and her typical workdays, telling Aunt Claudette how her least-liked shift was the dreaded Turndown & Activity Hour and how her favorite shift had turned out to be bartending.

"Anything you weren't expecting?" Aunt Claudette asked.

Adrienne left out the obvious, being Shane, but the truth was that many things about working at sea surprised her. A big one was living on "boat time"—the crew's way of referring to the drastic shift in their internal clocks. One day working on the *Amelia* felt like a week; a short six-day or eight-day trip, like a month. They were only four trips in, and the first cruise already seemed like an eternity ago. Unless they checked, the crew often forgot what day of the week it was altogether. But boat time made them grow close quickly. Being around the same fourteen people each day proved the experience an intimate one, regardless of whether they all got along.

Adrienne also hadn't expected such detachment from reality. Without cable or internet, there was no way to know the ongoings of the outside world. She supposed she could read the newspapers Connie stocked in the pax lounge, but with so little free time, reading periodicals wasn't how she wanted to spend it. Occasionally, she'd glimpse magazine headlines in the guests' cabins, but Adrienne didn't care much about pop stars, and the only topic *People* or the rag mags were covering was Britney Spears's very public decline.

The same went for keeping current on music. The only way to hear the hottest new songs was at bars when they went out at night. So far, Rihanna's "Umbrella" was unmistakably the anthem of the summer, with plenty of hits from Timbaland, Akon, and Justin Timberlake following close behind. Otherwise, they were clueless.

"Do you realize the president could get assassinated and we'd probably be the last to know?" Adrienne said to Noah one night.

"Girl, I kinda like living this way. It's like being off the grid."

It is peaceful, Adrienne admitted. Who would have thought being so out of touch could offer such introspection?

Another unforeseen surprise was how well the crew was treated at the bars they frequented. From Block Island to New Bedford and beyond, no one wearing a NECLA logo was ever carded, even though Noah, Hailey, Max, and Brynne were all still underage. The company had a reputation for bringing good business to ports big and small, and rumor was that NECLA crews had been well taken care of for decades.

It didn't hurt that they'd gotten acquainted with the local bar staff before tourist season began, receiving VIP treatment without getting lost in a shuffle of vacationers. The Oar on Block Island became a frequent haunt, popular for its outdoor picnic tables and seventy-five-cent PBRs, and in Providence, they flocked to the Fish Co.—a favorite of Logan's from her RISD days. On Martha's Vineyard, practically anywhere on

Circuit Ave. was guaranteed.

The bartenders serviced them immediately, the younger, college-aged ones always curious to learn about boat life. In return for their generosity, the crew always tipped upward of twenty percent. They were all industry workers in not-so-dissimilar capacities, and it went without saying that one hand always washed the other.

Hailey

SHE CRINGES when she thinks of her parents' reactions if they knew about all these bars, of the lectures she'd receive about following God's expectations. Already, they'd had so many *comments* when she went home for Memorial Day.

"You must miss church, don't you, Hailey?"

"Mrs. Higby has been asking for you. And the Milner girls want to know when you'll be back for good."

Tell them never!

She'd avoided all their questions about money, too. They don't need to know that she buys hoodies at every port. Or CDs. Lots of rebellious girl music they'd always forbade her from listening to. Fergie. P!nk. Gwen Stefani! She even buys the new Rihanna album after hearing Noah play her songs during galley clean-up at night. *Good Girl Gone Bad*. Now what would her parents say about that?

June 2007

29

By the time she went to bed at night, Adrienne was usually too tired to care how spatially challenged their living quarters were, glad the space only served as somewhere to sleep and bathe. She and her roommates had devised a schedule to clean the bathroom and tried keeping their bunks, lockers, and floor areas as tidy as possible. The arrangement had worked initially, but with the other girls always shopping, Adrienne was growing concerned at how fast *stuff* continued to accumulate.

Logan was an art collector. More than once, Adrienne had seen her admire some painting or piece in a store and have it shipped to her parents' house in Connecticut. But other pieces Logan would have wrapped and bring back on board with her. Then there were the clothes—bags of them. Hailey, with her sweatshirts in every port, was the biggest culprit, but Logan and Katherine were guilty, too. If anything, Noah was the most fortunate. Everything he bought was flung atop his regular-size, not-shared bunk down in guys' quarters.

On the first morning the *Amelia* docked in Portsmouth, Adrienne was applying her contacts in the bathroom when she heard a thud, followed by Katherine yelping, "Ow!" and then, "Darn it!" Adrienne capped her lens solution and walked to their bunk room to see Katherine cradling her foot. Logan and Hailey followed, stuffing their polos into their khakis.

"What's wrong?" Adrienne asked.

"I can't take living in this congestion anymore!" Katherine whined. "I just tripped over that water and stubbed my toes on the minifridge." She pointed to a case of Poland Spring sticking out from under their bunk.

Adrienne rolled her eyes. She'd stubbed *her* toes plenty of times over the past seven weeks. "There's no way around living like this," she told Katherine. "You knew that when we moved in here."

"Maybe I can drop some things off at my condo when we get back," said Logan. "I've totally been buying a lot this season, I'll admit it."

Katherine shook her head. "No. I'm *also* upset because I don't think Max is even living on the other side when *we* could be using it for storage. I think she's been living in her boyfriend's cabin this whole time."

"Why do you think that?" Hailey asked cautiously.

They listened as Katherine described her midnight encounter with Max two weeks earlier. "She was *so* rude to me," Katherine said. "And then she followed Marco off the lazarette and into his cabin."

Logan shrugged into her cardigan. "He was probably working late, and Max wanted to spend time with him. I'm not making excuses for her, but it seems totally improbable to make such a *thing* about having the port side if she wasn't planning to live down here."

"Too improbable for Max?" Katherine countered. "She's awful. I wouldn't put *anything* past her."

Adrienne opened her locker and slid her lens solution onto the shelf. "Why don't we find out?"

Katherine's foot fell from her hands. "You mean go on *their* side?"

"Why not? I don't trust Max either. This way, we'll have some answers."

Logan checked her watch. "I'll go, but we have to be upstairs in five minutes."

"Max is Galley Stew today …" Hailey said, looking at the schedule. "And Brynne is Galley Assist …"

"Then what are we waiting for?" asked Adrienne. "Their shifts already started." She led the way out of their room and rapped lightly on the portside door. "It sounds empty to me," she said, pushing down the handle.

Gasps and murmurs chorused behind her when Adrienne hit the lights. The first bunk room—Max's—served as a closet. Hot-pink hangers lined the bed frames, displaying scores of jeans, tops, and dresses. In place of her mattresses were dozens of shoes, all secured with bungee cords. Ziploc bags of makeup and jewelry were crammed into the wall cubbies, and a makeshift vanity topped her plastic storage drawers. Max's locker, which Adrienne unhinged to find her uniforms, was covered in magnetic photo frames of Max and Marco, and, of course, Max and Brynne.

"I knew it!" cried Katherine. "She *hasn't* been living down here!"

"Where are her mattresses?" asked Hailey. "They were here while we were working in the shipyard, weren't they?"

Adrienne sighed, feeling foolish that Max had gotten away with tricking them. "That's probably all the noise we heard over here when we were moving in."

Brynne at least had one mattress, sheeted in blue satin bedding. But her top mattress was also missing, a TV/DVD combo zip-tied to the bed frame instead. Her wall cubbies were full of Hollywood classics starring Audrey Hepburn, Doris Day, and Shirley Temple, and her book collection rivaled Wendy's—packed with thick romances and the complete works of Jacqueline Susann, Daphne du Maurier, and the Brontë sisters. *An old soul*, Adrienne noted. She pulled back the shower curtain, exposing tiered shelves of hair and skincare products.

"This looks like a *mansion* compared to our side!" exclaimed Hailey. "Look at all the room they have!"

"It's the same amount of space," Adrienne clarified. "Just three *less* people living in it."

Katherine spun toward Logan and planted her hands on her hips. "Is the rule about seniority *true*? Because this doesn't seem right. We could be storing all of our extra things in Max's room."

"Technically, it is," said Logan, "but there were seven girls on the *Beatrice* last year, and this girl Angelica was the only one who didn't share a bunk. She lived where Max's room is, but she wasn't a bitch about it. She let us put stuff in there if we needed to."

"Well, *I* think we should discuss this with Connie! The nerve of Max is appalling!"

Adrienne laughed. "Katherine, don't you see how Max tests Connie? There's no *way* Connie will do anything about this."

Logan nodded. "Adrienne's right, Katherine. Talking to Connie will paint *you* as the bad guy. You'll never get her to reprimand Max."

Katherine's foot tapped furiously against the carpet. "You know what? Sometimes I don't care anymore! I went to school for Hospitality Management, and I intend to remind Connie of that! I'll be happy to give her some pointers!"

She huffed past them, heading for the stairs, with Adrienne, Hailey, and Logan all hot on her heels, frenziedly trying to talk some *fast* sense into her.

Katherine

SHE NEEDS TO get off this boat before she screams! What kind of company lets a stewardess rule the roost? Has Max even gone to college? She doesn't think so. And better yet, what has *she* done to Max *or* Brynne for them to treat her so awful? Nothing, might you ask! She's even kept Brynne's secret! That's right—she hasn't told *anyone* about all of Brynne's midnight rendezvous at the Biltmore with Daddy Warbucks! She hasn't even spoken to Brynne! And they're partners in the rotation, working together at least twice a trip!

Speaking of the rotation, she doesn't care *what* the other girls or Noah say! She's convinced Connie gave her the worst rotation on purpose! *Constantly Nagging Connie*. Leaving her anchored at sea for so many LD days! Waking her up during an LD shift because of a thief! Scolding her for wanting to switch shifts on her birthday!

If she'd known in the winter that *this* was the reality of working for Northeastern Cruise Line Associates, she'd have declined Beverly's offer immediately. You'd think a businesswoman of Beverly's caliber would be more conscientious about her choice of staff!

Noah

OH, HELL THE FUCK NO.

This is the last thing he wants to hear when he's LD, okay? LD days are supposed to be their "days off." No galley. No cabins to clean. No tables to serve. Just *light duties* while listening to his girls on his iPod. *Not* hearing Katherine complain about being clusterfucked while the others try stopping her from going to Connie.

Anyway, of *course* he's not surprised to hear Max isn't living in girls' quarters. "What did I tell you?" he says to Adrienne on the laz. "Built-in booty call!"

Not that he wouldn't love to feast his eyes downstairs for himself, but he's trying to get off this boat A.S.A.P. Bethany's driving up so they can see Nelly Furtado's Get Loose Tour in Boston tonight, and *nothing* is gonna ruin it for him!

Thank God Boston's only an hour away. *And* that he has the night off. *And* that he has the funds for their tickets! Girl, of course he loves his bestie, but she needs to get off her ass and do more with her life. Someday he'll finally say something to her, but *today* isn't it.

30

WORKING THE T&A SHIFT that evening was a bore. The onboard lecturer giving a history of Portsmouth had a monotone way of speaking that made Adrienne start to doze. She busied herself by restocking the bar cabinets, making as little noise as possible. When her shift ended, she ran into Shane in the dining room, brewing hot tea at the coffee station. "Want some?" he asked.

"Sure," Adrienne said.

He asked her to join him for a cigarette, heading for the gangway instead of the laz. "It's a nice night out," he said. "We can sit on the pier."

The *Amelia* was docked at a wood-slatted pier called the Marina at Harbour Place. At the end of the gangway, Jordy was passed out in his chair, the sign-out clipboard falling from his lap. Shane nudged him. "Jordy, wake up, man. C'mon, before someone sees ya!"

Jordy jumped. "Huh? Oh shit! What time is it?"

"It's ten-oh-nine, buddy."

"Is everyone back yet?"

"Noah will be back for curfew," said Adrienne. "Maybe earlier."

"What about Nicky and Marco?"

Adrienne shrugged. "Where did they go?"

Jordy yawned. "They took a cab to Hampton Beach with the girls."

"Don't think so," said Shane.

He and Adrienne walked to the end of the dock and dangled their legs over the pier. When Shane asked about her day, Adrienne shared that morning's discovery in girls' quarters.

Shane puffed his Camel. "I'm surprised you're just findin' out now."

"Finding out what?"

"That Marco's girl lives with him. Nicky told me the day I got here."

Adrienne processed his words. "Wow. I can't believe she's been living in there all this time and we didn't know."

"There's somethin' wrong with that broad," Shane said. "Marco's a cool dude, but she's got a coupl'a screws loose. I'm not sayin' it's right what she did."

Adrienne laughed. "Thanks for the sympathy."

"Brynne seems sweet, though," Shane continued. "I've never said more than a coupl'a words to her, but I know Nicky really likes her."

Adrienne had never said much to Brynne either, but she was realizing that she didn't necessarily dislike her. She thought of telling Shane about the older guy who brought Brynne to the shipyard but thought the better of it. Brynne's personal life wasn't any of *her* business.

They talked for an hour. As usual, the conversation flowed naturally. Shane was so unfiltered, speaking freely about his daughter's developmental delays and his cousin's prison record. He told things as they were and didn't hide his truths. But Adrienne noticed he never mentioned his wife, sensing an unspecified resentment. And for how open he was, she was careful of the questions she asked in return, heeding Shannon's advice from her last day at Giovanni's. *Don't ever forget where you come from.*

Was this how Raina's affair with the Accountant began? Harmless chitchat at the water cooler? She already worried that her connection with Shane was not, in fact, harmless; that if he were single, they could've talked uninhibited and endlessly, never running out of conversation.

Eventually, they were interrupted by Bethany's Celica barreling into the parking lot. Out popped Noah, his hair a sweaty thatch of disorder. "Later, bitch!" he called, flashing the peace sign as Bethany sped away. He walked toward them, humming Nelly Furtado lyrics in his stride.

"How was the concert?" Adrienne asked.

"Fucking *amazing*! Ugh, this port is so dead. I didn't expect anyone to still be awake."

"She was tellin' me the woes of girls' quarters," Shane joked.

"Oh yeah!" Noah cried. "Can you believe that? What a wench. I still wanna see that pitiful palace."

"Well, they're not here now …" Adrienne said.

"Who's not where?"

"Max and Brynne. They went out with Marco and Nicky." She hoped she wouldn't regret what she was suggesting.

Noah pulled her up. "Then show me!"

Adrienne turned to Shane. "I guess I'll see you tomorrow."

She followed Noah inside, wondering if this was a bad idea. It didn't feel *too* intrusive. They were just going to open the portside door, look inside, and leave. "Don't make any noise," she whispered as they walked downstairs. "Everyone else is sleeping. And don't *touch* anything!"

Noah knocked sardonically, then pushed the portside door open. "Girl! Are you serious? The bitch has a walk-in closet down here!" He opened Max's locker. "Ha! Look at these magnet photos! What is she, back in middle school?" He turned his attention to the mile of hot-pink hangers, reading the clothing designers aloud. "Bebe … Juicy Couture … Ed Hardy … What a label whore. At least her friend has some taste."

"*Okay*, Noah," Adrienne said, "I think we've seen enough."

But Noah ignored her, walking into Brynne's bunk room and checking out her movie collection. He pulled *Love Story* from the wall cubby and read the back. "Ha! Guess she likes old movies *and* old guys."

"Noah, seriously!"

He put the DVD back. "All right, girl. We'll go after I see this bathroom."

Adrienne waited impatiently. Suppose someone caught them in here? She practically yanked Noah toward the door when he finished poking around, but it was too late. Her hand was on the light switch when they came face-to-face with Max and Brynne in the doorway. *Shit.* She hadn't even heard them coming down the stairs.

Max thrust a plush carnival frog to the ground. "What the *hell* are you doing in here?"

"Oh, hey, girl!" Noah said. "Just checking out the room you *don't* live in, apparently!"

Seeing her open locker, Max pushed through them. "You're going through my *stuff?*"

"Girl, please. I wasn't going through *anything*. I just wanted to see this

California Closet with my own eyes. You've got hella nerve, you know that? Making four girls share a side so you can have this cheap boutique? Why don't you move this shit into your boyfriend's cabin?"

"I have nerve?" Max retorted. "Get out of our room, you faggot!"

Adrienne froze. Yes, they'd entered Max's personal space without permission, but calling Noah a faggot was *not* warranted.

"Max …" Brynne spoke timidly, "just drop it." She looked embarrassed, and Adrienne couldn't blame her.

But Noah bristled with rage, wholly prepared to rise to the occasion. "I'd rather be a faggot than a fucking sea witch like *you*, Ursula! No one on this boat can stand your sorry ass! I bet your own fucking friend doesn't even like you!"

At the mention of Brynne, Max raised her arm to swing, but Noah grabbed her wrist just in time. "I wish you would, girl! I'll sue your family for so much money, you'll be living out of garbage bags like the *trash* you are!"

"*Noah, come on!*" Adrienne pleaded. "Let's just get out of here!"

Max wrenched her wrist free. "Like this wasn't your idea! Come in here again, and I'll have you both *fired* while we're on a fucking island!"

"Eat a dick, bitch!" Noah snarled, shoving past Max, and kicking her frog. He and Adrienne just made it to the stairs when the frog hit the backs of their heads. "That's *your* job, cocksucker!" Max shrieked.

Noah turned, but Adrienne pushed for him to keep moving. "Just go!" she insisted. "This is too much!" She was overwhelmed by how drastically the energy had shifted—how she'd just come from spending time with Shane, from Noah having an "amazing" night at his concert, from Max and Brynne enjoying some beach carnival—to physical violence and a barrage of F-bombs.

She refused to do the catty girl thing and rehash the drama with Noah. She believed in accountability, and she told him so. "We were *all* wrong tonight!" she admonished him out on the laz. "All of us, so leave it alone. I'm serious, Noah. Don't bring it up again."

A distinct strain circulated the *Amelia* on the last day of the cruise. Noah and Max were scheduled in the galley together, creating a noxious tension so pervasive it disrupted the energy on the boat. Adrienne was grateful she was LD and had limited exposure to them, but for Noah's sake, she feared Marco. Noah might be gay, but Noah was still a *guy*. It was murky waters that he'd grabbed Max at all. But as the day passed and Marco still seemed oblivious, Adrienne strongly suspected Max had left him in the dark.

With five months left, Adrienne hoped they could all move past the incident, that Noah and Max could put aside their animosity sooner than later. By bedtime, it already felt like a week had passed since she and Noah entered the portside quarters. Same as every other day, that's just what boat time did to you.

31

WHEN THE NEXT passengers boarded for the return leg of the cruise, Connie stopped Adrienne and Noah on the stairs after the muster drills. "Just a heads-up, guys ... Lorna called to say two passengers missed their flight into Portland. Kitty and Dell Chandler. They're meeting us in Portsmouth tomorrow."

Noah snorted. "Kitty and Dell?"

"Kitty and Dell," Connie repeated. "I believe they're from the South."

The next day, while cleaning her cabins, Adrienne heard Connie's voice coming from the dining room, accompanied by voices she assumed belonged to the delayed passengers. "Yes, unfortunately, the Strawberry Banke tour has already left," Connie was saying, "but there's a bus scheduled for the USS *Albacore* Museum after lunch."

"Oh no, sugar!" said a woman in the strongest southern accent Adrienne had ever heard. "My daddy was in the navy, and I sure didn't fly up North for any submarine museum! How 'bout lettin' us get settled right quick, and *you* just fix us a ride to the Strawberry Banke?"

"Of course ..." Connie said, turning around on command.

They'd now reached Adrienne, and she got a good look at Kitty and Dell Chandler. Probably in her early seventies, Kitty was a stout woman with mischievous brown eyes and a giant fluff of hair dyed the color of a carrot. She wore an outlandish blouse and held the arm of a balding, dour-faced man. Behind them trailed Jordy with two suitcases. Spotting Adrienne, Kitty's eyes bloomed impishly. "Oh, Dell, look, it's our maid! Look at that get-up she's in!" Then she turned her attention to Jordy.

"Which room's ours, sugar?"

Jordy lifted the luggage tag and pointed to the cabin number. "31S."

Kitty unlocked the door and left her husband in the hall. She was back out at once. "Why, that cabin's smaller than a mustard seed! I reckon there's not room for us to plumb fit two!"

Adrienne knew Kitty's claim was farfetched, even if the cabin *was* obscenely small. She also knew NECLA provided diagrams in the brochures and that Kitty and Dell must have known the dimensions of 31S beforehand. Still, customer service was essential to her job, so she said, "You'll get used to the size in no time. There's so much going on that the guests hardly use their cabins."

Kitty squinted at Adrienne's name tag. "Aye-dree-enne Dee-no," she said. "And Jor-dee Kell-ee. Tell me now, where're y'all from?"

"I'm from Connecticut," Adrienne said.

"Massachusetts," said Jordy.

Dell Chandler recoiled. "Heavens to Betsy! Y'all're *Yankees?*"

Adrienne looked awkwardly at Jordy. "Uh, sure?"

Kitty's displeasure contorted into a menacing smile. "Yankees! Well, don't that beat all! But I reckon y'all better run and fetch that cruise director to fix this pickle! Hurry up! Get on now!"

Adrienne had to wait until after lunch to tell Noah about her experience with the Chandlers.

"Yankees? Girl, the trip is *literally* called the New England Newcomer! The company is *literally* based out of Rhode Island. Who did they *think* they were getting for crew?"

"These people will be a pain in the ass, Noah. I can feel it."

Noah hooted. "I bet they won't even tip!"

Adrienne wasn't sure. "You really think they'd stiff us?"

"Girl, I *know* they will. You can see it in that woman's eyes."

"She does have conniving eyes," Adrienne agreed. Troublemaking eyes that said Kitty Chandler would be *far* from the average passenger.

Connie

UNBELIEVABLE, THIS COUPLE! And she thought Nita Cagle from the second trip was abusive! Not that Nita didn't have reason to be upset, but the Chandlers ... they're something, aren't they! Demanding a new cabin because of mildew? *What mildew?* The boat's been completely refurbished, for Chrissake!

She tries putting them at ease, but Kitty Chandler is *insistent*. Lord, this trip is almost sold out. The only cabins left are the ones down below—where Peter lives that NECLA doesn't sell—and 70P, a Category IV cabin. The Chandlers only paid for a Category II. Reluctantly, she gives them 70P, an outdoor cabin by the stern.

"Divine!" Kitty Chandler says when she brings them upstairs. "I reckon Dell and I'll get on just fine up here!"

She hopes so, too. The Chandlers have been here less than an hour, and already they've caused an entire trip's worth of commotion.

***

AT DINNER, Adrienne found it in poor taste how Kitty Chandler carried on about her cabin upgrade. "That's right!" she kept boasting. "The whole commode was moldy, so I *insisted*. That cruise director found us a lovely cabin up top, plumb overlookin' the water!"

A few passengers commiserated with Kitty, but others were unhappy. As crew dinner ended, a husband and wife rallied around Connie in the dining room. "I thought this was a renovated vessel!" the husband growled. "Where's *mildew* coming from so soon after the improvements?"

"That's what I was wondering!" his wife said.

With a throaty grunt, Hardigan pushed aside what was left of his chicken cacciatore and went to Connie's aid. Adrienne looked on with Hailey and Noah from the galley, while out in the dining room, Max started the vacuum to drown the couple out.

"At least Max is good for *something*," Adrienne joked.

Noah glared at her. "Feel like losing a friend tonight?"

The next evening, Noah ran downstairs just before dinner service. "Dri! Kitty is *smashed* right now! And her husband!"

Adrienne smirked. "Really?"

"Yes, girl! I made her, like, five G&Ts during Cocktail Hour, maybe six. Wait until they get down here!"

Adrienne waited. The Chandlers arrived carrying the reek of gin clear across the dining room. Kitty's head was thrown back, her braying laughter an instant disturbance.

"Isn't there anything you can *do* about that woman?" a solo traveler asked Adrienne. "She's been a nuisance since she arrived!"

Yeah, no kidding, thought Adrienne.

On Monday night in Plymouth, Adrienne and Nicky joined Noah in crew lounge to watch *Borat*—one of Noah's newest purchases. Midway through the movie, they heard footsteps plodding down the stairs. "Yoohoo!" a woman's voice called. "Yoohoo! Anyone home?" Kitty Chandler stumbled off the last step, grabbing the handrail for support.

"Well, I declare!" she said, drunkenly jovial. "I reckon I found y'all's little hideaway!"

Nicky jumped up in a flash. "No way, lady! Now, I already told ya that any place that says 'Crew Only' means *crew only*! Ya can't be walkin' around wherevah ya want to on this boat!"

"Oh, it's just a self-guided tour, sugar. I'm sure the rest don't mind."

"It don't mattah who minds! I already told ya that when ya came into the engine room. Some places ah off-limits to the guests, and this here's one!"

Kitty looked positively aghast. "Well, bless his heart! He thinks I came up North to be sassed? For seven thousand dollars, I'll go *wherever* I plumb please!"

Nicky stood his ground. "Lady, ya ain't leavin' me any choice but to get the captain down here, and he's not gonna tell ya any different!" He engaged in a pint-size staredown with Kitty until she turned, heading defeatedly back up the stairs.

"*Redheads*," Nicky muttered once she was out of earshot.

"What about them?" Adrienne asked.

"It's old sailor's lore. Redheads ah bad omens at sea." He chuckled. "That's why Bev leaves Lorna in the office."

"Hmph!" scoffed Noah. "What do they say about *platinum blondes?*"

Adrienne shook her head. It *was* going to take Noah time to get over Max.

On Tuesday morning, Adrienne had the Chandlers in her section for breakfast in Nantucket.

"Say there, sugar," Kitty said, showing no recollection of what happened in crew lounge the night before. "I've got a hankerin' for a mushroom frittata. I don't reckon y'all can whip one up?"

"I'm sorry," said Adrienne. "Those were yesterday's egg specials. Today we just have the lobster Benedict." She pointed to the platter centered on the table.

Kitty smiled devilishly. "Well, then, how 'bout bringin' that chef out right quick? I'm *sure* he and I can fix somethin'."

Adrienne gritted her teeth. There was making a request, and there was taking advantage, and Kitty Chandler was the sort of woman who knew the difference but didn't care. "Absolutely," she said. "I'll bring Chef Ray out right away."

By the end of breakfast, Kitty had ordered a fully customized meal, including three Bloody Bulldogs, even though bar service was only included with Cocktail Hour. She rationalized her demand by telling Connie that she and Dell were *entitled* to compensatory drinks for the liquor they'd missed on the first day of the cruise.

When Kitty finally exited the dining room, her arm linked through Dell's for balance, Connie shook her head and said, "It's good they declined the first launch ride to the island. She's in no condition to be on the water right now."

"Mmm," Adrienne agreed. This was the earliest she'd ever known someone to start drinking, and Kitty was far more inebriated than seemed moral for the eight o'clock hour.

Brynne

SHE'S VACUUMING her outdoor cabins when she hears the commotion near the bow—a heavy splash followed by a woman screeching, "Good Lord, he's gone over! My husband! He's gone over!"

She runs to the bow and sees Kitty Chandler frantically trying to climb the rail. A broken highball glass is at her feet, dribbling rivers of gin. *Shit!* Down below, she sees Dell Chandler struggling, flapping his arms and choking on water as he bobs around like a cork. Kitty stumbles forward and shakes her. "*Help him!*"

She yells, "Man overboard!" and rushes for the nearest life preserver, the entrails of rope unraveling as she runs back to the bow. "Here!" she tosses the ring buoy over the rail. "Grab on!"

Kitty shakes her again, "He can't swim! He's goin' to drown!"

He can't swim? She rips off her shoes and smock and climbs the bow in her tank and housekeeping pants. "Hang on!" she calls, positioning herself not to dive directly into Dell. Just before her body pierces the water, she hears Nicky yell, "Brynnie! No!"

The water is *cold* for June, but she secures Dell right before he goes under. She wrangles the buoy around him like they learned in training and treads against the bumpy waves. "Just hang on," she pleads. "It'll be okay."

The sirens start blaring above, and Nicky splashes into the water next to her. She hears the launch boat revving to life as Nicky helps her steady Dell. "C'mon, guy, don't struggle! We've got the launch comin' for ya now!"

The boat arrives beside them, and Peter and Marco grab hold of Dell. After he's on board, they pull her up first, then Nicky. Peter checks Dell over while Marco speeds back to the stern, and suddenly, she realizes she's surrounded by four men, her white clothes see-through now that they're soaking wet.

Nicky shifts his attention away from her cleavage when she catches him staring. "Good job back there, Brynnie," he says, pretending he hasn't just gotten an eyeful. "Ya did a real good job."

32

EVERYONE WAS BUZZING about Dell's near-death experience. Everyone except for Connie, who Kitty had *insisted* accompany them on the rescue boat and ambulance to the hospital. At crew lunch, the stews pondered how Dell managed to fall overboard in the first place—something about climbing the bow to photograph the *Nantucket Lightship* and losing his footing. They also whispered about Brynne's bravery for saving him, though no one felt comfortable telling her personally.

Hardigan was livid, especially with Nicky for his role in Dell's rescue. "That was one hell of a stunt you pulled, O'Hara! And for anyone thinking of jumping on his pea-brained bandwagon, know *this*—the next time, I'll let the sea have her way with you! You don't *ever* deviate from your maritime training!"

Adrienne wasn't exactly gobsmacked that Hardigan was singling Nicky out. He was known for being harder on the guys, mainly the ones he considered weak or defective in some way. Marco, Keith, and Shane all managed to evade his abuse, but when Hardigan wasn't yelling at Noah for playing his music too loud or harping at Jordy to complete some menial task, Nicky was given frequent tongue lashings for a litany of reasons—most often for forgetting to secure his cleat ropes.

Fortunately for his jolly disposition, Nicky nodded along with Hardigan's tirade and said, "Gotcha, Capt. No more jumpin' off the bow! Heard ya *loud* and *clear!*"

With most of the passengers off board during the excitement, the news didn't circulate until they returned for dinner. They gossiped like schoolchildren, playing a geriatric version of Telephone.

"He was trying to get a picture of the *Nantucket*."

"Yes, I heard that, too."

"Too bad *she* didn't fall over instead!"

Once Connie returned, everyone learned Dell was fine and would reboard with Kitty before the boat left for Martha's Vineyard the next day. Adrienne was glad Dell wasn't gravely hurt, but she wasn't thrilled about having *either* Chandler back for the last three days of the cruise. The couple were the rudest guests she'd ever waited on, and with boat time playing a factor, their final three days together were bound to be more like three *weeks*.

Sure enough, Kitty and Dell were acrimonious the following morning, instantly calling for custom breakfasts and complimentary drinks as though it was the crew's fault Dell had fallen overboard. They griped the whole way to Martha's Vineyard, giving attitudes to everyone and milking the incident for whatever they could. When Kitty let herself onto the laz and saw Adrienne and Noah, she grimaced and said, "Better turn *around*, Dell. I reckon we're someplace else we plumb aren't welcome!"

The Chandlers weren't the only ones afflicted by the incident. That night, Adrienne overheard Marco telling the officers Nicky was sick with a head cold. "He's already bunkered down," Marco was saying, "so I'll cover through ten tonight."

"You tell O'Hara he better have a clean bill of health by tomorrow!" said Hardigan. "Otherwise, I'll dock his pay. The little guy's not getting any get-well cards from me after that halfwit move he pulled yesterday."

Later, Adrienne walked to the end of Tisbury Wharf to smoke. In the distance, Noah was coming down the road, swinging a plastic bag. "Shopping?" she asked when he reached her.

"Girl, this is all for Nicky. I went to the pharmacy for him."

He brought Adrienne downstairs to deliver Nicky's items. It was Adrienne's first time in guys' quarters since the shipyard tour, and seeing the room in use felt odd. The first bed—Noah's—was shrouded in blankets like a cave. The bed at the end—Jordy's—was unmade, with piles of laundry strewn across the top bunk. A picture taped to the wall showed Jordy with a corpulent woman in a wheelchair. *His mother?* She reminded Adrienne of the mom from *What's Eating Gilbert Grape*.

Phlegmy hacking came from the bunk next to Jordy's. Nicky lay in the bottom bed, buried under used tissue balls. "What'd ya get me?" he asked Noah as a racking cough escaped his throat. He sounded like a dying seal, and Adrienne wondered how Hardigan possibly expected him to make a full recovery so soon.

"The works." Noah emptied the bag on the bed. "OJ, Robitussin, Theraflu, cough drops, and Tylenol PM."

"Jeez ..." Adrienne said, "the water was that cold, Nicky?"

"It's not the watah!" Nicky wheezed. "It's those people! Kitty and Dick, or whoevah the fuck! Those people ah *Jonahs!*"

"Jonahs?"

Nicky swallowed a capful of Robitussin and winced. "Don't tell me ya've nevah heard about Jonahs!"

Adrienne shook her head. "Guilty."

"Jonahs bring bad luck on boats. It don't mattah whethah they're pax or crew. Trouble happens whenevah they come around."

"Mm-hm," Noah confirmed. "I've heard that before. My dad had some Jonahs who worked for him."

Nicky took a swig of orange juice. "That lady's a double Jonah with 'er red mop, I'll tell ya that."

"Jonahs," Adrienne said. The name suited the Chandlers *perfectly*.

On her way out of guys' quarters, she glimpsed at Shane's bunk. His bed was commendably neat, his suitcase and sneakers lined orderly underneath. Shane's only personal effect was a framed photo on the nightstand—of a curly-haired toddler flashing two tiny front teeth.

There were no other pictures to speak of. Not even of his wife.

On disembarkation day in Providence, Adrienne watched Bev board the boat and join Hardigan in meeting with Kitty and Dell in the dining room. Bev nodded stiffly as the Chandlers griped about the catalog of affronts they'd experienced, conveniently leaving out their excessive alcohol consumption and carousel of over-the-top requests. Eventually,

Bev removed a pen from her lapel and signed a document before her, sliding it to Hardigan to do the same.

"That's right!" Kitty announced to some passengers while she and Dell walked off board. "The *owner* gave us half-off vouchers for all the bothers. But she said *we* had to cover our airfare! Can y'all believe that?"

That night, Adrienne hung around for the tip counting to see if Noah's prediction would come true.

"Cabin 70P," Connie finally said, "formally 31S—*nada*."

Noah smiled smugly and said, "Told you so," while still recovering, Nicky nodded righteously. "What'd I tell ya, Adrienne, huh? *Jonahs!* I hope to hell we nevah see those people again!"

Adrienne kept silent, trying to comprehend the Chandlers stiffing the crew after the accommodating lengths they'd gone to. Undertipping would have been bad as well, but to leave *nothing*? What on earth was wrong with them?

Hailey

HOW DARE THOSE PEOPLE? Those Jonahs! This might be her first job, but she knows everyone worked *extra* hard to keep them happy! Changing their cabin for no good reason after arriving late? All those gin and tonics during Cocktail Hour? Brynne and Nicky jumping overboard to *save* the husband?

If there's one thing being a stewardess is teaching her, it's how much industry workers appreciate their tips! How far they'll go to please even the *worst* kind of people!

33

THE NEXT NIGHT, after turnaround, Adrienne agreed to help Logan bring her port purchases back to her condo, but with the boat still docked in Providence, they'd have to take a cab to Riverside.

It was dark when they exited the gangway, carrying a bounty of shopping bags down the long dock where a taxi waited. Across the parking lot, Adrienne recognized the same Buick that had dropped Shane off five weeks earlier. He leaned against the car, smoking a cigarette. A woman faced him, her arms gesturing angrily.

As they got closer, Adrienne and Logan overheard what surely was supposed to be a personal argument. "I told ya I'm on 'til eleven!" Shane was saying. "What more do ya want from me, Jess? I hafta work!"

Jess? Was …? Was that Shane's wife?

"Work!" the woman said hotly. "That's all it evah is with you! Your cousin works, too! But *he*—*the ex-con!*—can find a job where he comes home at night, and you can't? I don't wanna hear this shit anymore!"

Shane tossed his cigarette to the ground. "Oh yeah? I don't hear ya bitchin' that I send home four hundred bucks a week! How many more times do I hafta say it, Jess? We *need* this money!"

"And the only place you can make *money* is workin' on that thing?" Jess spun and jabbed a finger toward the boat just as Adrienne and Logan stepped off the dock.

Adrienne glanced at her quickly. Jess was unhealthily skinny, wearing a belly T-shirt and short shorts that exposed protruding hipbones. Her straggly blonde hair was pulled back in a lusterless ponytail, exposing dark roots at the top. She wasn't what Adrienne had pictured at all.

Jess's piercing blue eyes shot daggers at the girls. She whipped around ruthlessly. *"Who the fuck ah they?"*

"Calm down!" Shane seethed. "I work with them, all right?"

"Oh, you *work* with them! Funny how you left that out! Probably because you're screwin' them, too! How many othah girls work on that boat anyways? And here I am—*the suckah!*—believin' you only work with a coupl'a guys and a bunch'a old people! No wondah you're so happy here!"

"They're in a different department!"

"You think I give a fuck, Shane? That boat's the size'a my pinky fingah!"

Again, Adrienne thought of Shannon. *It's not easy knowing your husband works around pretty girls all day.*

She was grateful the driver spotted them and got out to help load their bags into his trunk. When they were all inside the cab, he wagged a scolding finger. "That *voman,*" he said thickly. "She been out here yelling at that poor guy for ten minutes that I see." He looked from Logan to Adrienne. "You know her?"

They shook their heads.

"That voman, she is not a good voman," he continued. "And I tell you something else. That guy? He is not a happy guy. I know this. I vork vit people every day."

Shane

THAT'S ALL HE NEEDS is to get fired because of Jess's shit. He can't afford to lose this job. This money's gonna fix their future, and he's not walkin' away from it. Avery's not gonna grow up watchin' them live hand to mouth anymore. For once in his life, he's proud of the work he's doin' and the money he's gettin' for it.

Two weeks ago, he opened a separate bank account. One Jess doesn't know about. He's been puttin' some money aside for himself and the rest in a special purpose account for Avery. A little somethin' for her to maybe go to college one day. Maybe even pay for a proper ceremony, so she doesn't hafta get married at the courthouse like he and Jess did.

He's sick of Jess naggin' his cell phone five times a day, henpeckin' him when he answers. Now this? He tells her to go home before Hardigan comes out and cans him. "Go!" he says. "You're embarrassin' yourself, and you're embarrassin' our family."

"In front'a who?" she wants to know. "Your girlfriends?"

He walks away without answerin' her. He always thought a wife's someone you're supposed to be proud of, someone ya wanna show off to the world. Tonight proves Jess isn't that person. Never has been. Never will be.

Jordy

HE'S SEEN Shane's wife before. She used to work at one of the clubs in Providence's red-light district. He's been to them all. Desire. Cheaters. Fantasies. Foxy Lady. Sometimes he even goes to Woonsocket to see the Dolls.

Most people don't know indoor prostitution is legal in Rhode Island. There's brothels and rub-and-tugs everywhere. He's glad Providence is so close to Fall River. He's never had a girlfriend, so it's nice to have variety. Especially the Asian chicks at the rub-and-tugs. He gives them more than the going rate, and they usually return the favor. Sometimes it's not just about getting a lap dance or seeing chicks strip. He likes the sensual experience, too.

But chicks like Shane's wife aren't the type he drops his extra money on. She probably *used* to be hot, but her dead eyes and bony torso are turnoffs. And who wants a chick that acts like white trash in public? He thinks Shane could do better. He knows he would.

***

For Father's Day, Adrienne sent Jack a DVD player and a few television box sets. They were the last people in the neighborhood without one, and she knew he'd welcome the upgrade. There were many newer electronics, like iPods, that Adrienne was perfectly content living without, but a DVD player seemed a happy medium. They couldn't live behind the times forever.

She'd hoped to find a way to see her father, but the *Amelia* had already left for Fall River, embarking on one last Bay State Colony cruise before heading to Maine. Though scheduling hadn't made an in-person celebration possible, Jack assured Adrienne he was fine. He and Thany were going for pizza with a few other Scout dads and their sons, maybe even a game of mini golf after. *Maybe.*

In Hyannis that Tuesday, Shane found Adrienne after lunch and said, "Hey. I just wanted to say sorry, ya know, for what happened the other night with my wife."

His apology surprised her. "Don't worry about it," Adrienne said after a moment. "Every family has problems."

Shane nodded. "Yeah, but the things she said weren't right. I told her not to come around startin' trouble like that anymore."

Adrienne didn't understand why he was sharing this. Did she want to hear about conversations Shane had with his wife? Conversations she thought should remain inside the bounds of a marriage? No. It made her uncomfortable. "You don't need to explain yourself to me, Shane. I wasn't offended, and neither was Logan. I'd forgotten about it already."

But the truth was, she hadn't forgotten. She hadn't forgotten Jess's hardened face or the roughness in her voice. *Or how she conducted herself.* "Classless," Logan had commented in the cab. She also hadn't forgotten Shane's jaded expression as Jess yelled at him. A look that said he dealt with those arguments more often than he didn't.

Logan

SHE TOTALLY FEELS bad for Shane after what she saw in Providence. But she won't pretend she doesn't see a flicker between him and Adrienne, and she's a little jealous, to be honest!

She'd love to have a real connection with a guy instead of random hookups. And she'd totally love to settle down one day and have a family. But only with a guy she can enjoy life with. A guy she can trust. She's never told any guy about her money before and never will unless she meets *the one*. The truth is, sometimes she worries about her future. With her nomadic lifestyle, who knows if *the one* will ever come along?

34

THE NEXT TIME they docked in Plymouth, Katherine asked Adrienne to visit Plimoth Plantation with her after lunch. "It'll be fun!" Katherine said. "It'll be like bunkmate bonding!"

At the beginning of the season, the stews were raring to go during their afternoon breaks. They'd rented mopeds on Martha's Vineyard, hiked the Cliff Walk in Newport, and explored Quincy Market in Boston. But their boundless energy had since expended, and now everyone napped during their breaks. It was better to recharge midday rather than drag during dinner service. Katherine was the only stew who didn't follow this practice, doing her own thing in the afternoons and going to bed after galley cleanup each night instead of venturing out to the bars.

Adrienne was tired, but she was also intrigued by Katherine's invitation. Her curiosity about Plimoth Plantation was over a decade old, having missed out thanks to the stomach flu when her fourth-grade class took a field trip. She could still remember how let down she'd felt staying behind. "Sure," she ultimately told Katherine. "That sounds fun."

In the parking lot, Adrienne was confused to see Katherine waving her over to one of the vans reserved for the passengers. "Uh, we're not riding with the passengers, are we?"

"Sure!" Katherine said. "Why not?"

Adrienne looked around for Connie. She didn't feel comfortable hitching a ride without asking first. "I assumed we were taking a cab."

"It's fine!" said Katherine. "There's always extra room on the vans."

"You've done this before?"

"Lots of times! There's always room to ride along!"

"Right …" It wasn't like they'd be *hanging out* with the passengers.

But when they boarded the van, Adrienne had a funny feeling about how chummy Katherine was acting. Lightheartedly kidding with the guests during work hours was one thing, but Katherine took her off-the-clock socializations too far, prying too deeply into their personal lives, showing too much interest in the photos of their grandchildren, and laughing too hard, slapping her knee and throwing her head back at their jokes. Though this group didn't seem to mind, Adrienne's gut said Katherine's behavior wouldn't earn NECLA's stamp of approval.

When they got to Plimoth Plantation, Katherine said, "Come on! We'll tour with Barbara and Bill!"

Adrienne stopped mid-step. "Katherine, I didn't come to tour *with* the passengers. That's something they're supposed to do on their own. Or with Connie."

"But Connie isn't here," said Katherine. "Besides, I grew up next door in Barnstable County. *I* can answer all of their questions."

Well, fine. If the passengers were okay with Katherine playing Assistant Cruise Director, who was she to interfere?

She lagged behind all afternoon, detouring into the little houses to avoid Katherine's vigorous interactions. But although Adrienne credited Katherine's knowledge of Plymouth's history, she also thought Katherine's mile-a-minute rundown of the upcoming ports might ruin the element of surprise. Why *tell* the passengers everything waiting ahead? Why not let them wait to see all there was to marvel at?

Connie

SHE'S CERTAIN she's misunderstood Bill Atlee when he returns from Plimoth Plantation, singing praises about the guided tour he received from the stewardess with the headband. But when his wife, Barbara, says, "That Kathy sure is well abreast of this area!"—she *knows*.

Katherine's boundary issues are becoming problematic. Several times, she's caught her sitting and chitchatting with the passengers during meal service. Same during Activity Hour. But joining the passengers on an excursion? This is overstepping, and it's not good for business.

She pulls Katherine aside after dinner to discuss her trip to Plimoth Plantation. "I want to remind you about *boundaries*," she stresses. "It's important to keep your distance from the passengers, especially off the boat."

She's only half surprised when Katherine doesn't get her point. "What do you mean?"

"I mean that you need to respect their personal space."

"Well, I don't think I'm invading their personal space. No one's ever complained before, have they?"

She listens as Katherine tells her about joining the passengers numerous other times, carefreely, seeing nothing wrong with her actions. "Katherine, what makes you think that's acceptable?"

"Because *I* have dual degrees in Travel-Tourism and Hospitality Management. I was *trained* to do things like this."

"Katherine, you were hired as a stew. The company isn't paying you to be a tour guide."

Katherine's face drops. "Are you going to report me to Beverly?"

She hesitates. Imagine a boss of Macy's reprimanding *her* so young in life, not that Macy would ever encroach on company expectations. "Not this time, Katherine. But if it happens again, we may need to reconsider your position here."

Katherine

RECONSIDER HER POSITION? She makes a mad dash off the *Amelia* after her shift, straight to a picnic table at Pilgrim Memorial State Park, where she calls home. She's in tears when her mother answers. "Mommy? I can't take working here anymore! I hate this boat, and I hate everyone on it!"

She propels into a tirade of all her sore spots. "I get criticized at least once a day! And the worst part is that I'm the most qualified stewardess here! Most of them don't have *any* post-secondary education! And only one of them has a bachelor's degree! Even the cruise director didn't finish college!"

She thinks she has some solid points, but her father takes over the call and tears into her. "Now, you listen to me, Katherine Jane! You aren't leaving that boat unless you have something else lined up! And the benefits better be comparable to what you're receiving now!"

"But, Daddy! I didn't graduate *early* to work with so many under-qualified people! Especially not for the same amount of money!"

"Katherine! I refuse to believe you're receiving so much criticism unless you're struggling! You need to learn to follow orders and ask for help! Not expect to have everything handed to you because of your education!"

"But, Daddy, you don't understand!"

"I understand perfectly fine! The other staff must add *some* value on that boat, so if the only purpose of your call is to gripe about your coworkers, your mother and I are *not* interested!"

She hangs up while he's still bellowing. Whoever said your parents would support you through anything was wrong! Just plain wrong!

Nicky

HE CAN'T BELIEVE what he's hearin' on his way back from his toke in the pahk. Is Homegirl really knockin' the stews for not goin' to college? Does she know how many hahd-workin' girls he's seen in his six years at NECLA? Ya want his two Lincolns? Homegirl's been sheltahed all 'er life. Nevah had any sense knocked into 'er ... That's what he thinks.

He gives 'er a look as he crosses the street. *College.* Who needs it when ya can learn a trade? No book learnin', no student loans. He knows plenty'a guys that he graduated from Durfee with makin' more money in the trades than the college boys. Twenty, thirty grand a year for a piece'a papah? Homegirl can have it!

"Now, I ain't one to rock the boat ..." he tells some'a the girls when he gets back, "but Homegirl's not the brightest light in the hahbor. Ya should'a heard some'a the stuff she was bitchin' to 'er folks about on the phone."

The girls look pissed, and he wondahs if he should'a just confronted Homegirl himself. Probably no sense in makin' waves when the watah wasn't rocky to staht with ...

***

A STIFFNESS penetrated the dining room while the stews set up for breakfast in Boston. Adrienne, Hailey, and Logan had been present when Nicky shared what he'd overheard of Katherine's phone call, and they'd filled Noah in after his T&A shift. "Who the fuck does Katherine think she is?" Noah had flared. "She thinks we're not *worthy* of working here just because we don't have bachelor's degrees?"

Adrienne had been offended, too. Never mind that Katherine *knew* she'd gone to college, but they'd just spent the entire afternoon together. Where was all this badmouthing coming from?

"Having a bachelor's has nothing to do with being a stewardess," Logan had pointed out. "Mine is from art school."

But Noah had felt especially wronged. "Say I won't come upstairs before my LD shift so she can explain herself!" he'd threatened. "I'll wake up early and everything!"

Adrienne had hoped Noah wouldn't follow through with his warning, but ten minutes after everyone else started work, he entered the dining room as promised. He walked to the coffee station wearing sweatpants and a T-shirt, his feet clad in moccasins and his hair unbrushed. He'd yet to shower or shave, and five o'clock shadow sprouted from areas of his face none of them were used to seeing.

He slammed a coffee cup on the counter as Katherine filled a basket with fruit. "*Hmph!*" he noised. When Katherine returned from the galley with a sheet pan of Parker House rolls, Noah made the sound again. "*Hmph!*"

Katherine opened the pastry case. "Are you okay, Noah?"

"*Hmph!*"

Adrienne sighed. Why come upstairs to make a scene? When she caught Noah's eye, he said, "No, I better not, girl! I might go off and get *fired.*"

Katherine looked around. "Is someone upset with me for something?"

Adrienne rested her rack of juice glasses on a chair. "I think we're all upset about some things we heard …"

"What things?"

"You were overheard knocking all of us for not having bachelor's degrees. Is it true you don't think we're qualified to work here?"

Hailey and Logan glanced up from their table-setting tasks while Noah leaned against the coffee station and crossed his arms. Even Max was peering out from the galley window, her eyes full of their usual hate, daring Katherine to say the wrong thing.

Katherine scanned the room. Obviously, she'd thought no one had gotten wind of her conversation, but instead of denying her comments, she said, "Well, this *is* a cruise ship. And I graduated early to start my hospitality career. It doesn't make sense why the company would hire people who don't have the same education and qualifications that I do."

Noah opened his mouth, but Adrienne headed him off. "Katherine, I worked in a restaurant for *five* years. And I was a manager for two. How would that not qualify me to serve meals on a cruise ship?"

"Yeah!" called Noah. "And she went to college! And so did I!"

Katherine turned to Noah. "You said you only went for a year."

"That's right, girl! One year, and I'm proud of every credit!"

"I've never been to college," said Hailey, "and I think I'm doing a good job here."

"You are, Hailey!" Noah blew her an air kiss. "Love you, girl!"

"Okay," Katherine said, "maybe there *are* other qualifications. But I still shouldn't be getting paid the same as people who don't have four-year degrees. Being a graduate means I automatically deserve more."

"So, you think you're better than us?" snapped Noah. "Girl, it's not like you dumb yourself down to *our* levels. You mess up all the time!"

Adrienne was having trouble tolerating Katherine's mindset. "Pay increases are supposed to be merit and performance-based, Katherine. And Noah's right that we've all seen you do things differently from how we were trained. Why would *you* qualify to be first in line for this job or a raise? And what gives you the right to judge *us*?"

Katherine hung her head shamefully. "I just—"

Logan stopped her. "I think it would be better if you didn't say anything else, Katherine. A person's education doesn't define them, and everyone on this boat totally has as much right to be here as you do."

Adrienne was glad Logan had come to their defense, and gracefully so. As the only other employee with a four-year degree, Logan's clashing viewpoint left Katherine isolated in her opinions.

But the negative energy hovered. It hurt Adrienne that Katherine had no regard for the unique paths that led them all to NECLA. She was proud of her associate's degree. Proud of having a work ethic that got her promoted at nineteen. Proud she'd helped support her family when they'd needed it most. Yet another part of her felt guilty, as if the conversation should have gone differently. As annoyed as she was, Adrienne couldn't help putting herself in Katherine's shoes, thinking how bad she would have felt if *she'd* just been ganged up on like that.

July 2007

35

THE BOAT DEADHEADED to Maine, meaning there were no passengers on board, just crew. These back-to-back Maine Marvels itineraries would be the season's longest and most expensive trips. Twelve days and eleven nights of lobsters, lighthouses, and loons.

The *Amelia* cruised through an odyssey of coastal towns, docking in idyllic, boat-studded harbors. At night, the melodic calls of the Maine loons were heard for miles, and in the mornings, Adrienne found the misty marinas a serenity. She began getting ready for work early each day, sitting on the laz with tea and a cigarette, savoring the tranquility.

The waters proved choppier along the coast, where Adrienne experienced her first bout of seasickness. Nausea, she was told, was best remedied on the bottom deck, where the rocking motions weren't as prevalent. She lay stomach-down in bed, praying her Sea-Bands and Dramamine would be effective. When they weren't, she made it to the tiny bathroom just in time to lose her shrimp scampi, dry-heaving until returning to bed. After that, she was fine.

On the Fourth of July, they docked in Bucksport, a small town better known for its down-home hospitality than its larger, touristy neighbors. The passengers spent the afternoon touring Fort Knox, returning to the boat to find a traditional Maine lobster bake on the top deck, the forty pounds of seaweed delivered personally by a local picker. Dessert was an ice cream bar featuring a medley of flavors from Gifford's.

After dinner, Connie brought up a boom box and some oldies CDs for an evening of dancing. Noah got right out there jiving with the passengers, and Hailey followed his lead, extending her hand to a little old man named Bart. Even Brynne joined in, dancing with the guests to the tunes of their generation. Adrienne watched her move with elegant grace. Noah and Hailey were good, but Brynne was a *phenomenal* dancer.

When the sky was shrouded in darkness, Keith, Marco, and the deckhands drove the launch boat into the harbor and set off an impressive fireworks display. Adrienne leaned against the deck rail to watch, focusing on Shane. When he looked up, a profoundly personal energy transmitted between them, same as the first time they'd seen each other. Adrienne wished she could read Shane's mind, wondering if he was thinking similar thoughts.

Their next stop was Bangor. In girls' quarters after housekeeping, Adrienne heard muted weeping coming from inside Katherine's bunk. "Katherine?" She pulled back a blanket curtain and found Katherine crying into a stuffed koala. "Katherine? What's wrong?"

Katherine blinked tearily. "I don't want to be here anymore, Adrienne. Everyone on this boat *hates* me."

It was true no one had spoken much to Katherine since Boston. But that was two weeks ago already, an eternity in boat time. Adrienne tried imagining how it must feel going without peer contact for that long, ultimately deciding that she wasn't going to coddle Katherine, but she *would* try and make things right. They needed to move past this.

"No one hates you, Katherine. But you have to acknowledge what you said to us was really insulting. Those aren't things you say to people you want to be friends with."

"But I didn't *say* those things to any of you! I was having a private conversation with my *parents*. And then I defended myself, and now no one will talk to me. People are allowed to have opinions, you know, especially when they're angry. And I was angry that night in Plymouth!"

"Katherine, you acted like everyone here is inferior to you because of your education. Don't you realize how hurtful that was?"

"Don't *you* realize that's all I have here?"

Adrienne crossed her arms. "*What's* all you have?"

"Everyone else has been bonding since the shipyard, and I feel like none of you want me around. Hailey and Logan are always together, you're always with Noah, and then *those two*." Katherine pointed toward Max's and Brynne's room. "I don't have a *go-to* person on the boat. That's why I spend so much time with the passengers."

Adrienne could see how Katherine might sometimes feel excluded. *Sometimes*. But it's not like they hadn't made an effort. "I didn't realize you felt that way. Why did you wait so long to say something?"

"What was I supposed to say? I've felt like this ever since Logan excluded me from the sleepovers at her condominium."

"She didn't *exclude* you, Katherine. Hailey and I were sleeping over to save ourselves the commute."

"My commute was the same distance as Hailey's, but no one ever asked."

So, she was right. Katherine *had* felt left out during all those weeks in the shipyard. "I didn't know that, Katherine. And I'm sure Logan didn't either. She would have invited you if she did."

Katherine sniffled. "Well, *I* think I've tried to make the most of it. Just because I don't want to go to the bar every night doesn't mean I don't want to socialize. But what's the point anymore?"

"I get it, Katherine," said Adrienne. "But how are you planning on fixing this? I have an *associate's* and I was offended. How do you think Hailey and Noah feel without *any* degrees? Hailey hasn't even been to college."

Katherine wiped her face. "I've thought about that a lot. And, you know, I was referred here by one of my professors after I got—after I graduated early last year—so, *naturally*, I assumed I'd be working with other graduates."

"What difference does it make? How would working here have changed your experience if we had bachelor's degrees, too?"

"Okay, well, another issue is *Connie*. She's always picking on me but lets Max get away with murder. And I didn't go to school to serve food and make beds. I want more guest interaction and to be more hands-on with the itineraries. Hospitality means a lot to me, but no one understands that."

Suddenly, Adrienne made a connection that hadn't hit her before, something Katherine said all the time that had never registered until now. "You were born in 1986, right?" she asked.

Katherine nodded.

"So, you're the same age as me?"

"Yes. Why?"

"Then how can you possibly have a bachelor's degree already? I know you graduated early, but people *our* age aren't supposed to graduate college until next spring."

"Oh. I went to a college preparatory academy for five years. When I started Johnson & Wales, I already had credits. And Johnson & Wales operates on trimesters, so I finished last August."

Finally, it all made sense. Katherine had been groomed to be a student her whole life. Academics were all she knew, and that was where the disconnect lay. It didn't make her judgments of the crew right, but now that Adrienne understood Katherine's background, she could better align with her thought process.

"I don't think you should leave," she said. "At least finish out the season. Just think of it as an extended internship."

"But Connie is always—"

"There's nothing you can do about Connie. If you just follow her directions, you'll be fine. And you should probably stop complaining so much. *And* questioning the officers."

"What about the crew? Is everyone going to keep ignoring me?"

"I don't know, Katherine. At the very least, you need to apologize."

Katherine smoothed the koala's fur. "I'm still unclear *what* I'm supposed to be sorry about."

This was exactly why Katherine was so frustrating! Yes, she meant well, but her unassuming loftiness continued to get the better of her. How many others out there had graduated early? And what was the big hurry to finish so fast? Katherine might have her degrees, but where was her independence? Her life experience? Why rush to finish college if she didn't have the maturity or preparedness for the real world? Without any personal growth, the crew would just continue resenting her. *If* she decided to stay.

36

ON THE THIRD Sunday of July, Adrienne ended her LD shift with no plans for her evening off in Rockland. She changed into street clothes and headed to the gangway, where she found Nicky on sign-out duty. "Where ya headed tonight, lady?"

Adrienne took his clipboard. "Nowhere special. Just into town to walk around."

"Mind if I stretch my legs with ya?"

Adrienne turned and saw Shane. Freshly showered, he wore jeans and a wifebeater. His body wash smelled amazing, of refreshing woodsy tones. "You're off now, too?" she asked.

Shane grinned. "Yup. 'Til eight in the mornin.'"

What could she say—no? But did she want to say no? No way. She passed him the clipboard. "All right."

"You kids behave now!" Nicky lectured.

Shane laughed and followed her to the dock. "So, what should we get into tonight, Adrienne?"

Adrienne stared up, noticing how the sun glistened off his close-shaven hair. "I had my heart set on a beer and a lobster roll ... if you're *really* curious."

Shane's smile was unrestrained and euphoric. "Sounds like a plan."

Adrienne looked at him again. "What's that giddy smile for?"

"Who, me?"

"Yes, *you*. You look like my little brother on Christmas right now."

"Maybe because I finally get ya all to myself for the night. This is the first time we've both had a free night since I started here."

Adrienne's heart skipped a million inappropriate beats. "You're something else, Shane."

They walked up the hill toward Main Street. On the corner was a red building called Time Out Pub. They sat at the bar, where Adrienne asked the bartender for two Bud Lights and two menus.

"You know me well," Shane kidded her.

Across the room, a band was assembling on a platform stage. "Eighties rock tonight," the bartender told them. "If you're still here after seven, I've gotta charge you a cover."

When Adrienne asked what the area had to offer, the bartender immediately recommended the Rockland Breakwater Lighthouse. "It's the town gem if you can handle the walk. Three miles down the road, then straight into the harbor when you get there."

"That sounds cool," said Shane. "You up for the hike?"

Adrienne's heart hammered. They were about to *go* somewhere, not just hang out at a bar after work. She hoped Shane wouldn't detect how nervous she was. "Okay … but let's have another round first."

They headed north on Route 1. As they walked, Shane asked questions about Adrienne's family. Personal questions, to which her answers came relaxedly. She felt comfortable sharing the details of her broken home with him. Until now, no one but Noah knew that Raina had walked out, just that she lived in New Mexico. "It sucks when a parent doesn't wanna be in your life anymore," Shane said. "I went through it with my father."

He asked to hear more about Thany, showing particular concern for his epilepsy. "I'm sorry ya had to go through that," he said when she explained life before Thany started taking Carbamazepine. "I thought Avery's delays were rough, but the way ya talk about those seizures …"

Adrienne showed Shane a recent picture Wendy had texted of Thany at the park. He opened his phone and shared a grainy photo of Avery set as his background. Adrienne didn't tell him she'd already seen the picture beside his bed.

The breakwater began at the water's edge, a lengthy expanse of rock palettes splicing the West Penobscot Bay. A square lighthouse was erected at the end—their destination.

Shane eyed the crevices between the palettes. "You up for this?"

Adrienne looked on reluctantly. "We didn't walk all this way for nothing …"

He offered his hand. "Here, let me help ya."

As wrong as it was to touch him, it didn't mean she didn't want to. But her morals came first. Breaking her neck was the lesser evil than holding hands with someone's husband. "I'm all set," she said, stepping onto a palette.

"Don't fall!" Shane teased as they passed a boat ramp.

A jinx, Adrienne thought when she stumbled after catching her sandal in a crevice. Shane grabbed her, his solid arms sending paralyzing waves through her body, but she pulled away quickly.

The sun was setting when they reached the lighthouse. "Wow," Adrienne said, settling onto the last rock palette. "This is unreal." The burning orb emitted a radiant glow as far as their eyes could see. "Yeah," said Shane, "this is somethin.'" The smell of his body wash was still sharp, an acute indication of how close they were sitting to one another.

A quiet remained while they admired the placid beauty that rivaled every sunset Adrienne had ever seen. As dusk fell, she realized how romantic the location was at this hour. Had the bartender mistaken them for a couple? Is that why she'd suggested they come here? The setting was so intense that Adrienne had to stomach the nerve to break their silence. "Do you want to tell me the long story now?" she asked.

"The long story?"

"That night in New Bedford," she reminded him. "At the bar?"

Shane turned to her. "You really wanna hear it?"

Adrienne nodded.

"My wife and I used to work together," he said, bringing a cigarette to his lips. "She danced at a club in Providence I used to bounce at."

"Danced?"

"She was a stripper. I know ya probably have feelin's about that."

Adrienne flicked her ash into a crevice. "I'm surprised …" she admitted. "But everyone has a story, right?"

"I was young," Shane continued. "Just turned twenty and didn't know if I was comin' or goin.' I was seein' other girls, but Jess started pushin' up on me on her first day at work. Things just went from there."

Adrienne listened as Shane unloaded. Jess had quit stripping after learning she was pregnant. Not that Shane was convinced she'd been faithful, because he sure was vocal about not being faithful to her. He wasn't even sure Avery was his at first, resorting to a paternity test after nine months of arguing. When the results proved he *was* Avery's father, he chose to stick around for the long haul, eloping with Jess and working low-paying jobs while she stayed home with the baby.

The "long story" became a saga of Jess's abuse, of arguments that lasted for hours, usually ending in Shane nursing the scrapes and wounds he'd collected. He'd been assaulted with various household items, including a fireplace poker. He pointed to the fat scar below his tattoo, revealing its origin. "She's got somethin' wrong upstairs," he said. "But she's undiagnosed. Doesn't wanna get any help."

It was hard to brook Shane's stories. He was so open—sharing family secrets never supposed to be known to outsiders.

"Why do you stay?" Adrienne finally asked.

"I'm not gonna be like my father. He walked out when I was ten and we haven't seen him since. My sister doesn't even remember him."

"Where did he go?"

"Pennsylvania somewhere."

"Do you ever think about finding him?"

Shane shook his head, swift and firm. "Nah, no way. Now that I'm a dad, I can't imagine droppin' off and leavin' your kids like that."

Adrienne saw his point, but abandoning your kids and divorcing an abusive spouse were different animals. Didn't Shane realize he could leave Jess and still see Avery? Or maybe there was more to his story. There were always two sides, weren't there? What had Raina told the Accountant? What had Roman told Jenni? Did Jess have a story, too?

Shane changed the subject. "All right, my turn. Who's this ex-boyfriend of yours? What's the story with that?"

Adrienne watched the waves lap against the breakwater. If there were two sides to every story, she wondered what Rick's woebegone bullshit would be, knowing he'd probably twist things around to avoid responsibility. She told her version anyway, plunging into their history resentfully, being as honest with Shane as he'd been with her. The more she spoke, the harder it was to look at him. It hurt her pride to admit she'd put up with Rick for so long, to acknowledge that their relationship had been a one-way street, that she'd given everything and seen nothing in return.

"That guy sounds like a fuckin' loser," Shane said. "No job 'til he was twenty-one? I started workin' at fifteen. You're lucky to be done with him."

"Thanks ... I guess."

"I'm serious, Adrienne. Any guy who only thinks of himself doesn't deserve a girl. Especially not one like you."

"What's that supposed to mean?" Adrienne asked sharply.

"Look at how ya carry yourself. Any guy who wouldn't kill to give ya the world is outta his mind. Most girls only care about themselves, even some of your friends on the boat. But you've got depth. You deserve someone who shows ya what you're worth every day of your life."

Shane's playful smile was long gone, his vibe now conveying a solemnity that sent shivers up Adrienne's spine. But as inappropriate as his admissions were, Adrienne knew they weren't just words. They'd come from his heart, from his own life experience. She felt lightheaded but knew a response was necessary. "Thank you, Shane ..." she managed. "That's the nicest thing anyone has ever said to me. Really."

They got back with minutes to spare until curfew. Logan, Hailey, and Noah were leaving the pub, drunkenly singing Bon Jovi lyrics. Nicky and Brynne followed behind, equally tipsy. Nicky's arm was strung around Brynne's waist. "Adrienne! Shaney-Boy! Ya been gone this whole time?"

Marco, who'd taken Nicky's place in the gangway chair, stewed with annoyance. "Keep it down! All of you!" he ordered.

Max leaned against Marco, her head on his lap, half asleep. When Adrienne reached for the clipboard, Max opened her eyes and glowered.

On board, as everyone departed the dining room, Shane asked Adrienne to hang back. "I had a good time tonight," he said, serious and confiding.

"I did, too," Adrienne said quietly. "Thanks again for the nice things you said to me."

"I meant what I said, Adrienne. You only deserve the best in life."

The energy between them was blistering. Adrienne shuffled her feet. She had never experienced a moment that left her this magnetized to another person.

Shane stepped closer. "You know I wanna see ya again, right?" His voice was just above a whisper.

Adrienne fought the lump in her throat. "You see me every day, Shane. We work together."

"I mean like tonight. Just the two of us hangin' out."

She forced herself to swallow, hearing Shannon's reminder in her subconscious. *Don't ever forget where you come from. Or stray from your convictions.*

"I'm sure we'll have other opportunities," she said politely, stepping backward. "Have a good night, Shane."

In bed, Adrienne stared at the ceiling. It was getting harder to deny the rush she'd felt since May. Shane enamored her, and she knew he felt similarly. Until now, she'd forbidden herself from fantasizing about him, but what was the harm in letting her mind probe desires she would never act on? Wasn't she allowed to have secrets with herself?

She imagined they were back at the breakwater, Shane whispering huskily into her ear and lying on top of her, the two of them unable to control what happened next. She imagined their hands grabbing the others' bodies, over the clothes, then under. But when she imagined kissing him, it wasn't Shane's lips that her mind went to first. It was the translucent scar on his upper arm, so that he would know love instead of pain.

Shane

SHE KNOWS the struggle, too. He can tell by lookin' in her eyes. But she doesn't let it own her. She just carries on. Other girls all want the same thing—someone to take care of them in bed and out. It turns him on that Adrienne's so independent, that she knows how to grind. Not a lotta girls out there like that. He thinks of Jess. Without him, where would she be right now? Still on that pole at the club. He doesn't even remember how they got started. He drank a lot back then, he remembers that.

Adrienne's different. He's never talked to a girl about his life before, never felt the closeness he does with her. She makes him nervous. No girl's ever done that before either. It gives him goosebumps when he imagines bein' with her, puts a weird feelin' in his chest. She's beautiful, with such a nice body. And she doesn't flaunt it. Doesn't look for attention like other girls do. He figures there's no harm in thinkin' about her that way, but he knows better than to try somethin'. As much as he'd love to, Adrienne deserves respect. Doesn't sound like the last guy even cared what she was worth.

37

THREE DAYS LATER, Adrienne sat on the gargantuan boot outside the L.L. Bean flagship store, waiting for Noah as he shopped inside. She was on the phone with Wendy, confiding her guilt over her increasing closeness with Shane. Ever since their night in Rockland, she'd been overrun with shame. No matter how strongly she felt toward him, Shane was *married*. That was all there was to it.

"Technically, you're not doing anything wrong, Adrienne," Wendy objected.

"How do you figure?"

"Okay, so you spend a lot of time with him, but you guys work on a *boat*. You can't escape him any easier than the captain's daughter, or whoever she is."

"True ... but I don't hang out with Max."

"But you still see her every day."

"Not by choice."

"My *point* is that you're not seeking him out in an inappropriate environment," Wendy clarified. "If there's a closeness and you enjoy each other's company, well, that sucks that he's married. But he's allowed to have friends, Adrienne, and your social lives are pretty limited right now."

"So, you don't see a problem with us hanging out on Sunday?" Adrienne asked.

"You went for a *walk*," Wendy said matter-of-factly. "So what if it led you to some beautiful sunset on the water? So what if you shared a lot of private things with each other? It's not like either of you planned to have this connection. It's not like you *did* anything ... did you?"

"No!"

"Well, there you go! Adrienne, I know you have strong convictions about cheating, but as long as you aren't *doing* anything, you're not doing anything *wrong*. Not in your case, at least."

But even after hanging up with Wendy, Adrienne wasn't convinced she was in the clear. Wasn't there such thing as an emotional affair? The pangs in her conscience were constant reminders that Sunday's dialogue with Shane seemed far too intimate to have with someone who'd already committed his life to another woman. And that magnetic connection? That *definitely* wasn't appropriate.

Adrienne imagined what Shannon would say. Or her father. Or even Raina. Who knew what sort of feedback her mother would give? It had been years since she'd sought her advice and had learned to navigate life without it. They were practically strangers now.

Wendy

SHE'LL ADMIT she'd been expecting to hear from Adrienne more often. They're used to talking every day, but now she's lucky if they're in touch once a week. She knows Adrienne is busy and prioritizes her phone calls for her family, but does she have to spend so much of *their* conversations talking about the boat? When will she ever see those people again after November? Aside from checking how Sundays are going with Thany, it's been several calls since Adrienne's asked about *her* life. But don't get her wrong—she loves taking Thany out every week. It makes her think about life if she has a son one day.

She's been socializing more with the Giovanni's staff lately. She's spent a few beach days at Misquamicut with Becca and the drivers and another at the Pavilion in Old Lyme. Driving is giving her so much freedom, and she enjoys getting out of Westford with her coworkers. *Except* for the day Connor invited Rick along, and he pestered her about Adrienne the whole time.

She feels herself maturing at work, too. She's still shocked she agreed to take tables while Becca was out sick. And how much she made in tips! But Roman's been so quiet recently that sometimes she has to do things without his direction. Shannon hasn't been by the restaurant in months, so she has suspicions, but she doesn't ask. No one does.

These were all the things she's been wanting to tell Adrienne. Now she'll have to wait until she hears from her again.

* * *

THE DAY AFTER Maine Marvels concluded in Portland, the stews walked to Longfellow Books to commemorate the end of the Harry Potter era. The final installment had been released at midnight, and Adrienne, Logan, Noah, and Katherine had all preordered their copies in advance.

Adrienne and Logan were serious readers, but Noah was just into Harry Potter for the fanfare, claiming it was the only series he'd ever read. Hailey had never read the books, but she was aware of the hype and wanted just as much to be part of this historic moment.

Everyone had predictions about the fate of the characters.

"Snape is dead for sure!" Noah declared. "After he killed Dumbledore? No *way* J. K. Rowling is gonna let him live!"

"I wouldn't be so sure," Logan opposed. "She might think that's what we're expecting and throw a curveball instead."

"*I* agree with Noah," said Katherine. "I'm *positive* Snape will die."

No one responded to Katherine. In the sixteen days since Adrienne had spoken to her, Katherine *still* hadn't apologized to the crew. She'd obviously chosen to stay with NECLA and instead was being extra nice to everyone, trying to get back in their good graces with kindness.

Hailey walked beside Adrienne. "What do you think, Dri?"

"I think Snape will die, too," Adrienne said. "But I think J.K. Rowling will make us feel bad about it somehow."

At the bookstore, they waited in line with all the people who hadn't retrieved their books at the midnight extravaganza. While they waited, Adrienne noticed Brynne and Max had followed them. Max looked bored, like a bookstore was the last place she wanted to spend this beautiful July afternoon. But Brynne possessed an air of excitement, flexing her fingers together and wearing a hint of a smile. Adrienne thought of Brynne's book collection and vaguely recalled seeing Harry Potter paperbacks mixed among all the novels and romances.

If things were different, Adrienne wondered if Brynne would've joined their group instead, sharing their forecasts and excitement. *It's too bad*, she thought. Too bad there was such a divide. An *us* and a *them*.

Hailey

SHE FEELS so left out of this Harry Potter experience. Even though she's with everyone at the bookstore, she wishes she could participate in their debate about Snappy. Will Snappy live? Will Snappy die? Who *is* Snappy?

She'd never been allowed to read anything her parents didn't approve of. When *Harry Potter* first debuted, they said the content was inappropriate. Usually, they'd picked out books for her, but by high school, she'd lost interest in *Little House on the Prairie* and the Dear America series.

Partly out of curiosity and partly out of spite, she buys the first three Harry Potter books to see what the big fuss is. She's hooked immediately but feels bitter with each page she turns. How long had her parents planned to shelter her? Deprive her of *everything*? She knows she was meant to find the newspaper on the pew at church, that it was a sign from God. Otherwise, she'd never have met all her new friends. Still never have left New London County!

The more she reads … the more she realizes there is *nothing* wrong with Harry Potter … the more she doesn't want to be bothered with her parents during the upcoming three-day break. But she *is* excited to see Jeremy, and where else would she go? By the second chapter, she's shocked at how much she identifies with Harry. Her parents may as well have locked *her* in a cupboard under the stairs!

***

LATER THAT EVENING, Adrienne was passing through the dining room when she spotted Brynne on a banquette, engrossed in her copy of *Deathly Hallows*. Adrienne decided to take her chances. "Any predictions?"

Brynne peered over the book. "Are you asking me?"

"There's … no one else in here."

When Brynne still looked wary, Adrienne said, "I'm just curious about your opinion. I think Snape's a goner, but Logan isn't sure."

Brynne marked her place with a finger. "I do think he's going to die, but I think a lot of other characters will, too. The biggest misconception about *Harry Potter* is that it's a children's fairy tale when it's really about differentiating between loss and death and coming to terms with both."

Adrienne wished another stew had been there to witness Brynne speak. Her perspective was deep and thought-provoking, and for the first time since meeting her, Adrienne saw Brynne as an individual. For five months, she'd only seen an extension of Max, but now Brynne had emerged from her shell, unmasking a mind that moved all on its own.

Connie

ONE MORE TRIP until the next three-day break, and the homebound energy is ripe. She spends the week working on the midseason progress reports, knowing it's just as crucial to give the stews a fair assessment as it is to be truthful about her observations. And sometimes, the truth hurts.

There's nothing unfavorable in the reports for Adrienne, Logan, Hailey, or Noah ... but the other three? Katherine could use some lessons on maturity. Brynne could use some lessons on becoming a team player. And Max? She'll give that little urchin gold stars for guest service, but the act is smoke and mirrors. And if the passengers can't tell, what would Bev care? If only Max could treat the rest of humanity with the same civility and respect.

She *prays* for her vacation in September, her annual Florida trip with Macy. Forty days and counting, and it can't come soon enough.

Bev

SHE ASSUMES THE KNOCK on her door is from Connie, delivering the progress reports. So, she's surprised to see Hailey enter her office, positively glowing.

"I wanted to thank you again, Bev," Hailey tells her. "This is the best time of my life, and I … I'm so grateful you gave me a chance."

She's touched, really. It took a lot of moxie for this young woman to strike out on her own. "You're quite welcome, Hailey. I do hope you'll consider returning next season."

"Another season?"

"But of course, dear. I've added some new itineraries, one as far down the coast as Florida. You mark my words that you'll have no shortage of ports to traverse."

The girl's smile stretches up that precious round face. "*Florida?*"

"Yes, dear, you heard correctly. It's a tremendous world out there, Hailey, and you've only but *scratched* the surface."

38

ADRIENNE COULDN'T BELIEVE only two months had passed since she'd been home. So much had happened that it seemed longer. *Boat time*, she reminded herself. It felt good reuniting with her father and Thany, but Adrienne often wished Aaron were closer. So far, there hadn't been any news about his anticipated deployment. The last they'd spoken, he was busy assistant teaching on base. Knowing he was safe in North Carolina was a weight lifted from everyone's shoulders, especially Jack's. "Just as long as he stays stateside," Jack kept saying.

Now an expert with the new DVD player, Thany begged Adrienne to take him to borrow movies. She suggested playing outside, but Thany persisted, sticking his lower lip into a pout. "Pleeease, Adrienne? I just want to cuddle with you and Dolly on the couch and have snacks. I've been playing outside all summer!"

How could she resist Thany's adorable innocence?

"Serves you right," Jack said. "You never should've sent home that damn contraption. Now we're both addicted."

Not long after the DVD player had arrived, Adrienne learned Wendy had been taking Thany to borrow movies from the library. Occasionally, Jack would put in for a request as well.

"*One* movie," Adrienne said as Thany buckled his seatbelt. "And then you're going outside to ride your bike."

But when they got to the library, it was closed for maintenance. "We can go to the movie store …" Thany suggested. "Wendy says they have a *million* more movies than the library, but she never takes me."

Wendy would know, Adrienne thought as she drove to the nearest

Blockbuster. The money Wendy spent on her movie collection likely reached four figures annually.

Going Out of Business! signs were plastered all over Blockbuster. The store was selling its entire stock, and Adrienne realized that Wendy was right—renting movies in stores was headed for extinction. She drifted from aisle to aisle, astonished by the liquidation prices. *New Releases for $6.99. Buy 3 for $9.99. Buy 2, Get 2 Free.* The bargains prompted her to return up front for a basket. Who knew if Blockbuster would even be here the next time she came home?

"Need help finding anything, Adrienne?"

Adrienne looked up to see Rick standing behind the counter. *Damn.* She'd completely forgotten he worked here. Probably because she'd tried forgetting about him altogether. Aside from the uniform, Rick hadn't changed. His untamed scruff and boy-band haircut still weren't doing him any favors, and his skin was as pasty-white as she remembered, no doubt that he still dwelled in his mother's basement, letting life pass him by. But Adrienne was now looking at a stranger, unable to summon one fond memory or recall one occasion he'd even made her smile. The *only* thing she felt toward him was resentment. "I'm all set," she said coldly, grabbing a basket from the rack.

She turned toward the Horror aisle, but Rick was at her side, eager to make conversation. "You never answered my card," he said.

Adrienne dropped a DVD into her basket. "I had nothing to say, Rick, so you can quit following me." Couldn't he take a hint?

Blood rushed to Rick's ears. "I still love you, Adrienne," he whispered. "I still think about you all the time."

Adrienne looked over the aisles for Thany, spotting him piling DVDs into his own basket. *Great.* "Well, I never loved *you*," she said firmly. "I mean it, so get that through your head." She was becoming impatient, setting her basket down. Rick's presence repulsed her, and she needed to escape. "And don't ever contact me again. Do yourself a favor and get on with your life."

She pulled Thany to the registers with his basket, anxiously waiting while another employee rang them out. *Love.* Rick was ignorant to the depth of the word. Loving someone wasn't just a feeling but an action.

And what had he ever done to *show* her love? Not a single thing. He was needy. A taker. And nothing more. That's when it occurred to Adrienne that Rick didn't miss *her* but how she'd made him feel. How ironic it was that she didn't miss how he made her feel in the least.

Brynne

WHENEVER SHE'S AWAY, she leaves Pearl with Taylor Windmere, the fourteen-year-old girl who lives in her building. Asking Maureen to care for Pearl would be pointless. Her mother has no more interest in animals than she does in *her*.

She and Maureen live in a lavish Regency condominium secluded from the main road. They live in the only penthouse on the property—a spacious two-bedroom that allows for a fair amount of privacy. Taylor and her mother moved into one of the Tudor Suites a few years ago. She'd met them at the mailboxes one afternoon.

Taylor attends the private day school in town. Fortunately, neither she nor her mother know anything about her reputation. They like her, and she trusts them with Pearl. She bought Pearl after ending her first pregnancy, to fill a void she couldn't explain, to give her a companionship she knew she needed. It's hard to believe she was Taylor's age at the time.

When she goes to collect Pearl, Taylor invites her inside to see her new touch-screen cell phone. "It's called an iPhone," Taylor says. "It was *so* expensive."

She stays just for a minute. Gordon's coming down for the evening, and she wants to relax in the Whirlpool before he arrives. He calls while she's reading *The Notebook*. "I'll be late tonight, love, but I'll be there." Gordon usually makes good on his promises, but she worries. Of the six times the boat has docked in Boston this season, they've only seen each other once.

He doesn't show until nine. She can feel the aloofness in his kiss, and on the drive to Federal Hill. Tonight, he chooses Camille's, where their conversation feels forced. He asks about the boat. She asks about his patients. Her stomach tightens when they leave and he drives toward the highway. "Aren't we going to the Biltmore?" she asks.

Gordon acts like he doesn't hear the hurt in her voice. "Surgery tomorrow morning ..." he tells her. "But next time, love ... I promise."

Shane

IT'S LIKE WORKIN' a second job when he gets home. Same thing happened last time. Jess bitches about the busted fridge. The leak in the sink. The grass not bein' cut. How their landlord took off to the Azores for the summer. *He* fixes it all. Afterward, he tells Jess let's go do somethin' as a family, go to the zoo or mini golf. Just get outta the house.

They go to Roger Williams Park, where Jess rides him whenever he takes out his wallet. "You think you're *Mistah Hot Shot* with all that money, don't you? Eric's a piece'a shit for tellin' you about that job. Why doesn't he leave *his* wife and kids if it's so great?"

This is gettin' to be too much. *She's* too much. He tries talkin' to her in bed that night, asks what her problem is, why she's gotta be so negative all the time. But she pushes him away. Coupl'a hours later, after he's asleep, she rubs his leg. "I'm sorry, honey. Let's make up."

He tries, but there's somethin' different about sleepin' with her now. With your wife, it's supposed to be special, but it doesn't feel special with Jess. She laughs when he finishes, cruel and snarky. "Guess I was wrong about you screwin' those boat girls, Shane. Would'a lasted longah if you were."

He doesn't see Travis anywhere. When he asks Jess where he is, she says, "How the fuck should I know? You think I keep tabs on him?"

"Does he still live here?"

"Course he does! Comes and goes as he pleases, just like you!"

"So, where is he? He owes me his rent."

Jess laughs, she's enjoyin' this. "What do I look like? A private eye? You figure it the fuck out. Maybe he met a girl."

The next day, he takes Avery over to play with Eric's daughters.

"You like working for Bev Sanbourne, mano?" Eric asks.

"Yeah. I owe ya big time for that."

"You don't owe me nothing. That's what friends do. Help each other out."

He tells Eric about the boat, what he does, who he works with. He tells him a little about Adrienne.

"She sounds like a nice girl, mano."

"She is," he says. "It's too bad I didn't meet her earlier."

August 2007

39

THE EARLY TRAIN got Adrienne back to Rhode Island two hours before she was scheduled for work. She took a cab to NECLA, assuming she was alone in girls' quarters until she was startled by Hailey. "Didn't you go home for the weekend?" Adrienne asked.

Hailey smiled low-spiritedly. "I came back early. I had a disagreement with my parents."

The disagreement had clearly inflicted more pain than Hailey was letting on. Adrienne offered to buy breakfast at a nearby café, hoping to shed the negativity from their weekends before bouncing back into work mode. On their walk, Hailey explained the ongoing friction with her parents since pursuing NECLA in December. The problem over the weekend started when she brought up working a second season—a major grounds for war. "They thought I was getting the last of my *hormones* out of my system, and I was coming home forever in November," Hailey said.

"What did you tell them?" asked Adrienne.

"That's when we started arguing. I asked if we were *Amish* now. I asked if they would *disown* me if I came back next year."

Adrienne was fascinated by their polar existences. She'd been thrown to the wolves when she was just sixteen, and Hailey's parents were still hovering with shepherds' crooks at nearly twenty? Didn't the Deckers realize it was time to cut the cord?

"I *want* to come back next year," Hailey said. "And I want my life to be *my* decision, not theirs."

Adrienne couldn't blame her at all.

As they ate, Hailey asked, "What was it like growing up in the city?"

"The city?" In Adrienne's eyes, she hadn't grown up in the city. Sure, the city limits were a stone's throw from her house, but Westford was classified as a suburb. She tried explaining this to Hailey, but all of Hailey's curiosities—weekly grocery shopping, quick access to public transportation, neighbors that lived right next door—were things Adrienne had always taken for granted. To Hailey, Adrienne was *citified*, raised in an on-the-go culture rife with amenities.

"What was it like growing up in the country?" Adrienne asked.

"*So* different. Nothing like how you grew up."

"Is there anything to do out there?"

"Well … there's an apiary down the road from my house."

"An apiary?"

"It's a bee farm," Hailey said. "They raise bees and make honey."

"That's it? A farm with bees?"

Hailey nodded, furthering her description of Franklin to include shared regional resources and a population smaller than the student body at Adrienne's high school. "I'd love to visit your town one day," Hailey said. "Go to the mall … maybe go to the *real* city!"

Adrienne smiled. "Anytime. I'd be happy to show you around."

While she cleaned her cabins that afternoon, Adrienne couldn't shake the thought that however much working for NECLA meant to her, it surely meant ten times more to Hailey. If given a choice between their upbringings, she'd pick hers without question. She'd already concluded that the Deckers sounded completely unreasonable, making her appreciate *her* parents a little more. Even Raina, for whatever it was worth.

With every port in full swing for tourist season, all the bars the crew had enjoyed before leaving for Maine were now grossly overcrowded. Martha's Vineyard was such a nightmare that they'd stopped going to Oak Bluffs altogether. Instead, whenever they docked at Tisbury Wharf, the crew chipped in for a rack of beer and trekked to Eastville Point Beach to drink on the seawall.

They made an exception for Noah's twentieth birthday, braving the swell of Provincetown tourists to celebrate at the Boatslip Beach Club—

known for its barely-there pool parties and sprawling deck extending over the Cape Cod Bay. Adrienne considered it a clichéd coincidence they were in Provincetown of all places, but Noah said it was *fate*, the universe's present to him.

They'd been to Provincetown once, at the beginning of the season. That night, they'd gone to A-House, where Adrienne had loved watching Noah in his element, dancing and mingling with all the other gay men. But that was before seeing *The Laramie Project*. This time she had a newfound respect for the gay population, for their sacred communities like Provincetown. Not long after seeing the movie, Noah had said, "Now you know why I don't dance with guys in *regular* bars."

Before meeting him, Adrienne was oblivious there were gay hubs across the country. But Noah, forever educating her on the culture, caught her up to speed. "Provincetown is the gay capital of New England," he'd said. "And San Francisco and West Hollywood in California. But, girl, you *have* to see Fort Lauderdale, where my ex lives. I've told you about Devin, right? I'm supposed to visit him after the season."

Adrienne wasn't surprised at how fast gay men flocked to Noah. His looks were fetching, and it amused her when they entered the Boatslip and heads turned about the room. What did stump her was how many everyday-looking people came to Provincetown. There were plenty of obvious patrons—masculine women and lispy men—but so many others she *never* would've suspected.

She sat with Shane at the poolside bar, foregoing their usual Bud Lights and sipping celebratory cocktails as they watched Noah bump and grind in a pack of men, unquestionably the evening's showstopper.

"Are you uncomfortable here?" Adrienne asked, watching Shane's eyes circulate the pool deck.

"I wouldn't be in here if it weren't for Noah."

"Yeah ... he's definitely opened my eyes to the gay community a lot since meeting him."

Shane nodded. "I've never been friends with a gay kid before, but Noah's a cool dude. At first, I didn't wanna live with him. Now, sometimes I forget he's gay."

Adrienne watched Noah gyrate against a shirtless man who looked like Harrison Ford. "I find that a little hard to believe."

The next day, Adrienne walked to the post office to mail gifts and birthday cards. With Wendy's birthday on the fourteenth and her brothers sharing the twenty-first, they were all Leos like Noah. August had always been a costly month.

As she was leaving, Adrienne spotted a stand of postcards depicting images of the Cape. On a whim, she selected one for Aunt Claudette and Dickey, then another for Roman. It had been ages since she'd talked to any of them, and she knew keeping in touch was important. This way, they wouldn't feel forgotten.

Roman

HE GETS A POSTCARD from Adrienne dated August 10, 2007:

> Ro,
> I've been to Boston a half-dozen times
> & their pizza has <u>nothing</u> on ours!
> Loving (almost) every minute of it.
> —Adrienne
> P.S. Hi to Shannon & the kids!

That's nice of her to think of him. Can't say he doesn't miss having her around the place. Her absence makes a difference.

Doesn't sound like Wendy's told her about the divorce yet. Got served by a Marshal on July 16—one day after his and Shannon's seventh wedding anniversary. Now Shannon wants to take him to the cleaners. Alimony on top of child support. Hell, she makes more than he does. She kicked him out, says she's sticking a sale sign in the front yard the second the divorce is final.

"Whatever you want, Shan," he'd conceded. "Just don't keep the kids from me." He knows he's a good dad. He used to think he was a good husband, too.

He's found a small duplex nearby. Rent's reasonable, and there's an extra bedroom for when the kids stay over. Jenni keeps asking when he's gonna let her move in.

"When the time's right," he says, but he doesn't know if it will ever be right. Can't say he didn't see the divorce coming. He just didn't expect it to hurt so much, to leave him feeling so empty.

40

THE MISSED CALL from Raina came on a dreary morning in Newport. Adrienne saw it as she changed uniforms for lunch service. Her stomach flip-flopped as she pondered why Raina was reaching out. Had something happened to her father? To Thany or Aaron? No, she assured herself. Wendy would have called.

She was spacey throughout the lunch shift, hardly speaking to Hailey or Logan, who were serving on the floor with her.

"Is everything okay, Dri?" asked Hailey. "You're being super quiet."

Adrienne didn't want to go into detail. "It's just family stuff."

"Is it your brother? The Marine?"

She appreciated Hailey's concern. Having a brother working as a state trooper was probably just as nerve-racking as having one in the military. "No, he's still on base. I'm just not up for talking about things right now."

"That's okay. I'm here if you need me."

By crew lunch, the gloomy weather had advanced into a quaking midsummer thunderstorm. "Looks like a wet ride to Block Island," Hardigan declared from the officers' table. "I'll announce for the passengers to stay in their cabins if this weather continues while we're underway."

At break time, Adrienne grabbed her cell phone and windbreaker, but the deafening rain thwarted her attempt to return Raina's call on the laz. She tried the dining room next, only to find a group of ladies playing cribbage at the center banquette. The library and pax lounge were also occupied, the nasty weather restricting the passengers from venturing out. Even crew lounge was out of the question. The bottom deck was notorious for poor cell service.

Adrienne optioned calling Raina another time, but waiting would only induce anxiety. All the restraint she maintained elsewhere in life didn't apply to her mother. Ever since Raina had walked out, any unsolicited contact always left Adrienne on edge. Knowing her last resort was to place the call off board, she returned downstairs for her purse. She wasn't sure about finding shelter in Fort Adams State Park, but she had to try.

Marco was manning the gangway, with Max sprawled across his lap, her arms around his neck. Adrienne winced at the scene, a look reciprocated by Max when she turned her head, and they locked eyes.

"May I have that?" Adrienne asked, pointing to the clipboard.

Marco eyed the unremitting rain and pulled an umbrella from the stand beside him. "Here. Better take this, too."

Max glared at Marco in disapproval, then turned to Adrienne. "My stepdad said the boat isn't leaving at three-thirty anymore. He changed the departure time to four-fifteen because of the weather."

Marco furrowed his bushy eyebrows. "When did Peter say that?"

"He just told me after lunch. You know, in case me and Brynnie wanted to go shopping? He said he would mention it during his announcement."

"I wish he'd tell me these things."

Max smiled sweetly at Adrienne. "I just thought you should know!"

It's a little late for you to be doing me any favors, Adrienne thought.

Outside, the rain was brutal. Cherry-size raindrops pelted Adrienne while she fought to open the umbrella. It was cheaply made, quickly flipping inside out. Realizing her best bet at shelter was the Fort Adams Trust, she powerwalked to the colossal fortress and explained her situation to the woman behind the ticket counter. "I just need a roof over my head to make this call. There's nowhere private to talk on my boat."

The woman wore chain-link glasses and a name tag that read *Lydia*. "Go ahead, dear. Feel free to walk around. We don't close until four."

Adrienne found a bench beneath an overhang, fumbling as she dialed Raina's number. It had remained unchanged all these years, still with a Connecticut area code. She grew anxious during the interminable ringing, praying Raina was otherwise occupied. But Raina answered on the last ring. "Hi, Dri!"

"I'm returning your call," Adrienne said. "I was working earlier."

"Thany told me! It sounds like you have a great gig going for you!"

Adrienne ignored her small talk. "You didn't leave a message. Is everything all right?"

"Things are great! In fact, that's why I was calling." Raina took a breath. "I wanted to tell you that Vince and I are getting married."

Adrienne's heart sank. Outside, a sonorous thunder rattled the sky. *What an ideal setting.* "Congratulations," she said dryly. "You must be thrilled."

"Yes, I am, Dri. But the ceremony won't be as meaningful without you and your brothers here. Vince and I are planning for early October."

"This October?"

"Yes. It's a gorgeous time of year in Santa Fe. The air is—"

"You're kidding, right? October's a month and a half away."

"Well, I was thinking—"

"No, you *weren't* thinking," Adrienne said, tensing. "I have a job. I signed on *through* October. And Aaron's down in North Carolina. When's the last time you even talked to him?"

An uneasy silence hung between them. Adrienne visioned Raina pacing around nervously, unsure of what to say next. "I'm sorry, Dri," she finally said. "I do try to give you your space. I just wanted you three to be a part of this moment for me."

"Well, we've had moments we've wanted you there for, too! The world doesn't revolve around what *you* want."

"Maybe we should discuss this another time," Raina said, pulling chute. "I can always postpone things until all three of you can make it. Maybe next October would be better."

"Don't bother," Adrienne said. "I don't think I'd go even if I *were* free." She tossed the phone back in her purse. Raina was getting married? What did a piece of paper that legally bound her and the Accountant even matter at this point? A tax reduction? Insurance benefits?

She wasn't ready to head back to the boat. Maybe the storm was a blessing in disguise, the forty-five-minute delay gracing her extra time to digest Raina's news. She checked her watch. Wendy didn't go to

Giovanni's until 4:30 on Thursdays. She still had time to seek her advice.

Wendy answered on the third ring. Adrienne tried sounding upbeat, but Wendy wasn't buying her fraudulence. "Adrienne? What's wrong?" Adrienne's eyes welled. Just the sound of Wendy's voice brought an unnatural wave of homesickness. Through sobs, she relayed her conversation with Raina.

"Oh my God, Adrienne! I wish I were there to hug you right now! I just ... *wow*. I can't believe she wants to make it official!"

When Adrienne didn't respond, Wendy held no bars offering her honesty. "You know ... I kind of sympathize with her."

"You do? Why?"

"I guess spending so much time at your house recently, I can see why your mom wasn't happy. Your dad ... he can be so distant, Adrienne. I've actually tried putting myself in your mom's shoes a few times, wondering how that must feel for a wife."

"I never thought of it like that before," Adrienne confessed.

"Yeah, well, don't take this the wrong way, but your dad's never been the same since his accident."

Adrienne stared at the ground, watching her teardrops splash against the stonework.

"He's changed, Adrienne. Big time. You know he has. And that must've been *really* hard on your mom."

"You need to go back to school," Adrienne said, forcing herself to laugh. "You'd make a great therapist."

Wendy laughed, too. "But then I'd have to charge you."

"You're right, though," Adrienne said wistfully, remembering how life had been before her father's accident. He had been different, happier almost. "My dad hasn't been the same for a long time. I've just harbored so much anger toward Raina that I never considered her feelings. I always thought she was being selfish."

"I'd try being more sensitive," Wendy suggested. "But I wouldn't take time off for her wedding. You need to look out for *you* first. If Raina wants you guys there, she needs to wait until you're all available. Maybe by then, you'll reconsider."

Adrienne glanced at her watch. 3:45. "I've gotta get back to work," she told Wendy. "But thanks for listening. There are some things I'm just not comfortable telling my boat friends, you know?"

She lit a cigarette and thought over Wendy's take on things. Maybe Raina's nuptials weren't financially related. Maybe Raina wanted a family again, a binding connection that made her feel whole. She remembered the spring she was six when she'd helped Raina paint a wooden marker for the front yard. Raina had painted cardinals and blue jays while Adrienne practiced her letters, writing *The Deneaus*. The marker hadn't moved since they'd staked it in the ground fifteen years ago, and the paint was now peeling apart, just like their family. Maybe Raina wanted a new sign in her front yard in the desert.

The rainstorm had only worsened during Adrienne's time inside the Trust. Walking back toward the dock proved challenging among the heavy winds, leaving her no choice but to use the umbrella as a shield. She pulled her hood tighter, keeping her head down and praying the shower would be free upon her return, that she'd have five minutes to regroup before running upstairs to set up Cocktail Hour with Hailey.

Adrienne yanked the umbrella to her side as she neared the dock, vainly hoping no one aboard had seen her looking so foolish from the boat's windows. But when she looked ahead, the *Amelia* was nowhere to be seen. Was she at the wrong dock? She turned in a three-sixty, realizing she *wasn't* at the wrong dock at all. With raindrops machine-gunning the water before her, Adrienne was flooded with a sick revelation she didn't want to accept—the boat was *gone*.

She charged down the Fort Adams Bay Walk, straining her eyes as the rain besieged her visibility. She stopped to catch her breath—cursing herself for not trying to quit smoking—and squinted into the distance. But standing before one of the most supreme panoramas in all of New England, Adrienne had a front-row seat to nothing but the famed Newport Bridge.

She rechecked her watch. 3:59. One minute until she had to be in the lounge for Cocktail Hour. Frantically, she grabbed her cell phone and called NECLA. "*Lorna?*" she yelled against the wind. "This is Adrienne Deneau from the *Amelia!*"

"Oh, Adrienne! What's up, hon?"

"I'm in Newport! At the Fort Adams Trust, and the boat is gone!"

"Oh gahd! All right, hon … gimme a few minutes to get through to Connie."

Adrienne peered at her clothes as she listened to a sales ad. She was sopping wet, the rain having permeated her jeans, windbreaker, and everything beneath all the way through. Her Adidas had oceans inside of them, squishing terribly against her socks. Helpless and waterlogged, she stared at her shoes until Lorna returned. "Adrienne? Bad news, hon. The *Amelia*'s halfway to Block Island, and Capt. Hahdigan won't turn her around. You'll hafta get there on ya own."

What? Block Island was bridgeless, isolated in the middle of the Sound. "I'm already *on* an island, Lorna. How am I supposed to get to another one without a boat?"

"You're gonna hafta take the ferry. You got money on ya?"

"*Yes*," Adrienne said crossly.

"Good. Here, lemme give ya the address."

Writing down anything in the rain was pointless, so Adrienne memorized the address Lorna recited—39 America's Cup Avenue.

"Call me back when ya get a ticket," Lorna instructed. "I'll stick around the office until I hear from ya."

Adrienne slammed her phone shut. How was she supposed to get to the ferry? She was stranded on a peninsula with no clue how to get anywhere! Across the green, Lydia from the Trust struggled with her umbrella on her way to the parking lot. "Hey!" Adrienne called, starting to sprint. "Wait a minute!" She ran fast for how much rainwater was weighing her down, startling Lydia as she reached her Volvo.

"Oh my!" Lydia gasped, taking a moment to recognize Adrienne. "What happened to you, dear?"

"My boat left without me!" Adrienne panted. "Can you please drive me to the ferry on America's Cup Avenue? I can pay you."

"Oh, for Pete's sake!" Lydia shooed her hand at the mention of reciprocation. "Of course I'll give you a ride!" But at the ferry terminal, Adrienne was further distraught to see a sign indicating the last ferry to Block Island had left at half past noon. "Why don't you try the visitors center?" Lydia suggested. "They're very nice inside. They should be able to help you get to Block Island."

Adrienne thanked Lydia and waved her goodbye, then walked over to the visitors center. Fortunately, it was still open.

The visitor reps looked alarmed at the sight of her. After she explained her predicament, one said, "The next ferry doesn't leave until a quarter of ten tomorrow. Can we help you find accommodations?"

Adrienne called Lorna back. "I'm at the visitors center," she explained. "The next ferry doesn't leave until morning, and they're offering to help find me a hotel."

"I'll pass the message on for ya," said Lorna. "And, uh … Adrienne?"

"Yeah?"

"Capt. Hahdigan's got a real stick up his keistah about this. He's gonna wanna talk to ya tomorrah."

Adrienne heaved a sigh. "You got it."

"Good luck, hon."

The visitor reps volunteered to call the hotel next door, but the waterfront views implied the accommodations far exceeded Adrienne's price range. When she asked about the least expensive hotel in the area, they suggested the Motel 6, noting she'd have to take a cab unless she felt like further bearing the storm.

"I've had all the rain I can handle for one day," Adrienne admitted. "A cab sounds great."

41

THIRTY MINUTES LATER, Adrienne was staring at a king-size bed on the ground floor of the Motel 6. With taxes and fees, the room had set her back a cool sixty dollars. She wrung her clothes out and spread them over the heater. After a hot shower, she wrapped herself in a towel and sat on the edge of the bed. *My stepdad said the boat isn't leaving at three-thirty anymore. I just thought you should know!*

Max. Adrienne wanted to kill her.

What an awful thing to do to someone, regardless of their bad blood. Adrienne couldn't even imagine putting Jenni in this position. Not that the idea wouldn't have entertained her, but Adrienne had a conscience—something Max was devoid of. She wondered about Marco. Had he been in on it, too? As an officer, Adrienne hoped he hadn't. And now she was supposed to answer to Hardigan tomorrow? What was she supposed to tell him? *Your darling stepdaughter lied about the departure time to leave me stranded on Aquidneck Island?*

Without her phone charger, there was no point wasting what remained of her battery by calling anyone. Instead, Adrienne turned on the television, feeling guilty she was watching MTV while the rest of the stews were hard at work. It was 5:30. She should be helping them set up for dinner and wondered what they'd been told, deciding that although she wasn't going to tell the officers the truth about what happened, she had full intentions of alerting her friends of Max's deviance once she was back on board.

Three hours later, she was awakened by the nagging vibration of her cell phone. She answered it without opening her eyes.

"Hey, girl!" belted Noah. "Where are you?"

Adrienne sat up, realizing she'd dozed off. "Newport."

"Where in Newport?"

"At the Motel 6."

"Ew," he cringed. "I would *never*."

"It's called being budget-conscious, Noah."

"Okay, okay, enough of that. *Girl*, how did you miss the boat?"

"Well, if you *really* want to know ..." Adrienne began, briefing him.

Noah gasped contemptuously. "Oh, hell no! Ursula left you marooned? *On purpose?* You need to kick that bitch in the snatch!" He laughed daringly, then assured Adrienne the other girls were only concerned for her well-being, not upset for taking on her workload.

When they hung up, Adrienne placed a take-out order from a nearby restaurant. The storm had finally run its course, and she redressed in her damp clothes to pick up her food. She'd just returned to the motel room when her phone rang again, this time from a Rhode Island number she didn't recognize.

"Hey, Adrienne ... it's Shane."

Shane? How did he know her phone number?

"I asked Noah for your number," he said. "I wanted to check on ya."

It was comforting to hear his voice. "I'm doing all right."

"Noah said you're stuck in Newport?"

"I'm at the Motel 6."

"Sounds fun. Wish I was there to keep ya company."

Me too, Adrienne thought. She told Shane about Max's treachery, asking him not to repeat the details. "I'm not going to tell the officers," she said.

"Wow. And she's gonna get away with it scot-free," he mused.

"Yeah. I can't wait to get reamed out by Hardigan tomorrow."

Shane chuckled. "I'll protect ya."

"I'll be okay. At least I'm not getting fired."

Shane's lighter clicked in the background. "If ya did, I'd quit. Then we could find another boat to work on."

Adrienne waited for his laughter. When it didn't come, she felt strangely warmed by the sincerity of his comment. "I have to save my battery," she finally said. "I'll see you tomorrow, Shane."

"Sounds good," he said. "Can't wait."

Yeah, she thought. *Me either.*

Marco

HE PULLS MAX into their cabin after his shift. "What the hell's the matter with you? Why did you lie to that girl about the departure time?"

Max glares at him—that look he *hates*—and crosses her arms. "Because she had it *coming*, Marco! She's been starting with me since the yard."

He doesn't want to hear it. Not this time. "I'm an *officer*, Max. The crew needs to trust me! That girl Adrienne probably thinks I was behind your little prank, too."

"She won't say anything, babe. She knows better. Besides, who would she tell? Peter? Connie? *You?*"

"She better not start anything with me because I'll be looking at *you* if she does."

"She *won't*."

He shakes his head. "Don't pull any more shit. There's seven weeks until New York, and I don't need extra attention while I'm doing business for Frankie."

Max hears the worry in his voice. "I'm sorry, babe. You know I don't want anything to go wrong for you. Especially not in New York."

She gives him that *other* look. That wide-eyed look with those parted lips. The same look that's pumped his veins since he was sixteen. He swoops her into his lap. "Good. You can be a real hellion sometimes, you know that?"

Max leans in and catches his lower lip with her teeth. "Don't worry, babe. The next time there's a problem, I promise to keep it between me and *her*."

***

THE HI-SPEED FERRY got Adrienne to Block Island by eleven o'clock. She ran into Nicky at the gangway. "Hey, lady! Heard we left ya high and dry yestahday!"

"More like sea level and soaked," she corrected him.

She was changing her contacts in girls' quarters when Logan, Hailey, and Katherine returned from housekeeping.

"Don't worry about your cabins," Logan said. "Noah's LD today. He did them for you."

A true friend, Adrienne thought, knowing she would've done the same for him.

Up in the dining room, Adrienne encountered Hardigan leaving the coffee station. "*Ms. Deneau*," he said stiffly. "I was just made aware you were back on board."

"Yes, Captain."

"Please, then, come join me in the wheelhouse."

Adrienne followed him to the top deck. She had never been inside the wheelhouse and was surprised at its compactness. There were dials and switches everywhere, monitors and radios whose purposes were alien to her. She stood reluctantly as Hardigan settled in the pilot's chair. "I understand you missed the boat yesterday," he said.

"Yes, sir, I did."

"Would you care to explain how that happened?"

"I'm sorry, Captain. I wanted to check out the Fort Adams Trust, and I lost track of time."

Hardigan sampled his coffee. "Ms. Deneau, do you know where the daily itinerary is posted?"

"Yes ... of course I do."

"Then there shouldn't have been any confusion about when the boat was leaving port, am I correct?"

"No, Captain, I suppose there shouldn't have been."

He set his coffee on the bridge. "Ms. Deneau, are you familiar with Atlantic Embassies?"

Adrienne shook her head.

"No? As I understand it, Atlantic Embassies *terminates* crew members who miss the boat ... that they aren't even allowed to return for their belongings, which, I assume, is a reminder to the others to be timely."

Adrienne steeled her rising anger. "Again, Captain, I'm *sorry*. I made a mistake."

Hardigan nodded. "It is to your benefit that Ms. Sanbourne doesn't believe in termination under these circumstances but prefers her captains to issue discipline at their discretion. That said, I'll be docking a full day's wages, tips included. With an absence of twenty hours, I see no reason you should be paid for services you didn't provide, do you?"

"No, Captain, I don't."

"Very well, then," Hardigan dismissed her. "I'll inform the office we've agreed on a consequence."

When Adrienne returned to the dining room, Max smiled knowingly, ensuring Adrienne recognized yesterday was no accident. Though Adrienne tried not to let people's actions affect her, this time it was difficult not to feel dispirited. The events of the past twenty-four hours had just been too much. Raina's call. Max's trick. Unnecessarily losing her hard-earned money. The combination of everything was enough to bring anyone down.

One of these days, Adrienne thought as she passed by Max. *One of these days, everything will come full circle, and you'll get what you deserve.*

Connie

THE TENSION between the girls is palpable. Adrienne isn't talking, but *she'd* seen Max's face when she'd told the stews Adrienne missed the boat. Smug satisfaction. A sick glee.

It's been nearly a week now, and she *knows* Max was responsible. Somehow ... some way ... Max did this. But why? That's *her* question. Adrienne doesn't cause any trouble. What could she have possibly done for Max to plot such a scheme? What has anyone ever done?

Bev

HER WEEKLY CHECK-IN with Connie leaves much to be desired. "I don't care for your tone regarding Peter's stepdaughter and the Cavanaugh girl. Not in the progress reports, and not when we speak. I've *told* you ... unless they're jeopardizing my company, their positions are of absolute permanence until I say otherwise."

The call leaves her peeved. She went through this with Mattie last year and laid into him just the same. If it weren't for Peter stepping up in the sixties, there wouldn't *be* a company. Every day, she hears her father's reminder—*We owe Peter everything for carrying out your brother's legacy.*

Countless times, she's tried imagining Dawson fulfilling the fleet captain position that was built for him, but after forty-four years, it's too hard to fathom. Dawson would've turned sixty-four in June, but she can only picture a teenager leaving the family home in 1963. Freshly recruited by the navy, never to be seen again.

She's never missed her yearly visit to Portsmouth. She hires a boat to take her into the waters every April, the same waters where her parents' ashes were scattered after their deaths, knowing one day, her remains will be spread at sea, too. She's a tough bird, still plenty of years left, but Andrew and Mattie have her instructions just as well—the very instructions that will be handed over to the Hardigan family should another tragedy ever strike her own.

42

THE LAST WEEK in August, Michelle Hardigan boarded the boat to join her husband on the final New England Newcomer trip. "She was here last year, too," Logan explained. "I totally thought it'd be worse, that we'd have to wait on her hand and foot, but she didn't expect anything extra from us."

Thank God, Adrienne thought. Catering to Max's mother was the last thing she wanted to do.

"Don't worry," said Logan. "Basically, she just ignores us."

Looking at Michelle Hardigan was like looking at Max twenty years from now.

"Gold digger?" Noah sniffed. The others turned inconspicuously. Max's mother was at least two decades younger than Hardigan and positively stunning. She had the same sculpted face and sapphire eyes as Max and equally great blonde hair. She laughed spiritedly as Max jetéd across the pax lounge to greet her, her white-as-cotton smile radiating the room.

"Gawk at Ursula's maker all you want," said Noah. "I'll be drooling over that hottie over *there*." He pointed to a tanned thirtysomething standing beside a woman in a wide-brimmed hat. "Tell me he doesn't look just like Zack Morris!"

The guy *was* a dead ringer for Mark-Paul Gosselaar, more so from the cheesy Hawaiian movie than *Saved by the Bell*'s early years.

"I'll totally second that!" Logan admired dreamily. "He's gorgeous!"

"Is he a passenger?" Hailey and Katherine asked in unison. There hadn't been a single guest under sixty the whole season.

"He has a suitcase," Adrienne identified.

Noah patted his pompadour. "Ugh, finally some eye candy after all these wrinkles and age spots. I hope he sits in my sections for meals. You already *know* I'll serve him the secret menu!"

Adrienne looked at Noah hopelessly. "Hate to break it to you, but I'm pretty sure he's straight."

During Cocktail Hour, they learned the younger passenger had booked the cruise to celebrate his widowed mother's birthday. He drew lots of attention from the female guests, many of whom offered pictures of their granddaughters once word got out that he was eligible.

"I feel like I'm on another boat tonight," Adrienne murmured to Hailey. "The energy on this trip is so different."

Hailey nodded. "It's weird having that guy here. And Max's mom."

"Yeah …" Adrienne said, watching Hardigan parade his wife around the lounge. "I just hope Logan's right about her not giving us a hard time. You know what they say about the apple and the tree …"

Brynne

SHE'S BEEN EXPECTING Michelle's visit all season. As far back as she remembers, Peter has always brought Michelle on the boats during the last week of August. When Max and Desi were younger, the Hardigans would hire a nanny for the week, instructing them to leave Petey alone and care for *her* in his place. She and Max would spend their days lounging poolside, reading *YM* and *Teen People*, and their nights staying up late ordering trashy movies, which Max always blamed on the nanny when the cable bill arrived.

The summer they were twelve, she'd asked Michelle if Max could spend the last week of August at her house instead. "Desi can come, too," she'd offered. "I have a trundle and a daybed in my room."

Michelle's smile never faltered. "That's *very* sweet of you, Brynne, but Peter and I couldn't impose on your mother. Caring for three girls would be too much to ask."

She hadn't realized at the time that was Michelle's way of saying she wouldn't *dream* of leaving her daughters with Maureen. Who knew what behaviors they might learn from East Greenwich's resident whore?

In Boston, Michelle takes them to lunch on Newbury Street. "How is your mother, Brynne?" she asks, stirring her spritzer. "I've hardly seen her at the club all summer."

She doesn't know how Maureen is one way or the other but does know Michelle's inquiry is only meant to be courteous, not genuine. She suddenly wonders if Peter and Michelle actively participate in all the *Peyton Place* gossip back home. Women tell their hairdressers everything, and she suspects Michelle holds the key to East Greenwich with all the secrets that enter Salon Medusa. But before now she's never considered the rumors that must circulate the yacht club scene. The Hardigans have been members long enough to know the talk that goes on there, which likely includes a register of unflattering hearsay about her mother.

***

HAVING MICHELLE HARDIGAN on board proved to work in the crew's favor. Not only was she not demanding of them, but her presence put Hardigan in a noticeably better mood.

"Lady Hahdigan can move in for the rest'a the season if ya ask me!" Nicky said one night. "Capt. hasn't ridden my ass since she got here!" He started mocking Hardigan's most recurrent orders. "'Secure ya cleat ropes, O'Hara!' 'Get me the engine room log, O'Hara!' 'Mop the goddamn decks, O'Hara!'"

Noah smirked. "One guess says why."

"Why?" asked Hailey.

"Really, girl?"

"Really! I've noticed, too! Why has Hardigan been so nice this week?"

Noah laughed deviously. "Because he's been on a dry spell! Now, I bet he blows two loads a day. Her, *too*, the way she's always smiling."

Hailey's naivety erupted when she realized what Noah was saying. She clasped her hands over her mouth. "Oh my gosh!"

"Girl, I bet he gives it to her *hard*," Noah continued. "All those months away from each other? No wonder he has the hull to himself! No one down there to hear them? They're probably *hella* loud when they're going at it!"

"I can't listen to this," said Adrienne. The image of Hardigan and Max's mother having sex was the *last* thing she wanted in her mind. Even if it was the reason Hardigan had eased up on the crew all week.

"Good for him, though," said Noah. "At least *someone* on this boat is getting laid. I thought there'd be hella booty calls this season!"

Logan

THE JOKE'S ON NOAH, because Hardigan isn't the only one getting lucky this trip. She was game the second the Zack Morris look-alike passed her a note during dinner. *Drinks later?* Totally. Besides, she hasn't had sex since January, when she'd hit it off with a guy in Cancun. Sure, bedding a passenger is frowned upon, but this guy is *so* arousing. "I'll be off at eight-thirty," she whispers when she drops off dessert. "Let's meet at the end of the wharf."

After work, she slips on heels and a sundress and splashes herself in Flowerbomb. It turns out the look-alike's name is Craig. Thirty-three. An entrepreneur from Phoenix. "I haven't stopped thinking about you since I got here," he tells her over margaritas. "Let's go somewhere private."

She leads him to a secluded strip on the beach, where they tussle in the sand. He unzips her dress and eases the straps down, kissing her breasts while she gives him a hand job. When Craig rolls on a condom, she takes control, biting his shoulder as she grinds against him.

The next night, he suggests they get daring and do it in the elevator. She barely hits the stop button before he drives into her from behind. When they're finished, her legs quiver so fiercely she can hardly stand.

She doesn't say goodbye when Craig and his mother disembark in Providence. Why bother? Some people are only in your life for stolen moments. She'd known right away that he'd be one of them.

Wendy

SHE'S THOUGHT a lot about Adrienne's comment about returning to school. Honestly, she's been considering it for a while. It's a tough decision, though. If she'd stuck with CCSU the first time, she would've graduated with her bachelor's in May. Going back now means she'll be one of the oldest undergrads there. But she's already got thirty credits, and who says she has to go back full-time?

She decides to go for it and sets up an appointment with an advisor. Classes start next week, so her options are limited, but she finds a history course on Monday nights and a film class on Tuesday and Thursday mornings. Neither interferes with Giovanni's, which is good because she's just started waitressing and still can't believe how much money she's making. Or saving!

She tries calling Adrienne with her news, but gets her voicemail. Hours later, Adrienne responds with a text—*Long day, but I have the night off on Labor Day. Talk then?*

I'll be free all day! she texts back.

But Adrienne's become such a phantom that she wonders if she'll even remember. It's sad it's come down to this. They used to be so close.

September 2007

43

IT WASN'T UNTIL after arriving in East Bay on Thursday that the stews learned Connie and Hardigan were taking the upcoming trip off. Hardigan was leaving with Michelle that afternoon, presumably back to East Greenwich, and Connie was flying to meet her daughter in Fort Lauderdale.

"Girl, I'm jealous," griped Noah. "That's where Devin lives. We need to go down there when the season's over."

Personally, Adrienne thought it would've been nice if Connie and Hardigan had given the stews a heads-up, just as a courtesy. Instead, they were caught off guard when Lorna arrived with a rolling suitcase to fill in as cruise director, and an off-duty captain named Knowles showed up to replace Hardigan. Knowles was the same height as Hardigan, with short white hair and a toothy smile beneath his mustache. Together with the other officers, he and Lorna would oversee the upcoming Bay State Colony cruise.

This will be different, Adrienne thought, walking over to say hello to Lorna.

"Adrienne!" Lorna said. "How ah ya?" Lorna was all bubbles on the surface, but Adrienne detected an abnormal anxiousness. She was about to ask if everything was okay when Lorna leaned forward and whispered, "I just want ya to know I felt real bad about havin' to dock ya pay. Capt. Hahdigan's a real piece of work, isn't he?"

Adrienne chuckled stiffly. That was one way of putting it.

***

Connie

THANK GOD NECLA offers vacations for the officers. This season sure hasn't been what she'd expected, and she *needs* this break. She and Macy are off to Fort Lauderdale for the week, their annual trip before school starts. Usually, they visit with Mattie, but he's out of town, and it's just as well. Instead, they'll rent a beach cabana and order frozen drinks delivered on trays. This year, she'll be ordering *doubles*.

When she meets Macy in Florida, she can't believe what her daughter's done to her hair. Her silky strawberry-blonde hair is twisted in dreadlocks. *Dreadlocks!*

"What's wrong, Mom? Don't you like it?" Macy asks.

"No, baby, I don't."

"Mom, it's Colorado. No one cares what I look like there."

"Don't tell me that, Mace. Tell me it's just a phase."

"Okay, it's just a phase."

That afternoon, while they're lying on the beach, Macy asks about NECLA.

"It's been a headache, baby. Lots of headaches."

"What's it like working with Max Hardigan and Brynne Cavanaugh?"

She gives Macy a *look*. "You weren't kidding about Max. The devil sure broke the mold when he made her."

"What about Brynne?"

She's more thoughtful about this answer, especially after Bev laid into her last month. Her opinion about Max will never change, but the truth is, there isn't much that's negative about Brynne. "She's quiet, actually," she tells Macy. "Very reserved."

"Did you ever find out if she's a prostitute?"

"No, baby. And if you want my opinion, I don't think that rumor was ever true."

***

There were pros and cons to having Knowles and Lorna on board. The pro was that Knowles was a super nice guy. Right from the start, he made a point to acquaint himself with the crew. And when the passengers arrived, he announced he'd be giving daily tours of the wheelhouse and eating dinner with different groups at night. The con was that Lorna had no idea what she was doing. Starting with embarkation day, when she'd fumbled over the welcome speech, it was evident there would be problems.

"Girl, this is a shit show," Noah had whispered to Adrienne.

"Yeah …" Adrienne was stunned by Lorna's fear of public speaking, especially considering how friendly she usually presented herself. When it came to minding the stews, Lorna did fine, constantly double-checking the folder of notes Connie had left to aid her. But addressing the passengers as a group caused her to freeze up and stutter.

On the second night, Lorna began panicking when the Activity Hour lecturer canceled in New Bedford. "What am I gonna do?" she quailed to Adrienne. "I can't entahtain these guys for two hours!"

Adrienne popped a DVD into the player while Lorna ran to the cruise director's office. When Adrienne checked on her, Lorna was in the middle of a breakdown, shaking and blubbering at Connie's desk. "Oh gahd, Adrienne, do I evah wish I hadn't agreed to this!"

Adrienne was so confused. "Didn't you used to work on the boats back in the day?"

"Hon, I was a stew, for cryin' out loud! I was nevah a cruise directah!"

"What about all this other time you've been with the company?"

"Hon, I do the payroll! Numbahs ah my thing, not people!"

Adrienne sympathized with Lorna. She figured being a cruise director was probably more stressful than it seemed, making sure everyone was looked after twenty-four seven. But for all Lorna knew how to do in the office, it didn't show on board the *Amelia*. She rushed through turndown service, scrambled with boarding the passengers on the excursion vans, and was overall scatterbrained. Adrienne recalled Nicky's words from back in June, words she'd thought were just a joke at the time: *That's why Bev leaves Lorna in the office.*

If Knowles noticed Lorna's incompetence, he didn't say, but on Monday, some passengers expressed disappointment during breakfast, telling Lorna they thought she was disorganized. Lorna ran back to the cruise director's office and started bawling all over again. "I don't know how Connie does it! I just wanna be back in my cornah doin' the books! I wasn't cut out for this!"

Adrienne was curious. "What has the company done when the other cruise directors took vacations?"

Lorna honked into a tissue. "Mattie—Bev's son, ya know—he used to work through the whole season. And before that? Gahd, I think Bev used to fill in. But that was before Cecil died, ya know?"

Adrienne had no idea.

After lunch, a solution dawned on her. It might not be the best idea, and it certainly wasn't her place, but doing *something* was better than not. She caught Katherine in their room, filling her in on Lorna's insecurities. "Is there anything you can do to, you know, help her?"

Katherine shone with the same enthusiasm from when they'd first met. "Of course! Did she ask for *my* help specifically?"

"Well, no. But I'm sure you can see that she's struggling. And with your degrees and everything …"

"You mean like assisting her with Activity Hour and the excursions? Aiding her with general hospitality oversight?"

Adrienne shrugged. "She'd probably appreciate anything you can do."

Suddenly, Katherine's vigor disappeared. "I don't know. I don't think Connie would approve."

"Probably not, but Lorna is so out of her element, and we still have five days left. If you follow our routine, everything should be fine. Just don't go overboard … no pun intended."

Lorna was beside herself when they approached her with Adrienne's idea. "You girls ah so sweet, ya know that? I've been such a Nervous Nellie ovah here."

From that moment forward, Katherine was by Lorna's side whenever possible. And when Katherine asked to be the permanent T&A Stew for the rest of the trip, nobody balked. If Katherine wanted to work until ten o'clock every night, everyone was happy to let her.

For the next five mornings, Adrienne could hear Katherine climbing out of their bunk early to help Lorna buy the newspapers. During breakfast, she'd stand beside Lorna, exuberantly engaging the passengers about that day's local tour options. Katherine was completely at ease, excelling for being thrown into the role.

Her organizational and public speaking skills even made an impression on Knowles. "You've got a real knack for this, girlie," he said, patting Katherine's shoulder. "Never know … if you stick around long enough, Bev might give you your own boat someday."

On the last night of the trip, Knowles praised Katherine during the farewell dinner. "Let's give a round of applause for Miss Katherine Fowler, ladies and gents! She's done a tremendous job assisting Lorna with your cruise this week!"

The passengers, who'd all gotten to know and love Katherine, applauded loudly. Katherine's face flushed with joy as she waved at them with one hand, the other squeezing Lorna's tightly. Together, they'd found success in a struggle. Two fish out of water, working as their own little team.

Katherine

THERE! She's finally gotten the chance to prove herself! To show that her College Knowledge *can* pay off! And how about Captain Knowles's comment about having her own boat one day? How exciting! She finds an internet café to email Professor Dahl. Then she calls her father. "I got a standing ovation, Daddy! They all loved me!"

For once, he doesn't yell at her. "You see what happens when you tough through life, Katherine? *These* are the calls your mother and I want to receive. Not that nonsense about your coworkers!"

But the conversation shifts when her mother gets on the line. "Have you formally apologized to your colleagues yet, sweetheart?"

When she admits she hasn't, her mother sighs. "Katherine, people will always remember how you made them feel. It's a testament to your character to recognize their feelings and apologize if you've hurt them. They'll always remember that, too."

She thinks of Noah's dirty looks and how Nicky hasn't spoken to her for months and decides her mother is right. But she'll do it *her* way … when she's better prepared. Let her enjoy her victory tonight before she figures out the right words. She's making baby steps, working on herself first, then her relationship with the crew.

* * *

THREE DAYS AFTER Connie and Hardigan returned, Shane found Adrienne on the laz in Boston. "Wanna go out with me tonight?" he asked.

"Where are you going?"

The same giddy smile from their night off in Rockland inched across Shane's face. "Not sure yet, but it's my birthday and I wanna hang out with ya."

Technically, you're not doing anything wrong, Adrienne. Okay, okay, maybe Wendy was right. Maybe she should enjoy the night with Shane instead of beating herself up about it. Was going out on the town *really* the end of the world? "Sure, I'd like that," she said. "Happy birthday."

They decided to take in Rob Zombie's *Halloween* remake, walking to the old theatre on Tremont Street. Adrienne was glued to her seat, fascinated by the spin put on the original. Only the sex scenes made her uncomfortable, reiterating that she sat just mere inches from the one person she desired a deeper intimacy with. But they were only thoughts, and she pushed them away. She didn't have another choice.

After, they stopped at a bar, where Adrienne bought a pitcher of Bud Light. As they drank, she shared how Wendy's newspaper had started all of this, leading her to NECLA and changing her life. "Can you believe that ten months ago I didn't even know this company existed? And look at me now—scrubbing toilets while I sail around New England!"

"Are ya glad ya took the job?" Shane asked.

"I am. I couldn't do this forever, but right now, I'm happy. I love the water and all the places I'm seeing. I love that I'm learning so much about life." Adrienne smiled, humbled by her good fortune that Bev had selected *her* for one of the highly coveted stewardess positions. "What about you? Are you happy you're here?"

Shane leaned back reflectively. "There's nothin' besides my daughter keepin' me home anymore. How I've been feelin' lately, I'd do this 'til my body couldn't take it anymore if it weren't for her."

Adrienne stayed quiet, breaking down his words. Was he trying to communicate something indirectly? Proposition her in some way? Was this an opening? "What about your wife?" she asked tentatively.

But unlike their conversation at the breakwater, an awkwardness now loitered between them. Shane's eyes bore into hers, and Adrienne sensed a strong reluctance. She couldn't place her finger on it, but something was off. "I can't leave, Adrienne," he finally said.

She remained still, stifling her confusion. Was she missing something? What were Shane's motives, exactly? Why had he wanted to spend the night together? She had so many questions but couldn't summon the nerve to ask them. She turned the focus on herself. What was *she* doing here? Out for drinks with someone's husband? On his birthday of all days? But only one answer came readily. *Because this feels right. It feels like I was meant to meet him. It feels like he's supposed to be a part of my life.*

44

ON SEPTEMBER 18, the stews watched in confusion as Max and Marco passed through the dining room with their luggage. "See you next week, man," Marco said, fist-bumping Nicky at the gangway. He gave a courtesy nod to Connie and walked off board with Max.

"Where are they going?" Hailey asked.

"Vacation," said Connie. "They'll be back on the twenty-fourth."

"*Vacation?*" Katherine parroted. "For six days?"

"Marco's an officer," Connie reminded them. "He's allowed vacation time."

"But *Max* isn't an officer. Why is she entitled to time off just because she dates him?"

"Katherine, I don't know what kind of arrangement they have with Bev, and I don't ask. But if it makes everyone feel better, Max's time off isn't paid."

"Like that matters," Adrienne said under her breath.

"I thought you'd be happy, Adrienne," Connie said slyly. "After that farce in Newport, I thought you'd be over the moon to see her go."

For the past month, Connie had been pressing Adrienne for details about missing the boat, but whenever she brought it up, Adrienne was quick to shrug her off. Who knew what telling Connie the truth would bring, especially if Bev caught wind of it and decided she and Max could no longer work together? Suppose Bev terminated her? There was no way she'd risk not finishing the season just to expose Max. Refusing to be swayed, Adrienne said, "I think this next trip will be a nice break for *all* of us."

"Whoa there!" Noah said suddenly. "Does this mean we're all gonna have extra rooms to clean? Or are you gonna make whoever's LD clean Ursula's rooms every day, or what?"

"Actually," said Connie, "you'll have a replacement stew joining you this trip."

"Who?" everyone asked at once.

Nicky cleared his throat from the gangway. "You're lookin' at him."

"*You're* going to be a stew, Nicky?" gasped Hailey.

"That's right, lady! And everyone bettah treat me right, or I'll abandon ship!"

"Oh, we will, girl!" Noah laughed mischievously. "Don't you worry about that!"

With Nicky replacing Max for the penultimate Coastal Cape Cod & the Islands trip, a yard worker named Brennan was brought in to cover the engineer position. And to fill in for Marco, Hardigan's son, Petey, came aboard.

Hailey shook her head at the uncanniness. "Holy smokes! He looks just like Hardigan!"

"He *does*," Adrienne seconded, observing the younger clone. But neither Brennan nor Petey proved very sociable. According to Connie, Bev had difficulty getting the yard guys to leave their families when the boats were short-staffed. And even though Petey was single, he was content working as an assistant harbormaster and never fond of being uprooted.

Their indifference was overshadowed by the lively energy Nicky brought to the steward department. *He* fit right in but playfully warned the others not to get comfortable, that he was only doing this as a favor to Bev. Adrienne thought it was too bad Nicky wouldn't consider a department change. For once, everyone was working as a cohesive unit—how things should have been all along.

Stew work wasn't his forte, but Nicky had plenty of heart. He kept up with the girls and Noah, never complaining about the monotonous tasks. And though his napkin folds were too loose, and his silverware was spaced awkwardly, they'd gladly pick him over Max any day. He did show promise with how well he cleaned cabins, and even Hardigan remarked in his own ass-like way. "Not bad, O'Hara. Can't foul up stew work any more than forgetting to reel in the cleat ropes, I see."

During galley cleanup, Nicky donned an apron and took control of Noah's iPod, scrolling until he found music he liked. "None'a that Nelly Furtado shit this week!" he'd declared the first night. "We're gonna listen to my boy!" He began playing Eminem at a questionable volume, bopping along as he washed dishes.

The next night, Noah beat Nicky to the iPod and said, "Don't worry, girl! I have the *perfect* rap song for you tonight!"

Everyone dissolved into gales of laughter when Noah turned on Skee-Lo's "I Wish," singing the chorus as he danced around Nicky.

Nicky took the song in stride, despite the lyrics being a gibe at his height. He grabbed a dishrag and chased Noah around the galley while Noah stooped and dodged like he was in *The Matrix*. "Ya wish ya had a *girl*, aye, Noah? That's not what I heard!"

Nicky

SO, Noah's got jokes, aye? He *used* to wish he were tallah, but he's learned to live with bein' five-five ovah the years. And he won't front, sometimes he does wish he had a girl. Someone to talk about life with, a nice wahm body to hold at night. He asks Brynnie if she's still with that boyfriend. When she nods, he says, "As long as he treats ya right, Brynnie. You're a good girl. I know it."

He'd paht oceans for a chance with 'er, but he can respect that she's involved. Don't mean he can't have his own fun in the meantime. He's had a few hookups already this season. A waitress in Salem. A bahtendah in Gloucestah. Hell, there was even a summah girl in Hyannis who brought him back to 'er rental and gave him a blowie.

He tells Brynnie to let him know if 'er situation changes. "I'll always be good to ya, Brynnie," he promises. "Ya can count on that."

Brynne

SHE FEELS SO LOST without Max on board. Not talking to anyone besides Nicky, not having anyone to hang out with. It feels like the other stews hate her, though she can't pinpoint a reason as to why. She's never been cruel or unkind to them, but they've hardly spoken either. She envies their camaraderie. At least if one of them went on vacation, the others would still have friends left.

Last year, when Max and Marco took off the third week of September, she'd asked for the trip off, too. Mattie couldn't say yes fast enough, waving them both off the gangway. *You girls have a fab time now!*

She'd spent the week with Gordon in the Hamptons, him reading the *Globe* while she read her novels. They'd dined at the finest restaurants in the evenings, returning to the mirrored canopy bed and rolling around for hours. She still doesn't know which of those nights she'd become pregnant, but when she found out three weeks later, she'd sworn Max to secrecy, planning to tell Gordon only once they returned home.

His response was quick-remedied. "Don't worry, love. We'll take care of it."

She was shocked, assuming he'd want to keep the baby. There were plenty of men in their fifties becoming first-time fathers. But Gordon resisted, claiming if he wanted children, he would've had them by now. When she shared that she'd already had an abortion at fourteen and didn't want another, Gordon didn't empathize as she'd expected, shifting his eyes and saying, "I wish I'd known that before, love."

Before what, exactly?

She bawled when the ultrasound revealed she was ten weeks. Her baby had a heartbeat. Her baby had fingers and toes. She'd almost changed her mind then but knew Gordon would hold the decision over her forever, making her and the baby feel unwanted and burdensome. Now, when she'd called him in August to ask about taking time off in September, he'd seemed disinterested. "Maybe next year, love. The Hamptons can be such an albatross."

45

IN NEWPORT, quiet knocks prematurely woke Adrienne from her LD shift. She opened the starboard door to find Brynne on the landing.

"I'm sorry," Brynne stammered. "I came to … well, you wear contacts, don't you?"

Adrienne stared back at her, dazed. "Yeah?"

"So do I, sometimes. I was wondering if you had any lens solution."

Adrienne was floored. After seven months, this was the first time Brynne had actively sought anyone out. "In my locker …" she offered, opening the door to allow Brynne inside.

Brynne peered around. "Wow … it's pretty tight in here."

Adrienne took an extra bottle of Bausch & Lomb from her locker. "Yeah, I wonder why." But when she saw Brynne's hurt expression, she reconsidered her remark. "Sorry. It's not even your fault, really. It's just …" But there was no point in continuing. Brynne knew whose fault it was.

After she left, a curious thought crossed Adrienne's mind. There had been something longing in Brynne's eyes, and Adrienne wondered if she'd truly needed lens solution. Or was it only an excuse to see if someone would actually give her the time of day?

On the laz, Adrienne told Noah her thoughts. "Have you noticed it's not even Brynne who's the problem? I feel like we always group her into whatever Max does, but she hasn't done *anything* to us, Noah."

"Girl, she's friends with the bitch. That makes her just as guilty in my book."

"Really?" Adrienne challenged. "What if I did something horrible, and people blamed you for being *my* friend?"

Noah grew serious, a rare occurrence. "That's the difference, Dri. We would never be friends if you treated people how Ursula does."

"Okay, I get it. But, do you ever look at Brynne, Noah? I mean, really *look* at her? I think Max is her only friend in the world. Sometimes you can just tell that about people, you know? Maybe I'm wrong, but I don't think she has many people in her life at all."

Noah shrugged. "So what if she doesn't? We're outta here in six weeks, Dri. We don't owe her any friendship. And if she *wanted* other friends, she's had all season to do something about it."

Adrienne didn't agree that just because Brynne hadn't come looking for their friendship didn't mean she wasn't interested. Maybe she was afraid of betraying Max. "I think we should invite her out with us while Max is away. I don't care if she says no, but if she says yes, I'll feel better."

"Oh, you will? Why?"

"Because if I'm right, at least we'll have made a difference for her. Don't ask why that matters to me. It just does."

"*Fine*," Noah relented. "For *one* night. But if it backfires, don't say I didn't tell you so."

Adrienne waited until they got to Martha's Vineyard before approaching Brynne, finding her in a housekeeping closet. "Hey …" she said.

Brynne's eyes darted skittishly. "Nicky has the vacuum … if that's what you're looking for."

"I was actually wondering if you wanted to hang out with us tonight," Adrienne said. "If you're not doing anything."

"Where are you going?"

"Probably Eastville Point Beach, like usual. I thought this time you could go *with* us, like, as a group. Maybe we can get to know each other."

Brynne studied Adrienne, then nodded. "Okay. That sounds nice."

Logan told Adrienne that she had to pass. "My sister and her roommates rented a house in Oak Bluffs for the weekend," she said. "Not that I'm not *totally* interested in learning what Brynne's like without Max around."

Hailey and Katherine were also intrigued that Adrienne had

included Brynne. "I thought she hated us!" Hailey exclaimed.

"So did I," said Katherine.

"So, you'll both come?" Adrienne asked.

Hailey nodded. "I will."

"Maybe …" said Katherine. "I am working Turndown & Activity Hour tonight, after all."

They walked the half-mile to the beach in silence, Noah hauling a case of beer. At the sea wall, they each took a bottle and sat. "*So*," Noah said emphatically, "why are we all here tonight, Dri?"

Adrienne shook her head. Leave it to Noah to put them on the spot. "I thought we could get to know each other better."

Noah was in full diva mode. "*How?*"

Sensing Adrienne's annoyance, Hailey took the lead. "We used to do icebreakers in my church youth group. Whenever new members joined, we'd share things about ourselves to make them feel more comfortable."

"Okay, so do an *icebreaker*," said Noah.

Hailey's icebreaker was more of a confessional, sharing how her older brother was a state trooper and how overprotected she'd been growing up. Adrienne went next, telling Brynne about her background at Giovanni's, then focusing on Aaron and Thany.

At Noah's turn, he rolled his eyes and said, "*Tiverton. Only child. Gay.*"

Adrienne nudged him crossly, but curiously, Brynne spoke up. "I'm an only child, too. I thought I was the only stew who was."

"Nope."

"Did you ever wish you had brothers or sisters?"

"I never gave it much thought, girl," Noah said, loosening. "You?"

"No. Probably because I always had—" She stopped before saying Max's name.

The four of them were able to maintain conversation. Surface-level topics, but their reservations about Brynne were dwindling. Eventually, they were joined by Nicky and, shortly later, Katherine. Adrienne was amazed Katherine had come, even more so when Katherine plunked down next to her and accepted a beer.

She appeared contemplative, not eager to insert herself into conversations like usual, but waiting until the timing was appropriate to speak. When she saw her window, Katherine looked around at her crewmates. "I want to formally apologize to everyone for what I said in June. I think all of you have valuable skill sets, and I'm sorry I didn't recognize or respect them. I also want to apologize for making judgments about your education. It was very insensitive, and I want you all to know I'm sorry."

No one spoke at first. It had been so long since Katherine's remarks that everyone had moved on. Had it not been for their talk in July, Adrienne might have considered this apology too little too late. But she *knew* Katherine, if only minimally, and wasn't surprised it had taken her so long to recognize her faults.

Finally, Hailey said, "Thanks, Katherine. I appreciate that."

"Me too," said Adrienne.

Grunts of acknowledgment came from Nicky and Noah, and even Brynne gave a subtle nod. Adrienne didn't know what response Katherine expected to generate, but her apology was a step in the right direction. The right words were always better late than never.

When they got back to the *Amelia*, Logan was just getting dropped off. In the dining room, she passed around cardboard photo envelopes and said, "Sorry I couldn't hang out tonight, but I got a *ton* of pictures developed at the one-hour place and made copies." She handed one to Brynne. "Here. You were in a couple, too, so …"

Brynne smiled, thanking Logan, but the loneliness in her eyes made Adrienne take pity. Aside from being an only child from East Greenwich, the stews knew nothing about her. Whatever her origins, whatever she'd endured this far, Brynne's life wasn't something the rest of them could relate to. *Maybe not so much an old soul,* Adrienne reconsidered. *Maybe more like a lost one.*

Brynne

SHE'S HAPPY she went tonight. At least she can leave this season having associated with other stews besides Max, even if it was only for a few hours. It felt nice to be included, but she'll never tell Max that Adrienne invited her. If Max ever asks, she'll just explain that Nicky was there, too.

She doesn't think Max would ever do anything to hurt her, but she does know Max prefers to lie in wait when she feels she's been wronged. Just like she did with Lola and Emma. Just like she did with Adrienne in Newport. With Max, you never can tell when she'll pounce.

Marco

AT THEIR RESORT in the Bahamas, Max books spa appointments every day. "We work hard, babe," she says. "We deserve it." In the evenings, she runs up the room service bill. Seafood and pasta dishes. Expensive bottles of wine and tropical cakes for dessert. At night, she doesn't want to leave the suite, dresses in a white satin robe and tells him to lie down so she can massage his back. "We work hard at our relationship, too, don't we?"

"You know we do."

"Can you believe we've been together for seven years, Marco? *Marriages* don't last that long."

"Those people aren't really in love."

She kneads into his shoulders skillfully. "I fall in love with you all over again every day, Marco. You're going to marry me, right? And give me babies?"

"I'll give you whatever you want when it's time."

"*Boys.* Only boys. I want to be the only woman you ever love."

He laughs. "We can't control that, Max."

The night before they leave, Max rests her head on his chest. "Are you scared about doing business for Frankie?"

"No," he tells her. "The money will help give us a leg up. And Frankie won't touch me once I'm a captain. That should be a respectable enough reason for him to find another mule."

"I'm scared if you get caught. It's like Frankie didn't even give you a choice."

"I wouldn't have agreed to it if I thought I'd get caught. It's one day, Max. The exchange takes twenty minutes."

She kisses his chest. "You're my entire world, Marco. I don't know what I'd do without you."

He strokes her beautiful hair, the softest hair he's ever touched. "Don't think that way, babe. You'll never have to worry about that."

46

ON THEIR LAST DAY on Martha's Vineyard, Adrienne walked to Leslie's Pharmacy during her break. As she took her wallet from her purse, the pointy corner of Logan's photo envelope jabbed the back of her hand. *Oh yeah!* The pictures had remained in her purse for a week, unopened and forgotten about. She thumbed through them on the sidewalk, smiling at all the shots Logan had developed. There were some great ones of the stews riding mopeds, a hilarious candid of Noah caught off guard as he vacuumed, and dozens more from their nights out in various ports.

At the end of the stack was a group shot Adrienne didn't immediately recall, taken at the Oar sometime that summer. The crew had their arms around each other, with Shane at the end, resting one hand on a barstool and the other around *her*. Adrienne studied the picture carefully. Why hadn't she remembered this until now? She looked at ease with Shane's arm curved around her middle, but the expression on his face appealed to her more. Shane was beaming, happier than she'd ever seen him.

She traced his smile with a finger, lost in a moment she thought was private until being startled by the condescending voice signature only to Max Hardigan. "You *can't* be serious."

Adrienne turned around. Max stood directly behind her, wearing designer sunglasses and a taunting smile. "Serious about what?"

"That picture!"

Adrienne stiffened with embarrassment. How had Max snuck up on her during such a vulnerable moment? "What about it?"

"Don't pretend you weren't staring at it like a lovesick puppy! You're in *love* with him, aren't you?"

Never in these seven months had Adrienne wanted to hit Max as she did now, but she knew better, certain the outcome wouldn't be worth the momentary satisfaction. She tried sidestepping around her, but Max moved quickly, blocking her path. "Get *out* of my way, Max."

Max moved closer, relishing in her discovery. "Maybe you haven't been checking your calendar, but the season's over in five weeks …"

"So what?" Adrienne snapped.

"So, did you really think you and your *boyfriend* would still see each other after this?"

Had Max followed her here on purpose just to torment her? And Adrienne sure didn't like how she was talking about Shane. He might not have been there to hear it, but she felt protective of him regardless. But it was the unsettling coolness in Max's tone that caused Adrienne to lose composure, the pent-up anger she'd repressed all season reaching its boiling point. "Why do you act like this?" she demanded. "Why do you treat people this way? It wasn't enough to trick me in Newport? To cost me a day's worth of pay? *Why?* All because of some comment I made in February? I've been paying for it ever since!"

Max removed her sunglasses, her sapphire eyes dancing sadistically. "I just saw this as an opportunity to remind you."

"Remind me of *what?*"

"That you're not special, remember? You're *convenient.* Just like every other girl who signs up to be sailors' choice. And not to forget that your boyfriend has a *wife.* That's all."

Sailors' choice? Adrienne's blood froze as Max walked into the pharmacy. Her words were so vicious, so paralyzing, that Adrienne grabbed hold of a nearby bench to absorb their aftershock. Words, she was continuing to learn, were incredibly powerful. And Max's words were inarguably chosen with care, solely intended to cripple her.

For the first time since arriving on the *Amelia*, Adrienne couldn't sleep, dizzied by her shift in mood. *Had* she been checking her calendar? Not exactly. But what had she thought would happen after the season ended?

That she and Shane would still talk every day? Sit side by side at meals? Spend their free time together? A deep-rooted shame began to onset, worse than any guilt she'd felt since meeting him. How had they grown so close? How had she been so obtuse not to consider the future?

And that *Max* had pointed it out downright sickened her. But it wasn't Max's reminder that she was about to lose Shane that most gutted Adrienne, but Max's observation about *love*. She had been so cautious … had tried protecting her feelings and abiding by her morals for months … but now that the word had been spoken aloud, Adrienne had to face reality and accept that she was at a crossroads. Because the truth was that she *did* love Shane. That she had this entire time.

October 2007

47

THE CREW RETURNED to East Bay on October 1. They were in the home stretch now, with just three trips remaining: two Foliage on the Hudson cruises and Haunted Homecoming—the Halloween-themed final voyage.

They weren't deadheading to New York until Thursday, leaving the crew a day off to go home. When they returned, they'd festoon the boat for fall. Connie advised the stews that the task was a huge overhaul but an exciting one they should look forward to. Adrienne loved fall and wanted to be eager, but Max's scathing comments from Martha's Vineyard still had her rattled, and since then, she'd been keeping a lot to herself.

Logan was driving to Connecticut for her mother's birthday and offered to drop Adrienne off in Westford. As they crossed into Chaplin, Logan lowered her radio. "Is something bothering you, Adrienne?"

Adrienne snapped alert, realizing she'd ignored Logan most of the ride. "No, I'm fine. Why?"

"You totally haven't been yourself the last few days."

By this point, Adrienne considered Logan a friend, but she was protective of her feelings for Shane, never having confided in any of her crewmates on that level before. But when she reckoned how many opinions she'd get besides Wendy's, Adrienne figured at least Logan could offer the perspective of someone who *knew* Shane. It made a difference that Logan had observed their interactions, that she'd seen his wife in person. Adrienne took her chances, sharing her confusion with Logan but keeping the word *love* and Max's venomous input to herself.

"I won't say I haven't noticed," Logan said. "It was obvious that you two connected from the beginning, and I think you're both well suited for each other. You'd probably make a totally ideal couple if he weren't …"

"Married," Adrienne finished.

"Right. And I commend you, Adrienne … because *I* wouldn't have held back from a connection like that. What I see between you guys doesn't come along every day."

Adrienne was shocked. "And you wouldn't have felt guilty?"

"God no! Shane's *not* happy, Adrienne. Just one look at his wife that night in Providence? That anger she had toward him? Totally unhealthy!"

She had a valid point. "What would you do if you were in my position?" Adrienne asked.

Logan shrugged. "Do? That depends. Has he ever said anything to you about leaving?"

Once. He said he can't. But Adrienne kept that to herself as well. Speaking the words aloud only gave weight to their truth.

"I guess it'd be different if he were at least separated …" Logan continued. "Then, I'd *totally* pursue things if I were you."

But he's not, thought Adrienne. *He's married.* And despite Shane's unhappiness, nothing he'd said all season indicated that would ever change.

Hailey

SHE'S SO GRATEFUL that Logan offered her condo as an alternative to going back to Franklin, especially since Logan won't even be there. She needs more space after the argument during her last trip home, more time *away* from her parents.

Jeremy comes to see her instead. He picks her up from the shipyard and takes her to Riverside, where they walk the beach and he catches her up on his life. Work's been hectic, and he's still single, but he's finally saved enough money to buy a six-acre plot and was interviewing contractors. "You're saving *your* money, right, Hai?" he asks, getting big-brothery.

"I could be doing better …" she admits, thinking of all the CDs and sweatshirts, the digital camera, and all the nights out after work. "But I've decided I'm doing another season, Jeremy. I don't care what Mom and Dad say. Next year has trips going all the way to Florida!"

Her brother knows more than anyone what all this traveling means to her, especially how excited she is to see New York City this week. "The world is yours, Hai," he says. "Stay another year if you want to. Go see Florida. And don't worry about Mom and Dad. It's *your* life. Do whatever makes you happy."

***

IN WESTFORD, Logan idled her Mercedes in front of Adrienne's house. "Cute place," she said. Adrienne thought of inviting Logan inside but quickly rejected the idea. She had no clue what her father and Thany were up to, and worried Jack might consider Logan's presence an intrusion.

The house was eerily quiet when she entered. For her last two homecomings, Thany and Jack had met her at the door, but this time just Dolly came, pawing excitedly at her knees. Adrienne assumed the house was empty, jumping when her father appeared cross-armed in the living room. "That friend of yours has a lot of nerve," he said.

Logan? What could *she* have done to upset him? "What are you talking about, Dad? You didn't even meet her."

"Didn't meet who? The kid's lived next door for eleven years."

"Wendy?" Adrienne asked. "What did she do?"

"You didn't see the tree?"

"No, Dad! What tree? What is going on?"

Jack grimaced. "Last Sunday, your *friend* took Nathaniel to buy a yellow ribbon and tied it around the tree out front."

"A yellow ribbon?" Adrienne didn't make the connection until she spoke the words and remembered the song. "Tie a Yellow Ribbon Round the Ole Oak Tree." Raina used to have the Dawn record. "What's wrong with that? I thought a yellow ribbon symbolized hope?"

"False hope, Adrienne! What if something happens to Aaron? What will your *friend* tell Nathaniel then? He's only seven! She's got no place getting his hopes up like that!"

Adrienne was blindsided. What was she walking into? "Why do you always have to be so negative, Dad? What if something *happens* to him? Let's worry about that *if* Aaron gets deployed!"

"Adrienne, I won't tolerate this war with the Middle East under my roof. I lose sleep every night, praying to whatever *God* exists up there that your brother's unit never gets that call."

"So, why don't you take the ribbon *down*?"

"Oh, I tried on Monday morning! Nathaniel got so worked up that I thought he might have a seizure. He told me *his* ribbon wasn't going anywhere until his big brother and sister were home safely."

Adrienne stood rigidly. Thany had acted defiantly? And why was he worried for *her* safety? Where had that come from? She found him in his room, coloring. "Hey, Bud."

"I heard you and Daddy fighting," he said. "He's mad about my ribbon."

"Where did you get the idea to get a yellow ribbon, anyway?" Adrienne asked. "From someone in Cub Scouts?"

"No, from Wendy."

"From Wendy? The ribbon was *Wendy's* idea?"

"Uh-huh. We went to the movies, and then we got the ribbon from the flower store. The lady made it for us special."

"Okay … and what did Wendy tell you the yellow ribbon was for?"

"She said it was for soldiers like Aaron, and you tie it around a tree until they get home safely. But I told Wendy I wanted the ribbon to be for you, too."

"For me? Thany, I went away for work. Not because …" She wasn't sure how to finish her sentence. *Not because I left to train for the war?* "Well … there's nothing unsafe about what I do on the boat, Bud."

"But what about what Aaron does?" Thany asked. "Is being a Marine unsafe?"

Later, Adrienne walked to the front yard to investigate. Sure enough, a yellow florist's bow hugged the trunk of the dogwood tree. The longer she stared at it, the more Adrienne questioned what message the ribbon conveyed. It wasn't a subtlety, but a statement that carried far more weight than Wendy had probably given any proper thought to. Suddenly, Adrienne felt a sense of accountability for letting Wendy take Thany without setting ground rules. But after eleven years of knowing their family, she'd expected Wendy to use better discretion. The ribbon crossed a line, and she needed to make sure it didn't happen again.

She walked down Wendy's driveway and knocked on the hatchway. When Wendy pushed a door open, Adrienne stared, puzzled. Wendy's fiery blonde hair had grown *long*, her rectangle Vogues absent from her face, contacts aiding her eyes instead.

"Hey!" Wendy said. "When did you get home?"

"Earlier. I'm going back tomorrow."

"Oh. I'm watching a movie for Film Studies, but you can come in."

Adrienne stood back offishly. "No, thanks. I actually came by to talk to you about that ribbon."

"What ... about it?" Wendy asked warily.

"My dad's upset, Wendy. And to be honest, I am, too. I wish you hadn't done that without checking with us first."

"Upset? Why?"

"Wendy, you *know* how sensitive he is about Aaron and the military. And I'm upset that Thany's worried for Aaron's safety when he's not even deployed. Why instill that kind of worry in a seven-year-old?"

"I had no idea Thany was *worried*, Adrienne. We just ... in my history class ... the professor was discussing the origin of yellow ribbons. And the idea just came to me ... as an activity to do with Thany."

A surge of impatience Adrienne had never felt toward Wendy suddenly engulfed her. "I *appreciate* that, but you have no clue what it's like explaining war to a child, Wendy. I really wish you would've asked."

Wendy squinted. "Is there something else going on with you?"

"Like what? What are you talking about?"

"Adrienne, I haven't heard from you in four weeks! Do you even realize that? And now you're showing up here to *lecture* me about a ribbon?"

"I'm not *lecturing* you. But I have to do what's in my little brother's best interest."

"And what's that?"

Adrienne folded her arms. She was too stressed on the boat to worry about things at home and could do without the extra drama until she returned. "Maybe it's not a good idea for you to take Thany on Sundays anymore. I'm coming home in a month, so he should be fine until then."

"Are you serious? Adrienne, I don't know what's going on, but you're obviously projecting whatever it is onto me. You can't honestly be this angry with me over a *ribbon*."

"Projecting?" Adrienne scoffed. "I guess it's good that you went back to school, Wendy ... to *amplify* your vocabulary."

Wendy's face fell, and Adrienne knew the second the words left her mouth that she'd taken their disagreement too far. "Wendy, I'm sor—" she began, but Wendy was already tearful, reaching for the hatchway door. "*No*. That boat's changed you, Adrienne."

Adrienne cursed herself for being so cold to Wendy. Of course Wendy's intent hadn't been malicious. Wendy was one of the most thoughtful people she knew. The ribbon idea couldn't have come from anywhere but the good place in her heart that cared for people. So why hadn't Adrienne drawn that conclusion *before* confronting her? And why had she been so drastic, saying Wendy couldn't take Thany anymore? That was going to hurt him the most.

Adrienne couldn't sleep a wink. At dawn, the sun's rays declared that Logan would be arriving soon, that she still had a whole month left on the boat. A month of uncertainty with Shane. A month of continuing to bear the cross that was Max Hardigan.

She didn't feel right about leaving without smoothing things over with Wendy, but all her calls went straight to voicemail. Texting didn't produce a response either. *What did you expect?* her conscience challenged. *Especially after everything she's done for you?* Wasn't it because of Wendy she'd discovered the boat? *Wendy*, who'd encouraged her to seize the moment? And look how she'd treated her in return. How much of an effort had *she* made all these months? How many times had Wendy reached out that *she* couldn't talk? When Adrienne thought of it that way, she couldn't fault Wendy for needing time.

While she paced the living room impatiently, Jack entered and handed her an envelope. "Here, someone left this for you in the mailbox."

Adrienne worried it might be from Rick, that he'd somehow found out she was home and written her another love note. But the script on the envelope was tiny and neat—unmistakably Wendy's. Adrienne numbed when she opened it. Inside was every receipt for Wendy's and Thany's Sunday outings and one hundred seventy-three dollars left in change.

Shane

THERE'S SOMETHIN' UP with his cousin. Travis wasn't here when he got back yesterday, and he never showed up again last night. Every time he comes home, the guy's a no-show. Thinkin' about it now, he hasn't seen or heard from Travis since June.

Jess is in a mood, so he calls his mom and Caela to ask if they know what's goin' on.

"He's still living there that *we* know of," his mom says. "Still working with that chimney service."

Caela tells him the same thing—that she just saw Travis on Saturday when she drove up to visit Avery. Across the street, even Eric and Nati say they see Travis comin' and goin' every day. "He shouldn't be avoiding you like that, mano," Eric says. "You give him a roof, and now you come home and he's Harry Houdini? You think he's skipping out on the rent?"

He's not sure. Finally, he goes to the basement to look around. Travis's cot's still there, and some used furniture he's never seen before—a nightstand and dresser and a little TV. The books on the nightstand are all stamped in green ink—*Property of MCI Norfolk*.

So, Travis does still live here.

When he calls twice and gets no answer, he gets so heated that he knocks Travis's books on the floor. Then he confronts Jess in the kitchen. "You sure ya don't know what's goin' on, Jess? Where the fuck is he? He owes me eight seventy-five in rent!"

"He's probably *workin'*!" she sneers. "That's the excuse you all have nowadays, isn't it?"

47

CONNIE WAS READY with an extensive list of seasonal changes when the stews returned. October was a big month for NECLA, she told them, probably the biggest, and the remaining guests would be expecting nothing short of first-rate experiences.

The detail involved in the *Amelia*'s transformation was maximal. Artificial leaf garland was strung around the doorways. Candy corn and mellow crème pumpkins were added to the bar snack carafes. And the flower deliveries now included sunflowers and orange chrysanthemums. Lastly, the white and blue table linens they'd been using since April were replaced with new colors like saffron, burnt sienna, and chocolate.

The stews worked late, waking early on Wednesday to help Chef Ray unpack the food deliveries. Instead of going heavy on seafood, the new menus were fall-inspired. They unloaded pumpkins and squashes of all shapes and sizes; bushels of apples, persimmons, and beets; and jumbo containers of nutmeg, cinnamon, and allspice. Down in galley stores, the deep freezers were stocked with enough game and red meat to last through the end of the season.

There was no shortage of work. Out on the laz, Adrienne and Hailey reorganized the spare fridge to make room for cases of apple cider. Adrienne wasn't much for talking, but Hailey was too ecstatic to notice. "I'm *so* excited for these next three trips!" she gushed. "Especially New York City!"

"I've only been once," Adrienne shared. "When I was eight. This will be my first time seeing it as an adult."

"Look!" Hailey pulled up her sleeve, revealing goosebumps. "I'm so excited, I'm shaking!"

Adrienne had to smile. She felt for Hailey big time.

"The itinerary says we're supposed to get there at two," Hailey said. "Will you watch from the top deck with me?"

At two in the morning? "I'll think about it," Adrienne told her. "Two's a little late."

After Hailey left, Adrienne sat on her perch, watching the *Amelia* cruise west through Long Island Sound. She felt out of sorts, but blaming the cooler weather or change of scenery would be a copout. This emotion was something new, something heavier. She'd felt incredibly blue since the last episode with Max. So not herself. She prayed the feeling to go away, to not affect her final weeks on the boat. But Max's cutting words were a wake-up call, causing her to step back from Shane.

He'd also seemed stressed when they got back yesterday, and Adrienne wondered if something had gone wrong at home. But she couldn't keep checking in with him. And there was no way they could hang out anymore. There was no future for them, and she needed to accept that. Putting a stop to things now was the right thing to do. If only she could put her feelings into words.

Hailey

SHE'S SET HER alarm for 1:30. On vibrate, so it doesn't wake Logan. The crew doesn't understand how special this is for her, seeing The City for the first time. She remembers in high school when her American Government teacher made a blunt announcement to the class: "Washington D.C. might be the capital according to Rand McNally, but New York City is the true chieftain of the United States. It has anything, and it has everything. There is *nothing* you cannot find in New York."

Whenever she'd seen New York on television, she couldn't believe it was real. How could the Big Apple—the city with *everything*—be so close to Franklin, which had nothing?

As the *Amelia* reduces speed, she slides from her bunk and into her slippers and a hoodie. This is her moment, and no one can ever take it away from her.

***

Adrienne decided to wait up for Hailey, quietly following her to the top deck. Outside, she'd expected darkness to dominate, thinking of all the nights the boat had cruised through blackened waterways, using the navigation lights as its guide. But tonight, lights from all over creation surrounded them, the spires of thousands of buildings silhouetted across the skyline.

Nearing the portside rails, they heard Nicky's voice. "And that there's Lady Libahty 'erself!" he announced. Adrienne and Hailey turned to see Nicky and Shane approaching with a six-pack. Nicky parked on Hailey's left. "What're ya ladies doin' up so late?"

"I've never seen New York!" Hailey squeaked. "I didn't want to miss this!"

Nicky pulled out two bottles and handed them to the girls, then two more for himself and Shane. "Shaney-Boy hasn't eithah. I told him this here's the best way to see 'er for the first time—top deck, middle'a the night, with some nice cold brewskies."

Adrienne twisted off the bottlecap and took a long swig. She hadn't expected to see Shane up here, and his presence jangled her nerves. Besides, she'd had such trouble sleeping the past couple of nights she didn't see how a beer *couldn't* help her.

They stared in awe as they cruised by the Statue of Liberty, illuminated in all its glory. Hailey gasped at its mammoth size, inadvertently reaching her hand toward the woman. Even Adrienne was mesmerized seeing the iconic monument this close and unobstructed.

"Jaw-droppin', ain't she?" asked Nicky.

Hailey sighed. "I should have brought my camera up with me."

Shane shook his head. "Nah. Somethin' like this is better in your head. Pictures get lost, but memories stay with ya forever."

Adrienne thought back to their night in Rockland, to the magnificent views at the breakwater. No picture could have done that setting justice. It was one of those moments you had to witness firsthand.

Nicky nodded at their bottles. "Let's toast, mateys. Whaddaya say?"

"To what?" asked Shane.

Adrienne saw Nicky's mental cogs churning, probably conjuring a nautical quip per usual, but Hailey beat him to it. "How about to moments no one can ever take away from us?"

"Aye there, I'll second ya!" Nicky agreed, clinking his bottle around.

As they headed inside, Shane tapped Adrienne's shoulder playfully. "How's it goin'? Haven't gotten to say a word to ya since we got back."

Adrienne looked past him, concentrating on the metropolis. "I know. It's wild how busy we've been," she said, fishing for excuses.

"You okay? Things good at home?"

"Yeah. Just cold. And it's late. I really need to get some sleep, you know?" She walked away quickly, following Hailey down the stairs without looking back.

49

CHELSEA PIERS was unlike any port they'd docked before—a giant cobalt sports complex jutting into the Hudson River. All kinds of boats were docked at the Piers, from sports boats to private yachts to transients. The *Amelia* was docked at Pier 60, parallel to a glass-windowed fitness club. One dock down was the infamous Pier 59—the *Titanic*'s intended destination.

Embarkation was more hectic than usual. Many passengers had trouble navigating the complex, winding up at the wrong piers after getting through security. By eleven, the boat was full, but the departure time wasn't scheduled until tomorrow, and no one was staying on board. Two chartered buses waited on Eleventh Avenue, hired to transport the guests to New York's acclaimed landmarks.

"You guys may as well live it up tonight," Connie said after the muster drills. "This group will keep us on our toes."

"Yeah …" Adrienne knew the next four weeks would be intense, the three nearly sold-out trips certain to keep them busy round the clock. But given her current mood, she wasn't too sure about "living it up."

When Logan invited the stews to her sister's apartment after work, Hailey begged them to walk, wanting to see the sidewalks of New York in their gritty nighttime majesties. Her excitement reminded Adrienne of Thany's elation on Christmas. Hailey was enraptured by the city's magnitude, her eyes turning into discuses at all that was foreign to her—the copious amounts of homeless people, the swarming pedestrian traffic, all walking so fast, all in such a hurry. She took pictures of *everything*, craning her neck way back to capture the full scope of the skyscrapers.

Logan's sister rented a Village brownstone with two fellow NYU students. Alannah, who was twenty-two, bore a striking resemblance to Logan, but they differed cosmetically. Alannah's hair was pin-straight and two-toned—blonde on top and black on the bottom. And she had piercings—a hoop threaded through her nostril and gauges in her ears.

Adrienne found Alannah nice enough, but it was clear that living in New York had inflated her. A "student by day, scenester by night," she regaled the stews with stories of exclusive parties and warehouse raves, claiming to be friends with many a Village child star and a few offspring of famous actors and musicians, none of which Logan questioned.

They walked to Times Square, where Hailey was hypnotized by the buskers and street vendors, the behemoth billboards haloing the storefronts. "I can't believe this is real!" she squealed. "Franklin has *nothing*!" When they ran into the Naked Cowboy outside MTV Studios, Hailey asked for a photo even though she had no idea who he was. She jetted in and out of the tourist traps at the junction of Broadway and Seventh, buying as much I Love New York merchandise as she could carry. And when a stranger banged into her while they rode the subway back to Chelsea, Hailey laughed it off. "I don't even care! I've never seen so many people in one place before!"

Back at the Piers, they ran into Nicky, Jordy, and Shane, headed to grab drinks at the bowling alley. The others started following, but Adrienne was reluctant. "It's already after eleven," she pointed out. "Don't you guys think we should get some rest?" She felt foolish, using *rest* as an excuse to avoid Shane, but how could she continue acting like nothing was wrong without confronting her feelings head-on?

"*Rest?*" Hailey tugged Adrienne's arm. "Come on, Dri! This is the city that never sleeps! Hang out with us!"

Under different circumstances, the nightcap would've been tempting. But when Adrienne saw Shane's hopeful look, she freed herself from Hailey. "Sorry, but I'm exhausted. I won't be any fun. But you guys go. Have a good time. I'll see you in the morning."

Marco

IT'S OVER. Yesterday, in the back room of Alessio's, Frankie dropped a leather satchel on the card table. "There's eighty thousand dollars and a scale in there, Markie. You don't let Benny Giuseppe see a red cent until the product's weighed. He gives you a hard time, I'll send the boys to clean his clock. *Capisce?*"

He didn't say yes or no. The less you say, the better. Always, wherever you are.

Tonight, he'd done what his brothers, cousins, uncles, and father have done before him. It's not respectable, but it's what they do, their underground business. He took a cab to Hell's Kitchen, met the Giuseppe gang at the front to exchange with Benny, and took a cab back. His only worry was getting through security at the Piers, but with his uniform and proof of clearance, the guards didn't give him a second look.

He locks the satchel inside one of Max's suitcases and shoves it under their bed. That's it now. He can rest assured. Only four weeks until he delivers the weight back to Frankie. Then he can take his cut of the money and wash his hands of this.

***

AFTER NEW YORK, the succeeding ports up the Hudson didn't have much within walking distance. If the crew wanted to go anywhere, even just to the drugstore, they usually had to call a cab. Tarrytown afforded a grand view of the Tappan Zee Bridge but nothing except parking lot at ground level. And at West Point Military Academy, only the officers and passengers were allowed off board. Everyone else was restricted to the boat. Poughkeepsie had a walkable yet underwhelming downtown area, and the riverfront communities of Hyde Park, Kingston, and Catskill were no different.

Everyone was growing so bored that Noah began hosting nightly movie parties in crew lounge, but Adrienne continuously declined. Leaving to chance another encounter with Shane would undoubtedly lead to a conversation she knew she wasn't emotionally prepared for.

The entire vibe of Foliage on the Hudson was strange. "Depressing almost," Keith pointed out during one of his rare daytime appearances. "Not as liberating as the summer trips."

Adrienne had seen so little of Keith since April that she often forgot he was on board. He was an introvert who kept to himself, off in his own world. On the rare occasion that he joined the crew for a meal, he'd sit between Connie and Hardigan at the officers' table, not saying much. To the rest of them, Keith was a nocturnal nonentity, appearing while they set up for dinner and retreating to his cabin before their days began. Still, his observation about the seasonal change was valid.

It wasn't just all the humdrum new ports either, but the lingering cinnamon smell coming from the galley, the disappearance of the sunny warmth they'd grown used to, replaced by a pervasive chill that stagnated in Adrienne's bones. Then there was the repetitious cruising along the Hudson. The other itineraries had had the *Amelia* cruising through various waterways, but Foliage on the Hudson was literally just that—designed for optimum leaf peeping while the boat plied one hundred fifty miles upriver and one hundred fifty miles down.

Sure, the scenery was gorgeous, especially the Kaaterskill Wild Forest with its steep mountains rimming the water. The backdrop was exactly why the passengers had coughed up the big bucks. They spent lots of time frequenting the top deck, which meant so did the stews, bundled in scarves and fleeces as they cocktailed trays of hot cocoa and cider.

But when Adrienne looked around, her crewmates were still smiling, whereas she felt so sad for so many reasons. She was still reeling from her falling-out with Wendy, from her abrupt decision to cast Shane aside, trying to process it all. She cried soundlessly in the shower, her only place of privacy. When she wiped off the steamy mirror and didn't recognize the grief in her reflection, it was impossible to get Wendy's words out of her head. *That boat's changed you, Adrienne.*

50

IT WAS HARD to believe that in three weeks they'd be home again, that this would all suddenly be over. Adrienne began considering her future with the crew. Was it possible to spend this much time with a group of people only to never see each other again? Her gut said she and Noah would remain friends. At least once a week, he'd drop hints about her road-tripping to Florida with him. And though Adrienne wasn't sure about staying in touch with Katherine, she, Hailey, and Logan were close now, weren't they? Permanently bonded by this *opportunity of a lifetime?*

And for all the gnawing wonders about her future with Shane, Adrienne's answers came on a Friday night in Troy—the turnaround port for Foliage on the Hudson.

She was handing the sign-out clipboard back to Jordy when Shane approached the gangway and took it from her. "Goin' out?" he asked.

Great. Being caught off guard was exactly what she'd been avoiding. "I was planning on taking a walk."

"You mind if we talk?"

Shane looked nervous, worried even, which surprised Adrienne. Did he really care that she'd been stonewalling him these past two weeks? *He has feelings, too,* she considered. Imagine if he'd treated *her* this way. "All right," she said. "I think there's a park nearby."

They walked along the Hudson silently, both knowing the conversation wasn't to happen in stride, but once they were stopped, concentrating only on the others' words. Adrienne leaned on the fence that separated the sidewalk from the water. Shane did the same, staring upriver at the Green Island Bridge. He broke their quiet first. "Why've ya been dodgin' me, Adrienne?"

She shrugged. "It's finally hit me that our connection will end once we're off the boat. I didn't get it before, maybe I didn't want to, but I get it now. There's no point in spending any more time together when we'll never see each other after this, Shane."

His voice filled with suspicion. "Did someone say somethin' to you?"

Adrienne nodded. "Max. On our last day on Martha's Vineyard. I know she wanted to get a rise out of me, but everything she said is true."

Shane crushed his cigarette angrily. "She's one miserable broad. Wants to bring the whole world down with her."

"Was she wrong, Shane? Did you see us staying in touch off the boat?"

Shane stared past her, pressed and hard. The corners of his mouth twitched, restraining emotion. "You want the truth? I enjoy your company, Adrienne. I wish we could spend *all* of our time sharin' experiences. I've never met a girl I have things in common with, a girl I *like* bein' around. My marriage is so bad, ya don't know the half of it. That's why I stray." He paused. "But not since I met you."

Adrienne stood unnaturally still. It had to be difficult for Shane to speak his truths like this. She opened her mouth, but Shane wasn't done. "Adrienne, besides bein' with my daughter, these five months gettin' to know ya have been the best times of my life. I know I don't say it, but that's how I feel. You want the *truth*? The truth is I don't know what's gonna happen when we go home, but I do know I don't wanna lose ya."

Adrienne's anxiety buckled. They couldn't keep dancing around this anymore. She needed an answer. Now. "Shane, you're *married*. Do you plan on changing that? If you've been unfaithful to your wife before, that's your business, but I refuse to be that person. I won't compromise my morals because of my feelings for you."

Shane shook his head. "I don't want ya to be that person, Adrienne. I'm attracted to how ya carry yourself. Not countin' for family, you're the only girl I've ever respected. I mean that."

She hated herself then. Hated the whole situation. Hated that Shane was baring his soul to her while she repressed her truths. But she also hated that she wasn't getting a clear answer. Didn't he see how frustrating this was for her? She wanted to scream, *Then what* do *you want? Do you want to be with me?* But she didn't, too fearful of betraying where she came from.

"This has been the best time of my life, too," she said stoically. "And I'm glad I'll always have the memories."

Shane stepped back, stung. "What're ya tryin' to do here, Adrienne? Just write me off? Avoid me 'til this is over, and never see me again?"

Is that what she wanted? Not at all. But it was what needed to be done. "Yeah ... I guess I am."

Resignation stained Shane's eyes. He stared off at the Green Island Bridge until speaking the words that cemented their destiny. "Maybe in another life, Adrienne," he said quietly. "Maybe in another life, we could've had somethin' special." And with that, he stuffed his hands in his pockets and left.

Adrienne stayed in the park for hours, chain-smoking indiscriminately. Even when a pesky numbness invaded her body, she still didn't return to the boat. Her mind was so bogged down that she needed to be alone with her thoughts. Ever since the end of September, she'd felt ... what? Displaced, maybe? She needed this space, this place to think.

All her losses over the last six years were wearing her down. Losing the father she once knew ... her mother's abandonment ... Aaron taking off to the military ... and now Wendy? Adrienne was sure they would reconcile, but would things be the same? Their friendship had never taken a hit like this. And what about her relationship with her father and Thany when she got home? Would they have learned to get along without her and make her feel like a stranger? But it was losing Shane that hurt more than the rest combined. The person she knew the least, go figure. *Maybe in another life.* That's what truly crushed her.

When she finally returned, Adrienne slipped into a vacant outdoor cabin, crumpling onto a bed and sobbing into a pillow. Disconsolate pains rocketed up from her gut, searing her heart as they passed. What kind of fool had she been getting involved in a situation like this? It was like fate had played some cruel trick on her. Why bring Shane into her life if they couldn't be together? They had so much in common. They had chemistry. They shared pasts that were dark and deep, and they could relate to each other because of them.

All season, she'd been hearing Shannon cautioning her. But now, as she lay brokenhearted, imploding in a strange bed, it was Aunt Claudette's warning from nearly a year ago that resurfaced. *Those things never work out. And it's always the innocent ones who suffer the most.*

If only she'd known at the time what eleven months could bring. If only her aunt could see her now.

51

ADRIENNE'S SLEEPING TROUBLE resumed on the return trip down the Hudson, alternating between a recurring nightmare and the insomnia she developed trying to prevent it. The nightmare was slow and tortuous, exiling her back to Giovanni's, cornered in the kitchen while Jenni heckled her. "How does it feel, *hypocrite?* How does it feel to fall in love with a *married man?*" Then Shannon would appear, thrusting her palm out and demanding that she return the bracelet. "I thought you were different, Adrienne!"

She kept waking in a cold sweat, having to reassure herself that none of it was real. But the nightmare derived from a true enough reality that Adrienne couldn't fall back asleep, fighting off tears for countless reasons until they inevitably rivered down her cheeks.

She stopped going out at night altogether. Unless she was scheduled as T&A Stew, she'd go straight downstairs after work, avoiding everyone by plugging away at *Harry Potter*. It turned out she'd been right about Snape—killed off after the surprise revelation of his love for Harry's mother. The plot twist left her glummer, feeling cheated that she'd spent six books hating a character who could love so purely. She considered Brynne's theory about differentiating between loss and death, genuinely shocked by the accuracy of her prediction.

But even once she finished her book, Adrienne still turned down offers to watch movies or hang out with anyone. She wanted to avoid Shane however possible, going so far as to stave off her cigarette cravings until he wasn't outside. Their conversation had hurt her terribly, and

Shane was clearly affected, too. He hadn't shown up to a single meal since that Friday in Troy, and Hailey and Katherine both said they'd seen him eating alone in the galley, washing his dishes when he was done.

Ironically, no one connected Shane's absence with Adrienne's shift in mood. But during their next galley shift, Noah said, "Girl, *what* is wrong with you? Why are you in this funk?"

Adrienne felt horrible. Noah was her best friend on the boat, and she wished she could confide in him. But Noah could be judgmental, and Adrienne worried he'd chastise her. "It's nothing," she brushed him off. "Probably just the change of weather. Seasonal affective disorder … that's a thing, isn't it?"

She'd never felt so alone. Without Wendy, there was no one who *knew* her. She'd already gotten Logan's take on the situation, and she assumed Hailey and Katherine had limited, if any, experience with guys. Adrienne considered going to Brynne, remembering the passion in her kiss with that old guy, but Brynne had gone back to her antisocial ways ever since Max returned, and even so, a few hours hanging out at the beach didn't make them friends.

It didn't dawn on Adrienne until the last day of the cruise that *Max* was probably the only stew who recognized true love. That was why she could read the signs and throw them in Adrienne's face. But though Max had been cruel, she had also been honest. That's why her words had cut so deeply.

So why couldn't Adrienne be honest with herself? Honest with Shane? *Honesty* would've been throwing her arms around him that night in Troy, admitting that no one had ever affected her so strongly, that the mere thought of him made her heart smile, that she couldn't imagine feeling this way about anyone else in the world. But telling Shane these things would mean straying from her convictions. And worst of all, admitting to another woman's husband that she was in love with him.

Eric

IT'S PAST NINE when he gets home. Today's fish haul in Boston was four hours late. He hates that route. Always has. He finds Nati asleep on the couch. He loves that she never goes to bed without him. She stirs when he kisses her forehead. "Mmm, *papi* ... there's leftover *pernil* for you on the stove." He kisses her again. That's a true woman right there.

"I almost forget ..." Nati says when he comes back with his food. "*Jess* came again today. She say her fridge still *rota*. I ask why she don't call her landlord, and she say he still in Portugal."

He doesn't wanna hear this, not tonight. "What about Shane's cousin? Why can't that fool fix it?"

Nati laughs. "Travis? That fool can't fix himself!" Then she gives him *ojos de cachorro*—puppy dog eyes. "I tell Jess you come by ... I say if it just her and Travis, she need to wait ... tell her you work too hard all day. But I won't let *niña* go with no cold milk, no huevos, Eric."

She's got him there. He finishes eating and heads across the street. It's probably just clogged coils or the evaporator fan. If so, he'll give Jess a number for a guy he knows. Should only run her a few hundred bucks.

No one answers when he knocks. The TV's on in the living room, but no lights. He goes to knock again but remembers Avery's window is above him, so he walks down the driveway. It's dark in back, but the TV glows through the sliding door. Travis is standing by the couch with some girl bent over in front of him. *This stupid fool! With Jess and Avery in the house?* He laughs, ready to leave, when the girl's head turns. That's when he realizes he knows her. It's *Jess*. Getting rammed by her man's own cousin.

He jogs home and tells Nati what he saw.

"*Puta!* I always say I never like her, Eric!"

He falls back on the couch. "The fuck am I supposed to do, Nat?"

Nati looks at him like he's *loco*. "You tell Shane, *papi*! He help that fool at his worst!"

She's right. Shane'll be home in ten days, but he deserves to know now. He'll call him in the morning. First thing, if he can even sleep.

***

TURNAROUND DAY for Haunted Homecoming involved swathing the boat with web netting and Halloween décor. Max and Brynne were assigned to the dining room, while the rest of them bedecked the pax lounge. As they worked, 2008 became the topic of discussion.

"I can't believe we only have nine days left!" said Hailey. "I can't wait to come back next year!" She looked around hopefully. "Are you guys coming back, too? Please say yes!"

Logan hung a foil bat from a ceiling hook. "I need to start seeing some different ports. Next year will be my *third* season, so it totally depends on where we're going."

"*I* am," Katherine cut in. "I wasn't at first, but I understand now why this job is necessary to gain experience for a position like Connie's. I am going to ask if I can shadow, though."

Adrienne knew everyone was thinking the same thing—Connie would *never* let Katherine follow her around all day and ask questions.

"What about you, Noah?" Hailey asked.

Noah dumped out a bag of plastic spiders. "Poss. I'll hafta see how my winter in Florida goes."

They all turned to Adrienne. "I don't know, either," she said. "I'd like to, but I have things to figure out first." And that was the truth, mostly. She'd consider returning if her friends were, but with both boats in operation, who knew if they'd be together? And then there was Shane. Adrienne had no clue what his plans were. All that time together, and she'd never thought to ask. But given his comments about Avery, she couldn't imagine he'd leave her again.

They hadn't spoken in over a week—more like a month in boat time—and Adrienne didn't know if they ever would again. The truth, which she forced herself to acknowledge, was that in nine days, Shane would be living with Jess again, being a husband, sharing their marital bed each night. *Don't forget that your boyfriend has a wife.*

The thought was all Adrienne could do to keep from crying.

Shane

HE MAKES UP his mind as soon as Eric tells him. Season's over in nine days, and he's filin' for divorce in ten. It all adds up now. *All* of it. And he'll deal with Jess and Travis at home.

He's hardly spent any money besides what he's given Jess. Now, she's not gettin' another dime 'til a judge says how much. He keeps tellin' himself that he's not walkin' out on Avery. He'll fight for custody, whatever he has to do. He's not gonna lose his daughter.

He's stable now, plans on stayin' with NECLA. Nicky and Marco told him he's got plenty of skills the company can use. The Sanbourne family's got their hands in a lotta stuff. He can work in the shipyard, drive truck for the fish market like Eric ... For the first time in his life, things are different. He's got options now.

Nicky

HE TAKES Shane to some hole-in-the-wall and ordahs two Paul Bunyan breakfasts. "Aye, that's a wicked pissah, Shaney-Boy. Catchin' ya wife cheatin' with family? That's not somethin' a guy can go back to."

"It doesn't hurt," Shane tells him. "At least not because of Jess. That make sense?"

He nods, digs into his eggs. "Shuh does. Only hurts if ya love 'em, catch my drift?"

Shaney-Boy gets it.

"Got a place to stay when we get back?"

"Not yet. I just found out. They don't even know that I know yet. Might hafta crash at my mom's."

"Ya can crash with me if ya wanna. My pad's huge. I'll rent ya my extra room."

Shane looks interested. "We'll see, man. I might take ya up on that."

***

THE FIRST TWO DAYS of Haunted Homecoming were spent in Tarrytown—the waterfront village Washington Irving once called home. On Wednesday, the passengers toured Sunnyside, his former estate. On Thursday, they were bussed to Sleepy Hollow itself to view the celebrated author's gravesite. Activity Hour on both nights consisted of live performances by a local theater group.

On Friday, the crew bid their final goodbye to New York. They were Fall River-bound, where the passengers would get a private tour of the Lizzie Borden house. Nicky, proud "Rivah Boy" that he was, strolled through the dining room chanting the local tune: "Lizzie Borden took an axe and gave 'er mothah forty whacks! And when she seen what she had done, she gave 'er fathah forty-one!"

The next time Adrienne saw Nicky, he was dressed in street clothes, heading to the gangway with Shane. Shane wasn't in uniform either but jeans and a zip-up hoodie. He glanced over his shoulder, meeting Adrienne's eye for only a moment.

Nicky

POPPY'S WAITIN' outside with his pickup truck. He and Shane hop in, and Poppy drives to their tenement on Plymouth, yakkin' how the Sox bettah sweep the Rockies in the Series. When they get home, he takes Shane to the second floor and shows him around. "I'll chahge ya four hundred a month, Shaney-Boy. No lease. Everythin' included."

Shane checks the place out. The kitchen and the double pahlor. The bathroom and the extra bedroom. "This looks straight, Nicky. I'll take it. Thanks, man."

He's gotta give Shane credit for keepin' the news undah wraps. Makes sense, though. Wants to wait 'til he sees the wife and cousin in person to bust 'em. He feels bad for the guy, can't blame him for leavin'. What kinda woman gets it on with 'er husband's cousin, anyways? Only the kind who belongs on *Jerry Springah*.

Aye, it's not like Shane didn't have opportunities. The guy's a saint, stayin' faithful with that kinda temptation lurkin' on board. *Whew!* If he were Shaney-Boy, he'd have taken up with Adrienne months ago.

"What's goin' on with 'er anyways?" he wants to know. "Haven't seen ya hangin' out much."

Shane shakes his head, don't wanna talk about it.

"Ya sleep with 'er, and things go south?"

"Nah, man. Nothin' like that."

"Aye, Shane, whatevah happened, I'm shuh she'll come around."

He wishes Brynnie'd come around, too. He knows she'll be back next season, which means he will, too ... as long as Bev still needs help on whatevah boat she's on! Turns out workin' on board ain't that bad. He had himself some fun this season. And this year was just round one.

Shane

FOR FIVE DAYS, he waits for the chance to tell Adrienne. They don't hafta rush into things, but he wants her to know what's goin' on, thinks she'll have a change of heart. She's not a girl ya give up on. Not a girl ya walk away from without a fight.

But when he finally gets her alone, out on the laz on their last night in Boston, she goes for the door, looks like she's gonna cry. "Shane, *please*. I want to keep my distance from you. I'm serious, okay? I mean it. I *can't* do this anymore!"

52

HAUNTED HOMECOMING concluded after three *spooktacular* days in Salem. Once the last passenger disembarked, Connie pounced with her final turnaround assignments. The boat was staying docked in Salem for the crew's benefit only, awarding them an end-of-season celebration in the most ultimate setting. They'd deadhead to East Bay tomorrow, where the stews couldn't leave until Connie okayed their public areas and reviewed their final evaluations. Then it would be over. Sayonara. Farewell. Thanks for your service.

Adrienne was assigned to the sun deck, tasked with inventorying the housekeeping closet and stripping bare the outdoor cabins. Even with the nippy weather, she was satisfied working in an area where she didn't have to deal with anyone. There would be enough interacting tonight when the crew went out for their threefold celebration—Halloween, the season's end, and Hailey's twentieth birthday.

Halloween had always been one of Adrienne's favorite holidays, but her melancholic state hadn't altered in a month, and she didn't expect things would change today. It didn't help that this was the first year she wasn't taking Thany trick-or-treating, something she and Wendy had always done together. But she hoped maybe Jack taking Thany would start a new tradition between them, that her father would at least walk him around the neighborhood, not just to the top of the street.

Adrienne lost herself in her turnaround assignments. She didn't notice it had grown dark until Connie found her in the housekeeping closet. "That's enough for today, kiddo," she said. "Go get ready with your friends."

In girls' quarters, everyone was applying their makeup and changing into their costumes. Noah chattered frenetically in his Jack Sparrow outfit, rimming his eyes in black kohl. It had been his idea for everyone to dress in a nautical theme, but Adrienne hadn't gone costume shopping with them on Monday, refusing to waste money on something she'd never wear again.

If not for her foul mood, she would've partaken with enthusiasm. Instead, she borrowed a bandana from Katherine and hoops from Logan to call herself a pirate. At the last minute, not wanting to be a total spoilsport, she took her anchor bracelet from its jewelry box and clasped it around her wrist. Usually, Adrienne only wore the bracelet with her formalwear, but this last-ditch effort to cobble together a costume couldn't hurt. It was the best her friends were going to get out of her.

Katherine had also been frugal with her costume budget. She was going as a "feminine stewardess," pairing her formalwear shirt with a black skirt and pearl-buttoned cardigan. She modeled a pair of modest peep-toes for Adrienne. "I only spent money on these. What do you think, Dri?"

The others had spent a fortune. Noah's costume had cost eighty dollars, but Logan and Hailey had spent way more. Logan was channeling Cher in *Mermaids*, flaunting a sequined tail and humungous curls under a jewel-encrusted tiara. Hailey was also going as a pirate, but a risqué one. She pranced out of the bathroom wearing a satin bralette under a ruffle-sleeved top, replicating one of Gwen Stefani's outfits in the "Rich Girl" video.

"New decade, new you?" Noah joked.

Hailey smiled mightily. "My twenties will be *mine!*" she vowed.

Everyone gathered at the gangway. Max was dressed as a sexy gangster—in pinstriped suspender pants, a collared halter top, and a fedora. Brynne was dressed as a pinup girl, scantily clad in high-waisted shorts and a micro sweater that barely covered her breasts. Nicky's eyes popped cartoonishly as he approached with Marco and Jordy. "Aye now, Brynnie!"

Adrienne was relieved Shane wasn't with them, but wondered where he was, the only non-officer not joining their outing.

Essex Street was their preplanned destination. Downtown Salem was a mob scene, but the crew paraded through the crowd like they owned the streets, ready to "paint the town red," as Logan had declared. Inside Ouija Bar, the music throbbed loud enough to wake Salem's dead. They found room at the head of the bar, where Nicky ordered beers and shots for everyone, toasting first to Hailey, then to the crew for making it through the whole season without anyone quitting or getting fired. "Except Kyle, though!" he yelled, the alcohol taking control. "Fuck that kid!"

Adrienne wished she could let loose with them, but her heart wasn't in it. What began as a magical adventure full of hope and promise had been unraveling since Raina's phone call in August. Throw in her falling-outs with Wendy and Shane, it was all too much to bear. She declined Nicky's offer for a second shot and impulsively ordered a fishbowl of some house concoction called The Stuff That Killed Elvis, breaking away from the group and sneaking it out past the bouncer.

Outside, there were people everywhere. Hundreds of them, all screaming and stumbling about Essex Street like some costumed, alcohol-fueled apocalypse. Adrienne found a bench in an alleyway and sat down, taking a huge gulp from the fishbowl. The drink was more potent than anything she'd ever consumed, the perfect elixir to numb her mind for a couple of hours. She finished it in three gulps—a reckless decision. The spins came first, and then the sorrow, her mind running distorted *What If?* scenarios. What if she'd never seen Wendy's newspaper? What if Kyle had never gotten fired? What if she'd never met Shane? Would she have ever known love? Would she have ever known the mental purgatory of loving someone you can never be with? Only when she looked down and saw a tear splash against her Adidas did she realize she was crying. Again.

"Adrienne?" Shane was approaching her, smoking a cigarette. He wasn't in costume either. "You okay?"

Adrienne wiped her tears with Katherine's bandana and stood from the bench. She felt woozy, stumbling before catching her balance. Shane reached out to help, but she pulled away. "Don't touch me!" she snapped. "I want to be left alone."

"C'mon, Adrienne," he said. "Let me help ya. Let me take ya back to the boat."

Adrienne threw her fishbowl to the ground. "No, Shane! You have a *family* to get back to tomorrow, same as I do! I told you there's no point in continuing this anymore! You've led me on enough already, so *please*, leave me alone!"

Across the street, a group of drunk college kids who'd witnessed her outburst whooped and jeered loudly, mortifying them both.

Shane

HE DOESN'T wanna be out in this crowd. The only reason he left the boat was to find Adrienne. He didn't wanna leave tomorrow without talkin' to her ... lettin' her know what's goin' on. But seein' her now, drunk and cryin' in the alley, he realizes the pain he must've caused her, understands why she's so guarded.

He hates that she's yellin' at him to leave her alone. He knows she's drunk, but drunk words are sober thoughts, right? Fine. If that's what she wants ... he'll let her go. Maybe he didn't know her as well as he thought. Maybe their connection hadn't been that deep after all.

Hailey

SHE'S NEVER HAD so much fun on her birthday!

"Cheers to twenty years!" the crew hollers, toasting her.

Definitely! Cheers to a new decade! Cheers to the life-changing eight months she's had working for NECLA! Cheers to finding her freedom and coming into her own!

If this is what's so wrong about "gallivanting around on some boat," then she doesn't want to be right! She's coming back no matter what, and this moment defines it. She doesn't care *where* the boat takes her or *what* her parents have to say. Her life belongs to *her* now.

Connie

IT'S WELL AFTER midnight when she hears the crew tramping in drunk. She remembers the days.

She turns into Keith, wrapping her naked leg over his. They first got together last month, and no one has suspected a thing. Keith's supposed to be working right now, but she'll keep him to herself until things quiet down. This is the best sex she's ever had, and she'll be damned if they get found out now on the last night.

She's still working on the stews' final evaluations. Logan, Hailey, Adrienne, and Noah have nothing to worry about, but if things were up to *her*, Max Hardigan would be blackballed from NECLA permanently. The best she can hope for is passing Max and Brynne onto Mattie next season—if she doesn't wring his neck first. But she *can* do something about Katherine, and by this time tomorrow, Katherine will be waiting on the unemployment line. She doesn't like firing anyone, but it comes with the territory. She's given Katherine plenty of chances, but taking the reins during her vacation was the final straw. No guesswork required whose idea that was.

And her? In twenty-four hours, she'll be out of NECLA mode. She knows Bev would prefer she stick around to discuss 2008, but they can flesh out the details when she comes home in December. She's headed back to Florida to visit Mattie for a couple weeks, then it's off to Colorado to spend Thanksgiving with Macy. Right now, she needs a break from boat life just as much as the stews do.

November 2007

53

CONNIE LET THEM all sleep in the next morning, a fringe benefit Adrienne much appreciated. Of the few times in her life that she'd been hungover, this was the worst. Whatever was in The Stuff That Killed Elvis had stunned her into oblivion last night. When she woke, bleak recollections of the crew's walk back to the *Amelia* crystallized: Noah vomiting on someone's front lawn. Nicky's hand cupping Brynne's buttocks. Max dropping her fedora, and Katherine accidentally stepping on it, crushing it. Max pitching a fit in the middle of the road.

She recalled being in an alley with Shane. Had there been an argument? Had she yelled at him? She was positive that there had been, that she did. He'd wanted to talk, and she'd rebuffed him, yelled something about him leading her on. Whatever she'd said, she had no call to be so rude. She needed to find him before going to the train station. She'd booked the 5:30 out of Providence, and sometime before then, she was going to make peace with him. Her drunken state couldn't be his last memory of her.

Connie roused them at nine, calling, "Rise and shine, sleepyheads! It's not over yet!" She suggested they finish cleaning their public areas first, then pack their things. She was almost done with the end-of-season evaluations and would find them when she was ready.

Adrienne returned to the sun deck, stepping out for a cigarette. The *Amelia* had left Salem sometime that morning, and rain was bucketing down with a vengeance. Punishing rains, harsh as when she'd been stranded in Newport. Except now it wasn't August anymore, but November already. *Maybe you haven't been checking your calendar ...*

She completed her sun deck tasks right as Chef Ray clanged the handbell. On her way downstairs, she saw the deck department listening to Hardigan give some speech in the pax lounge. She tried signaling Shane, but he wasn't looking in her direction. This afternoon, then. That's when she'd find him.

Crew lunch was grab-and-go—sheet-pan grilled cheeses and what remained of the potato chip stash. Everything else was getting trucked over to Sanbourne's Fish Market when they docked. While the stews inhaled their lunch, Hardigan appeared, offering some eleventh-hour bullshit about what a fine job they'd done and how he hoped they'd consider returning, presumably the same speech he'd just given upstairs. "Girl, please," Noah puffed. "He doesn't give a *shit* if he ever sees us again."

They deep-cleaned the galley and dining room one last time. No one said much, letting Noah's iPod provide the background noise. They were all tired, hungover, and, dare anyone admit, burnt out. Adrienne wondered if anyone felt sad. She thought back to their first day in the shipyard, to their group dinner at Logan's condo. They'd been so talkative, so excited to begin boat life, and *this* was how they were leaving things? So quiet? So listlessly?

Once everything was gleaming, they headed downstairs to pack. The girls removed their personal effects from the bathroom, emptied their drawers and lockers, and stripped their beds. Over on the port side, thuds and bangs could be heard, same as on move-in day. Max and Brynne were packing, too, and Adrienne knew there would be no goodbyes between that side and this one.

Katherine stood on her bed to disassemble the blankets from the curtain track. When she began peeling the glow-in-the-dark stars from the ceiling, Adrienne climbed up to help her.

"Thanks, Dri," Katherine said. "And thanks for being a good friend to me. I hope we can be bunkmates again if you come back."

Adrienne smiled. "We'll see."

They brought their luggage up to the dining room. It was still downpouring, and Adrienne could see the shipyard ahead, the deckhands moving swiftly about the sun deck, readying the mooring ropes. And then there was Bev, standing by the rock jetty in her poncho, a mother awaiting the afternoon school bus.

It wasn't until that moment that Adrienne realized this was *it*. The adventure was over. The good times had rolled. She stared through the window, watching Shane and the guys bring out the gangway. Now was the time to set things right. Even if they never saw each other again, she couldn't leave on bad terms with him, knowing that would only cause additional hurt. She couldn't admit her feelings of love, but she needed Shane to know that she cared about him, that he'd touched her life.

As she started for the stairs, Bev caught her by surprise. "Adrienne! I see the boat's brought that dreadful weather back from the North Shore!" She shook off her poncho. "How did you enjoy New York, dear? It's beautiful in the autumn, isn't it?"

Adrienne wished she could be honest and tell Bev that she hated New York. That it was unstimulating, and she'd been depressed the whole time. But she staged a smile and said, "Oh, New York was nice."

"Wonderful! Perhaps you can point me in Peter's direction?"

"The wheelhouse?" Adrienne guessed. "I'm really not sure."

Bev started upstairs, calling, "Make sure to see me before you leave, Adrienne. I'd love to discuss next season with you!"

Adrienne couldn't deal with this right now. She needed to find Shane. "I have a train to catch," she said. "Can I call you?"

"Of course, dear! You call me soon so we can catch up."

Adrienne hadn't made it ten feet when she ran into Jordy, hauling a bulky duffel on his shoulder. "Hey, Dri. I guess this is it, huh?"

"You're leaving?" Adrienne asked. "We just docked."

"Hells yeah. Time to turn back into a pumpkin. You know I'm still a yard worker, right? Gotta be back in the morning."

"Oh yeah ... I forgot about that." Tomorrow was Friday. The non-seasonal employees still had work. "Well, it was nice working with you, Jordy."

Jordy raised his eyebrows. "You're not coming back?"

"Undecided. There's a lot up in the air right now."

"I hear that," he said. "Friend me on MySpace when you get home."

Adrienne had to chuckle. *MySpace*. When was the last time she'd checked her account?

On her way to guys' quarters, Connie appeared from her office. "Adrienne, good. I'm looking for stews." She guided Adrienne to a table and gave her a slip inviting her back for 2008. Adrienne skimmed Connie's handwritten notes. *Hardworking. Resourceful.* And so on.

"Truer words, Adrienne ..." Connie said. "I'd love to have you back on my team again. It was a pleasure."

"Thanks, Connie. I'm considering it."

It was then that Connie offered her a ride. "Let me take you to the train station," she said. "I'm going through Providence anyway."

"Uh ... sure," Adrienne stammered, assuming until now that Logan or Noah would drive her. But she hadn't asked them, so going with Connie it was. "When are you leaving?"

"Not for another hour. I still have stews to find."

"Okay, thanks. I'll meet you in here." Adrienne left the dining room quickly, heading to guys' quarters, where she expected to find Shane packing.

"I'm decent!" Noah called when she knocked.

Noah was transferring the contents of his locker into a suitcase. The rest of the room was bare, showing no sign of other inhabitants. Adrienne looked from the empty lockers to the empty bunks to the empty nightstands in between. No towels hung from the shower hooks. No razors or shaving cream lined the sink ledges. Nothing. "Where is everyone?" she asked.

"Gone," said Noah.

"Gone?" Adrienne repeated hollowly. "Who's gone?"

"Jordy ... Nicky ... Shane ... They all left."

Her chest compressed with torment. "But we just got back! We still have work to do!"

"No, girl. *We* still have work to do. The stews. Hardigan cut the guys loose."

Adrienne leaned against the doorframe, realizing she'd been too late, waited too long, that this *was* it. Now Shane was out of her life forever. Quick as a wink, as unexpectedly as he'd appeared.

Logan

SHE'S GLAD CONNIE is taking Adrienne to Providence. She just wants to get back to her condo and *sleep*. She's so tired, totally ready for a break. In only three weeks, she'll be packing again, meeting her parents and Alannah in Stowe for a Thanksgiving ski trip. For Christmas, the whole family is traveling to Oahu.

It's totally sweet of Connie to recommend her again, but she needs to confirm the new itineraries first. She's heard rumors of Florida, which is *totally* up her alley, but the world is too vast to experience the same ports three years in a row. And it depends on who else comes back. She liked this year's crew better than last's, and her gut says they wouldn't treat her differently if they knew her secret. Not that she'd ever reveal it.

When it's time to leave, she promises to stay in touch with them about 2008. Either way, she insists they get together after the holidays. Maybe she'll host a New Year's party if she's back in time. Who knows?

Out in the parking lot, she spots Brynne getting into Max's Infiniti. She nods cordially, but they don't exchange words. To Max, she says nothing. There totally isn't any point.

Brynne

SHE'S NOT SURPRISED Connie didn't call her or Max for sit-downs, just left their evaluations on a table. Does it even matter anymore? Let Connie hold a grudge.

She's got bigger concerns, starting with getting an answer from Gordon. They haven't spoken since she contacted him in August, and she's been a wreck these past eight weeks. She needs to know what's going on and intends to get her answer soon.

Besides, she already knows from Max that they've been reassigned to the *Amelia* with Peter and Marco. Max isn't sure who their cruise director will be—Connie or Mattie—but what's the difference? They both despise her and Max the same.

She's just glad to have a plan. If not for NECLA, what else would she be doing with her life?

Katherine

CONNIE'S FACE is flat as they sit for her evaluation. Not a good sign. And Connie doesn't waste any time mincing words. "Katherine, I don't know how else to say this, but I don't think you're a good fit to return here."

Not a good fit? This is like the Biltmore all over again! "You're terminating me?" she asks.

"Yes, Katherine, I am. It surprises me you didn't see this coming."

Well, forgive *her* for being so clueless! When she asks Connie *why*, the woman goes straight for the jugular. "Katherine, you've had too many issues this season. Your chemistry with the crew has been unstable, your inability to retain instructions and respect boundaries is concerning, and based on those things alone, I can't recommend you again."

Stay calm, she tells herself. *Don't do anything rash. Respond with professionalism and etiquette.* "But I fixed my relationship with the crew. Everything is fine now. And I haven't had any issues since you spoke to me in Plymouth."

"Yes, Katherine, you have. A major issue is interjecting your opinion all the time. This is not *your* company, and you aren't paid to express every thought in your head. I wish there were another way, but my decision is final."

"But what about all I did to help Lorna while you were gone? Doesn't that mean anything?"

"Katherine, stepping into my position wasn't your call to make. I told you before, you were hired as a *stewardess*."

Her lip quivers, but she's determined to stay strong. "Well, I respect the difference of opinion, Connie, but I was planning on working a second season here before pursuing other options."

"Then I suggest you try pursuing other boats. We're through here, Katherine."

She runs to her Volkswagen before anyone can see her cry. Other boats? *Other boats?* Well, maybe she *will* pursue other boats! But only after writing a strongly worded letter to Beverly, of course!

54

NOAH WAITED with Adrienne in the dining room while Connie swung by the office with the cash box. "Dri, will you *please* road-trip to Florida with me? I mean, what *else* do you have going on?"

Adrienne had forgotten about Noah's offer to join him. Really, she'd thought it was just talk. Of all the girls who'd left Giovanni's over the years, of all the times she'd heard "keep in touch," or "let's hang out," no one had ever followed through. This—Noah making an honest effort to continue their friendship—was all new to her. "You really want to go?" she asked him.

"Yes, girl! It was eighty-three degrees in Fort Lauderdale this morning! Besides, we need a vacation. And you need to get out of this *funk* you've been in." He said it in an accusatory, cut-the-shit sort of way.

"What about Bethany?" Adrienne wondered. "You've known her longer. Don't you want to go with her?"

"Hell no! I'm not paying her way the whole time! I love the bitch forever, but I'd rather go with you."

Noah was right. She didn't have anything else going on right now. "All right," she yielded. "Let's do it. As long as I'm home for Thanksgiving." The holidays were fast approaching, and Aunt Claudette was already leaving texts and voicemails regarding their plans.

"Really? Yes, Dri! We're gonna have a *real* road trip! We need to think of places to stop on the way!"

"We can visit my brother at Camp Lejeune," Adrienne suggested. The thought of seeing Aaron was warming, and maybe family was what she needed right now.

"A military base? Girl, bring me *all* the men in uniform!"

Adrienne laughed. At least road-tripping with Noah would be comedic. She listened to his excited yammering until Connie entered the dining room, jiggling her keys. "Ready to go, kiddo?"

Noah grabbed her cheek and kissed it. "I'll call you *tomorrow*! We have hella plans to make, girl!"

The rain was dying off as Connie parked in front of the State House. "It was one hell of a season, but we survived, didn't we, Adrienne?"

"Mmm," Adrienne murmured. It *had* been one hell of a season, unpredictable in so many ways. But if she could've changed anything about her experience, it would've been meeting Shane under different circumstances. And, of course, never meeting Max Hardigan at all. Shane's abrupt exit hadn't hit her yet, but the pain was bound to surface, and Adrienne worried it might escalate her depression—another reason she'd agreed to the road trip.

"Any thoughts on coming back?" Connie asked. But her cell phone rang as Adrienne started to answer. "My daughter ..." Connie said. "I'll just be a minute."

Atop the State House dome, the statue of the Independent Man gallantly guarded the capital city. Adrienne had learned from her time waiting at Union Station that the statue represented the trailblazing spirit of Roger Williams—founder of the great state of Rhode Island. Staring at the figure, she reflected on *her* journey, how she'd followed this blind path of happenstance like a proverbial calling.

A year ago, she'd known nothing about boat life. The ports she'd since visited were only destinations on maps. The people she'd since met were only cogs in the world's wheel. But she'd undergone an awakening since February, learning about the boating industry and stewardess trade, absorbing new diversities and appreciating the uniqueness of the people who'd taught her to see life differently. The boat *had* changed her, but was that necessarily a bad thing? And if she could gather all this insight in just one season, what else might be in store if she returned for another?

Her anchor bracelet remained on her wrist from the night before, and Adrienne spun it slowly, thinking of *her* anchors. Her father and brothers. Dolly. Aunt Claudette. And even Wendy, who she'd thought of every day since their fight. *Don't ever forget where you come from.* But who was to say that she hadn't inadvertently started building a new foundation? That she hadn't acquired new people and perspectives that were currently shaping her future?

She'd have to weigh the pros and cons, of course. Drifting further from her roots to carve a new path required serious thought. If she stayed home, what were her options? Return to school? Go back to Giovanni's? Find a new job altogether? Committing to another season meant she could forge on and see where this path took her. She'd come to NECLA for an experience, after all, and that she'd gotten. But it still felt enormously unfinished, like there was far more waiting ahead.